SHATTERED OMEGA: PART TWO
POISONVERSE NOIR

MARIE MACKAY

Copyright © 2024 by Marie Mackay

Edition 1.0

All rights reserved.

Edited by Caity Hides

Cover design by Marie Mackay

No part of this book may be reproduced in any form or by any electronic or mechanical means, including information storage and retrieval systems, without written permission from the author, except for the use of brief quotations in a book review.

CONTENT WARNINGS

Please note: *If sexual as$ault outside of romance and on page, or violence toward FMC is an extreme content note for you, read the last section of the content warning page (spoilers) in order to learn how to skip it.*

Alright! Anything I need to know before I start?

> Yes! The book contains dub-con and coercion between love interests.

> Outside of romance: Sexual violence and alpha bites (unwanted) + bullying and humiliation on page.

> There is also self branding, violence, experimentation, rejected mates, and depictions of mental health struggles.

> In passing mentions: Drug use (via experimentation), brief suicidal ideation. Brief references to human trafficking.

Anything else?

> Yes! Other content notes include: Somnophilia, public, spanking, BBS, rejected mates, and other explicit adult spice. This is a non exhaustive list.

!SPOILER! CONTENT WARNING BELOW!

SA: There is a depiction of SA on page in chapter 15. It begins at the start of the chapter (approx. 700 words).

Details: It depicts oral sex both unwanted, and outside of the romance. The passage includes action beats of event itself, though kept to a minimum, with the FMC focusing on her emotional state in order to maintain distance.

To Skip: When reach Ch15 you can skip to page from page 126 to page 130, searching for the symbol above to mark the end.

There are instances of brief flashbacks to the event throughout the book (one or two lines) none have any explicit detail of the SA.

If SA *and* Violence is an issue (more spoilers):

After the SA the FMC experiences violence via unwanted alpha bites that are also on page. If you would like to skip the entirety of chapter 15, the end of the book contains a Chapter 15 Summary which includes ***non*** explicit details of important information so that you can continue the book without missing plot relevant details.

This is my first 'skip' trigger. If you would like to note unlisted triggers, or have an issue bypassing of the trigger, please reach out to mariemackaybooks@gmail.com to suggest a way to improve the setup. *Thank you, and take care!*

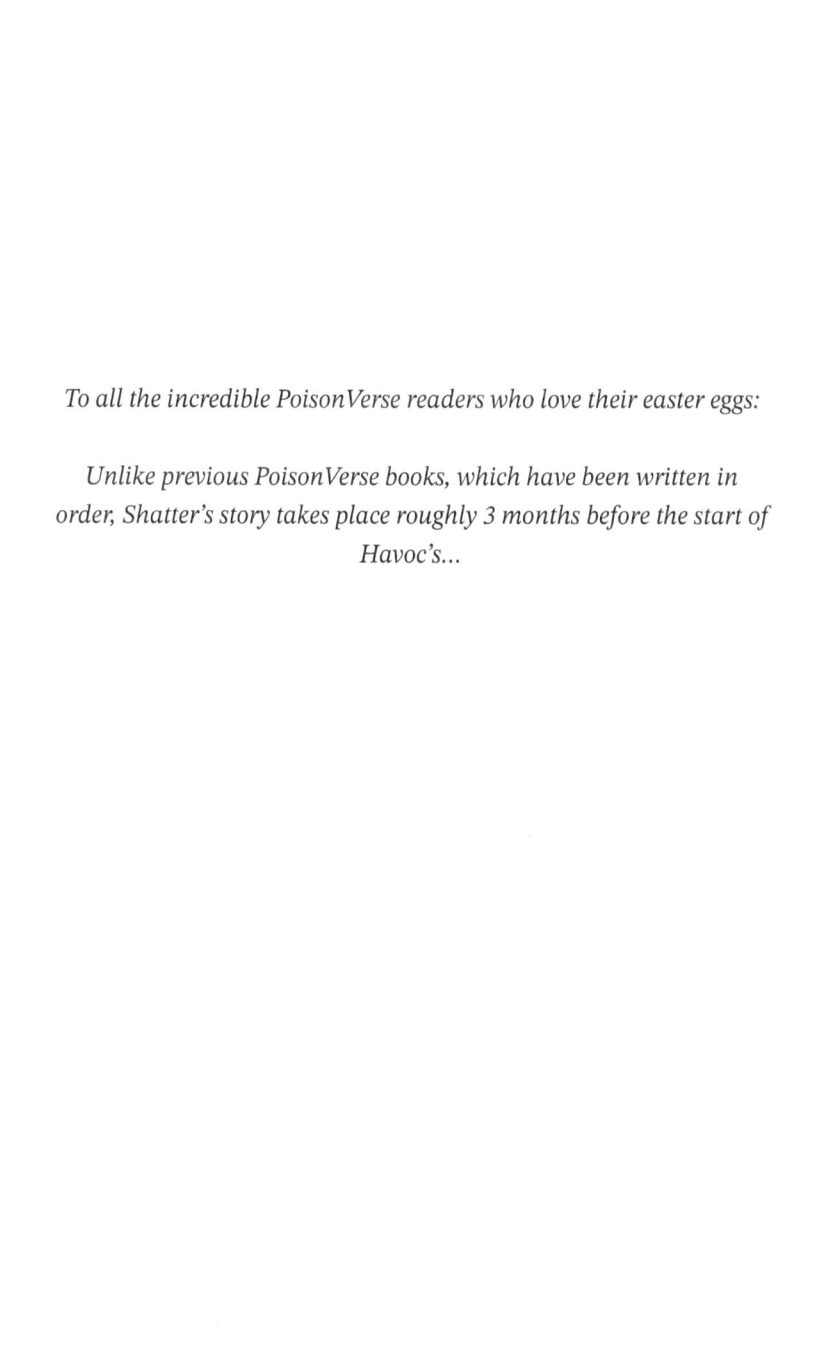

To all the incredible PoisonVerse readers who love their easter eggs:

Unlike previous PoisonVerse books, which have been written in order, Shatter's story takes place roughly 3 months before the start of Havoc's...

ONE

SHATTER

Another *BANG* from the room on the balcony made me jump.

I should check on that.

I stared at the locked door above, heart pounding, mind racing a million miles a minute. I'd just spent Lord knows how much time making sure Dusk and Umbra were safe. Now they were both wrapped up in blankets, their auras stable.

That noise couldn't be either of them—Umbra was still peacefully vacant in the omega bond I had. He was sleeping, just like Dusk was resting on a bed of pillows in the kitchen before me.

I was trying to catch up with what happened, and my pulse was still erratic.

I'd come out of the bathroom of the club to find Dusk gone. It had been so unexpected, I'd hurried out of the front doors, alarm bells going off in my head. There, I'd found him doubled over on the pathway, body shaking, aura flickering in and out.

Never had I even *read* about something like this, let alone seen it. He had been dying, I'd known it in my gut. There was something so, so wrong with what had happened to both him and Umbra... It was more than sickness... It was unnatural.

If I was being honest, I had no idea how I'd fixed it.

But now, they were both asleep.

That noise could *not* have been them.

The clinical side of my brain had already done the calculation, but it was just so wildly unbelievable that I was having a hard time processing it.

Because if that wasn't Umbra or Dusk, then there was only one person it could be, and that was—A KNOCK sounded at the front door, making me jump.

I spun, staring at it, then scrambled to look through the peephole. My heart bottomed out of my chest.

Flynn Lincoln was standing outside.

"One... one second!" I called. I pressed my back against the door, absolutely unsure.

Flynn was here?

Everything I'd just been thinking about running to.

My mate was outside. Right. Now.

Instead of elation, I felt a sense of dread creeping up my spine.

What about the sound upstairs? I couldn't just leave, right? My mind thought wildly to the registration card in my pencil case—which reminded me I needed to grab that before I even thought of leaving.

Stupid.

Stupid and rushed and... *damn it*, I wasn't ready.

But if Flynn caught my scent and knew I was his match, I'd never be able to check on that room.

I ran to the kitchen, almost tripping over Dusk, and opened his drug drawer. In it was a bottle of scent-dampening spray. It wasn't as long-lasting as the pills, but it was enough for now.

I sprayed it all over myself and the whole kitchen, almost choking on the thick mist.

The knock sounded again.

"Be there in a minute!" I called.

I wasn't giving up on my mates. I could wash this off and go back to them. After. After I'd checked the room and made sure everyone was safe.

Finally, feeling ready, I cracked the door, peering out. Coconut and plum were the first scents I caught in the air, and sure enough, Flynn was right there.

Right in front of me.

"Hi," I said awkwardly, still holding the door mostly closed.

He frowned, gaze meeting mine for a long moment, and then lifting to the kitchen beyond.

"Is your pack okay?" he asked. "Dusk left abruptly. He didn't look well."

"Yes," I said too quickly. "He's fine."

I couldn't explain the sudden sickness in my throat, or the absolute need that gripped me to lie—to ensure that the alpha before me never saw Dusk laying on the kitchen floor, asleep.

Vulnerable...

Before he could say anything, I slipped out and shut the door behind me so he couldn't see in.

I don't know why it was so imperative. It just was. Dusk had fought through hell to get back to Umbra. I might resent everything he'd ever done, but I couldn't deny the strength in that loyalty, just like I couldn't deny my instinct to protect it.

I fingered Dusk's keys in my pocket, making sure they were there. I *could* get back in.

I blinked, reality flooding back now there was a door between me and the alphas who had captured me.

Why was I worried about getting back in?

I should be *throwing* myself into Flynn's arms.

"I..." Flynn trailed off, looking unsure, glancing down at

where I was gripping the keys in my jacket pocket. Then he looked back up at me, and saw his pupils were blown.

Oh.., Oh my God. I'd had the door open for a while.

Had he caught my scent?

If he had, what would that mean?

Did he know who I was?

"I just wanted to check in," he said again. He looked intense. Too intense. "Are you sure I can't speak to him?"

"No. He's uh... doing something important with Umbra."

"Okay." He took a step back, then paused. His eyes fell to my shoulder, and I glanced down to see a stain of red in my hair.

Umbra's blood.

Oh... *crap*.

He looked back at me, eyebrows raised. "Are *you* okay?"

"Yes. I am. Definitely."

He didn't look convinced.

"I promise."

Promise? Really, Shatter?

Still, he continued staring at me with pupils that were definitely blown wide. "I..." He trailed off. "Shatter..."

My pulse raced out of control at the sound of my name on my mates lips... Thoughts of investigating the sound from the mysterious room faded away for the briefest second.

I was so fucking warm and my brain just wasn't working straight. It had taken far too much out of me, sorting out Dusk and Umbra.

Flynn was still staring at me.

I heard sounds down the hall and glanced down to see that Eric and Gareth were both waiting by the stairs.

They'd all come?

"I h-have to go," I stammered.

"Wait," Flynn rasped. "Just... wait."

"What?" My voice was weak, metal digging into my palm as I gripped the keys too tightly.

"I just... fuck." He straightened, running his fingers through his hair. "Forgive me, but..." He looked pained. "You came to us at the ball, and now I see you everywhere."

My mouth dropped open, completely caught off guard by his words.

"I'm not the only one. It's Eric and Gareth, too. You're... different."

I froze completely, staring at him.

"But Eric..." I trailed off, knowing I shouldn't say that.

Flynn frowned, cocking his head. "What?"

"I... I heard him..." My voice was weak. "He said I didn't belong here. He uh... doesn't like my hair," I said, but Flynn's eyes darkened. "I d-didn't mean to overhear—"

"Fuck." He leaned back, letting out a breath. "Eric's a fucking idiot, alright? And he doesn't... He's not used to..." He ran his fingers through his hair again, still so anxious. "We've never been interested in an omega like we're interested in you, Shatter."

Interested?

What?

This... wasn't the time.

I couldn't do this right now.

"And Eric," Flynn continued, "all of us—we see you with the Kingsman pack every goddamned day. You have no idea how it's killing us. So he pretends he hates you because he can't handle it."

"Hates me?" I shrank down, Eric's words still replaying in my head like they had so many times.

"He *doesn't* hate you. Please, don't let him blow this chance. Not because Eric can't keep his mouth shut."

I couldn't think.

He was asking me for a chance?

At what?

"I'll get him on his knees for you. He'll beg you for forgiveness, I swear it." There was the faintest smile on his face.

But none of this made sense.

What about Roxy?

He knew I was her friend. And what he was asking...

"I know how harsh he can sound. He's not... Look. I know this isn't going to sell you on us, but he's not always the best, alright? He's spoiled, but he can be better. I've seen it."

My heart slammed into my ribs uncomfortably.

I'd heard them say they wanted a princess bond—I swear it. And I'd *almost* fallen for Dusk, after everything he'd done. Was it possible Eric wasn't that bad either?

He wanted me.

They *all* wanted me?

Flynn's scent was too much for me to try and parse this out, I felt like it was weaving into my very soul. My fingers were clammy, sweat beading on my back.

My brain wasn't working right.

If it *was* Ransom in that room, could he possibly be as sick as the others? He might die if I didn't go to him. And he'd got me my registration card. Flynn would understand that.

Nothing made sense. I felt like I was splitting into two different people. One that couldn't understand why I wasn't throwing myself at Flynn, and the other that couldn't understand why I wasn't already back inside.

"I... I just need a bit of time... to..." I gripped my sleeve with my free hand, needing to clear my head. "To th-think." Goddammit, I couldn't think. Not with Dusk and Umbra nearly dying, and now Flynn's coconut and plum, and... oh... "...My registration card is a really big deal..." That was Ransom—He'd done that for me. And what if he was dying? I couldn't let the one alpha in the world who'd got me a registration card die because Flynn's scent of coconut and plum was intoxicating.

God, I was warm.

Too many people.

This was too much.

Dusk and Umbra. Ransom. Now Flynn and the rest of the pack. How was I supposed to think straight with all of these alphas?

"I just need time," I squeaked, then turned, grabbing the keys from my pocket and fumbled with the lock on the door.

It took me far too long to find the right key. By the time I had, embarrassment had set my blood on fire.

I didn't breathe a sigh of relief until I'd slammed it shut behind me, not even daring to catch a glimpse at Flynn's expression.

I kept a hold of the keys in my fist as I looked up at the room again, almost expecting another sound.

None came.

What did that mean?

What would I find, if I went inside?

But if I didn't go and look, I'd let my mate walk away for nothing.

TWO

SHATTER

Lily of the valley flowed through my system, smoothing every spike of anxiety, and every worry. Every doubt that had been clawing at me since the moment I'd shut the door on Flynn. The scent in the room was cool and earthy, like a forest beneath autumn rain. It was an alpha's scent: dark and curious in a way it shouldn't be.

It didn't have the magnetism of my mates, but it was still strange and overpowering, clogging my throat and lungs, a poison that invaded every cell of my body, slowly drowning me.

I'd just look. Make sure he was safe.

That's what I'd told myself, but a floorboard creaked underfoot as I stepped further into a broad room, the air growing thicker with lily of the valley. I peered around, taking a moment to adjust to the light of a dim wall lamp. There was another sound from ahead, this time more muffled.

That was when I saw him.

A shadowed figure stood at the head of the bed, fists balled at his side. There were dents across the wall, I noticed, and the side of the bed was in splinters. For a long moment we stared at one another. In the darkness I could just see the spark of light in dark eyes, a tall frame and shaggy, shoulder length hair.

Oh my God.

I had been right.

"Ransom?" My voice was weak.

He *was* here.

Had he been here since term started?

Ransom hadn't moved. His chest was heaving as he stood beside his bed, eyes fixed on me like I was prey.

But I wasn't afraid of him. It was a soul deep truth that he needed me just like they had.

His scent was odd... Not like Umbra and Dusk's had been, yet something *was* wrong about it.

I took another step into the room, tentatively, trying to make him out. He hadn't responded to the sound of me entering and the room dimmed as the door finally swung shut behind me.

At the sound of the latch clicking, Ransom reacted. His aura split the air, and then he made for me and—

Fuck.

Those were chains around his wrists. Dark iron chains.

I stumbled back as he crossed the distance between us, too afraid to even turn. The violent clinking of metal drowned the sound of Dusk's keys hitting the floor.

My back slammed against the wall, hand fumbling desperately for the door handle that I couldn't find. I flinched, breath catching, but with an almighty clang of metal, Ransom came to a jarring stop, his face was inches from mine. His wrists were suspended by chains in the air on either side of him.

A growl ripped from his throat and he threw his weight against his bindings. I flattened myself against the wall further.

I was shaking.

What the hell was going on?

The iron around his wrists *had* to be made of the metal that could contain an alpha's strength—otherwise, he'd be free by now. But it was rare and expensive.

Low rumbles rolled up his chest with each deep exhale, and his eyes, a shade of deep, forest green, were wild.

A thousand fears crowded my mind. Memories of Tom when he'd caught my scent. The way the light had died from his eyes. The fury in them as he'd leaped at me.

It was happening again.

I glanced to the side, and realised the door was to my right.

I jumped violently once more as Ransom fought his chains to get to me, but his wrists wouldn't budge, and this time a low, strangled whine tore from his chest. He looked as if every breath was killing him. I examined that, trying to calm my breathing.

I took him in, truly, for the first time. Messy dark red waves of hair reached his shoulders, and his olive skin was clear and smooth over the angles of his lean face. He had a strong jaw and a straight nose, and his expression was twisted into a snarl.

Not angry or hateful at all.

Pain wasn't what I expected…

That wasn't what Tom had been like. He hadn't been in pain. He'd been wild with fury and disgust, as if my mere existence was a threat.

But Ransom was *chained* in here—Dusk must have done that. Oh.

"You're…" My whisper was rough as I realised what I was looking at.

He was *feral?* An alpha ruled by nothing but base instinct. It was rare these days, but I'd read everything there was to read on Arkology—on the history of alphas and omegas.

He hadn't spoken yet, and I didn't know if he would. Following a wild impulse, I lifted my hand and dared to press it to his cheek gently. He shifted, his whole body loosening as he leaned into my touch, eyes closing.

Okay. Maybe he didn't want to kill me after all.

Our scents tangled in the air, saturated with fear and frenzy, but now... his was changing. As in... right at this moment he was becoming more present—more dominant. When he opened his eyes again, his pupils were so wide there was almost no green left.

This time, the growl in his chest sent goosebumps across my skin, and my chest became tight. With each inhale of the wild hormones in the air, my own—on edge and frayed as they were—began to tumble out of control. A familiar wave of blistering heat swept through my body.

Oh, *bother*.

Heat?

Again?

It couldn't be. That was ridiculous—my last was *yesterday*.

Was that even fucking possible?

For me and my stupid-ass heats?

Yes.

And I'd been burning through too many omega instincts with Umbra and Dusk when bundling them both into cocoons and saving them from rabid auras. Then Flynn and his stupid mate-scent. Add to that the alpha before me, with lust now literally seeping from his pores...

Fuck.

But my mates were close. Could I leave right now and get to them in time?

I felt a sharp cramp in my stomach and loosed a low whine. Ransom went absolutely still at the sound, eyes boring into mine. Slick was already leaking down my thighs, and he let out a rumbling breath. He knew.

Flynn was long gone. *What are you going to do, Shatter? Crawl out into the hallway and hope no other alpha finds you before you can get to them?*

Wait.

My eyes had fallen to his left wrist, above where the cuff was fixed.

Were those my *scrunchies*?

Dusk had been giving him my scent?

And Ransom didn't *seem* to want to kill me. He was staring at me like he *wanted* me, his whole body tense against the chains that held him. His chest heaved, pupils dark and blown wide in the dim room. More than Flynn's had been.

Another wave of heat rolled through my blood, setting my pulse pounding. He was here and broken and... I thought I could fix him.

But my mates... *dammit*.

I couldn't keep fucking other alphas. Plus. This one was kind of on me.

I rapped my knuckles against each other anxiously, losing a battle against another little whine.

What was one more dick, really—in the grand scheme of things?

At the sound, he growled, chains clinking as he threw himself against them once more.

Fuck.

The sound struck me to the core and I whined again, reaching up with both hands and taking his cheeks between them—so refreshingly cool beside my warm skin. I was panting, feeling the mass murder of brain cells as the tide of heat flooded my brain.

I was so fucking warm.

And he was the sexiest man I'd ever seen. He didn't even look real. Like some kind of fae-vampire-rockstar forged in the depths of an alpha hormone volcano.

The low rumble in his chest told me he wanted to give me everything my body was screaming for.

I wanted him.

Needed him.

So I took a breath and I stepped forward.

THREE

SHATTER

It was as frightening as it was freeing, stepping into Ransom's arms.

I didn't quite know what to expect.

His grip crushed my waist the moment I was in reach, and he dragged me against him. I reacted, hormones taking over as I wrapped my arms around his neck, dragging my body against his.

The cramps were duller, even from this brief touch. His breath was hot against my neck as he growled, low and desperate, then his teeth grazed my neck. I froze for a moment, panic setting in. But he wasn't pack lead, if he bit me, nothing would happen. He seemed just to want the feel of my skin beneath his teeth because then he drew back and crossed the room, lowering us both to the bed.

This was more control than I'd expected so far—but it didn't last long.

All I knew was his touch. He pinned me down, grappling for my dress, aura out—wavering and unstable. I should be frightened, but I wasn't scared of him. We were in sync right now.

I trusted that.

The dress and panties were gone in a moment, torn away, and I arched toward him with a breath, needing him to fix the way my body burned. He had his own sweatpants removed in seconds, and he didn't wait, grip absolute on my waist as he lifted my hips and drove into me.

The desperate sound I made pushed him over the edge. Any lingering presence died, and he caged me in, breaths rough as he rutted me into the sheets.

I let go to Ransom like I'd let go to Umbra. It was easy, with the surge of heat burning through my body. Somehow, despite everything, in the face of Ransom, it all melted away; even my mates.

The uncomfortable cramps in my stomach faded, and instead each stroke cooled me like icy clouds sweeping past my skin.

How wrong this was, it didn't matter. I lost myself to him—to his rut.

He was all I knew, and his scent shifted again in the room, to petals unfurling beneath the sun.

I was doing that.

His omega.

That thought sank its claws in, bringing with it bliss. He was everywhere, taking me how he needed, every strong thrust keeping my heat sated. He had my scent, and he wanted me still, giving me what my body craved. His hands, his mouth, his cock, his body crushed against mine as I clutched him, lost for words and breath.

Sometimes he would knot me, and my heat would stay at bay for a while. There was slick and cum dripping down my thighs and whenever he stopped or slowed, I felt the heat returning.

This was what heat could be like?

Not kept at bay between goosebumps and sweat as my body

battled with the temperature of a huge fridge, cramps cycling in vicious waves.

Consciousness drifted in and out, more sharply whenever he stopped.

A low whimper slipped from my chest and I raised my hips to him. My aches loosened as I settled into position, sure it would be enough. He'd just finished, but I still needed more. I pressed my cheek to the blanket, tilting my head so I could look up at him, letting out a little whine.

I needed him *now*.

He was taking too long.

I heard his purr of approval as I arched my back further, adjusting my hips. I loved his purr. It eased my impatience as butterflies swam through the heat swamp in my tummy, making me giddy. I smiled as his thumb pressed into me, working me while he gripped his cock. His dark eyes were a storm of lust as I shifted back against his thumb, desperate for more.

I whined again, demanding him now. My desperation flipped a switch. He fisted my hair crushing me against the bed, and—

"Mmm..."

I moaned contentedly once more as he stretched me out, grip bruising as he dragged my body over his length.

I fell again into the blissful throes of heat.

DUSK

I woke up in a soft cocoon of deadly nightshade.

A purr rumbled to life before I could catch it, relief searing my system like a hot iron.

Umbra was alive. I could feel him in the bond. Happy. *Really* fucking happy, which not only meant Shatter had got to him, it meant she hadn't left.

And *I* was alive.

And... *shit.* Ransom was there. Awake in the bond.

A huge ball of... *Woah!*

I sat up, rubbing my eyes and tumbling from a nest of blankets and cushions and right onto the kitchen floor.

That felt like a rut.

Ransom had never rutted while feral.

What was he rutting, though?

Still, he was here. Present. So I didn't care if a few pillows made noble sacrifices.

I was on my feet in a moment, scrambling to the stairs and taking them by twos. I reached his door, then froze. Instead of bursting in, I opened it just a crack. Then nearly choked on nightshade heat hormones.

How in the *fuck...?*

She'd gone into heat *yesterday.* Those pills were legit.

She *couldn't* be in it again.

But my nose didn't deceive me, nor did the instant bulge in my pants as I squinted to see what was going on within.

I could tell it was afternoon by the way the light was filtering through Ransom's windows, which meant I'd been out a long time.

I rubbed my eyes to focus on what was before me.

Sure enough, Shatter was in there with him. *Completely* unharmed as she knelt at his bedside.

Dear lord, she was cute. She was wearing one of his tops, and no bottoms. Lace beneath? Or nothing? I wanted to go in and find out, but I controlled myself, needing to watch a little longer.

"We've gotta get them on you," she was saying. I frowned, then realised she was trying to tug sweatpants over his foot. "See if covering your dick up will help."

I had to press my hand to my mouth to stifle my snort.

"You can't just keep *fucking* me," she told him seriously. "I gotta get us food or we're going to faint."

She was still in heat, though her hormones weren't out of control. She'd clearly passed the peak of it and had enough lucidity now that survival trumped mindless sex.

Ransom, it seemed, wasn't on board, as she tried to feed his foot through the sweatpants. His fist closed in her hair and she let out a little breath of surprise as he dragged her lips to his cock. Nightshade spiked with lust again and she dropped the sweatpants, fingers curling around his calf as she relaxed, eyes crossing as she looked up at him. Little moans of pleasure sounded from her as he fucked her ruthlessly, barely letting her get space to breathe.

God *damn*.

When he'd finished, she gasped for air, cheeks bright pink as she fumbled for the sweatpants again.

"Okay. Now I'm putting them on, and then you can let me go for a few minutes."

I watched as she tugged the sweatpants all the way on, fighting with him when he tried to stop her.

Then she got to her feet, tucking a wild strand of her bushy hair behind her ear and catching her breath.

"Okay. I'll be back. I promise. With snacks. And I have to make sure the others are... are okay. And then we'll—"

She let out a gasp as he dragged her onto his lap, grinding up against her. "Oh... fuuckk." Her moan was breathy as she grabbed him for support. "Okay—Mmm." He'd grabbed her hair and arched her against him, then caught her nipple in his teeth. I could hear his purr of satisfaction as she melted against him.

Then she stiffened as he tried to tug the shirt from her.

"*No!*" Her voice was strained. But Ransom was already fumbling for his own sweatpants, a frown on his face as if he didn't know why they were there. "No no no. Not again. *I want food,*" she whined.

That tone didn't do her any favours. He dragged her closer, grip on her shirt more insistent.

How many times had she tried to get away?

"Ransom!"

Oh. I'd never heard her voice *so* demanding, and her hand had snapped to his neck. He paused, chest heaving as he stared at her.

"Let go," she ordered him.

I grinned.

Slowly, she pried his hand from her shirt, then she pinned him down on the bed, hand still closed around his neck. "I'm going to fuck you," she told him. "If you stay here right like this. Okay?"

He didn't reply, just watching her curiously. He still wasn't *truly* present, but he was there. Alive. With us. A big ball of feelings—even if those feelings were mostly lust right now. And pride. And happiness.

Slowly, she slid from above him. He shifted, but she jabbed a finger firmly in his direction. *"Stay!"*

His nose wrinkled, but he remained in place. She nodded to herself, taking a breath, and then she began padding across the hardwood like a teenager trying to sneak away for a party.

Then she froze, her eyes locking with mine. "Dusk?" she squeaked. "How long have you been there?"

Ransom was on his feet in a moment, chains clinking as he crossed to her.

What was he—? *Oh.*

He swept her behind him, eyes predatory as he took me in.

Protecting her?

Well… this just got better and better.

"It's okay," she whispered to him, arms winding around his waist. He turned back to her, and I'd never seen passion in his eyes like I did in that moment.

Ransom's eyes slid back to me. Finally, there was something calculating in his gaze, like he was analysing me properly now.

Did he recognise me?

I didn't know. Not yet.

I folded my arms, nudging the door open further and leaning against the frame. No need to rile him up. This was already amazing.

"You like him," I said to her with a grin.

She'd stayed.

She'd saved us, and now…

Damn… she'd just banged Ransom through a heat—which *still* didn't even make sense, but I'd deal with that later.

"He seemed like he could use some… help?" she said weakly. "I went into heat. I didn't know where your pills were."

"You like him."

Ha.

He wasn't her mate. And she *did* fucking well like him.

Her fingers dug into the muscle of his torso and she looked defensive. "So what?" There truly was something bratty in her voice. "*He* didn't force his dick down my throat the first time I met him."

Uh… that was such a lie?

The only thing that distanced me from Ransom was heat hormones. She looked so well fucked she was glowing. But I drew up as I saw Ransom had gone stiff, eyes wide as he stared at me.

Had he… understood that?

"Say that again…" I said.

"What?" Shatter asked. "You want me to lie to him? Tell him you asked nicely instead of blackmailing me, and drugging me, and—"

She cut off as Ransom took a step forward, pulling from her touch, lips drawn in a hateful expression as his gaze locked on me.

He… understood?

My heart soared, a grin spreading across my face for half a

second, and then it froze as Ransom's low snarl vibrated through the room, an echo of unadulterated violence.

Ah.

Shit.

He understood.

FOUR

UMBRA

So.

Banana splits were a *whole* thing. Like. Really, really important.

"Banana splits were what you ate when a family got back together."

That was what someone had said once—I didn't know who, but the words stuck even when the memory didn't.

Anyway, problem was, we weren't *quite* there yet.

Earlier, I'd woken up feeling far more refreshed than I had any right to given the last thing I remembered. But I'd been wrapped in an omega poison burrito with a pretty bite on my neck.

Her bite.

A connection with Shatter.

And Ransom was awake. And both of them were fucking.

Obviously.

Puzzle piece A: rutting, and puzzle piece B: heat.

I hadn't even needed to open his door to know, though I listened for a while because fuck me, those were some *hot* sounds.

But that was his first time with her, and I needed to go and get us Indigo Berry Blast smoothies from a shop down the street. (They were, I decided, halfway to banana splits). A good compromise, since Ransom was still a bit feral, and Shatter still had her scent matches that she was all possessive about. So we really needed a halfway point.

I'd had to step over a Dusk-omega-rollup on the way out, which meant she'd even softened to him. *And* I had a bandage on my wrist held together by sellotape and hair clips, so we were in *really* good shape.

Except when I returned, tray of half-patched-family smoothies in hand, it was to find the apartment in a state of war.

It looked as if a bomb had gone off, and, in the midst of it, there was a colossal alpha brawl like no other.

Debris littered the kitchen island and couches. The balcony was basically gone, splintered wood all that remained, and the TV was cracked and hanging half off the wall like someone had been thrown into it.

Ransom and Dusk were absolutely off the walls right now—and I didn't find Shatter cowering in a corner as two alphas brawled across our apartment.

No.

When I walked in, Shatter was joining in—or trying to, bless. Right now she was wrapped around Dusk from behind as he backed up against the couch. Her fingers were woven through his hair, dragging his neck into an arch as Ransom sent a fist flying into his face.

Her hormones were thick in the air, and she was in heat rage. I hadn't even really known that was a thing—but I was definitely looking at it. I could feel it through our special bond. Lust and rage. She was wielding nightshade like furious wildfire in the air.

She sure might act all small, fragile and cute, but Shatter was unbreakable.

I placed the tray in the fridge, since they wouldn't be having theirs all that soon by the look of it, then returned my attention to the scene.

"I *said—!*" Shatter snarled, "*—Don't hurt him!*"

"*He's* attacking *me!*" Dusk tried to duck another blow from Ransom's fist while also shielding Shatter.

"*You deserve it!*"

Ransom was in full alpha fury right now, muscles taut, face contorted in viciousness as he launched for Dusk again. Dusk, who'd just managed to shake Shatter off and drop her on the other side of the couch, darted in the other direction.

"Come on, mate," Dusk was saying, though there was a hint of humour in his voice. "You should go back to banging her."

Ransom rolled his shoulders, then pounced.

Definitely still in a rut. Just now, he wasn't fucking it out of his system.

I scratched my head, then winced. There was a tender lump the size of an egg on it—though none of my memories quite explained that injury.

Strange...

I brushed it off, focusing again on the fight.

The question was, *how* was Ransom in the living room? There were still cuffs on his wrists.

Odd, really.

Philosophy class would tell me that rather than asking *how* he got free, instead ask *why* he got free.

Hmm.

No. It didn't fit, actually. The answer was pretty obvious: to beat Dusk into a pulp.

Not *quite* philosophy level questions.

It *was* strange that he was out here while fully chained. Dusk had installed metal strong enough to withstand alpha auras. Though now I was thinking about it, it wasn't as reliable as those alpha hooks that could be buried deep in the ground. This one had to be attached to the walls. I mean, in *theory*—

Aaahhhh.

I saw it now.

That *was* the wall of Ransom's room that made up the pile of debris across the living room.

I sipped on my smoothie. "Heh."

Ransom's chains jammed again as he reached for Dusk, tangled like a dog's leash across the couch, kitchen island, and bannister. Someone should probably take them off him. Bit of a task, really, since he looked ready to kill.

Only, then I felt his aura wane, and he sagged.

He crashed to his knees, a low whine in his chest. Dusk reacted instantly, diving for Ransom and pinning him to the ground.

Shatter hissed, scrambling toward them, her fists around Dusk's neck as she tried to wrench him off.

"Get *off* him."

"Shatter—" Dusk snarled. "He's going to fucking hurt you if you're not—"

Ransom's trembling growl ripped across the whole room and he threw his weight against Dusk, eyes wild. His aura was still waning, though, so nothing happened.

Oh wow.

Had he *understood* Dusk?

Shatter gave up trying to drag him from Ransom, instead scrambling to her feet and making for the kitchen. She hesitated for only a moment, fist around a knife handle as her eyes met mine.

Indigo Berry Blast burst to life on my taste buds as I offered her a wide grin. She paused only a moment longer, then seized the knife and darted away.

She liked knives, which was cute. She had a small switchblade she carried around in her school bag all the time. Dusk had found it the first time he'd gone scrunchie searching, and she'd had a fit at the suggestion we make her take it out.

"Let go of him." She shoved the knife against his throat. I cocked my head, erection raging as Dusk froze.

"What would your mates say if they could see you now, Gem?" he asked, voice a taunt, rather unphased considering there was a blade to his throat.

What I wouldn't give to trade places with him right now. My eyes snagged on the way her delicate fingers locked in his hair. So demanding...

"He's *mine*," she hissed. "I'm taking him to my nest."

Wait.

Ransom got an invite to her nest that quickly—after everything I'd done to get one?

That was all it took?

I was crossing the room in an instant and sitting on the ottoman beside them. "Nightshade." I tucked a lock of hair behind her ear, and her eyes darted to me defensively for a moment. "You should have just asked, I'd have done this for you on day one."

Honestly.

I sighed.

I'd beat the shit out of Dusk for free.

She stared at me for a moment, and then glanced back to Dusk. *"Move!"*

"Alright," Dusk conceded.

Slowly, she lowered the knife, climbing from his back. She watched him cautiously as he got up, a flicker of worry in her eyes as she dropped her gaze to Ransom who was now curled up and heaving ragged breaths.

That drew me up. It was worry in her eyes. Genuine worry. It was flooding down the little omega bond we had, too, weak as it was.

For... Ransom?

I mean, he'd be fine. His aura got way more unstable than this, but she didn't know that.

The world shifted in that moment, and I might have caught the same from Dusk down the pack bond as we both watched her.

Something about her changed, her scent becoming something I'd never felt. Protective. Seductive.

So *very* omega.

I'd do anything she asked right now. I'd get on my knees and kiss her cute little toes if that's what she wanted.

"Carry him to my nest," she said.

I was on my feet in a moment. "I'll do it," I offered—especially now I knew more nest invites were on the table.

"NO!" Her voice was shrill. *"You"*—She jabbed the knife in Dusk's direction—"will carry him, or I won't fix him."

I grinned. She just wanted an excuse to tell him what to do, I knew it. Also—such a little liar. Of course she'd fix him.

Dusk cocked his head, considering her for a long moment. Then, without argument, he went to the drawer and dug out Ransom's cuff keys. When he'd freed Ransom's wrists, he leaned down and dragged him to unsteady feet. Shatter hurried after them, trying to stifle her shock as Dusk began hauling Ransom down the hallway.

And she had no idea that she'd just witnessed something we'd been dreaming of for months.

"Food and... and tea," I heard her mutter once we got to the door of her nest.

"Tea?" Dusk asked, turning to her.

"Y-yes." She cleared her throat, lifting the knife again. "We need food and tea. H-he needs taking care of."

"Okay."

She glanced at me as Dusk failed to argue, as if she couldn't understand. Then I saw a little flicker of boldness in her eyes, and she flipped from nervous to brat, hedging her bets in an instant.

"Green tea. Marmalade on toast."

Dusk raised an eyebrow, a half smile on his lips. "What?"

She narrowed her eyes, snarl returning to her lips. "Green tea and marmalade on toast."

His grin was white teeth and crimson blood. "We don't have marmalade."

"Then fucking get some."

I was smiling like an idiot as Dusk got Ransom to the bed.

Indigo Berry Blast, turned out, was the perfect flavour for this.

Half-patched.

This *was* my family. She completed it.

"You're so fucking perfect, Shatter," Dusk murmured, drawing her close once Ransom was settled. She narrowed her eyes, fist squeezing the knife, even if it was down at her side. "Our sweet omega brat with so many things for me to punish."

I saw her shiver.

Ransom's growl rose in the air, but Dusk was already letting her go.

"Just getting her ready for you, mate."

Ransom lunged for Dusk, but Shatter intercepted—which was good because he could barely hold himself up. She turned on Dusk. *"Get. Out!"*

Dusk raised his hands in defeat.

Her scent had changed again. Not just soothing, but absolutely full of lust. I noticed how hot her cheeks were as she set the knife aside and began grabbing pillows from the bed to tuck around Ransom. He was still breathing heavily, and she paused to place her hand on his cheek. He relaxed, leaning into her touch.

Through the bond I felt him surface—a flicker of something human clawing its way from his soul to reach for her.

I smiled.

I could watch this forever, but then I sipped again, only to hear the loud slurping sounds of my straw reaching the end of my drink. She spun, fire blazing in her eyes as she took me in, smoothie still in my fist.

Only mildly sad that the drink—and show—was over, and I backed out after Dusk. I had to let her get to work. She was taking care of our pack mate in her nest, after all.

"Where are you going?" I asked as Dusk searched the apartment for keys before grabbing his spare set.

"To the store to get her knock-off jam. And *don't*—" He jammed a finger at me, looking entirely insane with a huge bruise blossoming across half his face "—even think about burning her toast. She gets my toast, or none at all."

The door slammed, but through the bond I felt nothing from Dusk but pure joy.

FIVE

SHATTER

This was just temporary. I kept telling myself that.

This pack wasn't mine, but Ransom needed me. For the first time, I felt like myself. A proper omega. As if this was something I could do.

Something I was *made* for.

I followed my instincts, for once never worried about if I was doing it right. I didn't worry about who I was or had been, or if I was too broken to fix someone else.

I wasn't.

I *was* an omega, and this was mine.

Ransom was coming back to me, tucked in pillows and blankets, and curled in my arms.

After a while I heard a polite knock on the door, and dared to leave Ransom's side long enough to answer it, unsure of what to expect.

It was Dusk. He was holding a tray with steaming tea and a stack of toast. Beside it was a knife and a pot of marmalade.

I stared at it for an age, eyes catching on one thing in particular.

A *teapot*...? That hadn't been in their kitchen before.

Heightened omega instincts sent stars to my eyes as I fixated on it. It was beautiful, painted with a scattering of rhombuses and diamonds that almost had me snatching it from the tray and burrowing under the covers with it.

Oh *boy*, did I need to shed some hormones. Especially since Dusk was paying close attention to my reaction.

"Umbra went out to get it?" I asked, much too hopefully.

"Umbra's been watching *Breaking Bad* since you came in here," Dusk said mildly.

Oh.

My heart sank, but I felt a giddy little thrill at the same time.

Dusk had fetched me tea *and* a teapot?

That shouldn't make me pleased. I hated him, still. Even when those dark eyes of his bored right into my soul, and brainless butterflies lifted in my stomach every time he looked at me like that.

"Do you want me to bring it in?" he asked, peering into my nest.

I seized the tray from him. "*No.*"

He grinned, and I almost stepped back, but something halted me. I blinked down at the teapot, a question trapped in my throat.

"Is Umbra okay?" I asked, suddenly guilty. He'd left earlier with Dusk. But he'd been so unwell...

"He'd say yes, but I could send him with the next tray?"

I chewed on my lip and nodded. "Best I look him over. Just to be sure..."

The smile that played on Dusk's lips made me want to kick him.

"And, just so we're clear, the answer is no," he said, leaning against the door frame, arrogance across every inch of his face.

"No, what?"

"No, me bringing tea and orange jam doesn't mean you haven't still got a punishment coming."

My gaze snapped to him, and I knew heat was crawling up my cheeks. My nest was saturated with arousal right now, which explained the wetness between my thighs as he said those words.

I stepped back before I could say anything that would get me in deeper water with him, then slammed the door in his face.

I hurried back to the bedside where Ransom was stirring, tray clutched in my grip. All my worries of Dusk slid away as Ransom's glittering green eyes found me in the dark.

He was awake, and more present than I'd seen him yet.

I set the tray down on the side table and crawled over to him. Ransom wasn't my mate, but he was sweet, and caring, and sort of *mine*. He'd even protected me from Dusk.

It was my job right now to balance him, and mates simply had nothing to do with it. It was just what a good omega would do. I was doing my best—I'd even tied his hair in a bun with one of the scrunchies, since it was a bit tangled. But he didn't seem ready yet for me to tackle that properly. He was much more interested in holding me closer. Or sex.

Sure, a pack as rich as this could pay omegas to fall all over Ransom to keep him well—I whined at the thought, dragging him close—but I *could* be as good as any of them.

The spark in Ransom's eyes was fading, though. He wasn't all back, and even as I watched his focus drifted, the muscles in his jaw tensing.

Dammit.

I needed to do better.

So I sat him up and fed him my favourite snack (though he refused the tea) and purred for him until he settled once more, and then I drifted off in his arms.

UMBRA

Despite my disgust at the mere idea of it, Dusk forced me to discuss what happened. And not the nice Shatter-in-heat shit, either. He wanted to chat *feelings* and all the negative shit.

"You nearly died." Dusk leaned back on the couch, pausing *Breaking Bad* and rubbed his face.

I glanced down at the bandages around my wrist, clenching my jaw. "I don't know what happened. I think I—"

"It wasn't you," Dusk said.

Usually, talking about the Lincoln pack would drag me into memories. My imbalance—my curse—surfacing. I tensed, ready to disengage, but Shatter's lingering bite was like a fortress, walling me in and keeping those demons out.

I stared at Dusk. It *hadn't* been me?

But I'd been sure...

"How do you know?"

"Flynn touched me, and the whole bond began to collapse," Dusk said.

I froze. *What in the fuck did that mean?*

I didn't like it at all.

"I'm done with these stupid games," I growled. "We—"

"Ransom's getting better," Dusk said. "And we *still* don't know enough."

I grit my teeth as he echoed Decebal and his stupid, rational advice.

"You can't kill them until you know what they've taken."

Fuck him.

And Dusk always listened. Decebal didn't know what it was like. Having your living, breathing demons walk the same halls, un-fucking-punished for destroying everyone you loved.

I didn't care if killing them killed me. I *didn't* care. Yet still, I was trapped. If I died and our pack fragmented, Ransom might die. It was why we'd bonded him in the first place. To save him.

"If they were gone, she would be free," I growled.

Dusk tensed, a tick to his jaw. "I won't have this conversation—*I won't risk it.* She saved you as well as him. She stayed when she could have left. That changes everything."

I felt a flicker of uncertainty. My aura was a shadowed threat I could never escape—and despite Dusk's determination, I knew we might never fix it. It might keep dragging me down and down until I never came back.

It almost had yesterday.

And yet, Shatter was a parting in the clouds—a light we'd never seen before. And I didn't know what to do with it.

"She's still hung up on them. But maybe, after this—"

"What she did for Ransom won't change anything for her," I said.

He cocked his head, curious at my confidence. The bond she'd left on my neck connected us, even temporarily. I could feel all her wild little omega feelings.

She felt safe here. She... damn, I think she might really... I swallowed. I think she honestly might love us. That hadn't happened overnight, and still, she was set on getting to her mates.

"There's something she's not saying," I said.

"How do you know?"

I shrugged. "I don't care what anyone says. *We* are everything she's looking for. If she hasn't let go of them yet, there's more to it."

Dusk said nothing to that, leaning back on the couch and tugging out his phone. Likely to update Decebal with everything he'd learned about her in the last few days.

He was desperate to learn where she'd come from. It could help, perhaps, but I wasn't convinced. Dusk had to know everything, and that need drove him.

. . .

For the second marmalade and toast delivery, Dusk bundled the tray into my hands and shoved me to her nest door. It was late—like super late—though I didn't think they were actively fucking right now. Dusk was confused about her heat, but I was quite clear on the matter: just like everything about Shatter, her heat was not behaving the way it should.

"She'll let you in," he said.

Would she?

But Dusk was already knocking and cracking it open. We both paused when we heard her voice cut off.

What I found within was the most precious thing I'd ever seen. She was curled up on Ransom's lap in the bed as she read from an Arkology textbook. It was extra sweet because, as far as I knew, Ransom still hadn't yet spoken a word. They both looked up at me.

"Umbra?"

"Yeh." I glanced down at the tray in my hand. More marmalade and green tea. Dusk had chopped up some apples to add, too.

"Do you need to stay?" she asked. "Are you stable?"

I palmed my neck, but Dusk answered for me.

"No," he told her, shoving me into the room.

I snorted. Stupid answer.

I was *never* stable.

Still, I didn't feel bad because then she was lifting the covers in invitation and my worry vanished.

I crossed toward her and set the tray on the bedside table. I sat at her side, drawing her close and ignoring Ransom's little growl. I grinned. He'd have to get used to sharing sooner or later. And he was looking good, even if he hadn't said anything yet. His deep red hair was a shaggy mess, but his green eyes were bright and full of life. I couldn't believe he was back with us, and out of chains.

I was getting my brother back.

He settled well enough when Shatter set the book down and took my arm—the one with the bandage—for examination. It was healing fast, but the cut had been deep.

"Is it doing okay?" she asked.

I nodded. Her bandaging skills needed work. I'd taken a photo, so that when Dusk replaced it for me he was able to copy all the outer layers exactly as they had been—hair clip included—so she'd never know we'd touched it.

Seemingly satisfied, she patted it, then glanced to the tray I'd brought.

Right. Nesting alpha was my job tonight.

I passed it over and she set it on her lap, smiling as she lifted one of the pieces of toast to Ransom. He took a bite without question, eyes drifting around the room.

"He doesn't seem to like the tea," she said sadly.

I cleared my throat, picking up the second mug for myself. Shatter cupped her own mug to her chest, watching for my reaction. I forced a smile as I tasted it, which was enough to make her beam.

A post heat omega picnic?

This was better than I could have expected, even if the tea tasted like musty asshole.

When we were done, I was expecting her to tell me to leave. Instead, she settled beneath the covers, adjusting Ransom's arm around her waist before looking up at me expectantly.

Excellent.

I wrapped my arms around her, feeling the rumble of Ransom's growl as my arms brushed his chest. I couldn't help my chuckle. I could feel him waning in and out of the bond. He was confused right now, a collision of protection and happiness, as if he knew who I was deep down.

I huddled closer. "You saved me, Little Nightshade," I breathed in her ear. She melted into my arms because, well, how could she not?

Oddly, her heat seemed mostly over, judging by the hormones in the air. "Where did your heat go?" I asked.

"My heats... they..." She cleared her throat. "They do their own thing."

"What does that mean?"

"Well... it's short. And instead of it being like... every few months or whatever, they just come when things are... intense."

"Intense?" I pondered on that, but she ducked her head, wriggling back against Ransom, who was happy to tug her further into his arms. "Like...?" Oh.

Oh.

"When you're all turned on?" I asked.

A grin spread on my face. I could feel my chest puffing up as she glared up at me. I'd put her into heat all by myself.

"Not just... *that*. If I'm stressed or like... doing too many omega things."

"Uh huh?"

Boy, would that be a problem once she was in our pack.

Well. Not a problem for *me*. But if she wanted to go and be all professional, and work on her studies like she loved, *then* it would be. There was no way we weren't going to make her hot *all* the time for us.

Maybe we could work something out. She could work from home when she needed. We could have heats, and she could do her job in between.

There was something so sexy about the idea of my sweet little omega trapped on my knot while she flipped through textbooks and did all of her calculations and smart stuff.

Could I get her glasses? Just... just to see what she'd look like in them. Would she wear them for me?

She could be paid to do amazing stuff—change the world, and all of that—*and* get fucked *all at the same time.* And I'd feed and water her and make sure she didn't shrivel up and die when she got too lost in her work...

Yup.

The dream.

This was going to be amazing.

I frowned.

Would I make it to see that? If what Dusk said was true about the Lincoln pack—what were my odds, really?

One touch, and I'd almost died. I'd take them with me—no two ways about it, but... the thought of death had never been such an inconvenience before.

Now, I *really* wanted to see Shatter in glasses.

Working on Arkology and shit.

There was a rock in my throat.

The thought vanished at her small gasp. I blinked as I realised Ransom was gone. And by gone, I meant he'd sank beneath the blankets and buried his face between her thighs, dragging her hips away from me.

I grabbed the depressing line of thought and tossed it off a cliff. I had better things to focus on. Like Ransom's jealousy, which was definitely working in her favour.

"Ransom!" Her voice was a squeak of surprise, and her cheeks were pink, which made me chuckle, because they'd just had filthy heat sex together.

I closed my hand around her mouth, dragging her back against my chest as Ransom spread her legs further, giving me a fucking beautiful view as he dragged his tongue up along her center and made her shudder.

"Let him treat you," I growled. "You deserve it after you saved us all."

Her moan was a siren's call as Ransom buried his fingers into her. Interest sparked in his gaze as he worked her, taking in every reaction so he could push her to the edge.

He was in love with her already. I could see it by the dazed look in his eyes as he watched her. I could tell from the bundle of feelings that kept surfacing in the bond.

I smiled.

My girl and my pack brother, right here.

SIX

DUSK

Shatter might have been surprised when I turned up at her nest door with tea and toast the first time, but she was still failing to understand one crucial thing: she was ours.

I would get her anything she wanted. And today was proof that my choice was the right one.

Ransom had been to clinic after clinic, to dozens of omegas, and even experienced beta Sweethearts. We'd tried every drug known to science for alpha instability. Nothing had ever healed him.

Until her.

Now, it was the next evening, and I slipped into her nest. The lights were dim, bathing the rich browns of hardwood floors and broad desk, side tables, and bedframe in a warm light. There were two slumbering figures on the bed.

I'd met with Bolin, our appointed support, today. He'd sat down to catch me up on curriculum as I'd claimed a heat break for the pack. There was no other way we would be allowed to stay on, Kingsman name or not.

I'd also booked in for the repairs on the apartment, which I hoped would be done before Ransom and Shatter finished balancing him. I would allow nothing to interrupt that, however, not when we were on the precipice of getting him back, so they were only allowed in for repairs during the day, when Umbra were present to make sure no one went *near* her nest.

Right now, our apartment was stranger-free, and since Umbra had stayed the night with her and Ransom, visiting her nest was all I'd dreamed about. She was no longer in full heat—Umbra had caught me up on the details—and Ransom's rut seemed mostly over. I settled onto the bed beside Shatter, careful not to disturb either of them.

She was the most beautiful creature I'd ever seen, sleeping beside Ransom, hair draped over golden skin in waves and tangles, splayed around her in a crescent moon as she hugged his arm to her chest. She was protective of him, and that alone was the hottest thing I'd ever witnessed. Her expression was peaceful, a stuttering purr bubbling up here and there as her chest rose and fell. She wore his oversized T-shirt, and her legs were bare. The sheets were pushed down around her as if she hadn't cooled down entirely since her heat had passed.

I'd wanted to check on them, but now I was here, my mind was derailing.

She'd definitely burned down my rulebook—even if she had saved Ransom. I wasn't beneath playing dirty since she'd leached heat hormones into our entire apartment for days on end, and I hadn't been the one fucking her.

I ran my hand gently along her thigh, lust hitting my veins as she let out a low breath that sounded needy.

Out of heat, but still horny as fuck, clearly.

I caught my lip in my teeth as I dropped my touch between her thighs. Nightshade spiked the air with desire, and she shifted, adjusting to her front a little.

My thumb and pinky ran along the back of her thighs as I pressed my index finger between her legs. She wasn't wearing underwear, and slick was glistening on her skin.

I closed my eyes to fight my groan, then curled my finger, finding her entrance too easily and pressing in.

She shifted, grinding against me, a little mewl breaking from her chest.

Damn.

My dick pressed against my jeans so hard it hurt.

Every time she broke the rules and let me punish her, I would prove to her how fucking perfect she was for us. It wouldn't be long before she knew we were better than any other pack the universe had to offer.

I added my forefinger, dipping both into her with care, loving how she squeezed them so tightly.

She shifted again, eyes still shut, stretching one hand out before her and—fuck. Me. She balled a fist into the pillow as she lifted her hips, back arched as she presented for me.

With that, I kissed sanity good-fucking-night.

I pushed the oversized T-shirt up to her shoulders so I could see her full body on display for me while I dipped my fingers into her glistening cunt.

I froze as Ransom shifted, hand searching across the sheets until he felt her arm. Lily of the valley calmed as he drew closer. She wiggled her sweet ass, pressing back against my fingers with another needy sound.

I could have come right then.

But Shatter was my fucking ruin, and I was going to wake her on my cock.

I readjusted myself, undoing my jeans and freeing my length, then pressed my tip to her entrance. Her eyes fluttered, her fingers balling on the pillow harder.

I nudged into her just slightly.

It was thrilling, seeing how far I could go without waking her.

Cute eyebrows bunched and her lips parted as my girth stretched her out, but I was only in half an inch. I waited until she relaxed her grip on the pillow before filling her some more.

Fuck, she was tight.

It was so hot, watching her brows bunch up each time I inched deeper, her body shifting slightly as it adjusted to my intrusion.

She was still asleep somehow, and I managed to sink my whole length, right to my knot, without waking her. Again, I fought not to finish.

Instead, I pressed in just the slightest bit further, enjoying the feeling of my swelling knot as it stretched her unsuspecting body just enough that she moaned, long, low, and desperate. Any further, and I'd be locked into her. I didn't want that just yet.

Instead, I drew out, watching her eyelashes flutter again. I did it once more, stretching her over my knot, and she frowned deeper as she tried to adjust to me. I didn't know if her expression showed confusion or need. I rocked into her a few times with the edge of my knot, blood on fire at her precious whimpers.

I was going to leave her body trembling for my knot before she'd even woken. I swear she was wetter than when I'd started.

Bowing over, I place my hands on either side of her. Her cheek pressed further into the sheets, fists balling tight as I withdrew one inch at a time. I could feel her pussy seizing me as I pulled out, and a frustrated whine slipped from her chest. Ransom shifted again, starting up a low purr as he listened to her sounds.

I stifled the groan; I'd never felt her as tight as this.

I set a painfully slow pace, watching the shift in her expression each time I buried my length into her heat. Occasionally, she would tense, goosebumps lighting across her flesh, and I would slow until they were gone. I could feel the most primal frustration from her needy body as I kept her on the edge.

It was so fucking hot, and I warred against my own orgasm at the thought that I might be able to fuck her until she came in her sleep.

I *needed* that.

To see her wake, shaking, begging, and disoriented to the bliss I would wring from her body.

I groaned as I slid into her again, hitting that spot that made her tense and her pink lips part in a little 'o'. Again, since I'd just pull her back from the edge of another orgasm, I teased her with my knot. This time her whine was more desperate as I stretched her pussy over it just enough to feel it, and then drew out. She arched further, breaths short and sharp as she tried to take my knot. Her tight walls squeezed me, desperate for what I was denying her. There was sweat glistening along her skin now, as if the tail end of heat was resurfacing with a vengeance as I denied her.

I would wake her to the most mind blowing orgasm of her life, and then I'd fuck her some more.

Finally, I could see her nearing the edge again, her chest rising and falling, her eyelids fluttering each time I buried my cock into her—again I pressed in the slightest bit deeper, letting her know how close my knot was.

And that was enough.

SHATTER

I woke to an orgasm that wiped my mind utterly blank.

The world was nothing but dizzying pleasure. A hand clamped down over my mouth, stifling my moans. I gripped sheets, bliss soaring through my veins, pussy full of an alpha's cock, stretching me around a knot just the slightest bit before pulling out and driving in again.

I was shaking, cross-eyed, and panting before the world steadied.

Before I realised what was happening.

Before he rode my orgasm out and then kept going and I realised who was pinning me to the bed and fucking me.

Midnight opium filled the air as Ransom slept at my side.

I whimpered, a trembling wreck, but his hand, which was still over my mouth, tightened. "Shh, Gem. If he wakes angry, it'll undo all the hard work you've done."

I couldn't help looking at Ransom sleeping at my side, fear spiking through my veins.

Dusk drew out of me, then slammed back in before leaning close. "If I let go, will you stay quiet?"

I nodded desperately. They'd fight again, I knew that, and Ransom had just started to truly settle.

Dusk's hand dropped from my mouth, and I instantly tried to lunge away. His grip was bruising on my hips as he dragged me mercilessly back onto his shaft. I had to clamp my own hand over my mouth to stifle my yelp as he speared me right to the core.

"You said you wouldn't come in," I hissed.

His voice was low and humorous as he bent over me, stealing the breath from my lungs with another powerful thrust. "You said you'd do as you were told, and instead I ended up with a knife at my neck." His breath brushed my ear. "You break a rule, I break one, too."

I tried to ignore my dizzying, building pleasure as he continued driving into me. He'd got me aroused while I was sleeping, riding my attraction to Ransom.

"You have so much punishment to take," he growled. "I would spank you, but it'd be too loud."

Again, I tried to dive from him, but I barely moved, and the result was him slamming so hard into me I saw stars.

"How about we try something else instead," he whispered.

One hand clamped back over my mouth and his other found my nipple, fingers biting down just hard enough that I let out a muffled squeak. Worse, heat pooled in my stomach again as he flicked the same area he'd just bruised. Then his fingers shifted to my other nipple. I froze this time, hand pressed over my mouth, tears pricking my eyes. Again, he delivered a shot of pain, and again, my body jolted with pleasure.

Then his touch dropped between my thighs, and he circled my clit. I squeezed my eyes shut, trying to wriggle away, hand still clutching my mouth as I realised what he was going to do.

What I wasn't expecting was the furious orgasm that hit my veins as his fingers bit down on my clit. He did it again, while I was still in the throes of my orgasm, slamming into me with a breath of pleasure.

"You're squeezing me so good, Gem," he purred, keeping up his slow rhythm, fucking me into oblivion.

SEVEN

DUSK

It didn't seem to matter that she knew it was me. Shatter was so turned on. Still, she struggled, even when I felt her body tightening again, readying for the third orgasm.

"Stop fighting, beautiful," I breathed. "You have no idea how special you are."

And just like I'd known they would, those words undid her. A little whimper slipped past the hand I had over her mouth and her body seized me like a vice as she came apart.

"Do you want my knot, precious?" I asked as I continued pumping into her and drawing her orgasm out.

She hadn't seen what I had, with her eyes squeezed tight shut, that Ransom was waking. I twisted her nipple again, rewarded with her nails scraping down my arm, another desperate moan slipping from her.

"I won't give it unless you ask."

I dropped my hand from her mouth so I could hear her breathless panting. I moved my touch from her nipple to her clit, circling it firmly. Her whole body seized over my length, and she sucked in a sharp breath as I tried for another orgasm so soon after the last had crested. But I knew her body was capable of more before she was spent.

Ransom was staring from me to her, his lips parted, clear confusion in his eyes as he tried to orient himself.

"Let me knot you, Gem. You deserve it, don't you? After what you did for him?"

The sound she made was half feral, but she wasn't fighting me anymore. She was too busy warring with herself for the answer I knew she so desperately wanted to give. I stopped as I sunk deep into her, letting my knot stretch out her pussy again, just enough to tease. Her broken moan almost had me losing control and locking myself into her right then, but I held on.

I drew out, and she panted, wriggling back against me, her face screwing up in a frown as if she didn't understand why she'd done it. She was overwhelmed and confused, with no idea that she was contending with her own body, which had been promised my knot over and over.

I chuckled, removing my hand from her clit, and instead tangling it through her hair so I could press her into the sheets and make sure she was facing away from Ransom.

He was going to see how I treated our girl so he could get off that high horse of his.

"Ask for it," I murmured.

Now unable to wiggle back against me, she paused, still panting. Suspended as she was, with just the tip of my cock filling her, she gripped me tight with each rapid breath. Her body was shaking from the last orgasm, and her scent was flooding the air like an aphrodisiac.

Ransom was fully alert now, pupils blown as he watched us. He was tense. I could see that, as if her answer here would seal my fate one way or another.

And I knew what it would be.

I withdrew from her entirely and her low moan set every one of my instincts on edge, leaving them clawing at me to fix whatever made her so sad. I loved that she could do that to me. I was long broken, but Shatter made me feel like an alpha in a way no other omega could.

There was a pause as I nudged her slick entrance with my tip, and she shuddered. The ragged whisper came at last, almost impossible to hear. "Please."

A smile lit on my face. "Please what, Gem? Say it."

I heard her swallow, and there was another pause. Her golden skin glistened with sweat, lit with goosebumps as she trembled. "Please... knot me."

The rumble in my chest was involuntary as I slammed back in. Her eyes went wide as the breath rushed from her lungs. She was liquid, completely wrecked as she gave in to me. "My poor little omega," I growled, gripping her hips and driving into her brutally. "Begging me to fill your perfect cunt." For three strokes, I fucked her so deep that she loosed little squeaks, leaving her a scrambling, desperate mess.

I felt stars light in my veins again, and I straightened, dragging her back against me by her neck so she could look Ransom right in the eyes. She let out a breath of shock as she saw him, but it was stifled by her moan as I stretched her fully over my knot.

"You feel so fucking amazing." I needed him to see she loved my praise as much as she liked my punishment. "Show him how beautiful you are when you come apart on my knot." I pinned her to my chest by her neck, and she clutched my forearm as I circled her clit with my other hand, all the while rutting her deep.

She shuddered, body seizing me as she desperately clawed at my arms.

Ransom had heard what she'd said.

"You're ours." A purr rumbled deep in my chest, and she let out another moan, still struggling against me as I rutted her and circled her clit. "Perfect, and beautiful, and everything we've ever dreamed of."

I thought the sound she made might have been half a sob, but then all thoughts wiped from my mind as she came over my knot, sending me into the throes of my own mind blowing orgasm.

She curled up when I sagged onto the bed, burying her face in my arms and refusing to look at Ransom, who still watched like a lost puppy. I loved the way she squirmed when my purr rumbled to life again, and with my chest against her back, I knew it must send vibrations all the way down her spine and into her core.

She wasn't done.

We would be locked together for a while. With my purr still the only sound in the air, I dropped my fingers between her thighs and began playing with her some more.

Shatter grabbed the pillow and tugged it against her face, and Ransom looked utterly unsure.

"You made him better, Gem," I breathed in her ear, circling her clit slowly.

She wriggled against me, and I had to bite my lip at how good she felt on my cock.

"You fixed him when no one else could."

Shatter fought to stifle a low moan in her chest.

Locks of dark auburn hair swung past olive skin as Ransom's green eyes remained fixed on her. The look in his eyes broke my heart. I felt what he was feeling. A flash of sorrow for the time he'd lost.

Missing time once more.

And I think he knew he'd missed something huge.

I leaned down, nudging her hair back and tugging the pillow from her grip. I drew her neck into an arch so she had nowhere else to hide as I sped up on her sensitive clit and pressed my teeth to her neck. Not a proper bite, but it was enough to send her over the edge—because she would deny it to the ends of the earth, but my claim was the one thing she couldn't fight.

Shatter wanted it more than she hated me, and it melted her every time.

"My gift," I breathed as Ransom watched her come apart before his eyes. I fought my groan at how fucking amazing that felt.

Shatter was a gift beyond our wildest dreams. One that might mean he wouldn't lose one more day for what he'd sacrificed.

Ransom swallowed, seeking Shatter's gaze, but she was still pressed against me, eyes squeezed closed.

"I chose her," I told him, letting him feel my conviction.

And in the process, I saved her from a fate worse than death.

She wasn't ready for that truth yet.

Ransom reached out, nudging her chin up until she was looking at him. His eyes scanned hers.

"Do you want to come again?" I asked. She shook her head, still breathing heavily. "For him?" I caught her firm nipple in my fingers, twisting it softly this time, knowing she would be sore from all of my punishment. I was rewarded with a beautiful moan.

Even so, Ransom's growl was a warning.

"Sounds like a yes," I murmured, rocking into her slowly. Her nails bit into Ransom's forearm as she scrambled to dignify herself while her body betrayed her once more. "What if he helped, Gem?" I breathed in her ear. "How hard would you squeeze me if he had his tongue down your throat?"

I loved how easy it was to learn her truths with my knot buried deep within her, feeling her body tense up whenever I said *just* the right thing.

I rocked into her again, and the nails digging into Ransom's arms were more insistent. Her eyes were wide, holding his, and there was pleading in them. Not for freedom. No, right now she wanted to be trapped between us.

"You're going to have to ask him," I breathed in her ear, rocking into her again and cupping her chin in my hands like a gift.

"W-would you kiss me?" she asked. There was something broken and vulnerable in that question.

Ransom was swallowed completely by her gaze, and I knew in that moment, no one else existed in the world but her.

I drove my knot deeper.

She moaned, and he caved, drawing her into a kiss more gentle and caring than I'd believed Ransom capable of.

Her exhaustion just made the orgasm stronger, and I loved how she trembled against me, her body clenching once more over my cock. I groaned, spilling into her again, and this time she was so full that I felt some of my cum drip between her thighs, my swollen knot unable to lock it all in.

I rode the orgasm out to its fullest, until she was a trembling puddle in Ransom's arms, and my knot finally released her.

EIGHT

SHATTER

Despite the week's events, I wasn't going to fail school for the sake of going into heat and nesting with Ransom—thank *God*.

On Friday morning, Dusk provided me with coursework, and I spent the morning with Ransom's arms around my waist in the nest while I studied.

I was interrupted in the afternoon when Dusk popped his head in, *rudely* ignoring the fact that *I* was ignoring *him*, and told me he wanted Ransom to do a trial night without me.

"The whole night?" I asked, my voice high.

"We have to know if he's stable without you, or we won't know what's going on."

Ransom remained voiceless, and I was trying not to take it as a personal failure. He was gentle and sweet, I just knew it, and he was *in* there. I thought he even understood what I was saying when I talked him through Aura Studies equations.

I fought the pout on my face as Ransom went stiff, drawing me close.

"Will you chain him up again?" I asked.

"No. Umbra will stay overnight with him—With you," Dusk amended, eyes darting to Ransom, and I saw his spark of hope again.

By four in the afternoon, I'd scent marked most of Ransom's room and tucked him in six times, despite the fact it wasn't bedtime, (Umbra was setting up video games).

The apartment had been fixed while Ransom and I were down in the nest, and his bedroom had been given life, with couches and a TV, and even a few posters across the walls featuring bands I didn't recognise. Not that I knew many musicians outside of the opera singers Aunty Lauren liked to hum along to.

I'd also given him a bite on the neck in case anything drastic happened, and I had to know right away. I wasn't going to do this by halves. Ransom was getting better, and I'd see it through.

The last I saw before Dusk dragged me away was Ransom's beautiful green eyes fixed on me longingly, video game controller in his grip as Umbra helped shoo me out.

"Just one night, Little Nightshade," he'd said before shutting the door.

Now, I'd been pulled onto Dusk's lap while he studied. I'd loitered too long in the living room, anxiously incapable of bringing myself to vanish back to the nest.

His hand trailed gently up and down my arm as he hugged me close, flipping through the pages of a Physiological Adaptations Arkology textbook.

Not my favourite, since there weren't many equations involved, and my mind drifted.

Finally, a question nagged at me, twisting my stomach and making itself impossible to ignore. I couldn't help thinking to the blue registration card in my pencil case. The one I carried everywhere I could get away with.

"Ransom uh... didn't sort out my registration and papers, did he?" I asked quietly, tilting my head and peering up at Dusk. I don't know why that made me want to cry.

"He would have," Dusk murmured without pause, barely glancing away from the textbook, though I noticed a distinct clench to his jaw. "Ransom fights for people with nothing no matter what it costs him," he said. "I did it because he made me what I am."

"Oh."

Okay.

"So," he said after a pause. "Are we going to keep pretending?"

I looked up at him with a frown. There was a slight smile curving his lips as his eyes drifted inattentively across the page. "You begged me for my knot, you bit Umbra, and you went into heat with Ransom—even though there were pills and mates nearby."

"I didn't know where the pills were, and I couldn't get to my mates in time," I said.

His grin widened. "You could have left."

"It wasn't... I *was* going to leave."

"But you *didn't*."

I shrank in his arms, hating that he was saying exactly what I'd been trying not to think about. Especially now that Ransom wasn't a present distraction...

Dusk tilted my chin up, and I found myself swallowed by piercing yellow eyes. "Tell me what I need to do for you to let them go, Shatter. I'll do it."

I blinked, completely lost for words.

"I..." He trailed off, swallowing, and I followed the movement down his throat, suddenly needing any distraction. "I don't know how to tell you the truth without scaring you away."

What truth?

My heart was thundering in my ears.

"Why do you need them?" he asked. "Just tell me so I can fix it."

It wasn't something he could fix.

What I needed from him was impossible: trust that transcended a dark bond. The kind of forever it would be foolish to trust to anyone but mates.

"You've seen us. All of us. You know our secrets, our worst parts, and it's not..." He took a breath. "If it's not enough—"

That word splintered every concern I had. *"Enough?"*

That's what he thought?

How could Dusk Varis not think he wasn't enough?

"That's... not the issue?" He seemed to see the shock on my face.

"I..." I couldn't think straight.

"Please tell me. Let me fix it."

I shook my head, heart slamming into my ribs. No no. He had it all wrong. "I'm broken. That's all."

"Who told you that?"

"The whole world," I whispered. "I don't fit."

He breathed a low laugh. "Then I'll break the world until it fits you."

"It's impossible," I told him.

"That's all this pack is: impossible fragments left behind. Just as impossible as you fixing us when no one else could." He cupped my cheek, yellow eyes a storm of momentary hope. "If there's one thing I *can* promise you, Shatter, it's the impossible."

I stared at him and his promise lodged, like an anchor and chain crashing into the ocean bed, refusing to move; it was as foolish as it was tempting.

I'd never wanted so badly to speak my truth out loud, but I stalled, knowing it wasn't a mistake I could afford to make. If Dusk knew the only bond he could ever offer me was a dark bond, that might push him to it. No matter how much I wanted it not to be true...

"Ransom's going to wake soon, *really* wake. That changes everything. You'll love him, I know it. He'll love you—already does. I can feel it—"

He cut off as I flinched back, panic closing like a fist around my throat.

Dusk's face fell, as if he knew he'd crossed a line. A strange silence passed as I found no words to that, mind racing out of control. After a long moment, he sighed and rubbed his chin.

"Roxy wants to see you," he said quietly, glancing down at his phone on the coffee table.

"Roxy?" My heart lifted slightly at the idea of seeing her. I could really use a friend right now.

"She texted me. Said to let her know when you're free, and classes just finished."

"A study session?"

"Yup."

My hopes tumbled off a cliff, though. "But... Ransom—"

"You bit him. You'll know if there's anything really wrong."

That was true. And I really could use a friend this afternoon. "Okay..."

I nodded. Yes.

It was a good plan. Everything was a lot right now. I needed some space to catch up and figure out what the hell was going on now the hormones were dying down.

Roxy met me in our usual study room, arriving with all the Omega Studies course material for the week.

We sifted through it for a while, and she caught me up on the coursework until I wasn't worried anymore. I made mental notes of the chapters I needed to reread to refresh what I'd missed—though I'd devoured the textbooks front to back already.

While we worked, I pondered the *other* thing. I didn't know how I was going to do it, but I had to find a way to talk to her about the Lincoln pack issue. The offer Flynn had made... it affected her.

The only issue was that I didn't know how to go about that without discussing the scent match thing. And if I didn't mention the scent match thing, would she be suspicious of why the Lincoln pack were interested in me?

I mean, it was me. Of course she would. There was no reason for them to be interested in me outside of that—Eric's comment had made that painfully clear.

But how much could I trust her with?

"I missed you," Roxy said, after I'd finished reading through her notes.

"You did?" I glanced up at her in surprise, a burst of warmth blossoming in my chest at her words.

"Of course."

That sounded like a friendship thing, right? Real friendship...

Not just study partners?

I did like her so much, but I had a bad habit of misreading this kind of thing.

"So..." Roxy prodded. "How was your week?" I spotted something mischievous in her sapphire blue eyes as she looked me up and down. "You look... well."

I bit my lip, cheeks heating up. "It was... good."

Oh, this was confusing. How much was I supposed to say?

"I uh..."

She giggled, elbowing me. "You don't need to tell."

Did omegas usually talk about things like this? Heats and... pack stuff?

"You're definitely going to take the school by surprise again."

Oh dear. "What are they saying?" I asked, voice high.

"Okay. People are a little obsessed with your pack to be honest."

"Tell me." I didn't know why I was asking. If it was bad, I'd just stew on it.

"Well, no one thinks you went to a clinic since no one saw you leave. So... you had a..." She side-eyed me. "I'm just saying what everyone else is."

"What?"

"So obviously it was a rut or a heat, and you chose to have it with them. But no bond—still?"

"Oh..." Shit.

Right.

I'd taken a week off school. There was clearly only one thing that could mean.

Being chosen by a pack didn't mean I had to spend heats with them—well, for omegas to which the rules applied in the first place, which I definitely wasn't.

Damn it.

We studied in silence for a while longer, and she seemed comfortable as I processed that. I couldn't keep track of what all of this meant for my reputation. Was it good or bad?

Was Roxy judging me?

She didn't *seem* to be.

"What would you do if you met your scent matches?" I asked after a while. I needed to find a way to get the conversation where I needed it.

Roxy considered that, a sly smile on her lips. "Why?"

"I don't know, I just... I wanted your opinion."

"Well..." She looked thoughtful, pen tapping on her cheek. "I think if I met my scent matches, and they were... rich, *and* enamoured with the same studies as me, then I don't see myself holding back." She gave me a meaningful look that was anything but meaningful to my stunned brain.

What?

"You... know?" I stared at her, chest tight.

She let out a giggle at my expression. "Come on, Shatter, it's been clear from the start." She was still smiling, which wasn't right at all.

Clear?

"They are *obsessed* with you?"

My brain finally rebooted as I caught up.

The Kingsman pack.

She thought we were talking about the Kingsman pack.

I stared at her, wringing my hands, realising how completely impossible this conversation was always going to be.

"They built you a nest, and they keep your scent hidden like they own it—a bit possessive for me, but... I don't know." She shrugged. "It's sweet. There aren't many omegas who would have held out this long. What are you worried about?"

"I..." I didn't know why, but tears burned my eyes at her words.

Roxy reached for me. "Oh, babe... okay."

She pulled me into a huge hug, and I clutched her in surprise, still fighting not to actually cry in front of her.

But why was she saying all those nice things about the wrong alpha when I didn't know how to process it? It wasn't her fault. She didn't know—dammit. But this conversation had gone nowhere close to where I needed it.

I was such a mess.

I blinked furiously. My confidence was shot. I had no idea what to say to explain any of it. The hormones were gone, and I felt like I'd fallen into a hole.

A very confusing hole.

And now she was going to see me crying.

What would she think? That I was crying because my scent matches wanted me?

She was so kind, and held me so tight. And I hadn't told her about what Flynn had offered me. Or the fact that the pack who had sponsored her were my mates.

More tears burned my eyes.

When she drew back, I ducked my head, letting my hair fall in front of me like a curtain. I pretended to stare at the textbook.

Get it together.

I took a breath, blinking furiously, but it didn't work. I tried to rub them without her noticing. I froze as I felt my contact crease in my eye.

Fuck.

I was never supposed to rub my eyes—especially not when crying. I didn't—I'd trained myself out of the habit when I'd run from the Estate. But right now, I was such a mess.

"Is this just about them?" Roxy asked me. "Or did something happen?"

She sounded so concerned, but I barely heard in my panic.

I blinked carefully. Desperately.

Flatten.

Please flatten.

Instead, I felt the contact get caught on my eyelash.

"Shatter?"

My fists balled in fear. If I looked at her now, she would see the colour of my eyes.

How could I leave without her seeing? There was no way...

I dared reach up in a last-ditch attempt, hoping I could push it back in and undo this mess.

Of course, at the nudge, it fell.

I watched it tumble from my eye as if in slow motion, and jerked forward to catch it. But the contacts that hid golden eyes were clear, coated in a sheen that subtly shifted gold to brown.

They were almost invisible to spot. One second too late, and it was gone.

My breath caught, and my gaze raked over my skirt, my knees, the floor which was made of old hardwood, with dozens of cracks it could slip into.

Gone.

My breath caught.

"Shatter?" Roxy sounded worried. "Are you okay?"

I tried to force my voice calm, but my knuckles were white on the edge of the table. "I have to go," I whispered.

Could I get back to the apartment with no one seeing?

I was still searching my skirt and the floor desperately. Maybe it was caught in the crease of my clothing—

"Babe." I saw her reach out in my peripheral, and then she took my hand, squeezing. "If something happened, you can tell me, I promise—"

I felt the brush of her touch too late as she swept my hair out of the way. I glanced up on pure instinct for a split second before I slammed my eyes shut.

My blood ran cold in the darkness, knowing I had been too late.

I heard her little inhale of shock.

The sound that meant that Roxy knew I was gold pack.

NINE

SHATTER

"Shatter—"

Roxy cut off as I shifted my chair back. "I have to go."

"No." She grabbed my wrist with a death grip. "Don't move. It... it fell?"

"I..." I swallowed, eyes still firmly shut. "I need to—"

"You aren't going out there like this." I could hear her moving, her fingers brushing my skirt as if searching.

She was worried for me?

But I didn't understand. Why hadn't she said anything else?

"Fuck." Her voice was muffled, like she was under the table.

I dared peek out of one eye to see my assessment was correct; she was on her hands and knees with her phone flashlight on.

"I can... I can never find them once they're gone," I said weakly.

I still didn't understand.

"You have spares?" she asked, backing out and glancing up at me from her knees and poking her head out from under the huge desk. I met her eyes fully now, then panicked again.

But she knew.

She already knew.

"In my bathroom," I whispered. I couldn't carry spares with me. Having those discovered put me at far higher risk than what had just happened.

I wasn't supposed to rub my eyes.

"Tell me where." She got to her feet. "I'll be right back."

"But..."

"Oh my God, Shatter..." She trailed off. "They don't know? Is that why you're upset?"

I stared at her in shock.

I hated lying to her, but I was such a mess that I didn't know what I should say and what I shouldn't. She knew my most dangerous secret already, and she'd barely flinched. She didn't even seem to want not to be my friend anymore...

Roxy sat back down, looking at me in surprise. "Shatter, I don't think you have anything to worry about. They can't keep their eyes away from you when you're around them. I've never seen a pack as obsessed. They're in love with you."

In... *love?*

It rang of what Dusk had said earlier. The word that had already turned me into the disaster I was tonight.

"No—they... they know." I didn't know how to process this. I hated the lies between us more than ever.

"Oh." She looked relieved. "That's... that's good, right—if they don't have a problem with it?"

"I..." I winced, still scrambling between this conversation and the tail end of the terror I felt at being found.

"Are you worried about their reputation?" she asked quietly. "Even if that mattered to them, their name is big enough they don't need to worry about that sort of thing. You... you know that, right?"

I swallowed, feeling another round of tears coming on.

"First the contacts." She got to her feet. "Tell me where they are."

Once I'd given her the details of where they were, she vanished in a hurry, and I was left in a strange silence. My shoulders were hunched, head ducked down, afraid someone might walk in.

My anxiety was still buzzing.

What had just happened?

Maybe this was all a joke and she'd never come back. Except, I didn't think it was.

I think... *Could* I tell her everything now?

I wanted to.

Even about the Lincoln pack. We could find a solution. I still didn't know what to do with that offer, but Roxy was too important to get hurt because of this mess.

She returned ten minutes later and produced my contacts case from her pocket.

I stared at it for a long, stunned second, something stuck in my throat. She'd actually got it?

I took it from her, glancing up. "He let you in?"

"I told Dusk and he didn't ask any questions."

"Thank you." My voice was weak. I fumbled to put them in, relief flooding my system as I did. But I waited for her questions, unable to fully dispel my nerves.

How was I going to answer them?

"Are you alright?" she asked.

I blinked, gaze flitting up to her again. Her dark blue eyes were full of concern, rather than judgement.

"I think so."

Kind of. As well as I could be, I thought.

There was another heavy silence, and I broke it, too anxious to wait. "I uh... I have amnesia. I don't remember anything before I was 19."

She frowned. "Nothing?"

I shook my head. "So I, uh..." I trailed off awkwardly.

Becoming gold pack—not turning up for the Institute's injection within a year of perfuming—was a choice. One that most judged harshly. "I don't know why my eyes are gold—"

"You don't owe me an explanation, Shatter."

I bit my lip, suddenly feeling like I was going to cry again.

"It's illegal," I whispered. If I was discovered to be hiding my gold pack status, I could get in a lot of trouble. Would she be in trouble if I got caught and someone found out she knew?

"Well." Roxy cleared her throat. "Last year when my car broke down, I made seven grand from mailing scent marked clothing to lonely alphas and betas, and I, uh..." She dropped her voice to a whisper. "I didn't declare a penny of it. So I guess we're even."

Wait.

What?

That drew me up.

I suppose she *did* have a lovely scent. I didn't think many omegas smelled like Christmas.

"What kind of clothing?" I asked with a frown.

Her smile grew positively devilish, but before she could answer there was a knock on the door.

I glanced up, heart pounding until I reminded myself that my contacts were secure and present.

When the door opened, I was surprised to see Eric peering in. At his scent of passionfruit, my stomach did an uncomfortable swoop.

"Oh. What's up?" Roxy asked.

"It's ten minutes later than when you said you'd be done," Eric said, frowning. "We don't have much time to study before the party."

"Right," Roxy said, glancing at me. "Actually, I might have to bail—"

"No. That's okay," I said, quickly. I didn't want to be the reason Roxy looked bad in front of the Lincoln pack. Not after everything.

"I have... everything I need." I smiled awkwardly at Eric before meeting Roxy's eyes.

"Are you sure?"

"Yeah. Absolutely."

Roxy got to her feet, then looked at me curiously when I didn't join her. "I just... I need some time to figure myself out," I said the last part quietly so Eric didn't hear.

She nodded. "Just... find me if you need anything else, okay?" she asked.

I nodded.

"And I mean anything," she whispered, as she bent down to pick up her bag.

"Thank you."

After she left, I sat for a long time, trying to untangle everything.

I was so confused.

Was Roxy really the friend I'd dreamed of for so long?

I couldn't quite get my head around it. Even with all the proof, it just seemed too good to be true.

I hugged my bag to my chest, mind racing through everything that had just happened.

Roxy had said it... that she thought the Kingsman pack wanted me, too. And it didn't matter how many times I heard what they claimed was the truth, I didn't know how to make it fit with me.

Why *would* Dusk love me as I was?

Umbra and I... I fought the little smile on my lips. Umbra was like me. Different. And for some reason, that was easier to accept.

Ransom... Well, I don't know. He was rich and good-looking, and I was worried about when he woke up properly.

But Dusk was the enigma. Completely and utterly.

I didn't fit with a person like him. Not really. Up until now, it had been easy to be angry at him. To put him into a box and say he was having fun—taunting me, and taking things from me. I might not understand it, but I'd seen it before.

But now he wanted me to smash that all to pieces. To convince me he was serious?

He *couldn't* be serious.

I jumped at another knock on the door.

I frowned, then hurried over to it, cracking it open.

I was met by a set of green eyes and the sweet scent of passion fruit once more.

"Eric?" I asked, voice high. I tried to look past him, but I caught no scent of oranges and fir trees. "Where's Roxy?"

"She wasn't feeling social."

Oh.

"Why are you here?" I asked.

"Thought I'd wait for you, but you didn't come out."

Had he been outside the whole time I'd been thinking? "You said you had to study?"

He folded his arms, watching me intently. "This was more important."

"Important?"

I couldn't have another conversation like I had with Flynn. Not again, not when I hadn't told Roxy. And—dammit. I hadn't. I'd been distracted by the eyes, and then the scent-marked clothing. She still didn't know.

"I... I should go." I was determined to push past him no matter how good he smelled.

"Shatter. Please, would you give me a minute—"

"I can't." I edged by him and into the hallway, but he followed me.

Fuck. His scent was everywhere, and I was confused enough as it was.

"Five minutes, no more," he said as he reached the stairwell on the second floor. "You are very hard to get alone."

I glanced up at him in surprise, halting for a moment. "We..." I trailed off, averting my gaze to the floor as a pretty red-haired beta woman passed us.

I hoped she didn't notice who we were.

"We shouldn't be seen together," I told him, stepping toward the next flight of stairs.

He held out a hand to stop me, eyebrow raised, then stepped toward a door nearby, opening it.

"There. No one will see us."

I glanced inside to see a small closet, then I checked the hall. It was empty now.

"Look," I whispered. "I really can't—"

"I want to apologise," he said, voice low.

That caught me off guard. "Apologise?"

"Five minutes. I'll never live it down if I don't make every effort to say this to you."

I don't know why we needed a closet for that. "I—*oh*—!" His fingers closed around my arm and he easily tugged me in before I could protest.

Shit.

It was just me and him, alone, crammed between dusty shelves and boxes of cleaning supplies. Passionfruit smelled so fresh and sweet, overpowering the sharp scent of cleaning supplies that it tangled with.

There was nothing *hostile* in his scent, though I wasn't as in tune with it as I was with Dusk, Umbra, and Ransom's.

He was handsome, that was impossible to ignore, even with that frown as he considered me carefully. He had thick dark brown eyebrows that were perfectly shaped and intense green eyes. His skin was pale in that porcelain way that Roxy's was, and it did suit him.

I wasn't comfortable, though, not the way I should be with my mates. Flynn said he hadn't meant it, but Eric's words in the library stuck with me, weighing me down whenever I was feeling most insecure.

"Flynn spoke to me," Eric said, as if reading my thoughts. "It seems to have got around that I said a few unsavoury things about you."

I took a breath, the torment echoing in my mind again. *"...Doesn't even own a hairbrush..."*

I shoved the memory away. "He uh... he said you didn't mean it..." My voice was weak.

"Actually, I believe he claimed I only said it because I was infatuated with you."

"What?" My heart tripped over itself. "He... it wasn't phrased quite like that..."

"Shame. Because it's the truth."

My lips parted in surprise but he continued before I could speak.

"I've been..." He cleared his throat. "I've been so angry since the ball."

"Angry?" I asked, startled.

He leaned back slightly, jaw ticking, and it was enough to make me shrink down. "We messed up," he said simply. "That's been clear ever since. I should have known, the moment you came to our table, how special you were."

Shit.

This was the same as when Flynn had come knocking, but worse.

"We didn't," he went on. "And then you turn up at school with their star and I..." He wrinkled his nose, looking away from me. "I'm just angry at all of it. I even checked your entry scores. You're the most intelligent person I've ever met. It's incredibly intimidating."

"Intimidating?" My voice was high pitched. "But you have Roxy, and she's smart and really—"

"She's not *you*." Eric cut me off, looking so intense it was hard to keep eye contact. "But I have to pretend she is when I'm... with her."

I froze, cheeks going bright pink. "You... no. That's wrong."

Guilt turned my stomach. She didn't deserve that.

"I know," Eric said. "That's why we're dropping her."

Wait. No. "You're *what*?" My voice was hoarse.

That would be terrible for Roxy's reputation.

"We don't want Roxy caught up in this, but the others... they can't take it."

"The others?" I asked. "What about you?" Could I talk Eric into not dropping her?

"I... Well..." He rubbed his chin. "I had a different idea."

"To keep her on?" I asked.

He nodded. "I'm sure you know that the Barclay pack has two omegas?"

What?

My lips parted in shock. But... if they picked two, Roxy wouldn't lose her place. "Two omegas? Like Roxy and...?"

"You."

My lungs felt too big all of a sudden, and my eyes darted to the door.

Oh *dear*. This was *really* bad timing.

He was offering me everything.

Actually everything, because Roxy wouldn't even get hurt. And he was offering right when it was impossible for me to say yes.

I tripped over that thought violently.

Shit.

Shit, shit, shit.

Even one week ago, everything would have been different. But now there'd been the heat, and I'd met Ransom and I was all confused about what I was supposed to be doing with myself.

Eric smiled, flashing those perfect teeth for me like he so rarely did. "You're very cute when you're nervous."

I realised I'd been wringing my hands together.

I dropped them.

"I..." My words were failing. He was close, far too close, beautiful green eyes I could get lost in. I realised his hands were pressed to the wall on either side of me.

"You are worried about being seen with me, but did you know there are already rumours out there that you don't want the Kingsman pack?"

Uh... fuck.

"Are there?"

That wasn't good. If people thought I was disloyal—

"Well, how *could* you?" Eric asked. "When you can't take your eyes off us?"

My fists balled in my skirt as I stared at him. "I... I don't... not on purpose—"

"I hope the rumours are right."

My mind raced a million miles an hour.

"We're going to make you a formal proposal. We'll give you our star, and then you'll have a real choice."

Their star?

He *had* to be joking.

This was madness. "Why would you risk that?" I asked. If I said no, it would be humiliating for his pack.

"Because I think there's more to this than meets the eye." He reached out, and I jumped as his touch grazed my cheek. "I think you want us as much as we crave you, and I'd risk rejection if there's the smallest chance you say yes."

I tried to shift away from his touch without being too obvious. "But i-if I say no, and then you drop Roxy, you'll still have to take another omega."

"Yes," he replied. "And it won't be her, and she won't remind us of you every day."

He took a step back thank God, clearly done, but before he turned the door handle he looked back at me. "Did you go through heat with them?" he asked.

My mouth popped open. Was he *supposed* to ask something like that?

I didn't think so. It absolutely couldn't be good etiquette, no matter how out of the loop I was.

"If you had, I think I would be rather relieved."

"Why?"

"Because if you had a heat with them and there's still no bond, then perhaps we do have a chance after all."

When the door of the closet shut, I was left in a terrible silence. I waited a long time, mind numb. When I stepped out into the hall, for a moment it was as if the fading scent of passion fruit was drowned in midnight opium.

It was my own imagination, forcing me to realise that my mates had fallen for me without ever having caught my scent.

And they were too late.

TEN

DUSK

Eric: You know what I hate? How hard she wants us to work just to get some.
Gareth: You're the one who picked her.
Eric: You wanted the crazy roses chick.
Gareth: Apparently she puts out whenever. What's the point of this place if I can't get my dick sucked when I feel like it?

I was reading through the transcriptions Decebal had sent me this week. Any pieces of information that he thought might be relevant. This one, like most, turned my stomach. A part of me wanted to take them to Shatter and read them to her so she would understand the kind of vermin her mates were. But this wasn't the worst of it, and these alphas were so foul while she was so fucking pure that I ran the risk of her thinking it was a trick—that I'd fabricated it to convince her to commit to us.

It's the only way I saw that conversation going right now.

Instead, I read on, committing to memory everything as I always did.

Eric: I'm bored of this stupid school. Four years? Can't we just wait for his parents to kick the bucket? We already fixed his fucking problems.
Gareth: He was right to be paranoid. Don't tell me you wouldn't be the same if it was you.
Eric: It's not me. He wants sympathy? Then he shouldn't have blackmailed us into keeping pack lead. Fuck him. I almost hope it blows up in his face.
Gareth: Yeh. Fucking. Right. How much of his money did you spend last week?

My eyes dropped from the transcripts as another text came in. My heart skipped a beat at the words.

> Decebal: I found her.

The text stared up at me from my phone before the next popped up.

> Decebal: It was the interest in Eugene Howard. Sending it with encryption. Delete it. This isn't shit you want getting around.

> Decebal: There was more, but we were kicked the moment we got into the server. Couldn't get back. This stuff is locked up tight.

I tapped it open, already walking back down to my room.

I'd print it and the electronic files would be destroyed. There were some things that couldn't be left to hack. Some things I only trusted in my hand, able to be burned at any point.

Like the photo I'd snapped of her golden eyes. It was long gone.

After I'd printed out the information, I went to my safe in the back of my closet and unlocked it, pulling out the folder I'd been building. It was the only place I felt safe keeping this information. Anything incriminating about Shatter would end up in here. Nowhere else, just like the information I had kept on our pack. I sat down on the bed, finally finding the courage to read what Decebal had sent.

It was a photo of a handwritten report. I recognised the Institute stamp on the top to match ones I'd seen a thousand times before. My heart skipped a beat.

Centre for Omega Enhancement.

The underbelly of our government, responsible for managing unusual aura cases. I knew of them because they were one of the groups that wanted to see us captured.

Why was it on a document about Shatter?

It was confirmation that my draw to her wasn't a fluke—she *was* one of us.

My eyes scanned the page. It was a report by Arkologist, Dr. Eugene Howard. The man Shatter had been interested in—the one who had sponsored the Lincoln pack.

Subject: Subject Number One - Failed Experiment
To: The Center for Omega Enhancement.
From: Dr. Eugene Howard - Lead Researcher
Objective: Evaluation on Omega Subject Number One's safety in society by assessing her well-being and identifying risks to her and others.

I scanned the sheet, sifting through them, and my blood chilled as I read the contents. The words blurred together, painting a picture of the true nature of what had been done to her.

Shatter was a victim of experimentation, just like we had been.

...Unforeseen incident constituting sabotage...
...Incident involving the omega subject Number One...
...Instead of the anticipated Dr. Balch serum, the subject was inadvertently injected with a substance later identified as "Atropa's Poison." A drug used in illegal experimentation of alphas in the same facility prior to repossession by the Institute...

Two words stuck: *Inadvertently injected.*

Something had gone wrong, just like with Ransom.

I re-scanned it. *Illegal experimentation of alphas?* I checked the details again, and my heart sank as I recognised the location.

It was the same facility.

The experimentations me and Umbra had been a part of, those had been illegal. Run by scum looking to make a profit with no ethics involved. When it was shut down, it had been repossessed by the Institute. We hadn't dug, too afraid to poke them, for fear of them discovering who we were. Whatever happened there, it was supposed to be better.

Yet, she was the same as us.

As I read on, everything fell into place. Guilt was a fist around my throat as I forced myself to continue.

...The sabotage, which resulted in the deaths of four members of staff, was a vengeful act by an alpha previously subjected to experimentation in our facility during a separate program that was shut down due to severe, illegal and unethical practices...

The program me and Umbra had been a part of.

...He had intimate knowledge of the facility's workings, ultimately leading to the injection of Atropa's Poison into the omega subject on the day of the program's launch...

Most of those alphas—the ones like us—had died. We'd seen their bodies, but maybe a few had escaped. I had never considered what that could mean...

But one, at least, *had* escaped. They'd returned with vengeance, and Shatter was the one who had paid. She'd been injected with the same substance we believed Ransom had been injected with.

A drug that was dangerous, and never designed for injection at all.

I was scanning papers from the documents I'd had before—the old papers containing details of our pack. I'd read all of them a thousand times, but I had to see it for myself. Finally, I found an old report: Blood tests from Ransom, right after he'd begun to deteriorate.

The laboratory findings reveal the presence of 'Atropa's Poison' in the patient's bloodstream. Atropa's Poison is a restricted substance, toxic to alphas, inducing symptoms of paranoia, anxiety, loss of aura control, and heightened aggression toward others. Most significantly, Atropa's Poison results in delusions compelling them to harm others for self-preservation, driven by a fear of imminent death.

Atropa's Poison is conventionally administered via inhalation rather than injection.

Symptoms from injection: unknown.

Prognosis from injection: unknown

I knew the poison back to front. It was a weapon of war, not intended for use on betas or omegas. I grabbed a pen, scribbling a note and taping it to Ransom's old records.

"Did she become Ransom's cure?"

I had to keep it logged. It happened rarely, but sometimes I was swept away by the past just like Umbra, my own instability catching up with me. When I woke up, I didn't always remember what had happened. Nothing here could be lost.

I took a picture and sent it to Decebal, then returned to Shatter's logs.

...Given recent revelations and ethical considerations regarding both staff deaths and the Institute's methods of subject acquisition, I, Dr. Eugene Howard, have decided to step back from the program. Subject One is now under ethical monitoring and resides in my home with restricted access to citizens. Presently, she is confined to the Estate for ongoing observation and care. Continued updates will be provided to assess her readiness for reintegration into society...

That must be how she'd met the Lincoln pack. They'd visited the Estate, and she'd been there. She'd caught their scent, and they'd never caught hers.

In the latest assessment, I aim to provide a comprehensive overview of Subject One's symptoms.
...Mood swings and heightened instinctual omega behaviours... Irregular and shorter heats... No memories prior to injection... Scent of deadly nightshade remains, and, significantly, is incompatible with conventional pack matching.
Another unfortunate revelation has come to light. Subject One is not able to establish a conventional pack bond. My hypothesis suggests that she can only form a princess bond or dark bond. This,

> *combined with her inability to scent match at all, and her gold pack status, leave Subject One immensely vulnerable in society.*

I froze, almost dropping the paper as I read those words.

No.

Unable to form a conventional pack bond?

I blinked, swallowed by terror that was rising in my throat, everything about Shatter's determination to reach her mates in the face of everything, suddenly making perfect sense.

There were three types of bonds: regular bonds, princess bonds, and dark bonds.

A princess bond could only be offered by mates. If we couldn't offer her one, that meant... *All we'd be able to give her was a dark bond?*

I read and re-read the words, not processing them, scanning the rest of the page as if it might undo the truth before me... The rest was jumbled and irrelevant in comparison.

> *...Barring the day of the incident itself, Subject One's symptoms pose a danger primarily to herself and not others... I request that she continues to reside under my care for life, advocating against her transfer to the Institute.*

No.

Fuck.

This couldn't be right. My hands were shaking.

That was it?

Nothing else? Nothing undoing the truth that I'd just read.

"Shatter..."

I got to my feet, the world spinning.

Everything made sense. Her panic when I'd claimed her. Her desperation to paint her mates as saviours, no matter what... She thought they were her only chance.

And was she right? Now I knew all our pack could ever offer her was a dark bond?

I would fix this. I *had* to fix this.

I got to my feet, making for my door. I had to tell Decebal I needed the thumb drive. We were careful about it, keeping the data offline.

The information on it—the vile truth of what had happened to us—didn't just incriminate the Lincoln pack; if anyone realised Umbra and I were in those records, it could get us a one-way ticket to an Institute cage—that's if we weren't killed on sight.

But Shatter wasn't holding out on us because she didn't want us. She was afraid of a dark bond. If I showed her what was on it, then I could show her these transcripts, too. She'd know why we had them.

I had hoped the Lincoln pack would incriminate themselves beyond doubt from the apartment bug alone, but they hadn't yet. Not enough to outweigh the suspicion she would have when she discovered we were bugging their rooms.

But if I showed her everything... all of it, even the parts that put us at risk...?

That had to be enough.

I reached for my phone, only to realise there was another text from

> Decebal, along with a missed call.

> Decebal: These were from today. Just got them.
> Urgent.

I read through the data, stomach sinking.

Gareth: What do you think about the Kingsman pack? They've been out all week. Heat?

Flynn: I don't know. Ransom still hasn't shown. What are they playing at? They can't stay here if he won't attend.
Eric: I always get the feeling their pack lead is mocking us. Just me?
Flynn: He was so fucking pissed when he caught you eyeing up his omega.
Eric: She's the one who can't stop staring at us. Fucking weirdo, if you ask me. They gave her a nest, and she still wants us.
Flynn: What pack gives an omega like that a star before term even starts? It's a fucking insult. She doesn't fit here, either.
Eric: She looks ready to burst into tears if you speak to her wrong.
Gareth: I'd still fuck her.
Eric: Think they'd drop out if we got her to give us that star?
Gareth: So... fuck with their omega and take her star?
Flynn: We'd blow up any chance of an alliance.
Eric: Fuck the alliance. They're not serious and they're not going to last. Besides, they're obsessed with her, they might just go packing if we fuck that up. Once they're out, we're top anyway, right?
Gareth: Or they'll come for us. Not really that bothered, though. Never even seen Ransom.
Flynn: They won't. Not if we get her to give us the star.
Eric: I think I have a way to do it. You said she overheard me talking about her? What was it she said?

> Decebal: Nothing else. They left the apartment.
> This was at lunch today. Be careful.

Sickness turned my stomach at what I'd read. *Where was she?* Roxy. She'd gone with Roxy.

I was already crossing to my door. I couldn't risk Shatter getting anywhere near the Lincoln pack, not if she was their target. I reached the hallway, heart pounding in my chest. I tried to keep my panic to myself so I didn't disturb Umbra and Ransom tonight.

I just needed to know where she was, and I'd settle. Plus, they didn't know Shatter was gold pack, which kept her safer.

I knew a thousand vile truths about the Lincoln pack and what they were capable of. They had no boundaries when it came to omegas, not when pride was involved.

We'd tracked them for a while, digging into their every move, above or below board. Before the academy, they frequented social clubs that hosted gold packs for entertainment—places that all but owned the omegas in their 'employ'. All were gold packs with outcast designations—omegas who had broken the law or were deemed dangerous.

And they especially favoured establishments with the least rules possible. They were particularly competitive with other packs. One night, they'd lost a lot of money to another pack. The next, they'd paid for an evening with the omega their rival pack favoured. We couldn't find the exact details, but whatever they'd done was so bad the establishment had removed her from their roster.

I wouldn't let something like that happen to Shatter.

Scanning the hallway before me, I spotted the room she and Roxy studied in, but when I opened it, I found it empty, and my blood chilled as I caught the faintest trace of passionfruit in the air.

Eric had been in here?

Where was she?

I was left, frozen for a long, panicked second before I ripped my phone from my pocket, opening the tracker I'd hadn't used since I'd caught her sneaking off to the library.

ELEVEN

SHATTER

Numbness settled over my body as I reached the Kingsman apartment.

The door was unlocked, which wasn't normal. Had Dusk left it like that so I could let myself in when I came back?

He wasn't in the living room anymore, but the TV was on, playing a show I didn't recognise. I hugged myself, eyes darting up to Ransom's room.

What was I supposed to do?

The Lincoln pack were my mates, and they wanted me.

It was everything I had ever dreamed of. My own poisonous scent would no longer put me in danger, and I would never be under threat of a dark bond again.

The Kingsman pack... they couldn't offer me what my mates could.

The only ending with them was a dark bond.

My fingers crept to the tiniest scar on my neck. It was almost completely faded now. Tears burned my eyes.

But I stood for an age, desperately wondering why those

moments with Eric paled the more I replayed them—as I understood, at last, the truth I'd been running from.

I was stepping down the hall to Dusk's room before I could think, stopping at his door.

What *was* my plan?

Talk to him. Tell him everything.

Tell him that I wanted his pack, and hope he had an impossible answer?

But even breathing in midnight opium in the hall, I felt it.

I'd have to tell him why I was scared of a dark bond, though even admitting that put me at risk. Before, I'd been afraid that if he found out that was the only bond he could ever give me, he would do it right then, knowing he had to keep me from my mates.

But if I told him I *chose* him... It would change everything.

Dusk could have dark bonded me by now, and he hadn't. It was the truth I couldn't let go of, the tiny daring part of me that believed everything he'd ever said. Because if it wasn't true, if this was about a claim and nothing else, he could have stolen my freedom forever.

He wanted more.

He *was* the impossible, already breaking rules I'd been caged by. A new path was lighting before me, one unknown... Where before, the only option was to run to my mates—claim a life safe and protected where my scent wouldn't put me in danger, there was now them.

I could choose *them*.

I don't know how they slipped beneath my defences. I didn't know when Dusk had become safe, but my life was made of dead ends, and Dusk broke all the rules.

Maybe... no bond? Could we make that work?

Could they protect me, anyway?

I wasn't sure. I didn't have the answer, but we would figure it out.

A brief moment of hope lit in my chest. A thrill, as I truly realised what I was about to do. Through the fear, the unknown, I had something... mine.

This pack was mine.

A family who wanted me for who I was.

Outside of fate, it was a piece I could claim back. *My* trade, I would face my fears for this choice. Give up safety for the first true freedom I had ever claimed.

Daring and terrifying, it gave me a piece of *me* for the first time since I had woken as no one.

With this choice, came a thousand possibilities I'd never dared dream, not even with my mates. I'd known I wouldn't be their ideal, that I would have to beg them to accept me. But the Kingsman pack wanted me as I was—that's what Dusk had said... wasn't it?

With them, could I maybe have something *more* than just normal?

Pages of an old book rustled, buried beneath tomes dedicated to years of survival.

Would the Kingsman pack mind if I wanted to take a serious job in the Arkology field? And what about a library? And I'd always loved looking at Uncle's aquarium. I wanted my own Angelfish one day... And then, what about...?

Hmm.

I shrank, fingers finding the star on my necklace.

That was probably too far, right?

Once, I'd collected picture after picture from magazines, building the image of another dream. One so daring for a person with eyes like mine that I ripped it up the moment I'd finished making it.

Too far, Shatter. Definitely too far.

I rapped my fists together anxiously, eyes darting back down the hallway.

But what if *they also* happened to want a beach wedding? Barefoot at sunset, with an archway decorated with seashells... It looked so pretty in the pictures. Even if I didn't think I'd ever been to a beach, memories of smells didn't come when I tried to imagine it. But I needed to pull myself together. We didn't even know how bonds would work yet....

I pushed Dusk's door open, a daring smile on my lips, but the room within was empty.

My gaze dropped to the bed.

What was that...?

That warmth I felt flickered as I crossed toward the open binder and stared down at it.

I blinked, all the daring, blinding, brilliant hope vanished at once, leaving me in the cold.

I found myself confronted with a photo of me. Years old. I was in a white gown—though in this photo I was as far from a beach wedding as it was possible to be. My hair was tied back, expression drawn, and my face gaunt. Seeing it was like a shot of memories injected into my brain.

White walls.

Machines and pain; needles and drugs.

'Subject One', I was named. I knew where that was from.

Why did Dusk have this?

I sifted through the stack, heart growing heavy, chest constricting with every second.

There were more. And not just of me. Dusk's handwriting scrawled across a file on Ransom.

"Did she become Ransom's cure?"

My blood chilled.

I picked up the file, a high-pitched ringing in my ears, and scanned a few of the pages, eyes drawn to the handwriting on top of the printed text.

There was a list of what I thought were potential cures, some crossed out. I stopped on one.

'Omega bond—potential to balance and heal'.

Beside it was the note:

'Too risky. Can't justify a permanent bond unless we are certain it will work as a cure'.

I read that twice, ice crystallising in my stomach. I glanced back at the first note I'd seen. The one about me being Ransom's cure.

Dusk... knew?

For how long?

Claiming me at the ball. Playing into my deepest fears. Whispering worship—and had he known where I'd come from and what I was missing?

My hand jumped to my mouth.

A fix for Ransom—was that all I'd ever been?

A cure.

A pill.

An experiment.

Not worth anything beyond what my broken body could do...

But... I'd come in here to tell him the impossible, a truth enough to rip my world in two. Without answers, just a confession and trust that he might be able to find a solution.

I'd come to tell him that I chose *his* pack.

That I'd chosen him.

That dream was turning to stone—not at all what I believed it was. Not if he'd known. He'd pretended all this time, knowing it could only end in a dark bond.

There was more here—a whole folder of information. I had to read it. Would it have answers—

"Shatter." I jumped as I heard Dusk's voice from down the hall.

He was back.

"Shit..." I dropped the file, digging fingers into my scalp as I got to my feet, my breathing ragged. If he knew I'd read this, what would he do?

I needed... I needed help. This was all too much.

Roxy.

She'd said I could come to her with anything.

I managed to take a few steps back before I heard him calling for me again, sounding urgent.

I fixed my expression just in time to see him appear at the doorway. His eyes were wide and he looked frantic.

"Shatter!" He stepped toward me and it was hard not to stumble back. "I thought... *Fuck.*"

"Are you okay?" I asked, forcing my voice steady.

What did I do?

I had to make an excuse to get to Roxy.

"Yes, I..." His eyes fell on the papers on the bed and he frowned.

"I just got in," I said quickly. "I was looking for you."

"So was I. We need to talk."

Talk...? I tried very hard not to look back at the bed. To give away what I'd just read.

"Things have changed. I..." He trailed off, eyes darting to the papers again.

Changed? *What had changed for him today?*

"You stayed with us when you could have left, and now Ransom..." He trailed off, wonder in his eyes. "He's almost back. I should have let you in before now."

Ransom... That was it. He was maybe hours from being fixed...

My stomach twisted in terror as my mind wandered to the notes. He'd not wanted a bond with an omega until he could be *sure* it would work.

And now he wanted to talk... To let me in?

A dark bond I would never see coming...

I tucked my fist behind my back so he couldn't see me digging my nails into my palm, fear spiralling out of control. "I... I came to you about Ransom," I said.

I had to stall him—to escape and get to Roxy before anything else happened. She knew I was gold pack—I could tell her everything. She would tell me if I was overreacting, or if my fears were real. She would know what to do.

Dusk frowned. "What about him?"

"He... He took a turn for the worse."

Dusk's eyes went wide. "He did?"

"Not physically. It's his aura... It's hard to explain, but I can feel it in the bond. That's why I came to find you. I think he should come back to the nest tonight."

"Oh..."

"It's urgent. I don't know what's wrong or if I'm just not... not enough."

He crossed toward me and it took every ounce of my control not to run. He cupped my cheek and tilted my chin up. "You are enough, Shatter. Of course you're enough—you're a miracle. I'm sure it's just a setback."

I nodded.

"Once he's balanced, then we can talk. Just tell me what you need tonight."

"I think I just need to be with him alone," I said.

"Absolutely. I can go and make some tea—"

"No." I cut him off too fast, panic rising in my chest. I couldn't handle his sweetness. The reminder of what he had been to me. His brows came down. "I just mean... I think I need to be totally alone with him. No interruptions. I just... I want him to get better. Maybe... if I do a good enough job, he'll be back with us tomorrow."

Dusk's smile was devastating, and it was hard to shove the tears away.

"Okay. I'll bring him in." He pressed his lips to my hair, a purr rising in his chest as he held me against him. It vibrated through my body, soothing and beautiful. "Don't worry," he breathed. "You'll fix him. You're perfect, Shatter."

I almost cracked before I'd shut the door of my nest behind me.

Ransom was right on the brink of being healed.

A low sob sounded in my throat, but I clutched it, needing to hold it together just a little longer.

Was that the only reason I wasn't dark bonded?

He had to know I could fix his pack first. He already knew all he could ever offer me was a dark bond. A bond for life. A way to force me to stay forever.

They weren't my family. They were using me as Ransom's cure.

What would happen after—when he no longer had to pretend?

Could there be more to this?

I wanted, so desperately for that to be true. There were more papers in that stack, maybe papers that had more story to tell...

But if I gambled on that truth, I might be dark bonded by tomorrow.

TWELVE

SHATTER

I pretended to sort out my pillows when Dusk and Ransom arrived at my room. Umbra wasn't there, thankfully. I didn't know how I'd face Umbra. Umbra had always been different... like me.

My heart ached, and I didn't know how much was heartbreak, and how much was fear.

I tucked Ransom in, forcing back my grief, unable to help cuddling close to him once again. There was a frown creasing his brows as he looked down at me, and he lifted a hand, stroking my cheek with his knuckle. For a strange moment, I thought he was going to open his mouth to speak.

He held me tighter as I tried to pull from his arms, a low whine in his throat as if he knew I was leaving.

"No matter what happens, you're going to be okay."

It mattered to me more than it had any right to. He wasn't my mate, but I had to make sure he was okay. I'd tell Roxy it had to be a part of the plan we made: somehow, Ransom would wake up. He was a part of this, but not by choice.

My alpha...

The one I'd claimed. The one I'd saved. It was almost enough to change my mind.

But I had to leave now, or I might never.

"I'm not scared of a bond with you," I whispered to Ransom. "I just... I don't know if he's who..." My chin quivered. "Who I think he is."

The man I'd been about to hand everything to.

Yet, all he'd ever said and promised might have been a lie.

Ransom was still frowning, but I peeled his grip away. He tugged me back to him, desperation in his deep green eyes.

"I can't." There were tears in my eyes. "P-please let me go. I promise to come back for you. I just... I need Roxy to help me figure this out."

I would be safe when I was with her. That's what friends did in emergencies. They protected each other, and I think she would do it for me. I didn't know what it involved, but she was really clever and kind. Dusk would never come and dark bond me in front of her.

W-would he?

They both knew I was gold pack now.

Surprising me, Ransom pulled me closer, cupping my cheeks with both hands and drawing me into a kiss. I clung to him for a second, inhaling his scent, a cool forest after rain, lily of the valley making me feel so safe. And then, when he drew back, he let me go.

Stifling my sob, I grabbed my pencil case and hurried from the room. Dusk was down in the living room, and it wasn't hard to cross to his room without being noticed.

The folder and its contents were no longer on the bed. I didn't dare spend more than a minute looking around for it, hoping I could get the rest, but the shadows of the dim room revealed nothing. I stopped when I saw the iron safe in his closet.

Within, I knew, must be the pages. Information that could, perhaps, change what I'd seen?

But it was out of reach, and I might never get away if I didn't go now. I fumbled for the window that was still unlocked just like I'd left it, picking up my pencil case from the sill before I climbed through.

I wiped a tear on my sleeve as I slipped into the cool night air.

The metal fire escape was just to the right of his room, and it wasn't a hard climb, even with shaking hands. I tried not to think at all as I dragged myself over the railing. It was cool out, and the early evening air was heavy with the promise of rain.

I had to wait until I got to Roxy before I panicked.

She'd told me I could come for anything.

I needed her hug; her calm words. She had been rational and level even when she'd seen my eyes. Her answers to all the questions that were making me dizzy with fear.

Was I better off taking my chances with mates who wanted a princess bond, or a dark bond for life with a pack who just wanted to use me?

That shouldn't be a hard question, but I'd fallen for them... I'd only taken a few unsteady steps around the edge of the building when I curled in on myself, hand on the stone wall beside me as I almost crumpled.

I took a shuddering breath. No tears. Not yet.

Wait until I was in Roxy's arms.

But I didn't want any of this...

Despite spending so long struggling to believe it, I didn't want what Dusk offered to be a lie. For the first time, I'd finally admitted the truth I'd fled for so long.

That he mattered.

And what about Umbra?

That thought almost broke me. I thought I knew Umbra, I'd bitten him and felt him through a fleeting bond.

"*He* couldn't have been lying, right?" My whisper was to no one but the stone wall of the academy. Was... some of it real?

Was that enough?

I forced myself onward, hurrying around the building, shoving back memories that choked up my mind, forcing themselves present even as I tried to ignore them.

Dusk held me in his arms, wanting me even though my scent was wrong...

He'd become something so beyond my wildest imaginings that I had been willing to give my mates up. I'd been willing to step into the unknown... to risk a life with no answers.

Scrambling to shove together my broken heart, I took deep breaths, carrying on to the front doors. I shoved back thoughts of Umbra's boyish smile, of when he'd held me all night, purr rumbling in his chest.

I reached their door on the second floor, hearing the sounds of talk and laughter spilling out from under the door, so different to the home I'd just fled.

The party. Eric had mentioned a party.

Shit. Would Roxy want to see me with that going on?

But I was out of options.

I patted my hair down aggressively so it wasn't such a mess. I didn't want her to panic when she saw me.

Bracing, I lifted my hand and knocked.

I waited as the seconds passed, then I heard someone approaching. I jumped as the knob turned and the door before me swung open.

Eric's green-eyed gaze dropped to where I stood, and his expression brightened. "Shatter?"

I swallowed, trying to find my voice. "H-hi. I'm here for Roxy."

THIRTEEN

RANSOM

Years before...

I drove in numb silence, speeding through the pitch-black road to the city of New Oxford.

I didn't know what I was doing or where I was going. I just had to get as far away as possible. There were two alphas crammed into the single passenger seat of my Bugatti. The one with dark skin and piercing yellow eyes clutched the other in his arms as if he'd never let go. The second was vacant, with a sightless gaze and blood smearing his face and chest.

Dead...

All of the others were dead...

It was all I could think, fixated on the road as I felt that alpha's eyes weighing me down. I reached for the air conditioning only to realise it was already on full blast. The air in here was still too hot.

I drove until we were deep into New Oxford, then parked in a back alley near a local club I frequented. Tugging out my phone, I scrolled to a number I'd thought I would never need. One of my cousins had given me this contact, in case I ever got in trouble with my dad. He was a hacker that didn't work the regular channels and wouldn't be on my dad's radar.

I jumped when I heard a voice answer the call.

"Yeh?"

"I'm Ransom Kingsman. I need to hire you."

"What's the job?"

"I..." I trailed off, glancing over at the two alphas. One was still vacant while the other watched me intently, piercing yellow eyes guarded.

"I... I need help." My heart was racing, my mind sluggish. "Or they're... they're going to die if I c-can't..." I trailed off, panic seizing me.

There was a pause, and then I heard loud typing on the other end of the phone. "Alright man. One sec. I'm pulling in my pack mate. He's going to talk you through it while I do the work."

"No one else can know." My voice cracked with desperation.

"No one but me and him. That's how this works, alright?"

I nodded, then realised he couldn't see me. "Okay."

There was a long pause, then muffled voices. Finally, a new voice appeared on the other end of the line.

"Ransom, yeh?" he asked.

"Yes."

"I'm Decebal. You're going to talk me through this, and we'll fix it. You said someone would die?"

"I'm with some alphas, b-but my dad can't know."

This was my fault...

The truth hit me.

This was *my* fault.

I'd shut the experiments down... I'd blown the whistle.

"You're at The Crimson Bullet right now?"

I froze, terror seeping through my system. "How do you know that?"

"There's a GPS tracker on your car. It's not well hidden. If you didn't know, I'm guessing it was Dad?"

"N-no..." My throat was closing. "But I went... He's going to know where I was—"

"Back it up. Where do you want him thinking you were?"

"New Oxford... Here at the club. C-can you do that?"

"Yup..." There was a pause. "Already done, alright? One thing fixed. It's an old tracker, not an instant feed. Have you got any photos of you at the club from another night?"

"Um..." I fumbled with the phone, putting it on speaker as I dragged up photos with shaking fingers. "From a few weeks ago." There I was, getting piss drunk beneath the cage.

And all the while, these guys were going through hell...

"Send them over. We'll take care of the timestamps and socials. Tonight you were getting plastered at The Crimson Bullet, no one'll know any different."

"Okay."

"Now, you said someone was in danger? They're with you?"

I glanced over once more. "I need somewhere to take them, they're sick. But they're d-dead if my dad finds them."

There was a pause, and then the voice on the other end of the line became clearer, as if he was paying more attention now. "I can sort it. How many?"

I was caught for a moment; the words stuck on my tongue. My voice cracked with tears that suddenly flooded my cheeks. "T-two."

Only two.

Out of how many?

This was my fault. It was my dad connected to the place, and when I'd discovered what they were doing with it, I'd told him. He'd acted surprised—had asked me not to call the authorities, telling me he would deal with it discreetly. Safely.

I'd believed him.

"I'm getting it shut down, Son," he'd told me.

I'd believed him, yet something had itched at the back of my mind to go. To see for myself.

So I'd gone.

Sickness turned my stomach.

The bodies of dead alphas had littered sterile rooms as barren as prison cells... All dead. Not just dead—executed.

They'd have seen it coming, staring down the barrel of the guns pointed at them. Nothing more than animals... I could barely focus on the words over the phone. "...Need access to your funds, and a list of stupid shit you might buy that won't draw suspicion. It has to be expensive—like safe-house-expensive, yeh?"

"I can do that..."

"You said they're sick?"

"I... don't know... They're just n-not well."

What had happened to them in there?

"Do they need to get checked out?" he asked.

My voice raised with panic, still choked with tears. "I s-said *no one* can know about them."

There was a pause. "How about this, yeh? We get you booked for a long vacation in the Bahamas or something? You can stay with them here, but you won't draw suspicion from your dad? Everyone will think you're gone."

I ran clammy fingers through the locks of hair that were tumbling loose from my ponytail. "Y-yes."

"I have some medical training. I could come if you'll let me. If not, I could talk you through some checks."

"I..." My mind was fuzzy. I couldn't think straight.

"Are you alright?"

I... I was... I had to get them to a safe place...

"Ransom?" Decebal's voice was urgent but too far away. The world was spinning. *"Ransom!"* The phone was slipping down my

cheek, but I jolted at his tone, lifting it back.

"Are you hurt?"

"I... *me?*"

"Yes. You. Are *you* hurt?" His voice was fading in and out. *"Ransom?"*

"He was injected." The low voice beside my ear was new.

I blinked, realising it was the alpha with piercing yellow eyes. He was holding me up, and my phone was in his grip. I stared at him. He was so steady, while I was shaking and falling apart...

How... How wrong was that?

When it was him I'd almost got killed.

"Who is this?" Decebal asked.

The world was still spinning, worse now with black spots in the corner of my vision. The soothing voice of the alpha sounded again, but I couldn't see him anymore.

"He was injected by something when he saved us. I don't know what."

The low curse on the end of the phone was the last thing I heard before the world went black.

RANSOM

Present

I drifted in and out of reality like a tide that couldn't quite reach shore.

I *think...* I'd banged an angel.

?

Impossible.

Probably.

Unless I'd died without realising. An angel of death, maybe—beautiful all the same... But in flashes of reality, she was everywhere. We were one, breathtaking and entangled.

It felt like I had been absent for an eternity. Meeting Dusk and

Umbra was a blur in my past. My hands shook as I introduced myself to the two strangers now bonded to me.

No other choice, I'd been told. *Too unstable. I would have died without the bond.*

I didn't resent it, though.

Instead, I felt unworthy of it.

Then came the darkness. I was plunged into a pitch black nothingness that lasted an eternity.

Their scents, midnight opium, wolfsbane and blood, were my only connection to time and meaning, giving me threads of presence even in the deepest void.

But now the darkness flickered as I'd found the beautiful eyes of my angel. The tunnel, finally, had an end.

I'd thought at first, she was a reaper. An angel with poison, here to finish me at last. But instead, her poison had been vicious enough to claw through my cage of darkness.

Now, she was everything, and I was alive.

I was alive, and I could feel her with me. She resided in my mind, tied to me by the bite she'd left me with, an ache upon flesh I hadn't even felt until her teeth had sunk in.

Only... I was restless.

She was upset. So, so upset. This plane I existed in, these bonds, they were the only reality I could hold onto. I felt every shift, every echo and movement.

And then...

She was leaving us...

I didn't want her to, but she'd begged me to let her go. She'd been so afraid, but she'd promised to come back.

She'd *promised*.

She was my angel, I knew she would, but I still felt her every step of the way as she left. She was devastated, anxious, on the verge of cracking.

I started to worry.

How... long had passed?

I fought again to surface.

Come back...

I clenched a fist, flesh connecting with my mind again.

Real.

Controlled.

Body and mind truly finding one another for the first time.

Not enough.

How long had passed?

Her hope vanished.

It was her wash of terror, in the end, that saved me. A tide of fear and pain that shot through our connection like a lightning bolt.

My angel...

I fought to wake, fear gripping me. I *had* to wake. I had to go after her... The walls that had held me hostage for so long, shattered.

I staggered to my feet, the world crashing in around me. My life was above, and one piece at a time it was crashing through a broken ceiling, breaking across the floor, out of order, and out of place.

I knew only one thing, absolutely.

She was in trouble.

Weak palms flattened against the wall as I dragged myself to the door. Then I was outside, staggering to the hallway.

I was so weak. I'd missed so much.

Again.

They were both there, both my brothers in the room beyond.

Dusk looked up first, and he was on his feet in a second, making for me, and I grabbed him by the shirt when he arrived.

She wasn't an angel at all. She was *my* omega. Claimed and bonded to me.

And she was in trouble.

An alpha's claim at her neck...
A claim she didn't want...

Her terror burned through the old cobwebs of my mind, and I finally spoke the first word my brain was able to form.

"Shatter."

FOURTEEN

SHATTER

"I need to talk to Roxy," I said.

"Roxy?" Eric peered down at me oddly. "She wanted to dodge the party tonight. She's out."

Out?

I swallowed, clutching my pencil case close to my chest. "Do you know where she is?"

"Coffee shop or the library. Here, I can text her for you—"

"No. That's okay." I was already taking a step back. I needed to find her myself. My head was pounding. I was so confused and on the verge of tears again.

"Wait." Eric caught my arm as I stepped away, and I dared a glance up at him. "I'll text her. You can wait with us."

"Really. I-I'm okay—"

"I have no intention of letting anything happen to you if you're in trouble." Those words stopped me dead.

"I'm not…" I trailed off.

How bad did I look? My eyes must still be red.

I *was* in trouble, though. That's why I needed Roxy. She would know what to do. And she'd kept my secret.

But Eric was already tapping on his phone.

"I c-can't come in." They were having a party. He was dressed differently than earlier. Instead of his white school button-up, he wore a black dress shirt with a breast pocket, the top few buttons undone so it looked a bit more casual. "I'm not dressed right, and my hair—"

"Is perfect," Eric said, looking up at me sharply. There was something stiff in his words, and his jaw clenched. "It's always been perfect, Shatter."

I stared at him. Something caught in my throat.

"I told you, you're important to us. Please, just wait here until Roxy's back—I'll worry otherwise. She shouldn't be long."

The mention of Roxy settled my nerves.

"I've already texted her," he added, taking a step back and nodding inside. "She'll be on her way."

Oh.

Shit. Now if I went searching I might miss her.

I could wait here for a bit, and he knew I wasn't here for the party...

Still, I took a breath before entering the party, letting Eric walk in front of me so he could take the lead. It was loud, with music playing and people in each room. Alphas, omegas, and betas chatted on couches, playing games or standing about with red cups in hand.

"Let's get you a drink," Eric said as he led me into the kitchen. "You look like you could use one."

"I..." I trailed off as I saw Oliver Ryder and Jasmine Lynn staring at me from through the door to the living room. Jasmine had frozen, a drink halfway to her lips, eyes wide. "I really shouldn't be here," I said. "I can wait for her outside."

The omegas already thought so badly of me. I didn't want them getting the wrong idea about me and the Lincoln pack.

What if Roxy came in and read it all wrong and then she wouldn't talk to me?

And I'd brought my pencil case. It had my registration card in it and was super important, but even I knew that wasn't something you were supposed to bring to a party.

Eric brushed a lock of my hair, and I looked up at him sharply. "I'm taking care of you until Roxy gets here." He turned and picked up a red cup from a stack, handing it to me, waving at the selection of glass bottles along the counter. "What do you like?"

Uhhh... I glanced at them, unsure, trying not to shoot a glance back at Jasmine and Oliver. I edged closer to the counter, trying to read the labels as if I knew what any would mean. I'd barely ever drank at the Estate—maybe a glass of wine here or there.

"You alright?" Eric asked.

"Yes." I reached for one with golden liquid at random, trying to seem confident. He was being so nice. I needed to pretend to be normal for five minutes until Roxy arrived. I couldn't look foolish in front of Eric.

I wasn't stupid enough to believe he was the kind of man who wanted a beachfront wedding with a gold pack omega. It was unlikely he'd even want me pursuing a career. I knew that, but I might be back at square one, and my scent matches might end up becoming my only option.

No. *Don't cry.*

I was so scared of what the future held now—or the idea that the Kingsman pack might not be in it...

Don't think about it, not until you talk it out.

I looked between the bottle and the glass desperately, wishing someone else would come in and make one before me. I shouldn't fill the whole thing, definitely not, but how much should I use?

I glanced back at Eric who was watching me curiously, a faint smile on his lips.

"I can pour it for you?"

I stared at him.

"Um..." I stammered, when too long had passed. "Sure, just... not too strong."

"Half strength," he said, almost to himself. Then he glanced back up as if he couldn't take his eyes from me as he unscrewed the top. "Don't party that much?"

"Not really."

Would he think that was strange?

"Where did you grow up?" he asked.

"Around here," I lied.

He grabbed one of the small glasses on the counter. I watched carefully, flashes of my first meeting with Dusk coming to mind.

He drugged your drink and stole you from the alpha right here. Why are you sad about running from him?

Eric tipped the bottle, eyes sliding back to me for half a moment. I smiled nervously, trying not to seem too intense.

I crossed my arms, forcing my gaze down the hall to the rest of the party, but as soon as he turned back to the bottle, I watched again. He poured the alcohol into the glass twice over, then filled the rest of the cup up with coke.

I memorised it so I didn't look stupid in case there was a next time. Easy: two of the little glasses, fill the rest with coke. Double it if I wanted a normal drink.

And no pills to drug me. But Eric was my mate—he'd never do something like that.

I hugged my drink and my pencil case to my chest, trying to shove Dusk from my mind again as Eric led me back to the lounge.

Roxy was coming.

We arrived at a set of couches in the far corner where Flynn and Gareth were waiting. Flynn's eyebrows shot up when he saw me, and Gareth straightened.

"Shatter?" Flynn asked, getting to his feet, cutting his conversation off with an alpha from the Hargrave pack. He crossed toward me, eyes intense as he took me in, and I saw a little frown crease his face. He glanced at Eric, then back to me.

"Are you okay?" he asked, and I was grateful that his voice was low so no one else would hear.

"She's waiting for Roxy. In a bit of trouble."

"It's not... not a big deal," I lied again.

"You look..." He trailed off, clearly aware of the stares we were getting. "Are you in danger?"

I opened my mouth, then shut it, glancing around. "I... really sh-shouldn't be here."

"You're waiting with us." His voice was firm, and his hand was on my waist, leading me to the couch.

I sat between him and Gareth, anxiously hoping no rumours would start before I could sort this out. I was sandwiched between the scents of sesame seed and sunflower, and coconut and plum. Each was as mind scrambling as Eric's passionfruit, which wasn't what I needed right now.

"You alright, love?" Gareth asked. He was well built, with tanned skin and blond hair. I remember how much he'd caught my eye when I'd first seen their pack. But now his bright blue eyes and sesame scent seemed wrong. So far from sandstorm irises, or the dark woody scent of wolfsbane... So far from what I knew.

I nodded, taking a large drink and blinking harshly.

It tasted horrible, and nothing like the one I'd had with Dusk at the bar the other day. I must have picked an awful-tasting alcohol. Or maybe this was how these sorts of drinks were supposed to taste when they weren't full of sugar like the one at the bar.

"You don't like it?" Eric asked, clearly catching my poorly hidden reaction. I glanced down at it.

"It's great."

Roxy better hurry. They were being too nice. It was muddling me up.

Oliver and Jasmine entered the room, and I abandoned my dislike of the drink, hoping it would at least keep me from bursting into tears in front of other omegas before I could leave.

They took the couch on our left, where Oliver's pack was lounging. I could feel Jasmine's eyes burning into me, and had trouble figuring out where I was supposed to look. Eric was watching me occasionally, perched on the arm of the couch, poorly hiding his concern.

The conversation was rowdy, and the Hargrave pack were discussing sports with Flynn and Gareth. I sipped on my drink and dug my nails into my pencil case, trying not to count the seconds.

"You're the only omega who will ever belong between us." Dusk's words sounded in my head, and I shoved them away.

I hadn't realised how deep those thorns had sunk until they'd been ripped free. Now, breathing felt like trying to hold air within shredded lungs. I took another long drink, forcing back the heartbreak and pain.

My fault... foolish and stupid for ever listening to them, for falling for them...

Usually, I would be taking note, trying to memorise everything Flynn and Gareth were saying about what team they supported in Aura boxing, but I just couldn't.

I felt a slight buzz settle over my mind. Good. Calmer was good.

When far too long had passed and Eric glanced at his phone again, I got to my feet and edged to him. "How long until she's back?" I whispered.

"She got delayed," he said.

Eric caught my expression. "We're worried, alright. I can tell everyone to go home if—"

"No." Oh gosh, no. My cheeks heated up just at the thought of it. That would be so much worse.

"Tell us what you need, Shatter," he said.

"I just..." I failed to stop my glance over at Oliver and Jasmine. "I don't want anyone thinking anything that might hurt Roxy," I said. *"I really need her."*

"Alright. Come on." Eric got to his feet and nodded for me to follow.

"Where are we going?" I asked. When I stepped to follow him, the world spun a little.

Oh. Damn.

I shook it off, looking down at my cup and realising it was empty.

"Somewhere quieter," Eric said, as we reached the next room, which was just as loud, but at least didn't have Oliver and Jasmine in it. "You said you wanted to talk to Roxy alone anyway, right?"

"Yes."

Thank God.

"I get the impression you find crowds a bit overwhelming."

I thought back to the way they stared at my stupidity at the bar last week. "Was I...?" I swallowed. "I'm probably making a fool of myself."

"Nah." He shrugged. "I don't do well in crowds either, though Gareth still insists on hosting these damn things."

"Oh..."

Either he was telling the truth, or he was making an effort to make me more comfortable.

I set my cup down on the counter as we passed the kitchen and hurried after him down the hall where it was quieter. Eric opened a door for me, but before I stepped in, I noticed one of the Hargrave pack alphas–Jericho, I think, watching from the doorframe he was leaning against in the kitchen as he chatted to another party-goer.

That was okay. It was a relief to be away from all the watching eyes, and if anyone talked about it, Roxy would know I was just waiting for her.

"Um..." I paused as I stepped in. This was a bedroom—Eric's bedroom, I knew straight away from the scent of passionfruit. "Is this right?"

Eric just gave me a strange look.

Was I asking stupid questions? My mind was slower than usual. Calm, which was good, but slower.

"She knows to find me here, right?" I asked, glancing around again.

The large bed was neatly made, and there was a desk with an open textbook. I was in my mate's bedroom. And it was so... normal looking and straight and all lined up.

What would he think of how I nested?

Stupid.

No decisions. Not yet.

He was leaning against the closed door, watching me curiously. I think I was imagining the intensity in his gaze.

"Roxy doesn't know about what you said... earlier." I twisted my hands together anxiously. "She should know."

"Does that mean you're considering us?" he asked.

"I... no... I don't know."

I was.

I had to.

I just... didn't want to. Not anymore. Not now that Dusk had offered something better.

Something that was never real...

I dragged myself away from the train of thought. "If you want to go back to the party, I can wait here for her," I said.

"Actually, I hoped to get you alone."

"Again?" We'd *just* spoken.

I looked back to see him tucking his phone into his breast pocket, then fixing his intense eyes on me. "I... really should speak to Roxy first."

"This doesn't affect her."

"It doesn't?"

"It's about what you said, about hearing me say you didn't fit in."

I shrank, everything else tumbling out of my head as he said that. "Oh."

"*Where* did you hear that?" he asked.

"Just from..." I trailed off, brain working too slowly. "From rumours..."

As if I was with the in-crowd enough to know what rumours were going around. I couldn't blow this with Eric, though. Not when everything was so uncertain. And he was being so nice.

He straightened and stepped toward me. My eyes darted around the room nervously, but his knuckle brushed my chin.

Okay.

He was close. Way too close. His scent was sending my mind into a spiral—and the drink had hit harder than I thought it would. "I have only mentioned your hair one time, Omega."

My gaze snapped up, meeting intense green eyes in absolute horror, and I took a step back only to feel the wall behind me.

Oh...

Oh no.

Eric placed his hand on the wall between me and the door, then hooked his finger under my chin, holding me in place.

Dusk did the same thing sometimes, but he did it when he was being all serious with me. Never when he was actually angry.

Was Eric angry?

"Where did you hear me say it?" he asked.

"I..." I trailed off. My chest was tight with panic, every warm drop of blood in my body hitting my cheeks at once.

He knew.

I could see it in his eyes.

"Did you follow me and Roxy to the library that night after we left?"

Again, my mouth opened, but no words came out. A long, silent second passed.

"You did, didn't you? You watched us?"

"It... it was by accident."

"Accident?" he asked. "Yet, if you heard what I said, you stayed right to the end."

My lips parted as I scrambled through my sluggish mind to find an answer to that.

"I told you, people notice how much you watch us. *I've* noticed. I've been wondering about it for a while."

"It's not what it looks like," I said, trying to untangle this all with a swamped mind. I didn't understand. Earlier he'd said he liked that.

"Tell me why you were there."

I had to set this straight. "I... followed you."

"And?"

Fuck. But he knew, already. "I... I saw you and Roxy in the library, and then things got heated—"

"Did you leave?"

"No..." My voice was weak. But he knew that, too.

"Why?"

"I..." My eyes dropped to the floor, crushing my pencil case in my grip.

Because Dusk found me before I could... You'd have stayed anyway, Shatter.

Because you're my mate...

I couldn't say it.

Not before I'd talked to Roxy, and she'd helped me figure this all out.

But how did I make it not sound that bad? I couldn't figure him out—if he was angry, or disappointed, or what? He was changing too often, and the world was still unsteady. "I was... I was interested in you."

"Me or the whole pack?"

"Um..." Fuck. "The pack. But it doesn't mean anything, I swear."

"You stayed to watch me fucking your best friend. But it doesn't mean anything?"

My stomach dropped. I couldn't let him discover we were mates yet. "No. It... It was just... like a crush. It was stupid."

His eyebrows shot up like he hadn't expected that.

Fuck.

"A crush?" he asked. "You have a crush on us?"

I swallowed. Not the characterization I would choose. Not great if Roxy heard, either, but I couldn't find a way to uncommit, and I didn't know how else to explain this away. "Y-yes."

"Yet we offered you a chance at our pack, and you're here to see our omega, not us?"

I stared at him, lips parted, unable to come up with an answer to that. "It's complicated."

Dammit.

I wish I could read him.

"Complicated?"

"With the Kingsman pack," I explained. They still had that photo. It put me in danger, even now. The moment Dusk realised I'd run, he could send it out.

I *needed* a game plan.

"You're following me around with a crush, but you're wearing their necklace, and won't consider our offer—" He cut off, leaning away, all calculation falling away for understanding. "You... don't have a choice?"

"What?" Adrenaline hit my veins at those words.

"With the Kingsman pack. You don't have a choice."

"I..." *Shit.*

My mind was swimming. If he knew I was being blackmailed, would he guess what the blackmail was?

This was all happening too fast.

I *needed* my friend now.

I jumped as the door beside us opened.

Relief flooded my system as I looked over. But it wasn't Roxy. Gareth and Flynn were stepping into the room.

"Where's Roxy?" I asked, trying to push the whine out of my voice. I was too panicked. I needed to calm down.

"Answer my question first," Eric said. He glanced over at Gareth and Flynn.

Flynn was looking between us curiously. Gareth's gaze was fixed on me in a way that twisted me up. It was far too intense.

"She followed me and Roxy to the library, watched the whole time."

"I swear," I whispered. "It's *not* what it looks like."

"What do you think it looks like?"

"I... don't know..."

Oh dear...

This was it.

He knew.

He'd just figured out I was their mate. What was he—? "It seems like we have a sweet little omega stalker," he said. My gaze snapped to him in a moment, but he went on. "One promised to the Kingsman pack."

"Promised?" My voice was weak.

What did that mean?

Like... *betrothed?*

That was crazy.

"As if you don't know the kind of circles the Kingsman family deals with," Eric said, glancing back at me. "Especially Ransom's father."

"She might not," Flynn said, glancing from me to Eric. "It explains why she's so..." His gaze fell on me for a minute, sweeping up and down appraisingly. "Different. Some of those families keep their daughters hidden, hope they perfume and trade them out like cattle for good alliances."

"One of them got a damned good deal," Eric snorted. "Trading you for a Kingsman alliance."

What?

Keeping up was so hard. One small drink shouldn't have me this slow, I was just so exhausted, and broken, and now things were spiralling quickly.

"I'm not promised to them," I stammered. They had it all wrong.

"What family did you come from?" Gareth asked, totally ignoring what I'd said.

"I don't know what you mean."

"None that'll be a threat to our name?" Eric asked, looking to Flynn.

"To a Lincoln?" Flynn snorted. "No one in my family needs to trade their daughters away like animals."

"So...?" Eric pushed.

Flynn shrugged. "If we mess it up, they'll take the blame."

Mess it up?

Gareth grinned, eyes darting to me in a way that made my skin crawl.

"I already have her confessing to stalking us," Eric said, tugging his phone from his breast pocket and tossing it to Flynn.

"W-what are you talking about?" I asked, eyes wide.

What did that mean?

Flynn was looking at the phone with a smile.

Had he been recording what I'd said?

Why?

"That's why they picked you so fast at the ball?" Eric asked. "And why Dusk watches you like a hawk? I bet they have something riding on it working out."

No, no. This was all wrong.

I could fix it.

All I had to do was tell them I was their mate, then they'd understand and it would all stop. I hadn't wanted to, but then I'd made this all happen with my stupid crush lie...

I opened my mouth, but froze as Flynn turned and casually flipped the lock on the door.

The world seemed to slow, and the words got stuck on my tongue as fear gripped me.

Instinct warned me to silence, adrenaline flaring in my veins as I looked between them.

"Wh-where's Roxy?" I asked, my voice cracking.

Eric snorted. "She's in her room. Wanted to dodge the whole evening."

In her room?

Dread crawled up my spine as I stared at him. He'd had planned this since the moment he'd opened the front door.

"W-what do you want?" I tried to keep my voice steady, but I saw the truth Dusk had been warning me about all term. He... had been right about them.

I tried to edge toward the door, but Eric shoved me back against the wall easily. The movement was almost casual, predatory.

I swallowed, glancing to Flynn and trying to hold myself steady. "I w-want to leave."

Flynn grinned. "When you've finally got us all to yourself?"

My pulse picked up as I saw the malice dancing in his eyes.

Despair rose in my chest like vomit, but I shoved back my tears.

I'd... I'd misread everything.

Again. Over and over again, I didn't know how to translate this world I'd fled to beyond the Estate.

They can't discover you're their mate. That warning was sure, despite every misdirected instinct that had led me here.

If they knew, it would be worse. I didn't mean anything to them—not really. This was a game for them. Right now, I could see that.

It *had* to stay that way.

I bit my lip so my chin didn't quiver as I glanced at last to Gareth, in hopes I might find something on his face in the way of mercy.

I found nothing. He was tense, blue eyes fixed on me with anticipation.

Masks had fallen away for monsters beneath.

My mates...

My scent had always been a secret with sharp edges, ones that had been cutting me open from the inside for so long. And in one moment, it became something completely different. Something precious, something mine.

Something I needed to protect.

"What... what are you going to do?" I dared to ask.

Eric's voice was low, and full of delight as he offered me his perfect smile that had once tripped me up in its beauty, now cruel. "We're going to ruin the Kingsman whore who's been stalking us all term." His voice was low and full of delight "So that no one ever wants her again."

FIFTEEN

[*] Beginning of serious content trigger

SHATTER

I tried to close my eyes.

I'm here because I want to be.

I'm not afraid.

Fear was my enemy. My scent blockers were strong, but if I was afraid enough, my adrenaline could burn through them.

The hardwood ached beneath my knees, and I came up with a million reasons why that was okay.

It was okay. These were my mates. It was good I was here, even when Eric roughly forced his length down my throat.

I'd arrived at Rookwood Academy at the start of term. I'd found my mates. They were sweet and caring and they wanted me.

I was with them right now.

Eric's fist wasn't so painful in my hair.

Flynn was behind me, kneeling too, one hand at my waist, the other constricting my throat.

It was good.

He liked me.

If I closed my eyes, I could pretend that. But when I did, Eric held me deep enough I couldn't breathe, and I had to open them again. Then, I could see his cruelty. I could see Gareth leaning against the wall with his phone, filming me. My pencil case was in his grip. He'd taken it from me when Flynn had forced me on my knees.

I fixed my gaze on the lamp by the bedside as Eric dragged me over him again.

Don't cry.

I was with my mates. I had everything I'd come for. They knew who I was, and they loved me.

"You feel so fucking good, little stalker," Eric groaned.

My world began with pain, metal walls, and silence.

I was strapped down, and one word flashed on the blaring screens. Big, red, blocky letters.

ERROR

ERROR

ERROR

The word blinked over and over into the cold silence, branded into my brain with the pain that racked me timelessly.

My beginning.

The moment my memories began.

Alone in a room—or so I'd believed until the scents from beneath my gurney began to curdle with the sterile air.

Flynn roughly tugged at my shirt, ripping past the first few buttons.

There was no reason to be afraid.

Flynn's hand fumbled at my neck, searching for something.

What was he doing?

It didn't matter... *I was like that blinking sign. An error. Broken. Told I would never be wanted. But now, they loved me.*

I was their *omega.*

This was everything I'd come for—

The story I told died in an instant as Flynn tore away my necklace.

N-no!

Dusk. Umbra. Ransom.

A sob caught in my chest, panic surging in a torrent as I tried to cling to the lies.

I loved them. They were my mates, and I loved them—Teeth grazed my skin and I jolted in terror.

No no no. My mates loved me. They wanted to bite me. A princess bond, like I'd heard them dreaming of.

But I felt the flicker of a real bond, and it tore through every delusion, dragging me into a void. It was a lurking shadow. A promise like I'd never felt as Flynn's teeth broke my skin.

I went deathly still.

A dark bond.

My mind went blank, terror constricting my heart, another whine in my chest.

I wanted Dusk.

Eric groaned, yanking me forward and choking me harder, as my body seized with fear.

I wanted Dusk.

I almost broke then, tears nearly flooding my cheeks.

I wanted Umbra's huge arms wrapping me tight.

To feel Ransom at my back, purring as he slept.

But I'd left them.

I'd run.

I don't know what happened or how much time had passed,

but the teeth remained, the threat of a bite violently shaking me to the soul.

Incomplete.

It... it wasn't complete. I held onto that as I felt the warm trickle of blood down my back.

Then Eric pulled back, and Flynn's teeth were gone. I didn't have time to catch my breath as Eric groaned again, finishing.

I was going to throw up. With fear. Disgust. I didn't know.

A hand clamped over my mouth and nose.

"Swallow, little stalker. That's what you wanted, isn't it? A taste of us?"

Once more, I shoved back tears as I did what he asked.

It was over.

I'd done what they wanted.

[*]

"She's fucking terrified." I could hear the laughter in Gareth's voice as he dragged me to my feet. "Why?" His grip was painful on my arm. I wasn't steady. I saw Flynn picking himself up out of the corner of my eye and cringed away. "You didn't think he was actually going to bond a freak like you, did you?" Gareth shook me, forcing me up to look at him. I... I had to give him what he wanted so he'd let me go. I tried to shake my head through his grip.

"Why did biting you feel *that* good?" Flynn asked, and there was fleck of red on his lips. I hated the way his gaze was fixed on me. The way his pupils were blown.

The scents in the air were wrong now, and I had to remind myself he hadn't completed any bond. It had just been a threat...

"Because she's obsessed with us?" Gareth had me by the arm and was dragging me to the bed. "Think it makes omegas taste sweeter?"

A low whine rose from my throat. "W-wait. I did what you wanted—"

Gareth laughed as he shoved me onto the blankets.

I threw myself against his grip in terror. "You can't—"

"Get a grip slut. You think we'd fuck you?" Gareth asked as he pinned me. "After you had a heat with them?"

My breathing was rapid as he pinned me down.

"We're going to make it so no alpha ever wants to have a heat with you again." Panicked sounds rose in my chest, but Gareth clamped a hand over my mouth. "Make a sound and I'll take a turn just like Eric."

It didn't matter if I tried anyway; the music outside was loud enough, no one would hear.

I couldn't do this.

I couldn't be here.

I reached for a piece of me I'd only ever fled from as I lay on the bed. For the first time, it was a relief when time became meaningless, as I was swept back into the place where I was no one.

It wasn't absolute like it had been, but it was something. My eyes traced the curve of the vase-shape that made up the bottom of the lamp on Eric's side table. The pebbled texture along the surface. My pencil case rested beside it.

They were hurting me and I didn't dare make a noise. It was Gareth above me now, he said something with a laugh but I didn't hear it. His teeth hurt, digging into my flesh, nothing like the bite Umbra had left me. Not soft or passionate or loving...

Eric's fist was bruising on my wrist as he repositioned me. He wanted to bite me again.

Again?

I don't know how many I'd endured... Would they heal?

Alpha bites that weren't intended as bonds healed fast, but... but these were deep. Deliberate.

I clenched my teeth, battling tears through the pain, and kept silent. It would end eventually.

I focused on my pencil case. In it was my registration card.

That I could walk away with.

I clung to that, telling myself it didn't matter what they did to me here. The blinking ERROR sign had branded me since the moment I'd woken. I was broken already. Used by Dusk. Unwanted by my mates.

It didn't matter what they did.

This was my fault.

I'd been so stupid, coming here thinking it would be different.

Why? When my uncle had warned me.

My mates were matched with a broken omega, one stupid enough to want more. And I was the one who'd fled the only place that had ever offered me safety.

How much time had passed?

I hurt so badly. Even my mind ached from trying not to be here. How much of my life had I lost to silence, a nightmare of wishing I was present when I couldn't be, and now…?

They were talking. The words drifted in and out, forming meaning somewhere in my mind.

Again, the silence flickered and tears pricked my eyes, but I shoved them back seeking the cold room with bright lights and cold metal against my back.

The room I'd woken in, when shock had won, and I'd had no tears despite the agony shredding me, bone to soul.

I could hear the sounds playing from a phone. My own voice, echoing back at me.

"You came to watch me fucking your best friend?" Eric asked, his voice tinny in the recording.

"It… It was just… like a crush. It was stupid."

Gareth's laugh was sharp. "No way did she say that."

They were going to send it out… to… to who?

Everyone?

Would Roxy see?

Would Dusk?

I shattered for the millionth time since I'd been left to watch that blinking ERROR sign for hours.

My gaze focused as Flynn picked up my pencil case. The quiet in my mind flickered, waning again.

That was all I had.

He searched it, pulled out a marker and tossed it to Gareth who was above me again. I shut my eyes as I felt its cool tip upon my forehead.

He was *writing* something on me?

Why was he doing that?

I was... different. Not just about territory, it was cruel... They were my mates. They were supposed to love me. To cherish me.

I reached up at last, trying to grab his wrist, a choked sound escaping my chest, but he laughed and Eric pinned my arm to the bed as Gareth crushed my chin, holding me still.

I tried to calm my breathing.

He hadn't taken the card.

It's all that mattered. My only chance at... at anything.

Then Gareth was gone, and I tried to ignore the echoes of the sharpie on my skin. The dark bond they'd threatened hadn't been completed. I could still get away.

Every muscle in my body remained frozen in fear.

It would be over soon.

There was a thundering knock on the door, and I jumped. I lifted my head, but Flynn was pinning me to the bed in a second, hand clamped over my mouth, dark eyes holding mine in threat as Eric crossed the room.

The knock sounded again, and I heard the lock click as Eric opened it.

"Where is she?"

Roxy?

I tried to turn, eyes wide, but Flynn's grip became painful and his dark irises glittered with threats. He lifted a finger to his lips, tongue pressed to his canine. My blood still traced his lips.

"She left. She was looking for you." Eric replied.

"Someone said she was in here."

Roxy was looking for me?

Finally, one tear broke free. Not for them.

I... I think she was my friend for real. I had to leave after this, and I would lose her.

Eric snorted. "Nope."

"Let me see—"

"Enough." Eric's voice was cold and edged with an alpha command. "We didn't choose you expecting you to question us at every turn. If I say you aren't welcome, then fuck off."

"Open the door." Roxy's voice was vicious. I jumped as Flynn's hand on me became painful, and I realised I shifted, reaching for her. I was torn between screaming for her and keeping my silence.

But if they locked the door...? She couldn't push past three of them.

Then what would they do to me?

Gareth's threat stuck in my mind. And if she saw me... what about the video? I think Eric had cut it to sound like I'd betrayed her—as if I'd come looking for them, not her.

She already knew I'd lied about my eyes.

"I don't give a shit about you and your stupid ego," Roxy snarled. "If she's not in there, then show me."

Eric laughed. "Get fucked, Roxy."

I heard the door slam and the lock turn.

I trembled as they spoke, the words not sinking in.

"...She's throwing a fit..."

"...We're almost done..."

Almost done...?

I clung to that until Gareth's voice broke through my hope.

"We're really letting her go that easy?"

I blinked, surfacing fully, something about those words sinking deep into my consciousness, dragging me up.

He was on the bed at my side, fixated on me. There was something... not right in his eyes.

Don't let alphas bite you, Shatter. We don't know what will happen.

My uncle's warning rang in my ears. My mates weren't becoming violent from the bites they'd left, but that wasn't the only threat I faced from the Lincoln pack.

"Nah," Flynn said. "I'm not done."

Instincts rose, the tone shifting. I knew it, even as I lay still, waiting for it to be over. But I could feel that possibility slipping away.

Were they realising the scent match?

They'd had a plan, but it was fading now. Even their scents were shifting. Before, I was in a room of predators, now... now they were changing.

Claim tangled with their scents.

"Dusk..." My voice was a desperate whine. It was the first time I'd spoken in what felt like an age. I don't know what seized me in a moment, but I knew what I had to do. *"Dusk,"* I choked out.

I wanted Dusk.

All this time, he'd protected me from this.

He would never do that again now, but it didn't matter.

The frightening edge of their scents dulled, claim dying for arrogance as Gareth laughed. "You think he'll take you back? After you came crawling to us? He's going to find out you've been chasing us all term."

It... it was working. Eric dragged me up, fist back in my hair. *"Are* you going to run to him, little freak?"

I hugged myself, eyes closed.

"Look at me."

I shook my head. "I want... Dusk," I whispered, and in my voice was real desperation.

That was where it had all started: on the first day at the ball, when they'd only had eyes for him.

A competition.

A challenge.

And they hadn't seen *me*.

Now, I needed that.

Fury spiked, and then Eric hauled me to my feet. "Go on. Run to him, little stalker. Show us what happens when he finds out his omega's been ruined."

It was almost over.

I clung to that.

They'd done what they'd set out to. My body was marked but not claimed. I would never be wanted by another alpha again.

It was pitifully ironic. Today, I'd learned Dusk's love hadn't been real. They *were* the only others I had the chance of a future with.

It was Eric who hauled me out. I fought him at first, panic constricting my throat as I realised my pencil case was still in the room, but he just laughed as Flynn tossed it to him. Then he was dragging me out, and there were people around us. I hugged myself, but... they'd done up my shirt, I realised. No one could see what they'd done.

I felt a thousand curious eyes on me, some dropping to my neck.

The only bite they'd left there was at the back, hidden by my hair, but my necklace, it was gone.

Shock numbed me. I barely heard the laughter, the words exchanged.

"Came to our door begging to be let in..."

What was he saying?

"...Turns out she's a little stalker freak... started crying when we wouldn't give her a bond..."

Someone laughed.

No—that wasn't true.

I hadn't cried.

Not for them.

I tried searching for Roxy, but I couldn't see her anywhere. I saw Oliver, and the look of derision on his face.

Then it was quiet.

We were in the hallway, and the door shut behind Eric.

"One last bite, just for luck, since you are so in love with us."

His hand was tight around my throat. He was so much bigger than me.

I sucked a breath through clenched teeth as his teeth grazed my shoulder, pushing back the neckline of my shirt and breaking skin.

Balling my fists, I buried my whine of pain.

I wanted to go.

He didn't let go of my neck when he drew back.

When I glanced up at him, I regretted it, gaze instantly falling to the floor. I'd never been more afraid of my contacts failing. Of them realising I was gold pack.

Not with the strange look in his eyes.

The cruelty kept flickering out for something else. His jaw would tick, muscles on his neck going taut as if shoving me out of this apartment had been the plan, but he didn't want it to be the plan anymore.

It looked like madness. A monster I didn't want to provoke.

I just wanted to go.

He had the sharpie in his hand again, and he was writing something across my skin, below my collarbone.

"For Dusk, if you crawl back to him." He pressed the pen into my hand and drew my chin up roughly, thumb crushing my lips.

"I wonder what they'll do when they see we've defiled their precious little prize after she came begging us for attention," he murmured. "How angry will he be? Maybe he'll take you back, and the whole school will know they're nothing but worthless pricks, picking up leftovers from other alphas."

I don't know when he'd become angry, but his eyes were burning when he dragged my chin up to face him.

His lips were drawn in a sneer. "But I don't think any pack will ever want you again."

I was shaking to my bones, adrenaline scoring my system, horror and sickness drowning me.

This was wrong.

So wrong.

His scent was still cloyingly sweet. He shouldn't be able to do this to his own mate, but I... I was so broken.

He let me go at last, stepping back, that depravity shadowing his eyes for the briefest second as he took me in, gaze drawn to the bites before he ripped my shirt back over my shoulder. It was dark, I realised. The blood wouldn't be visible.

That was good.

He held my pencil case to me. I stared at it, desperate need rising in my chest. With my registration card in there, it was the most valuable thing I owned. I reached for it, but Eric pulled it away. Then he turned it, unzipping and upending it across the floor.

I flinched with each clatter of pens and pencils upon hardwood, my breaths tight again. Eric took a step back, glancing down. I took the chance to look, seeing my blue card grazing the toe of his shiny leather shoes.

When I looked back up, he was watching me, something cruel glinting in his eyes. A dare. To watch me scramble at his feet one more time.

It wasn't dignity that stopped me; it was the pure rocketing fear still in my system. The fear that he might realise, even now, who I was. Or what I was.

My contacts had already failed once.

He was cracking, and my scent could come out at any moment, breaking through the drugs from the terror I hadn't been able to control.

So, I fled, stumbling down the hallway, side pressed to the wall, too afraid to turn my back on him. He didn't pursue, and I almost fell down the stairs as I made for the exit.

SIXTEEN

DUSK

Ransom had just woken, made of nothing but terror in the bond, when there was a banging on the door. Umbra reached it first, ripping it open to reveal a deathly pale Roxy Vasilli.

"*What?*" Umbra's voice was more full of fear than I'd ever heard it.

"Th-they have her." She sounded close to tears.

"Shatter?" I demanded.

She was in her nest.

"I-I didn't know what else to do. They wouldn't let me in, but I know she's with them. I think she's in danger. You have to—" She cut off as Umbra shoved past her.

"*Umbra!*" He had to wait. He couldn't go charging in there. Not with what had happened with Flynn. He'd nearly died.

But...

How?

I paused only a heartbeat to tear a key from my keychain and shove it into Roxy's hand. "If you think they know you came to us, stay here," I told her.

She nodded numbly.

Ransom was already halfway down the hallway after Umbra, but I caught up to them by the time they were down the stairs.

"Umbra!" I snarled, reaching him as he got to the Lincoln pack door. "You can't—!"

Just... he had to wait. *He* couldn't be the one—

"Don't fucking tell me what I can't fucking do!" he hissed, spinning on me. I hadn't seen him this wild in years. "If they have her, I'll kill them."

"We *will*, but you need to back—"

Before I could argue, Ransom flared his aura for a brief moment, and the experience was downright unnerving. He'd ripped the front door open before we could say another word.

Shit.

I exchanged a glance with Umbra, and then I was after him.

"Where is she?" Ransom's furious growl ahead was met with a crash. Yells echoed around the apartment, and then a few betas and omegas were shoving past us, terror on their faces as we shoved into the room ahead.

Ransom was crossing the kitchen to a living room beyond.

I could see the Lincoln pack, but—where was Shatter?

"Ransom fucking Kingsman shows his face at last." I recognised Flynn's voice.

"Looking for your omega?" That was Eric. "Turns out she's a little stalker freak. Been obsessed with us since—" He cut off.

Ransom—still not fully present even in the bond—honed in on Eric in a moment.

Before I could stop him, he was crossing the room, shoving Flynn out of the way. I felt a flash of dread, but nothing happened. Nothing like before, when Flynn had touched me.

Ransom's aura exploded out, an invisible shockwave as he grabbed Eric's shirt in his fist.

Eric and Gareth matched him, but both auras paled next to

Ransom's, and Eric barely had a chance to flinch before Ransom slammed him into the wall, crumbling the drywall to dust.

His aura was harrowing. Broken. Leaving silence in its wake.

Eric's face was pale, his eyes wide.

"Where is she?" Ransom sounded more animal than human.

"Sh-she's gone."

"Where?"

"She r-ran out of the building."

"DUSK!" Umbra's voice from behind me sounded urgent. I spun, taking a step back to see Umbra was still the door, picking something up from the floor.

At his feet were scattered the insides of Shatter's pencil case, and in his hand was her registration card.

She wouldn't have left that, not unless she was terrified.

I would kill them.

I would tear them limb from limb. Peel their skin from flesh and watch them bleed. I would listen to their screams until they died down to nothing.

But Shatter came first.

SHATTER

It was a cool evening, chilly droplets cascaded around me, shimmering in the dim light of the academy grounds. The wet pathways glistened beneath my boots.

There was nothing left for me.

Dusk had been right. I choked back my sob. He'd been right, and I still didn't know if anything had been real between me and him. Even... even if it had been, they would never take me back now.

Their necklace was gone.

I was marked by other alphas.

Alphas he hated.

There was nothing left for me here.

Could I go back to the Estate? Beg Uncle and Aunty Lauren to take me back? Would they? Or would they send me to the Institute if I showed my face there again?

I sank to my knees on a garden pathway, body trembling.

My mates.

I never... I let out a low, pained sound. *I never wanted to see them again.*

Or think about them.

Not ever.

This shouldn't have happened.

They should never have been able to hurt me like that...

And Uncle was their sponsor...

Would he blame me for this?

Could I try to make it on my own?

I had the set of contacts in my eyes right now, but even my registration card was gone. My teeth chattered in the cold air as the truth hit in full force.

Eric was right. Dusk, Umbra and Ransom would never want me, even if it had been real...

I'd given up the safety of the Estate. I'd given up the Kingsman pack.

And they were cruel and horrible.

Footsteps thundered, and I looked up.

"There she is!"

Rough hands grabbed me, and there was a sound of laughter. An unfamiliar scent of chamomile flooded my senses. That was an alpha. I tried to pull away, but an aura hit the air.

"W-Wait—"

There were two of them.

"Said you ran off into the grounds after they rejected you," one was saying. "Didn't seem to mind the idea of another pack picking up their seconds."

"Let go!"

I heard a laugh. "No one's going to believe you. We've got a video saying the Kingsman slut is looking for out-of-pack company."

They'd seen the video?

My... my mates had sent it out to everyone...

"N-No." The world was still spinning. I couldn't think straight.

I was shaking. My scent. I had to calm down.

How much stress had I been under tonight?

I'd fought so hard to keep calm, but my scent could come out at any second, adrenaline burning through the blockers.

I'd be dead.

My breath caught as a pain shot over my scalp. Someone was dragging me up. I wasn't going to make it.

Pathetic. Weak. Five minutes on my own and—

I whined as the alpha's grip tightened, dragging my arms behind me. *"Don't!"*

"No one's buying it," a nasty voice said. "You're a little freak, stalking alphas who don't want you."

I whimpered as a hand clamped around my neck. Shock burned through my system, a fissure scoring deep into my sanity.

I wasn't ready.

I'd survived my mates. *Just.*

This was too much—

Another aura split the air; it was shaky static and held so much power that it drew the alpha up. He spun, searching for the source.

Umbra.

I saw him standing just up stone steps from the alphas who held me, sandstorm eyes dark in the night as he looked down at us.

He'd come for me?

It was one, tiny flicker of hope in darkness as the fragments of my shattered life tumble down around me.

My whimper slipped out as I tried to reach for him, his storm of wolfsbane and blood in the air. But it was different—the iron tang of blood consuming it.

He was different.

His eyes were fixed on them, devoid of the tender, caring alpha I'd come to know. His low growl echoed around the space, and the alphas let me go, turning tail and fleeing.

Umbra moved faster than I thought possible, taking the steps in fours as he threw himself after them. There was nothing human left in his expression.

Then I caught sight of Dusk.

What were they doing here?

He made for me, but I took a few steps back, that flicker of hope snuffed out as panic seized me.

I gripped my shirt, terrified. He could never see the bites.

The truth.

What they'd done.

Dusk drew up, seeing my fear, holding his hand up as if in surrender.

His aura wavered, furious, threatening.

I couldn't focus.

They were here. Not to save me… To tell me I wasn't even enough for them anymore. I knew it.

"Shatter…" Dusk's voice was broken.

Another whine rose in my throat at the sound of my name.

He closed the distance at that sound, drawing me against him. And I wanted to lean into that touch. To let it sweep me up and carry me back to my nest.

But…

"You… you can't." The words left me as hollow as they sounded. Still, he drew me closer.

I lashed out as he tried to wrap his arms around me, my nails catching his cheek.

I didn't want this. For him to pretend, only to take it away once he saw what they'd done. The fissure in my sanity cracked further, but he didn't let me go as I slammed my fists against him, a scream in my chest as I tried to get away.

I couldn't do it...

And then I caught lily of the valley, and another set of hands dragged me from Dusk.

Ransom...?

Ransom was here?

Awake.

I sobbed.

Too late...

Too late...

"Shatter?" His voice was low, melodic. As beautiful as he was. "My omega."

Finally, tears flooded my cheeks as I shook my head.

No.

Not anymore.

He was too late, and I never wanted him to see what they'd done to me. He drew me close, but his arms were like barbs, promises I'd dreamed of, and could no longer have.

The fissure became a chasm, and the last of my sanity drained away.

SEVENTEEN

RANSOM

There was a harrowing irony to the fact that I woke as she vanished.

From the bond she'd left on my neck.

From reality.

When she saw me, her eyes went wide, and a shadow of fear crossed her face.

Fear at... at me?

A low, wounded sound rose in her chest. I tried to reach for her, but she recoiled.

She fought me, distressed sounds rising in her chest as she tried to get away. I let go, heart beating a mile a minute, but the moment I did, she staggered, turning and trying to run.

"Shatter!" Dusk caught her arm, but at the touch she spun on him, eyes wild and empty as she lashed out.

Again, I saw what was written in black lines upon her skin. The word *'Stalker'* was written across her forehead.

A prank?

I couldn't understand. She was terrified. An angel worth the whole world twice over—and someone had tormented her?

The alphas back there... I didn't know who they were, but I hadn't done enough. I would go back—

"Enough!" Dusk's aura split the air, his word weighted with command. It was for her, not me, and it had her frozen still.

I took a step forward, but Shatter flinched from me and Umbra grabbed my arm.

When had he got back?

"Look at me," Dusk growled at her.

Her gaze darted around wildly, anywhere but him, until his fingers closed around her chin and he dragged her to face him. "We had a deal, Gem. Rule number one."

Her expression crumpled, her breaths becoming sharper, but her eyes locked on him.

I frowned, but Umbra's grip became firmer as I tried to take another step forward. Something flickered in her eyes at Dusk's words, finally, something human surfacing in our connection.

Dusk didn't take his eyes from her. "You aren't going to run from me."

She was shaking still, face ghost-like in the moonlight.

"Do you understand?" he asked. His yellow eyes were piercing in the night.

Finally, she made the slightest motion of a nod, and when Dusk let her go, she didn't move.

I stepped toward her again, but she recoiled, this time her fist closing around Dusk's sleeve as she cowered behind him.

I shoved down the aching wound at seeing terror in her beautiful eyes at the sight of me.

She was my angel. One that scattered the darkest of voids. She didn't need to be scared of me. Not ever.

Dusk didn't let go of her as he dug into his pocket, but his eyes found mine.

"Are you okay?" he asked, voice rough.

I nodded, though it was a lie. How could I be when she wasn't?

Dusk drew out his keys and tossed them to Umbra.

"We're going to the cabin."

"But—" Umbra began, and I felt the tense hatred in him through the bond.

Dusk cut him off, the full weight of pack lead in his words.

"We're. Going."

DUSK

The moment Shatter was in the car I shut the door behind her.

She needed a few moments alone—safe. Ransom was staring at the tinted windows looking lost, and I'd never felt Umbra this dark in the bond before.

I was shaking.

Everything I was terrified of had happened. They'd got ahold of her. Tormented her, humiliated her—

"They sent a video around campus." Umbra's voice was low, and he looked a second from cracking his phone.

I shoved it down. "Don't watch it."

"We don't know what happened—"

"*She's* the priority."

The cabin wasn't just for Shatter.

I needed Umbra out of here, too. His demon had surfaced, his side of the bond nothing but fury. I hadn't seen this side of him for a long time. I needed him on a different hemisphere from the Lincoln pack, or they'd both be dead by morning.

Ransom, at least, had been able to touch them without nearly fucking dying, though. I had no idea why, but I'd deal with it later.

I couldn't say I wasn't at risk of getting us both killed either.

Dread was a swamp at the back of my mind, threatening to drag me in.

I would kill them.

We would.

Just... *Fuck*.

Not yet.

"Her first."

I was dialling Decebal's number, leaning against the closed door, praying he'd pick up. And she could have a few moments alone and I could figure out what the fuck to do.

My hands were shaking, her fear piercing me to my marrow.

What had they done?

How long had she been gone?

Why hadn't I noticed?

Their scents were all over her. How long had she been with them?

"Yeh?" Decebal's voice cut me off from my thoughts.

"Decebal." My voice was rough. "We need help. Shatter, she..." I trailed off, searching for words.

"She's feral, Dusk," Ransom snarled. "Fully fucking gone, alright. She vanished from the bond with me."

"Is that Ransom?" Decebal sounded stunned.

I paused for a moment, finding Ransom's eyes, the little flutter of hope in my chest lighting again before reality came slamming down. "She... woke him."

"And now she's fucking gone!" Ransom's voice was low. *"What happened?"*

"I... I fucked up. Decebal. I need you on this. We're going to the cabin. Her mates, they..."

The world tilted violently at the thought, dread had me in a stranglehold.

This was my fault.

I pushed her.

I'd sent her running.

Umbra's hand was on my arm, and Decebal's voice sounded in my ear. I blinked, realising I'd lost a few moments.

Not now.

I didn't have time for stupid fucking aura shit and disassociation while Shatter was hurt. This stupid fucking sickness could wait.

"I swear, Decebal, I won't watch this happen to her." Not again. Not when I'd just got Ransom back. "What do we do?"

"I can meet you there." Decebal was saying. "Check her over—"

He cut off as I heard another voice in the background.

"Alright, give me a few hours. We'll come up with a plan. Do you know what happened?"

"Her mates," I said. "They... they hurt her..." Again, I was almost ripped from reality as I tried to piece it together. A video around campus? And what was written across her face— *Stalker...*? They thought... Bitter relief flooded my system for a moment. If they thought that, they hadn't figured out she was their scent match. "I don't know how. Like... like it was a game."

"Yeh. I know the kind of things they think are games." There was a pause. "They're her mates, Dusk. If they hurt her, rejected her—do you know what that can do to an omega? And she's unstable already. Sounds like she's regressing to how she was back when she was at that Estate—when she was off the meds."

"I'm not giving her anything," I hissed.

"Wouldn't suggest it. Until I get there just... just do your best —" He cut off again and I heard another voice distantly. "Ah Shit. I can't tonight, not anymore, I got work—"

"Decebal!" I growled.

I *needed* him.

"Rain check, mate." His voice became fainter as he spoke to someone else in the room. "It's important." There was a pause.

"You'll be fine. Gavin's really isn't my scene anyway—and Eliott was meeting us there, right?"

His voice got louder again as he returned to the call. "Alright. I'm on my way. You remember the protocol with Ransom. Same shit. Make sure she's safe. If there's anything that seems to trigger her further, don't push her. Anything you can do to ground her, do it, remove anything that makes it worse. I'll meet you at the cabin, alright?"

RANSOM

The massive Lexus SUV we'd arrived at wasn't one I'd seen before. I used to be into cars, but the model was unrecognisable.

How many years had I missed?

I wasn't ready to ask yet.

Dusk hung up the phone, then opened the door to the back seat. Shatter was curled up in the far seat, clutching her knees to her chest, eyes wide with terror as Dusk got in.

I took the front beside Umbra even though it killed me. But I didn't want to frighten her more. Decebal had said to remove anything that made her worse, and right now, the only one she was okay with was Dusk.

"Are you hurt?" he asked.

She didn't answer.

He reached for her but she choked a sob, pressing herself against the far door, covering her face and neck with her hands, fists balled in her hair to obscure herself from view.

My heart cracked in two again as Umbra turned the engine on.

I couldn't stand it.

She was everything. She'd saved me, and I'd woken too late to protect her.

"Shatter, if you don't tell me, I will check myself," Dusk said quietly.

She shrank further against the door, tugging on her hair viciously, but shook her head.

Good.

I met Dusk's eyes and nodded. Whenever she answered like that, I felt a flicker of her in the bond.

She was hiding from us, as if she was afraid of us seeing her.

Shatter remained curled up in the back seat, silent, almost catatonic for the whole ride. Dusk was beside her, but she flinched every time he reached out, and nothing he did soothed her.

Her scent became more frightened the more we drove.

When we arrived, he took her in his arms and carried her to the cabin. He set her up in his room, but when I got a glimpse inside, she'd curled up on the bed, hugging her knees to her chest, eyes blank.

She was my angel. The reaper that had brought me life, instead of death, and I wouldn't be okay until she was.

EIGHTEEN

SHATTER

I remembered, in vivid detail, what it was like to lose myself to the instincts that ruled me. Back to the time when I was taken off the meds and the world would fade, and I would return to myself, my room in ruins. Or locked in a pitch-black cellar after losing my temper.

It had happened again when I'd seen Ransom out in the dark and rain. I had felt myself fading, panic taking over.

Until Dusk's command.

It had been jarring, suspending me in a reality to which I couldn't have clung by myself. He'd stared down at me, rain-flecked hair stuck to skin that was umber in the night, a stark contrast to piercing yellow eyes that held mine.

Absolute.

Sure.

I was coming apart at the edges, and his voice had held me together.

Time passed in a blur, and there was a rumble of a car engine around me. The warmth of a car speeding along a highway. All of their scents were tangled in the small space.

Lily of the valley, wolfsbane and blood, and dark opium.

Mine rose, too. I knew the scent blockers must have failed by now, even if I didn't know exactly when.

The car ride had gone on forever.

I'd shivered in Dusk's arms, but he hadn't let me go. The affection was false, though. It would only last until he discovered the truth.

Time tripped over itself, scattering like beads across the floor. Sometimes I was with Dusk in the car.

Then I was back there.

In a room that smelled like them. It was slowly lodging into my consciousness like a great pillar, roots diving too deep to ever be dug up.

Passionfruit scented the sheets, and their teeth were on my flesh.

I knew what they were doing, even when I didn't want to. Marking me with bites deeper than Umbra had ever given. With everything but a true claim.

Marking me with bites so vicious that they would scar, and every alpha who saw me would know...

Flynn's were the worst, his bites ripping me from the silence of my mind with the threat of a dark bond. His eyes danced with joy when I clutched him. Terror a knife in my heart. Yet the dark bond never completed.

My body ached.

Finally, the car stopped and Dusk picked me up in his arms. We were outside for a moment, and I inhaled the smells of trees and rain before I heard a front door opening and boots upon creaking hardwood. Everything inside here smelled of pine, and there was comfort in its unfamiliarity.

Dusk's territory.

He set me down on a large bed with faint traces of dark opium.

"*Stay.*" His aura flickered and his command came through, gripping me. I listened. Not because I wanted to be on the bed, but because there was a frightening safety in letting his dominance, his aura, take over.

And because I think a small part of me was terrified of finding out what his punishments might look like after he saw my body—when he realised it held no interest to him anymore.

He left me for a time, and I didn't know how long I spent in silence. When the door creaked, I growled.

I don't think I'd ever done that before. The first time was followed by the scent of lily of the valley, wolfsbane and blood, but the door creaked no more and they were gone.

Safety returned with the silence as time slipped by, fading in and out.

Finally, the door creaked again, and my growls were ignored. The bed shifted as the weight of a body offset it.

I couldn't look up and see him, but dark opium could give him away from a million miles.

I curled up tighter, afraid.

Again, the bed shifted, and then his warm touch was everywhere. I reacted, fighting him, a rough wail in my throat as he held me down. Just like always, he didn't care what I wanted. Something warm was on my face. A damp cloth... He pinned me in place, washing my forehead.

I didn't understand. I fought him harder, but then the cloth was gone and he curled up around me until I could barely breathe. I wailed louder, unable to stand his touch.

"I'm sorry." His whisper was rough.

I shuddered.

Why was he saying that?

"I failed you."

He was purring, but there was something desperate in the sound as if, for the first time, he wasn't sure it was enough to drag me to the surface again. And like an avalanche, all my feelings came crashing down, and I was bawling my eyes out.

I couldn't take it.

I wasn't ready to feel this or face this.

Not yet. My breaths were choked, ugly tears tracking my cheeks. And he held me tighter, even though I didn't know why.

I didn't understand.

I didn't understand why I was here with him right now.

Was it possible they hadn't seen the video? That it hadn't reached them yet?

Nothing he offered would last. He would see the marks that seared across my body and he would vanish.

Ransom was awake, though. Would he dark bond me to ensure he would stay that way—even if I disgusted him?

I shoved Dusk away, terror blinding as sanity faded once more.

In a flicker of violence and rage and fear, he was gone.

I was left panting and alone on the bed.

I don't know how bad it got, but the midnight opium that lingered in the room was edged with fear like I'd never imagined it could be.

My mind had vanished again, tugged down into murky depths at the fear of what would happen when they saw. I still had that sharpie in my pocket, the one Eric had pressed into my trembling fingers.

When they saw what I was, now...

I dared tug at my shirt and look down, and was met by the blossoming, angry bruises of their bites. Dried blood smeared my skin.

Marks of my own failure.

My own stupidity.

Not enough. Never enough. Not even for my mates...

I crossed toward the closet, desperate for anything that could protect me, the pen Eric had left me with clutched in my grip as reality faded completely.

DUSK

I waited an hour, and then I couldn't wait any longer, my own fear of leaving her alone getting the better of me.

I'd had to leave.

She'd tumbled so far from sanity that her nails had dug into her own flesh until I pinned her by her wrists. Then she'd lost it, low wounded wails coming from her chest. Her scent was free in the space, and it was broken.

It wasn't until I'd let her go and backed across the room that she had settled. Her body wracked with heaving sobs as she curled up in the bed, barely able to breathe.

But I couldn't leave her alone for too long.

This was her sickness, I realised. I was witnessing what those logs described. The boundless agony of the instincts she was chained to.

She was an omega, and her mates had rejected her.

They hadn't *just* rejected her...

I knew her history. I knew she'd been in states like this before, and I knew she'd been suicidal.

When I finally dared return, it was to find her huddled up in the corner of my closet. She was wearing one of my bathrobes, and it was much too big for her.

That was good—at least, I thought it was.

But their scents were still here.

She'd slipped back into stillness. Her scent had settled, a bed of deadly petals rustling only slightly in the breeze.

"Come on," I said quietly, holding out a hand.

I would get their scent off of her.

She didn't move, fingers clutching her hair so tight I was sure she'd pulled some out.

"Get up." I used my alpha bark again. She flinched, but then she shifted to her knees, fumbling with a shelf to stand. Her eyes were still distant, not meeting mine.

Her scent settled further, and I wasn't sure why. It was far from calm, but instead of the vile sickness that had saturated it before, it had changed.

Fear?

It felt like it.

Of me?

I frowned.

She was disobedient at every possible moment, but right here she'd stood without argument.

"You're safe," I told her.

She didn't look at me.

I noticed her cheeks were too pink, and a sweat glistened on her forehead. I pressed my palm to her cheek.

Far too hot.

It couldn't be her heat again, could it? She said they were erratic.

I don't know what we'd do if it was, but nothing in her scent gave that impression.

I slipped my hand in hers and tugged her forward a step. She came with me to the bathroom, expression still empty.

It took me a while in the bright lights of the bathroom to realise what was off. She looked wrong... her figure, even with the robe, was strangely shaped.

She fought me, but I tugged the robe open. It was then that I realised why she was so warm. And what I'd missed—even in the short time I'd been gone.

I should never have left her alone. Not for a second.

Beneath the robe, she was wearing a dozen layers of fabric, as if she'd put on every piece of clothing in the closet. There was a shirt wrapped around her neck, but when I reached for it, her breathing became desperate as she flattened herself harder against the bathroom wall.

"I'm not going anywhere," I told her. Not this time. I couldn't. She was overheating as it was, and if she'd lied and she was physically injured beneath it all, I needed to treat it.

I knelt, every movement feeling like lead as I realised how terrified she truly was. How much shame she was carrying.

I'd failed her, if she was still afraid of that.

I cupped her cheek. "I'm going to take some of these clothes off."

She just shook her head, the slightest movement. A glittering tear tumbled down her cheek.

I shut my eyes for a moment, then reached out and undid the messy buttons of an outer shirt. Then the zipper of a hoodie beneath.

More tears began to leak down her cheeks, and her tremors became violent. Nightshade had lost all threat. It weighed in the air as heavily as it did on my soul, edged with fear.

I was afraid of what she was scared of me seeing.

Finally, I reached the last layer, a long sleeve button-up, and massively oversized.

She clutched the hem down, with short sharp breaths from her nose as her eyes fixed on the ceiling. She still had the other shirt wrapped around her neck.

"Show me."

She shut her eyes at the command, fingers trembling on the first button. She undid it, but didn't open it.

Her breath caught, her eyes on the ceiling as her chin quivered.

"When I came to your room, I wanted to…" Her voice caught. "I wanted to tell you I chose…" Her voice broke beyond repair.

Relief flooded my heart as I heard her speak, even if the words broke my heart.

She'd been about to reject them.

To choose us.

"I read… some of the documents…" Her voice caught. "And I know you only wanted me because I could f-fix Ransom…"

I froze.

"And I just… I was just… I was just looking for Roxy. I was s-so confused."

I shut my eyes, fingers tangling in hers again as I held her tight.

"Shatter…" *Shit*. That's why she'd left? It all clicked. If she'd read the notes I'd just made…

"But you…" Her voice was cracked and hollow. "You won't… you won't want me. Not even to dark bond me."

No…

"I never wanted that," I whispered.

Fuck.

Why hadn't she told me she'd seen them?

But… She must have been terrified that if she told me she knew I would bite her right then.

"I swear to you, Decebal found those files today."

There was a long, long silence as she stared at me, then a broken sob shook her whole frame. "It's too late. H-He said, no alpha is ever going t-to… to want me ever again."

I reached up, cupping her cheek. "*Nothing* has changed, Shatter," I told her. "Not since the day I met you."

"You won't…" Her words were breathless, and her eyes darted to the door. "I c-can't. You don't understand." Another whine shook her. "Y-you don't know what they've... th-they've—"

"You think I care if they've marked you?" I asked. She thought I didn't know what they were capable of.

They had, I knew that much. I knew it by her terror.

She thought I cared about that? As if the Lincoln pack weren't already a bleeding scar across my entire fucking life.

"I told you I love you—"

I cut off as a strangled sound tore from her. Her grip became vicious and she tried to pull away, true panic in her eyes.

I got to my feet in an instant and tugged the shirt from around her neck. There were no marks there, but the necklace was gone.

I wasn't expecting how much that cut, seeing the arbitrary symbol of the claim the academy handed us, taken by another.

I pressed her against the wall by her neck, gently but firmly. She grappled with my arms, wild eyes losing their humanity again, but I wouldn't let her run this time. "There is nothing I love that hasn't been broken and put back together. That someone hasn't tried to take. You are mine, Shatter, and there is no bite on this planet that can change that."

Tears wet her cheeks as she shivered, each breath wracking her whole body. She just shook her head, expression so broken.

"Show me." My command was absolute, and she did what I asked, fumbling with the last of the buttons as tears dripped from the chin to the floor.

Fuck—

I saw her skin at last.

A low growl of fury tore from my chest, making her jump.

Her eyes met mine, her whole body freezing as if ripped from a daze. She tried to pull the shirt closed in desperation, but I caught her wrists.

The Lincoln pack hadn't just left a mark on her skin, they'd brutalised her.

Each bite was clearly visible, a dozen, at least. Even through the mess of blood and blackness. They weren't dark bonds, but Shatter *herself* had—I placed my hands on the vanity, needing to steady myself.

This went beyond a claim or a prank.

Bite after bite marred her skin and torso and arms, and the wounds were angry, covered in thick lines of black ink—scribbles that covered most of her skin, all made by a sharpie.

She'd done that, I realised. In the time in which I'd left her alone. I'd seen the sharpie laying on the floor of the closet.

She'd made each dark stroke in a desperate moment of panic, trying to hide the marks beneath sharpie as if that might erase what had happened.

It was denial. Self hatred.

Hatred they'd given her.

And I had failed her.

She was fading again, and I looked back up at her, cupping her neck once more, getting myself under control.

"Nothing has changed," I whispered.

She couldn't understand me, I saw it in her eyes.

I tugged my shirt off and led us to the shower, but before we got in, I gently removed her contacts. She didn't fight me. Instead, she went deathly still as I turned the water on, waiting for a comfortable temperature. Those wounds were fresh and angry and would need healing, but I wouldn't allow another second to pass with their scents on her.

Not after what they'd done.

She shivered in my arms as the warm water streamed over us. I was gentle using the soap, trying to avoid her wounds as I freed her of their scents.

My pulse was erratic as I worked, alpha instincts trying to rip me apart as I saw, again and again, their marks. But those instincts had been long warped, overwritten by drugs and madness, and none worked the way they should—the way the Lincoln pack wished they might.

I wiped her face again with the cloth, the word across her forehead was faint now, but I needed it gone.

I saw the other message left for me. Almost entirely scribbled over beneath her collarbone.

'Dusk's little whore'

It was the last confirmation I needed. This went beyond a vendetta. Brutalising her like this? It wasn't a calculated prank, it was the sharp edge of insanity I recognised. Obsession and hatred.

Arrogant, entitled alphas twisted by a draw they felt but could not understand.

Hating her for what she couldn't control.

Hating me.

I should have never, for one moment, doubted her. I should have shown her everything sooner.

Her eyes were distant, not feral now, but reserved, as if she didn't know what was happening as I drew the cloth along her skin. I was caring for her, and I knew she didn't trust it.

She believed that these marks meant I couldn't still love her.

I washed her hair, fingers running through her thick locks with conditioner before I rinsed it out, then sat her on the vanity, towelling off her hair and drying her skin in patches so as not to touch her wounds.

I hadn't been able to get the black ink off, but her beautiful, tawny skin was mostly free of it.

Then, before I did anything else, I drew my jaw along her temple, leaving my mark.

Her scent shifted, panic turning to something... desperate. Like the faintest trace of hope trying to break through—as if a part of her was daring herself to believe what I was doing.

"I didn't know," I told her. "The papers you found about your history... I only just got them. I swear it."

Her lip trembled as I said that, and she looked away.

She blamed herself for not believing.

How could she have?

I hadn't given her that space or allowance.

"I've had so much worse stolen from me, Shatter," I murmured, drawing a towel over her long hair again. "All of it, I dragged from the edge of hell itself. Carrying you back—I could do that with my eyes closed."

She was still and her eyes fixed, body trembling as I drew new undergarments on. Umbra had made a trip to the store to stock up on food and essentials since we hadn't had any clothes for her here.

The bralette was soft against her skin, and wouldn't tug against the bites. The sharpie had mostly washed off, but I pulled the medical kit from the cupboard and got to work cleaning the bites. They were deep, deep enough to scar, but they weren't bleeding anymore.

There were some truly deep ones across her breast and shoulder. They would need dressing, but I would do that after. Every bite, or red mark where their nails had dug in to keep her still, every bruise, they all carried her terror. All surfaced a thousand imaginings of how frightened she must have been, reflecting the moment in which she realised what her mates truly were.

As much as it frightened me, there had always been something beautiful about how much light she could see in darkness—her faith in even them.

And now they might have stolen that from her forever.

So, I committed each mark to memory. They were for me, not her. I would deliver this back to them ten-fold.

The pain and the humiliation.

The agony.

And the earth shattering moment in which they realised they had lost.

I loved her more than I had even known when I'd dared say it to her today.

She didn't believe me, not yet, still fading in and out of reality. Still trying to run. I understood that more than most.

But running wouldn't help her heal.

I left her only for a moment, to change into a dry pair of sweatpants before I took her in my arms and set her down on the edge of the bed.

Then I got the fireplace going, so there was a flickering, warm flame dancing in the hearth.

She was exactly where I'd left her when I returned, damp hair dripping down her golden skin and over her bites.

The room would warm up quickly. It was beautiful here, the whole cabin was—a slice of heaven to host what had, for the longest time, been our pack's hell. But I'd never stopped appreciating it. I think I'd come from somewhere that had taught me things like this were worth never getting used to.

The bed was set before the far wall that was barely a wall at all. Timber beams held together great windows that arched over the bed. The clouds had cleared and the stars twinkled down from above.

I wanted her to see them, when she was ready to see beauty again.

I sat on the bed and shifted behind her. She tried to turn, but I placed my hands on her shoulders. Then I retrieved a belt from my drawer and drew her arms behind her back.

She flinched, trying to turn again, her body tense now.

"Still," I murmured.

She listened, not fighting me as I secured her hands behind her and made sure the buckle was positioned at the back so it wouldn't dig into her skin.

Why *was* she listening with such ease?

If anything, I thought her scent was less afraid than before.

"What are you doing?" she asked, voice quiet. Her eyes were wide, golden orbs as I returned to stand before her.

"Showing you the truth."

She might listen to what I said now, but if I didn't restrain her, she'd fight me.

There was a metal poker in the fireplace. One with ridges that Umbra used to favour, to make the payments on his skin before we moved out of the cabin.

I shifted her so she was laying back against the pillows, tear-tracked face still a mask of emptiness as I leaned close, pressing my lips to her neck.

"Nothing has changed since the day I met you." I'd say it until she understood. "You are mine, Shatter. Every mark they left on your body, they're mine, too."

NINETEEN

SHATTER

Shock blistered through every other emotion as Dusk shifted closer, lips caressing the first bite.

The one at my shoulder.

Eric's.

Then he drew back and ran his lips along the next.

Gareth's.

There was one upon my breast.

Flynn's.

I'd been frozen as he'd given me that, the lurking promise of a dark bond chilling me to my bones.

Over and over, Dusk kissed the foul marks my mates had left. It took too long. There were far too many. He pressed his lips to each, and the memories threatened, each blow was duller than the last. His grip curled around my thigh and waist, holding me in place, and yellow eyes pinned me every time he drew back.

Absolute and sure.

Safe.

Eric had sworn he couldn't, yet somehow, Dusk still wanted me. He could look at me. He could kiss me.

I didn't understand.

He pulled back at last, leaving me to stare up at him, finally a stirring of something that wasn't horror in my chest.

That was until he crossed to the fireplace and drew a metal rod from it. At the end, which glowed red, was a thin, straight line.

I tensed.

What was he doing?

He settled in front of me and, before I could open my mouth in protest, flipped the iron and pressed it to the same spot on his shoulder where Eric's bite was on mine.

His expression tensed through the pain, but he didn't waver.

"*No!*"

I understood, all of a sudden, why he'd restrained me. I tried to sit up but couldn't, eyes wide with shock.

"I failed you," he growled.

"You d-didn't."

"You don't trust my claim, Gem. If you did, today would never have happened."

"I..." I couldn't say it, though. That I trusted that he loved me? That he wanted me—even now? Even after everything. "It's not your fault," I choked.

He'd never wavered, but *he* wasn't the problem—how could he think he was the problem?

I'd been promised I would never have anything, while he'd promised me the world.

It wasn't that I didn't *want* to believe him—I did. I wanted it so badly it had driven me to run at the slightest possibility of having that dream stolen.

"Please..."

He couldn't... those marks would scar forever.

Dusk gritted his teeth as he pressed it to his skin again. A hiss of hot iron upon flesh rose in the air, but he held it there.

"Stop it!" I cried, managing to struggle into a sitting position, but it was too easy for him to cup my neck and hold me in place as he branded himself again, his aura splitting the air this time as a low growl of pain rolled through his chest.

He went on for what felt like forever, his body shuddering from the agony of it.

Agony he was enduring for me.

How many bites?

Five? Ten? I didn't want to count.

When he finished, he set the iron back on the fireplace and returned to the bed. His aura lingered, not for physical strength, I realised, but for the tolerance to the wounds he'd put on his body. As an alpha, he had faster wound healing which was increased by the presence of his aura.

I was silent, my heart racing a million miles a minute as my eyes traced the angry red wounds across his body. He drew my chin up as he settled on the bed before me and pressed his lips to mine.

The kiss was shocking, and familiar in that, too.

He had a habit of kissing me when he absolutely shouldn't. I swallowed, eyes tracing the wounds again, now he was closer. The patches of flesh were warped and angry. So much more painful than mine. But he drew my chin up, so I was swallowed by piercing yellow eyes.

"It's my job to protect you, Gem. From them, from the world. Even from yourself, if that's what you need," he murmured. "Your scars are my scars. My weight, my burden."

"It sh-shouldn't be."

There was a faint smile on his lips.

"It's no more your choice now than it was then. I claimed you, Shatter. I decided you were mine. I took you from your mates, and

I never asked you. I won't abandon that claim because it costs me." My lip trembled as he still found new words to knock me flat.

"If this is what it takes to put you back together, this is what I'll do." He tucked my damp hair behind my ear, the smallest smile playing on his lips. "And see, now you're far more concerned about my scars than yours."

At his gall to smile, I burst into full-blown tears. "B-because you b-*branded* yourself."

"Do you believe my claim now?"

I couldn't answer that, but he hadn't released my chin, and I was still drowning in his intense eyes and the comforting scent of midnight opium.

"Do you?"

With a choked sob, I nodded.

"I love you. It should never have taken you this long to be sure of that," he said, wiping my tears since I couldn't. "I've wanted you every day, from the moment I met you. They never had the power to change that, Shatter." His hands traced my body, somehow perfectly avoiding all the wounds, as if they were already fixed to his memory.

I stared at him. He had seen it all and still hadn't wavered.

I think... I think this is what love meant.

I didn't realise until now how much I hadn't dared believe I was destined for love. Not even with my mates.

Dusk was sitting up and freeing my wrists. "Decebal's on his way. He's going to wait until tomorrow to take a look at you, but he'll flay me if I don't clean these."

"Who?"

"Ransom's contact. He helps us with... a lot of shit, actually. But he's medically trained."

"Oh. Okay."

Dusk got to his feet and headed to the bathroom. I sat up

watching him open the medical kit. After he began digging inside it, I clambered out of bed and crossed toward him, nursing a little anxious ache that rose now he wasn't in the same room as me.

He glanced up when I clutched my arm, leaning against the doorframe and trying not to look too creepy as I hovered. Maybe I should act like I came here for a reason.

I peered through the huge pile of clothing on the floor as a distraction, trying not to think about what they had meant for me, even an hour ago.

"Ransom... he's awake...?"

Dusk's eyes lit up in a way I'd never seen, a smile curving his lips as if he couldn't help it. "You saved him," he said as he pulled apart some gauze.

I tried to bury the flutter of panic in my stomach at that thought. Tomorrow I would see Umbra and Ransom after... after everything.

I don't know why Dusk was safer.

Perhaps, it was what he'd said... He'd never asked. But Umbra was different... Dusk had claimed me, but Umbra was stuck with me. And he was such a beautiful person, and I was such a mess.

And Ransom...

Oh...

I swallowed.

He'd grown up in one of the wealthiest families in New Oxford. What was he going to think of me when he met me? *Really...* really met me. I had just been an omega with a scent he didn't hate (somehow) and I was just there at the right time.

"He already loves you," Dusk said, catching my expression "He'll only fall harder when he meets you."

I said nothing, chewing on that and trying really hard to believe it.

I felt like I was teetering between this safety with Dusk, and a void of darkness below. He dressed his wounds and then mine, and when he was done, he took us back to the bed and held me close, still careful around the bites.

"Now." He knelt before me on the bed. "Lay down, and let me finish proving to you that you're mine."

I tensed, suddenly nervous, but he was lowering me down against the pillows. "What do you mean?"

He couldn't. Not when I was like this. Shame lingered, my own mistakes scorching me to the bone.

Fighting him with his aura out, though, was useless, and before I could gather the breath for another protest, he'd tugged the black lace of my underwear out of the way and found my clit with his tongue.

I let out a low moan, my back arching, and he dipped his finger into me.

Fuck.

I arched into the touch as his hand clamped over my stomach, trapping me so he could work me deeper, his tongue drawing a low moan from my chest.

"Relax, Gem," he breathed, drawing back for a moment. Again, I didn't fight his command, and my body unwound, succumbing to his touch.

It wasn't until that moment that I realised how wound tight with terror I'd been. Not until the shock at what he was doing hit me with such force that tears pricked my eyes.

My vision swam and I blinked, glancing up and finding myself staring up into the starry night sky, pleasure building with each deep breath as Dusk drew me more firmly against him, drawing my gaze back to piercing yellow irises shadowed by the sweep of short, raven hair.

Another low moan escaped my chest as he pumped a second finger into me, slower and deeper, drawing the sounds out with each thrust. I could feel the slick pooling between his fingers as he worked me, tongue pushing me further and further toward the edge.

Tonight I'd tumbled lower than any point in my life. I'd made every mistake it was possible to make, and somehow, he was still here.

How was he still here? When I was covered in their marks. He was an alpha.

In a flash of panic, I was back there. *The grip Eric had on me was painful, he was smiling, finding delight in my fear—*

A low growl cut the thought off, something guttural in the sound as Dusk dragged me from the memory. He'd drawn his tongue from my centre and moved in a flash, palm pressing against the mattress at my side, rich dark skin inches from mine as he held my gaze.

I reached up, hands cupping his cheeks, but he caught my wrists and pinned them above my head.

"You're mine," he breathed, leaning down, teeth grazing my ear as he drove his fingers into my core again as if in echo of that claim. I moaned again as his breath tickled my ear. "You're not theirs. You won't go back there. Do you understand?"

I nodded, teeth catching my lip with another whine as his fingers found that perfect spot. Then the dark vanilla of his midnight opium sent me into a daze as he scent marked me again, jaw running along mine.

"Good girl," he growled, pumping into me slowly enough that goosebumps lifted across my skin and I tried to arch against him once more. His lips trailed my neck, warm breath tickling my skin before his teeth found my nipple.

"Mmmm." I shuddered, thrown right to the edge of pleasure before he released me, drawing his fingers back, too, before pressing them back in.

I gave in to him, letting it hold me, an impossible safety as my wounded body melted beneath his touch. With each breath my moans grew as he began working me faster.

"That's it, Gem. You're so fucking hot when you're right on the edge." He remained like that for a while, head cocked, pupils blown as he watched me writhe beneath his touch as he slid two fingers into me at an agonisingly slow pace.

Then he drew back again, grip returning across my stomach as his tongue found my clit once more.

I cried out, an orgasm scoring my veins as he drew it out, adding a third finger as he sped up. He didn't stop as it died down, dragging me against him more firmly as I shook, breathing heavy as I tensed, body already alight with one orgasm.

He worked me harder, fingers driving in over and over as I shuddered.

"Again, Gem. Relax for me." This time, when my muscles loosened, it threw me over the edge of the next violent orgasm, desperate whines sounding in the air.

He didn't stop, fingers still working my channel. "I can't—"

"You can. One more release, beautiful."

My eyes rolled back, heat and pleasure and hormones leaving me a trembling mess.

The world swam and a fuzzy cocoon of warmth felt like it was encasing my mind. It was safe here. It felt good, and warm and... I think I was purring.

I didn't think that would have been possible tonight.

Then he was beside me, rich scent like another layer of that cocoon.

I... I wanted more of this safety.

I think that was a moan, rising in my chest, I had reached for him, needing more, needing... something. I felt something soft against my skin, and realised he was tugging a T-shirt over my head. "To keep the dressings safe," he murmured, "But I'm not going anywhere."

I let out a breath of a whine, feeling the edges of the cocoon weaken, threatening to fade. I felt how hard he was against me and I shifted back, nails digging into his arm. I didn't want it to go. In here, even the aches of my wounds faded into the background.

He'd scent marked me.

He'd claimed me.

He was safe when nothing should be.

I didn't want this to end. I thought of that night with Umbra. Of a cocoon of safety just like this, wrapping me tight until I fell asleep.

His whisper was soothing and then he drew me against him, his chest warm against my back. "You're so perfect."

And then I felt his touch between my thighs, circling my waist and rubbing my clit again. My purr rose again, warmth spreading through my body.

I shuddered with another orgasm, but I was glad when he wasn't done. I tried wriggling against him, and I thought I might have heard his chuckle.

I felt him adjust, then let out a sigh of relief as he entered me. Bliss swept me away as his length stretched me out, sinking deep into my core.

Another claim.

My purr was louder than ever as he slid into me over and over, a lazy tide of pleasure washing in, over and over until my eyelids became heavy.

Finally, he drew me against him and my purr cut off for a groan of need as his knot rocked against my entrance, pressing in until I shuddered with another orgasm.

Dusk hadn't left me behind.

The last thing I thought, before sleep swept me away, was that the only thing that was missing was his claim on my neck.

TWENTY

UMBRA

I woke in my old room.

The cabin was one we'd lived in for a long time, and its strong attachment to nature was probably one of the things that had saved me during those years.

But it carried with it a heavy weight.

Ransom's tumble into insanity painted every inch, it was in every scent, or creak of hardwood. This was the place where we'd lost our brother.

Slowly.

Agonisingly.

Yet, this time when I woke, things were different. Because in my room was the scent of lily of the valley. Morning sunlight filtered in through the huge windows, as if an offer of new hope.

And he was here beside me.

Ransom had climbed into my bed like I'd climbed into his a hundred times when he was fading.

He was sleeping like he did often—clutching a pillow to his

chest. His auburn hair was tied up in a messy bun, and he was snoring loudly.

I found my own slippers tucked just beneath my bed, then glanced back at him. Ransom's long-ass limbs were sticking everywhere, and I realised I'd been pushed to the edge of the bed.

Pretty rude, to be honest. That was what girlfriends or omegas were for—platonic pack mates were *not* supposed to be bed hogs.

I got to my feet, yawning and scratching my belly. One of the marks on my abdomen had healed into a keloid scar and it always itched.

Right. Breakfast.

Dusk used to always make it, but I'd beat him to it this morning.

"Dude."

I glanced back to see Ransom rubbing his eyes and blinking around the room.

"What?" I asked.

There was a lot to get through today—including patching up a very wounded omega, but hearing Ransom's voice lifted my heart every time.

"You still hum when you're happy," he snorted.

Did I?

"So what?"

Ransom grinned, dragging himself into a sitting position and blinking sleep from his eyes. "It's cute."

"I'm not *cute*." What a ridiculous notion.

I'd nearly ripped the spines out of those alphas in the rain yesterday. Decebal had told me he'd been on clean up duty, and that they were both in hospital. I'd told him I was just disappointed they weren't in fucking caskets. I stuffed violent flashes of that memory into a little box, refocusing on Ransom—and the fact I was happy. (And the original *point*, which was that I was perfectly vicious, thank you very much.)

"I bet she *loves* it," Ransom chuckled.

My humming?

"She's never mentioned it, actually."

"Very polite of her," he said with a grin as he crossed to the closet door and unhooked the night robe and shrugged it on.

He had stuff in his room, but I suppose he didn't know that yet.

"Pretty impressive, really," I said as I passed him and made my way into the kitchen to start the coffee.

"What is?" he asked, taking a bar stool at the kitchen island and examining the connected kitchen and living room in the morning sunlight. It was a grand place, with thick timber beams supporting huge windows that opened out into the forest beyond.

I eyed him, with his robe hanging open, showing off his lean, tanned torso. A few auburn strands had escaped his bun, swinging about his face. He hadn't lost much muscle mass being sick, he'd spent too much time fighting us. Or the bed. Or the wall.

"Four years out feral, and you still manage to look like one of those rich trust fund kids."

He grinned as I pulled out the sausages and eggs. I'd left last night with Decebal to grab some essentials, including more clothes for Shatter since she was the only one who didn't have a stash here.

Decebal had taken the spare room in the basement as usual, but he slept in when he visited so I doubt we'd be seeing him for a bit.

"She'll see us today, right?"

I nodded. "Dusk's going to fix her up." He was good at that.

"Why... why did she want him and not us?"

"He's like... the Shatter whisperer. Don't let it hurt your feelings, they have a whole language."

"Language?"

"Mostly involves brattiness and spankings and shit."

Well it *had*. Now it was something else.

"Excuse me?" Ransom froze as he grabbed orange juice from the fridge, doing a perfect 'blinking guy' meme.

"Hard to explain," I said.

"Yesterday, when she was really upset. He…" Ransom trailed off, unsure how to put it to words. I knew what he was talking about. She'd been on the edge of madness, and he'd brought her back, sweeping in and giving her commands like only Dusk could.

"She didn't… *choose* us, though?" Ransom asked. "At first." Ah yes. Ransom had apparently been a bit distressed about that. It was why he'd torn apart our living room back at the academy on the Indigo Berry Blast day.

"Not at first," I said.

Ransom tapped his fingers on the oak table, nodding slowly, eyes narrowed. "He… chose her?"

"Mhmm," I said, turning on the stove and grabbing the oil from the cupboard.

And *that's* why Dusk was still safe when no one else was. I hadn't seen it until yesterday: the truth of the strange structure he'd built between them.

She'd been faced with the ugliness of the world in a way that could break a person. Her monsters had come for her, and she wanted to hide. I understood that. But hiding from monsters didn't take their power away, and she needed support she didn't know how to ask for.

For me to push into her space, though? What was between us would have to change. I would have to speak out loud the parts she was too afraid to look at. But Dusk could step behind her defences without asking because he'd always stepped behind them without asking. He could be what she needed without drawing attention to anything. He didn't have to change at all.

When the ground was crumbling from beneath her, he was absolute.

I dumped the sausages into the pan, listening to the satisfying sizzle.

Dusk was like that for me, too, now I thought about it, if on a different axis. That was value beyond what could be put into words.

Hmm.

Was that the payout?

She'd endured what he'd done, survived it, then chosen it. In return, she got something back. I thought so, anyway.

There was balance to that, I thought, as I tossed the sausages about.

Not a balance Dusk could have predicted—he played with fire when it came to the universe, but this time...

Maybe it had worked out.

I didn't really care. Right now, all I cared about was that *someone* was with her.

I peered back at Ransom, who still looked unsure.

"It's just who he is," I supplied. "Has been ever since you saved us."

Ransom's expression darkened and I had to remind myself that he was years behind on healing. Everything we'd all gone through at the facility, the things we'd seen... How fresh were those memories for him?

And us, too—*we* were different. I had to catch him up.

"We'd switched somewhere," I said. Last Ransom knew, the fragments left of me from that place had made up an entirely different person. "I broke. He stepped up."

Ransom knew me back when I hadn't found the person Dusk let me become. I remember the night he'd taken pack lead from me. I'd fought him and lost, and woken as someone else. The first lights of dawn after an unending night.

"He was only able to do that because of what you did in that place," Ransom said quietly. "You protected him. He deserves the chance to make it up to you."

I snorted. "Doesn't matter anyway. Turns out Dusk's a control freak. Give him power and he never gives it back."

Ransom grinned.

"Plus," I added. "We're even now. He found her, and she fixed you, so…" I shrugged.

That was it. Shatter was the best gift in the whole universe. I'd go through those experiments all over again if that was the price of having her in my life.

"She *is* ours," Ransom said quietly. He was tense, eyes drifting to Dusk's door.

Oh good. Ransom was on board. "'Course she is."

"What's she like?"

"I don't know… she's… Shatter. She's just perfect."

DUSK

I woke to sunlight streaming through the huge windows of my room in the cabin. Outside, I could hear the familiar sounds of tree branches rustling in the wind and birds singing in the late fall air.

It was impossible to escape the scent of earth and pine here; it lingered in the bones of this place, sweeping in with every open window or door. The air had a texture to it, the heavy exhales of a thousand trees—so different from the city. And all of that, I'd woken to a thousand times before.

Except this morning was different.

Because in my arms was an omega.

My omega.

Tangled with the bark and earth, were the light petals of nightshade, a balance of sweet and bitter that complemented the smooth earths of the cabin.

She was facing me. We'd come apart during the night, and I'd readjusted her shirt, making sure her dressings were safe. Even then, when I'd slipped away briefly for the bathroom, she'd been restless when I returned.

Now, her slender arms were wrapped around her waist, her cheek pressed to my chest as little purrs shuddered through her body with each exhale. I was quite sure she was drooling on me, which was oddly adorable.

Her wild, honey hair was ruffled and messily spread across the pillow behind her. The sunlight spilled past unclosed curtains, and her golden skin looked like it glowed with the morning rays.

I felt a moment of sorrow, seeing her peace, knowing that it wouldn't be so simple when she woke.

My omega, a survivor when she should never have had to be.

I slipped a hand through her hair, unable to look away, guilt swallowing me whole. Her purr rose at the touch, and golden eyes creaked, large and beautiful, as she blinked away sleep, getting her bearings.

Her brows bunched for a moment before her eyes met mine.

Then she drew back, one arm drawing away from me as she wiped her mouth, a little warmth blooming on her cheeks as she glanced down at the small trail of drool on my chest. I grinned, taking her chin between my thumb and forefinger, and pressing my lips to hers before she could get embarrassed about it.

I drew away, and there was a flash of a smile on her face. Breathtaking beauty contained in a perfect bubble.

A bubble that couldn't last.

I saw the moment it popped—when her eyes darted around the room, taking it in. It was the moment her memories came crashing back. Like a storm blowing in, I saw a shadow cross her eyes. Her smile dissolved, the glow of her cheeks draining away.

Her purr stuttered out to nothing, and she squeezed her eyes shut for a moment, her chin quivering.

"I'm sorry," I breathed, sitting us up gently and letting her sink against me, clinging tight. She was shaking.

"If there's anything else you need to feel safe, will you tell me?"

She drew back, capturing me in those beautiful eyes once more. I could see her mind working, something desperate forming on her face. She opened her mouth, then closed it again, as if unsure.

"Tell me."

"A-anything?" she whispered.

I frowned. "Name it, Shatter."

She swallowed, that odd look lingering in her eyes as she regarded me.

"Today," I added. "I'm going to show you everything, so you know I'm telling the truth—"

"I believe you. You... and your pack. You are everything I wanted. I just didn't see it."

"We're not leaving you." That was a promise I wouldn't break.

"Would..." Her breath caught. "Would you bond me?"

A chill slithered through my spine, setting my hairs on end, and my heart turned to stone. I leaned back, taking her in.

There was only one bond I could offer her.

What?

"Shatter—"

"You... you said anything. I thought... you wanted—"

"I want you in our pack," I breathed. *God*, I wanted that more than anything in the world. "But we'll find another way."

Not a dark bond.

Her expression fractured.

"There's..." Her voice trembled. "There's no princess bond.

There's nothing else but that, and I d-don't want... I don't want to be afraid anymore."

"Because we can find another way—I told you Shatter. I don't care who says it's impossible—"

"And if I get bitten while we wait?"

"I won't let that happen," I growled, chest tight.

Never.

But tonight...

That had shaken me, when Umbra had opened the door to Roxy and I realised she was gone...

I finally spoke out loud the thing that lurked at the corners of my mind every moment I was with her. "What if we were supposed to be your mates? What if...?" Could I tell her I had no intention of letting the Lincoln pack survive?

"Dusk..." Her eyes clouded and she shook her head. "If th-this is what mates mean. I don't want them."

I stared at her, believing that truly. And it didn't matter. "I can't."

A dark bond?

"P-Please, you said..." Her breathing was short and sharp. "You told me you would bite me if I begged—"

"Not like this."

"You d-don't want me?"

"I can't—" I began, but she cut me off.

"I lost everything. You and Umbra and Ransom, I want... I want your pack to be my choice before that's taken from me, too."

My pack?

The words gave me whiplash, hearing that she wanted to choose—not just me, but Umbra and Ransom too? She would be ours forever...

"Is it a choice if you make it when you're scared—?"

"I chose you already when I came to your room. When I wasn't scared, and Eric told me they wanted to offer me a place with them and I..." Her voice became choked. "And I believed him, but I still... *I still chose you.*"

My mind raced. "You aren't in a good place tonight—"

"I hurt." Tears beaded in her eyes again. "I hurt so fucking much. Dusk please, I don't want them to have any more power. I want you to have it—"

"You don't know what you're asking—"

"Don't!" Her fingers closed around my neck, her voice suddenly harsh. *"Like I haven't spent all my life afraid of this."*

"I can't be your monster—"

"I was wrong about what I should have been scared of. I was wrong and I ran from you, and you were my choice and I don't..." She choked on a sob. "I don't want that taken from me, too."

Her eyes glittered, tears finally tumbling down her cheeks, a thousand wounds in golden orbs.

My fault.

And she was begging me to fix it.

I never knew, until that moment, how weak I was in the face of her pain.

"We're going back," she whispered. "And I'm going to see them again." Her voice trembled, and I could see her fear so starkly. "They're going to be so angry, and what if... if they learn who I am..." Her voice cracked. "I was wrong. They never wanted a princess bond—"

"A princess bond?" I asked.

Why had she believed they wanted that? It wasn't common, even outside of gold packs.

"I... it doesn't matter. I think I made it up. I know they don't want me, b-but I don't want to live in a world where it's possible that they bond me."

My own blood turned to ice at those words. I knew she believed that they didn't want her, but the marks across her body

—they told me a different story. The Lincoln pack had brutalised her.

No. I didn't believe they didn't want her at all. I believed, down to my marrow, that the only reason Shatter had escaped today without a dark bond was because they didn't know who she was, and they didn't know she was gold pack.

"I won't let them dark bond you, Shatter. Never in a million years."

"Will you..." She swallowed. "You can make that promise real. If you—"

"No."

"P-Please, Dusk."

I realised what she was asking for.

Safety.

That's what my bite offered her.

I'd always wanted to bite her. Dreamed of it.

Just... not like this.

"I-I'll do anything." Her voice was thick. "You said... you said if I begged you."

I hated that she was.

That after everything she'd gone through tonight, her fear led her to this.

I stared at her, the picture of beauty: a wounded goddess, with tears trickling from pleading eyes, illuminated across the golden tan of her cheeks. Her nose was pink, and her lips blood red.

"P-please. I can't... I can't go back alone."

"You will never be alone."

"I will. You have the bond. I don't."

I'd never seen her so wholly as I did in that moment, chained by fear and begging for freedom. The centre of the whole world.

"I c-can't face them alone."

She cupped my cheeks, and I was swallowed into eyes shimmering gold.

The most beautiful omega in the world. In pain. The ebbing tide of nightshade stuck to my throat and lungs, coating my skin—a scent so beautiful and powerful, and wounded how it should never be.

I couldn't do it...

"You can keep me safe from them," she whispered.

The world slowed at those words. Dizzying in their truth. I *could* protect her, not just in this moment, but every moment from now until forever. From monsters so much more evil than even she had seen.

I *could* bite this fragment of heaven into our pack, where she would never be alone again. Where she would be safe. Where the horrors of what had just happened, would never happen again.

Her lip trembled as she begged me, and each of her words was a hook, sinking into my heart, demanding action, a jarring, desperate ache building and building.

"P-Please, Dusk."

TWENTY-ONE

SHATTER

Teeth sank into my skin once more.

Different this time: gentle, loving, and desperate.

For a long moment, I felt nothing. He drew back, his piercing eyes finding mine. I shook my head, realising he must have tried a normal bond—a last attempt to save me from what I was begging for. Just like the first time I'd been offered a normal bond, I felt nothing.

I curled my fingers around his neck, breathing growing rapid as he paused, every desperate nerve in my body alight.

I wanted this.

"If I got a princess bond with them, it would have been because I had no other option," I whispered. "But you are my choice, the only choice I've ever made because I wanted to."

There was a long beat, and midnight opium was filled with despair. He wasn't going to do it.

A sob caught in my chest, and fresh tears flooded my face.

He wouldn't do it.

But then he growled, fingers weaving through my hair, dragging my neck into an arch, and his teeth found my skin once more.

A bond lit—stronger than anything Flynn had threatened. This was real. I collided with his pack, and for the first time in my life, I wasn't alone. For the first time in my life, I had a family.

TWENTY-TWO

UMBRA

One blink, an explosion of light in the pack bond, and suddenly... we were four.

Ransom straightened where he sat, eyes wide as he looked at me.

I was on my feet in an instant, instinct on high alert.

Shatter was... She was pack.

Then the realisation hit me.

"No..."

Dusk had... *No!* I was crossing the kitchen in a daze and ripping open the door to his room.

They were on the bed. Shatter was beneath him, hair scattered around her, an oversized t-shirt riding up her hips. Her golden eyes were wide as Dusk pinned her to the bed, his teeth at her neck.

My aura split the air, and Dusk looked up, bright yellow eyes finding me in a second, a glisten of her blood on his lips and trailing down his umber skin.

The world came to a halt.

I *knew* we were different, me and him—I thought, I believed that he had been right for her tonight—but this?

I was upon him in an instant, ripping him from her and slamming him against the wall.

"What have you done?"

After everything she'd gone through.

He was pack lead—I'd never once, before this moment, regretted that. Only, I wasn't met with the defiance I was expecting. Dusk's eyes were shocked, darting between mine, absolutely unsure.

"Umbra!" Shatter's voice caught me off guard, and then she was shoving her petite frame between us, fingers gripping my shirt desperately. *"W-wait!"*

"Shatter..." My voice was rough. I couldn't take my gaze from the poisoned mark on her neck, leeching darkness across her skin.

"I..." She was breathing heavily, and she looked afraid. "I asked him to."

"You what?"

"I..." She trailed off, glancing back at Dusk. "I wanted..."

With me and Ransom in the room, she was getting overwhelmed again, only this time I could feel her panic like it was mine. A twisted ball of darkness and self-doubt—no, no.

That was wrong.

"I wanted..." She pressed back against Dusk, spiralling viciously. But I could feel what she wanted, bundled away deep and hiding behind panic and darkness.

I sank to my knees before her. "Oh, Nightshade..."

She wanted everything I wanted.

She wanted a pack.

"Please d-don't be mad," she whispered, voice thick.

Mad that she was ours? I cupped her cheek as she stared at me, still so unsure. "Never."

But as for Dusk, *he was a goddamned*—

She stumbled into my arms, gripping me so tight that she crushed the thought to dust. I drew her against me as an uneven purr rumbled to life in her chest.

Ah... Fuck.

"I love you," I breathed.

It was done; she was ours, and even I couldn't contend with my rising tide of relief.

The Lincoln pack would never be able to touch her.

My eyes found Dusk's again as he vanished from the bond. I'd never seen him look this shocked in my life.

Shatter broke from me only when she spied Ransom in the room. Her eyes were nervous again.

"He's been dying to meet you," I told her, nudging her forward.

She blinked, swallowing, clearly trying to find words. "H-hi."

Ransom cupped the back of his neck, and was doing that freakishly-still-reptilian thing he did when he was observing something he didn't quite know how to process. "A dark bond?" he asked, voice rough.

"I... I asked for it." I nudged another step, and she stepped toward him awkwardly, wringing her hands. "I um... I guess I'm in your pack and you don't even really know me."

"What's new?" he said, a smile twitching on his lips. His pupils were blown wide as he took her in, and there was nothing but a primal curiosity from him down the bond until he snapped it shut, eyes flicking to me like he'd felt me prodding.

"You're uh..." Shatter swallowed, her head flinching in our direction like she wanted to look at us again. "...Really pretty."

Ransom's grin was cocky this time.

She shouldn't be throwing compliments around like that; they went to his head quick. I grinned too, then caught Dusk's eye, which reignited the building volcano of fury that had built as I'd rushed in here.

"*What the fuck were you thinking?*" I mouthed.

He rubbed his face, looking lost.

He replied under his breath as Shatter said something else to Ransom. "She was... Very..." He trailed off with a wince. "...sad."

Oh, for fuck's sake.

"Of course she was, you fucking prat—after everything?"

I still couldn't say truthfully I was unhappy, but a dark bond was for life. And she was... well, even with her state of panic, she was... pleased. Really pleased.

It was *Dusk* who wasn't.

He was supposed to be the calculated one. The one who listened to Decebal and his stupid good ideas.

Right now he looked... Well, actually he looked horrified, running his fingers through his hair. *"She was crying."*

"Oh, now that's a problem for you—?" I cut off as I took a proper look at his torso. What in the fuck had he done to himself?

They'd both gone and cracked.

No fucking warning.

"Next time you need a babysitter, fucking well tell me—" I cut off at a spike of surprise from Shatter down the bond, and then a thump across the room.

We both looked over to see Ransom had pinned her against the wall. Her legs were tangled around his waist, and they were making out intensely.

We both stared for a long, long moment, before what they'd been saying clicked in my head.

"Did you just command her to kiss you?" Dusk snarled, shoving past me.

Ransom broke from the kiss, looking defensive as he eyed Dusk's approach. "She was nervous."

"Five seconds with a dark bond and you're already—"

"It's fine." Shatter looked flustered, cheeks pink, and her lip definitely wasn't trembling anymore. Her eyes were wide as she glanced up at Ransom, and I felt the little spark of—huh. Okay. This whole... possessive alpha-omega situation hadn't changed one bit with Ransom waking.

"Uh, guys, is everything—? Oh." Decebal cut off as a snarl ripped from Ransom's chest. He dropped Shatter instantly, spinning on the door. Her T-shirt tumbled down to cover her to mid-thigh, which settled my little spike of defensiveness. He was an out-of-pack alpha, after all, and she was ours.

Decebal took a step back, lifting his hands. "Shit. I'll be outside."

TWENTY-THREE

DUSK

"A dark bond?" Decebal asked as he seated me in the kitchen chair to inspect my wounds. His tattooed arms were folded, a pierced eyebrow raised as he peered down at me with dark eyes. "And what in the fresh fucking hell did you do to your body?" He prodded one of my burns like the prick he was. I let out a growl, wrestling with my aura, though many of the coverings I'd applied last night had fallen off. "Don't you start."

I wasn't ready to hear it. My ears were still ringing with shock, and I'd left her in the bedroom with Umbra and Ransom.

I'd fucked up.

It had been a moment of weakness.

"Let me clean them," Decebal was saying. "You and Umbra are as bad as each other."

"She's the one who has wounds that need—"

"Let them fuck, or celebrate or whatever else they're doing, I'll check those after."

I gritted my teeth but allowed him to unzip his med kit and get to work, containing flinches and growls.

His scent of cranberries and roses was obscenely settling to my frayed nerves.

How many times had he come out to this cabin for a desperate call because Ransom had taken a turn, or Umbra's void had dragged him down for too long, and I was scared he would go too far, and I couldn't stop him. Not on my own.

Or the times we'd never talk about because some of those calls, they'd just been me. At the start, when Umbra was still in and out, and Ransom was deteriorating, and Decebal would get a call with an emergency that turned out not to be an emergency at all.

He'd never said a word about it.

He'd crack a bottle of whiskey, sit out on the porch with me with a cigarette, even if it was the dead of winter, and we'd drink in silence until my aura went away, and everything seemed manageable again.

Once he'd even brought his packmate, the seer, who'd sat on the couch, trashing all the top scores on one of Umbra's favourite fighting games until he'd surfaced.

Umbra was still pissed he couldn't even rank, and 'RedEyedBandit' still dominated the entire scoreboard.

Finally, Decebal spoke into the silence. "The two alphas in the hospital, they're no longer in critical condition. Paid off the pack. They won't say a thing."

"What?" I blinked, trying to figure out what he was saying.

"I went to the campus first to clean up after you. Thought you might need it—and I was right. Umbra nearly killed those two alphas. I assumed it was to do with the... incident."

"Oh."

That tide of burning fury rose again, and I fought to keep my aura down as the memory flashed in my vision. Panic had me in a vice, blurring the world. *It was dark and rainy, and she was beside the archway in the grounds. Two alphas had her.*

They had their hands on my omega.

She was terrified, crying, and in that moment, Umbra and I were one. Only he got there first.

Pure fear was the only reason they weren't dead. Umbra had returned the moment he'd felt us through the bond—that was when she'd started screaming, feral and broken.

"They should be dead," I muttered.

"Umbra had the same sentiment. But if it makes you feel better, from what I heard, they're going to wish they were," Decebal muttered. "I'm not blaming you, but that kind of shit is going to ruin your plans if it keeps happening."

I shut my eyes as he continued to work, peeling off the covering on my chest this time.

"*Why* are the brands all over your fucking chest, mate?"

"They're her..." I trailed off, still not recovered from the last wave of hatred. "The scars they gave her."

There was a long pause and I heard him breathe a curse. *"Bites?"* he asked at last, as if he didn't really want the answer.

"Never..." I grit my teeth as I felt him prod at another wound. "Never seen anything like it."

"You'll get revenge."

Not soon enough.

We fell into another silence as he worked.

"Have you checked your texts?" he asked, when he was about half way done.

"Phone's dead."

I didn't want to charge it. Not with the video I'd been sent. I didn't want to see it—I didn't even want the possibility of seeing it.

"I went into the apartment," Decebal said. "That friend—Roxy—is in there."

"I told her she could. She told us Shatter was gone."

"Figured. Sent an email to the Dean to get her into the apartment on your floor. Thought you'd want her close."

"The Lincoln pack—?" I began.

"Dropped her."

That meant they knew she'd ratted on them. It meant she may not be safe.

This conversation wasn't enough to keep me grounded in sanity. Not with the searing pain of each brand as Decebal cleaned them. Not knowing that this was her pain.

And I couldn't kill them.

I couldn't do *fucking* anything.

Instead, I'd fucked up—I'd goddamned dark bonded her.

Had it been fear? Had the Lincoln pack, stupid fucking idiots that they were, baited me into that?

I'd never seen her hurt like that—I didn't know how weak I would be, faced with it.

"A bond was a decent solution given the circumstances," Decebal murmured.

"Decent solution?" I asked. "It was stupid."

"Then why did you do it?"

I glared at him. "When *you're* faced with an omega begging you to do what you know you absolutely shouldn't, telling you they *need* you, and you can... can fucking fix everything—then tell me how you fucking do."

Decebal snorted. "I'll get back to you on that when we find ours."

We'd spent a fair amount of time with Decebal over the last few years. His pack didn't have an omega because they were waiting for a scent match. He'd admitted once, with a few drinks in him, that he was holding out for his scent match more than any of his pack brothers. A secret romantic.

"She asked," he added. "It's not... unheard of. And you have an omega who loves you. For all the goddamned plans we've come up with to fix things—she just walks on in and brings Ransom back."

"Are you jealous?"

Decebal gave me a half-smile. "Once you get it registered and a seer assesses it, everyone will know she asked," he said.

"I know."

Dark bonds were absolute. For life. But seers—alphas and omegas who had the ability to visualise auras—could determine whether the dark bond was taken or given with permission. It didn't affect the bond itself, but it did affect reputation.

As if we gave a fuck about reputation.

"Problem is..." He tore off a piece of tape to dress my last brand. "You just gave up one of your healing options."

"What does that mean?" Shatter's voice carried through the living room.

Ah *shit*.

I looked up to see her in a T-shirt, leggings, and a fluffy white dressing gown, golden eyes bright and scared as she stared between us.

Decebal glanced over, frowning, and then looked back at me. "I assume you're going to tell her."

Great. "Well, now I fucking am."

She wouldn't be pleased.

She was crossing toward us, nightshade scent carrying in with her. Umbra and Ransom both entered the room behind her.

"You know that we're... sick," I said.

She looked between us. "You mean... like what happened the other week?"

As on edge as I was, flashes of that night threatened to rip me away at the mere mention of it.

. . .

Wading through agony to get to Umbra, so terrified I'd be too late, so terrified she'd leave...

One touch. One fucking touch from Flynn, and that was enough to almost kill us...

I hated it.

"Yes." I cleared my throat as I caught her giving me a funny look. "One of the possible solutions to our sickness was a... a princess bond." I winced, knowing she'd be upset.

"You mean it's happened before?" she asked.

"We'll explain everything. Decebal brought the information."

"But... you needed a princess bond?" Shatter pushed.

"Princess bonds are the only absolute cure to aura sickness. It doesn't seem like a huge jump to assume—"

"*Except*—" I interrupted. "—I was never going to risk biting an omega into our pack just for that."

"They would have been a scent match... you would have wanted to...?" She looked pale all of a sudden.

"Oh no," I spluttered. "*You*"—I jabbed my finger at her—"don't get to seduce me into dark bonding you with '*scent matches are worthless*' rhetoric and then throw *that* in my face."

Shatter pouted, folding her arms, but didn't seem to have a response to that.

Umbra chuckled as he crossed to his huge pan of sausages and eggs and began serving up.

SHATTER

We'd had breakfast, and Decebal had retrieved a USB from his car. "It has everything on it," Dusk had said. Umbra was printing it out right now for us.

Until then, Decebal had wanted to look at my wounds. I wasn't ready for Umbra and Ransom to see them, so me, Dusk and Decebel were in another room in the huge cabin. It had a pool table, a home theatre and a big cove of couches. I liked it here. Every room had huge windows showing the trees outside which reminded me a bit of the gardens in the Estate.

"The two on your shoulder and arm, could I check them over and make sure they're not getting infected?" Decebal asked. "I could check them all—"

He cut off, catching my expression.

"But I..." He cleared his throat. "I assumed you might not want me to, given where some are. We can just see if Dusk did a decent job."

Oh. "Okay." I nodded. "How do you know where they are?" I asked.

"Dusk informed me he matched yours," Decebal snorted.

"Right."

Decebal was tall, with deathly pale skin, a scar across his left cheek, and tattoos that crept up to his jawline. He looked super badass, though he was gentle as he peeled back the dressing that Dusk had put on.

"It's alright?" Dusk asked at my side.

"Yeh. Just want to make sure. Going to give it another clean."

I tried to settle as I felt the cool touch along the wound. It didn't hurt as much as yesterday.

"Are you okay with my scent?" I asked, hyper-aware that I was no longer on any scent blockers. He was an alpha, with a nice scent of roses and cranberries.

"I think so," he said with a shrug.

"But... it's not good?" I asked. I knew he'd read over the files just like Dusk had. I heard Dusk's rumbling growl at my side and darted a look in his direction.

"I don't get much information from other alphas," I whispered.

I just had to live in fear. And Decebal seemed calm.

Dusk rolled his eyes.

Decebal chuckled. "I can understand why it might be... unexpected, but it's not too much." I heard him rooting around in his kit. "You were told one of the solutions was bonding a pack?"

"Yes." My voice was small.

"I can't say for sure, but I think the bond balanced it out. It's not aggravating like it was described in some of the logs I did read."

"It's like... worse for alphas if they're near a rut, right."

Decebal chuckled. "I'm perpetually near a rut," he said. "But it's not bad, though I've never been much into the super sweet omega scents anyway."

"What's mine like to you?"

"Floral, earthy. When we match an omega, I hope it's like that."

I smiled as he finished and moved around to my arm, where Dusk helped me tug the shoulder of my shirt down.

"You watching?" he asked Dusk.

"Yup."

"Do it properly. It'll help with the scarring."

"What about him?" I asked. "Should I learn so I can do his?"

"He doesn't want help with the scarring."

I frowned, but Dusk folded his arms stubbornly.

I paid attention anyway. I had to help patch Umbra up, and it was looking like there was a lot more to it than I'd thought.

"So you're waiting for your scent match?" I prodded, interested in that.

"Yup."

"They built a nest and everything," Dusk put in.

"Really?" I asked, eyes wide.

Decebal grinned. "You don't think I look the type?"

"No. I didn't mean..." I trailed off, cheeks going pink as my eyes darted across his tattoos.

He *did* look intimidating. I'd even noticed the scar down his cheek, peeking from the loose strands of wavy raven hair that had escaped his ponytail, and his piercing eyes were beetle-black and a little unnerving.

Definitely not the kind of alpha who looked like he'd built a nest for an omega he hadn't met.

Decebal didn't seem offended, though, as he covered up the bite on my arm. "Right. I think they're good. I'm having a smoke, then Umbra should be ready."

"What kind of stuff are you going to show us?" I asked.

"There's some things that you and Ransom need to know. About us. About the Lincoln pack, things I should have told you before."

The Lincoln pack?

I swallowed back my nerves, nodding as Decebal shut the patio door.

"Before that, I just... need to ask him something," I said. "Alone, if that's okay."

I didn't want Dusk hurting more, but the mention of my mates brought up lingering worries.

Dusk stiffened, gaze darting from me to Decebal, who was settling on a chair on the porch. He nodded, though it looked difficult for him. "I'll be just in the kitchen."

I followed Decebal outside, and he looked up at me curiously as I sat opposite him. It smelled like sweet pine and day old rain in leaves and soil. Decebal's cigarette tangled with his cranberry and rose scent pleasantly as he peered up at me, taking a drag.

"Can I ask you something?" I asked. "But you can't... can't tell them."

His scent was calm, and I couldn't help but trust him.

"Depends on if it puts them at risk. They pay me."

I shook my head. "It's nothing like that."

"Then my lips are sealed."

I repositioned in my seat a number of times, gaze fixed on a squirrel that was scurrying up a tree trunk. Finally, I found the courage to speak.

"Some of the bites..." I chewed on my lip. "There couldn't be any... half bond or part bond, right?"

Decebal frowned. "What does that mean?"

"Well, for some of them..." I fisted my shirt tight to try not to let my voice shake. "When it was Flynn—the pack lead... It was like I thought there was going to be a bond—a d-dark bond. But then there wasn't."

Decebal's eyes darkened. "If he didn't complete it, you're safe."

"Okay. Good." My chest loosened. "I might have just imagined it anyway—"

"I doubt that." There was a twisted expression on Decebal's face. "That is something a pack lead can threaten—an intimidation tactic for cowards. If he was, it wasn't by accident."

I stared, unsure what my face was doing right now. I tried to fix it, and Decebal was kind enough to look away as he took another drag.

"I've worked with your pack for a long time," he murmured. "Seen some fucked up shit—on their case and others. There are no vermin lower than alphas who abuse their power to hurt omegas." He looked sick. "Not how it's supposed to work."

The cigarette smoke rose in the air, much less sweet than Uncle's cigars had been. I didn't hate it, though.

"You're still worried?" he asked, after a long pause.

I tugged my knees onto the wooden patio chair and hugged them to my chest. "What if me being in the bond hurts them?"

"It won't."

"How can you be sure?"

He looked back at me, a smile playing on his lips.

"You are the only good thing that has happened to that pack in a long time."

I considered that, finding it hard to argue with. And Decebal seemed to know everything about me, Dusk, Umbra, and Ransom, which was a little unnerving. But comforting, too, when he said things like that.

"You remind me of him," I said.

"Dusk?" He asked.

I nodded.

Decebal laughed. "We couldn't be more opposite."

"Why?"

"The pack Dusk was given was broken, and he put it back together piece by piece. I was given an amazing family, and I..." He trailed off, turning the cigarette in his hand. "You're worried you're poison, Shatter? None of you are. I'm the poison in my pack. I know it when I see it."

I frowned. "Is that why you want an omega?"

"For me?" He asked. "No—well, yes if you ask me on a selfish day, but I don't have anything to offer, not really." He took another drag of his cigarette, nearly finishing it. "An omega might balance us, though... Bring Bane out of his shell, make them all happy—maybe soften up my pack lead. He carries a lot—he's done a lot, for all of us. He deserves that."

"And you don't?" I asked.

"I don't deserve any of my pack, let alone the omega destined for them."

I frowned, sad at the resolution in his eyes, the absolution of his scent, the edge of roses turning bitter. "You'd have to be a part of it," I said.

He grinned, seeming rather unphased. "I would be. If we got an omega, I'd spoil the shit out of them. I'd make sure they had the world. Dusk and I, we have that in common: pack is everything."

I considered that for a long moment. He'd said he was nothing like Dusk, but I didn't believe it.

Was it possible Dusk felt like this sometimes?

I was his omega now. I think I had to watch out for that.

TWENTY-FOUR

SHATTER

"This is everything we have."

With Ransom at my side on the couch, I stared at the pile of documents. Umbra had been concerned when Dusk sat us down, worried I wasn't ready—that I needed more time to recover, but he didn't understand.

I needed this.

I tentatively reached for the top paper, eyes scanning the sheet, my heart sinking as I read. The words before me wiped everything else away. Paper after paper outlined fragments of trials: alpha experimentation.

Illegal practice... Shut down upon discovery... No survivors...

My heart turned to stone as I understood, at last, the connection between us.

"You were..." I trailed off, looking up at them. "You were at the same facility?"

They were like me? All this time...

"Same place, different owners," Dusk said. "The Institute took over after it was shut down. That's when you arrived."

I read through everything: the snippets of logs of what was done to Umbra and Dusk, the pain they had suffered. The information was sparse, some were accounts from Dusk and Umbra, compiled by Decebal. I drew up as I read about the death of... shit. "Your pack mate died?" I asked.

"We didn't really know him," Umbra said quietly.

"But the pack bond didn't break?" I asked.

That should be impossible. There had only been three in the bond at the time.

It *should* be, and yet, I was in that very bond right now. Dusk hadn't spun fantasies the other night. He was right. They *were* the impossible—a green sprout breaking through snow.

Umbra was sitting at my side, and I was glad for his arm around me as I read on. He'd been the most present in this new bond that occupied a part of my mind. I leaned on him, needing to be reminded that no matter what I read, he *had* come out the other side.

Ransom had the smallest list. He hadn't been a part of the experiments. He'd been injected with Atropa's Poison when they were leaving. His symptoms came on more rapidly, but they were clear-cut.

For Dusk and Umbra, that wasn't the case. The symptom list was long, even if many had been crossed off with dates beside them.

Insomnia, headaches, seizures that were unique to Dusk, and Umbra used to get phantom pain that would last for days. PTSD wasn't crossed out. Decebal had drawn an arrow toward it with the scrawl that read:

Dissociative flashbacks, sometimes entirely impossible to rouse them from. Auras become unstable and shift to something unrecognisable. Same aura instability progressing over time. Patients claim the aura is

—I frowned.

"Hostile to its own host?" I asked, looking up. Decebal had to be the one who'd done the examinations on them.

"It's not an official diagnosis. They can't risk seeing a real doctor. I have a bit of experience, but I'm out of my depth."

"I saw the sickness." I glanced at Dusk. He was seated in the armchair, one leg propped up. His chin rested on his knees as he watched me and Ransom scour the notes. "When you collapsed. That's what it felt like, like it was trying to destroy you."

I looked up to Umbra.

"I manage them with the knife," he said. "Keeps me grounded. And Dusk..."

"I lose time." Dusk shrugged. "It's not as bad as Umbra. Barely happens anymore. He... he took most of the experimentations."

"These are mostly the symptoms," Decebal said. "The aura shit, that's the real sickness."

"That was more extreme than it's ever been. It's slower usually, creeping closer."

"Like... your auras are poisoning you?"

"Tell me about the other week?" Decebal asked. "I didn't fully understand from your message."

"It was like your auras were untethered," I whispered.

"What?" Ransom looked at me sharply. "But that's..." He swallowed. "That's deadly."

"I've never considered that," Decebal said, gaze fixed on me. "But I've also never seen it as bad as you have."

"It felt like... it wasn't his aura anymore, or... or something."

When an alpha lost their pack suddenly or violently, their aura broke.

The missing pack bond left a wound that would never close without help, leaving them unstable—as if they were walking around with a wound that never stopped bleeding.

To seal the wound they had to do one of three things: take another pack, sever their ability to join a pack completely, or do the last option of the three. The worst option—make the choice to release their aura entirely: to untether it.

Once they'd done that, their aura would then draw energy from the alpha's own body when used. For a short time, they could gain as much strength as they wished—could become frighteningly strong and dangerous, but once that energy was gone, the aura died, and the alpha died with it.

"That's what it felt like. Like... it was burning *you* up." I frowned. Umbra hadn't chosen to untether his aura—he couldn't have since his pack was intact, even if he had lost a pack mate. "It's the closest thing I can think of, but it still doesn't quite fit."

I'd read lots about untethered auras; any time I managed to sneak from Uncle's study I'd read an obscene amount on anything alpha-related.

"Even when untethered, the aura should only exact cost when used," I said. "Umbra's was out of control, consuming him no matter what he did."

It was similar, but it wasn't the same.

I was staring down at the black and white documents, something sick in my stomach. Ransom was right. Untethering was deadly almost every time. If the sickness wasn't cured, would it... would it kill them? The truth was creeping in slowly.

I could feel numbness swallowing me whole.

I had a family at last. A family I loved. And now I might lose them?

Lose Dusk or Umbra? The thought was so charred and horrifying I had to shove it back. Something thick stuck in my throat.

"But I balanced it..." I whispered, looking up into Umbra's sandstorm eyes. "I anchored you. It couldn't consume us both. Maybe it won't come back now?"

He drew me closer, but wolfsbane wilted, the traces of its sweetness fading. "Maybe."

He didn't sound hopeful, which wasn't like him at all. "*What*... What was the goal of the experiments?" I asked, my voice weak. If I could just get a better understanding of this I could try to help fix it.

"No idea. They locked it down tight," Decebal said. "If we knew that, we might not still be here."

"What about *how* you ended up there?" I asked. "Do you know?" Maybe that would help.

But my question was followed by an odd silence that I couldn't read.

"I just thought, if you came from somewhere...?" I swallowed. "What?"

Decebal cleared his throat, shifting uncomfortably, but Dusk shrugged. I noticed his jaw was clenched and his gaze fixed on me. "The organisation that ran experiments before it was shut down, got their alphas from the Cimmerian Vaults."

My blood ran cold, lips parting as I stared between him and Umbra.

"What?"

I understood his words, but they didn't make sense. The Cimmerian Vaults was a fortified prison that held the most insane and aggressive alphas. Alphas that cracked and lost their sanity entirely. Not alphas like Dusk and Umbra. They were... different, I'd always known that, but they weren't insane. Not like you had to be to end up in a place like that.

"I don't like it, but the experiments did one thing right," Dusk said quietly. "Brought us back from... wherever we were."

"But why the Vaults?" It was another alpha-specific thing I'd honed in on in my Arkology textbooks. The Cimmerian Vaults had a whole chapter. It was a logistical nightmare keeping the alphas contained and safe. "Why would the people running the experiments want to deal with containment?"

"All the alphas that were taken ended up registered as dead. Not uncommon in a place like that. It was untraceable."

I nodded, mind racing a million miles a minute. "And... typically alphas like that are stronger, right?"

"Their auras?" Decebal asked.

"Yes," I said. "The auras of the alphas who end up there are typically at least twice as strong as the average."

"And you think that might be why they wanted alphas like that for the experiments?"

"If they were doing experiments on alphas specifically, I would assume auras would play a part in it."

"We just assumed they used the Vaults because no one would look into missing alphas," Dusk said. "And if we'd be less likely to rat on them if we were insane to start with."

"But..." Decebal was rubbing his face. "It's not like there aren't other ways to get ahold of alphas. Probably *easier* ways. The New Oxford Trafficking ring is no stranger to alpha trafficking... I just... never thought about it like that."

"So... they didn't just need alphas," Dusk said. "They might have been looking for alphas with particularly strong auras."

"Does that... change anything?" Ransom asked. I noticed he'd vanished from the bond, and his jaw was clenched. I reached out and took his hand, I wasn't sure what he'd think of that. But he squeezed it, rich, green eyes finding mine. I swear he settled a little.

"You know where you came from? Before, I mean?" I asked. "Before the Vaults, even. They might have your history."

"Yeah," Dusk said. "Decebal found our files."

I straightened. They had those answers? A little flicker of

warmth lit in my chest. That was something I'd never had.

"We don't want it," Dusk added. "Not until all of this is over."

"You don't?" I asked. I couldn't imagine that. Not looking when the answers were right there.

"But all of this. It's not…" Dusk took a breath. "It's only half of it."

"What does that mean?" I asked.

"We both came to the academy for the same reason."

I frowned, shrinking against Umbra at the look on Dusk's face.

"The Lincoln pack."

I opened my mouth, then shut it. It took a while for me to find my voice. "My mates?"

"This part is rough, Gem," Dusk said. "If you're not ready—"

"I need to know."

I knew they were monsters. With every movement or shift, my body ached: evidence of that very fact, but all of that paled next to what he was telling me.

Dusk tugged the bottom folder from the stack and handed it to me. "This is new to Ransom, too. We found out later. There's a video, but you don't need to see it. It's transcribed."

I opened the file, and ice crept up my spine as I read, horror scratching at the corners of my mind.

The last piece of the puzzle.

TWENTY-FIVE

DUSK

1 Year Before

"Sit down."

I stared at Decebal, jaw tight. "Show me."

"I said, '*Sit*'."

What did he need me to sit for? He said he'd found the truth at last. The video paused on the screen before us held all of the answers.

The truth of our nightmares.

"Insurance for the organisation who ran the trials—"

I winced, and he paused.

Trials?

He meant torture. Death. We were nothing but numbers, lab rats, lower even, than humans. Decebal didn't press play, beetle black eyes pinning me until, finally, I sat down on the couch, nodding that I was ready.

It was the one and only time I ever saw the video. Decebal kept it on a drive, locked away. We hadn't been recognised on it, but that didn't mean we couldn't be.

It didn't matter, though; every second had stuck with me forever.

The flickering, low-resolution video was a camera feed. It showed a lounge with upper class couches, and a glass coffee table. Across the wall was a huge screen—another video feed—and on that screen was a room of white and metal.

A room I knew intimately.

"What is this?" My voice was rough.

Decebal had seen some shit. He'd grown up in the Gritch District—and he looked like it too, with tattoos to his jaw, and darkness in his eyes, even in the face of the worst we'd uncovered. But right now, I could see how tense he was, pale skin almost sickly. He just shook his head as he glanced at me.

"Whatever you thought this was, Dusk. It's worse."

On the screen, three alphas entered the room, glancing around and making themselves comfortable. One began pressing buttons on the remote, and the feed on the screen changed. Each time it flickered, it landed on another room. A black identifying number in the top corner. And each time, the occupants changed.

"What is this?"

"An observation room," Decebal said.

My heart tripped. "For... us?"

"Yes. For all the subjects."

Something was stuck in my throat.

"To fund the trials, they ran..." Decebal grimaced. "Bets."

"Bets?" I asked, voice hoarse. "They're betting on us like... racehorses?"

Decebal nodded. "Which subjects are going to live, which will die. Who will survive with enough strength to be useful for the experiments they're running," he said.

My world shook with every word. At the horror of what he was saying.

That place had been my worst nightmare. For them, it had been a game?

"The only good news is," Decebal went on. "The packs that placed bets were also... benefactors of the trials. This pack—they were the ones who bet on you and Umbra. They were the ones involved in what was taken."

"And we still don't know what they were trying to do with the experiments?"

"No. But the pack in this room, they took something. As far as I can tell, it's linked with your pack."

"You think... if we know what they took, we could figure out why we're still sick?"

Decebal looked uncertain. "It's the only lead left."

My memories had long collided with those videos, moments merged—torture with entertainment.

I felt the moment 31 died, a splintering tear through the pack bond.

He'd got free, and Umbra had followed, but I'd been too scared to take more than a step out.

I heard the gunshots in the distance.

Flynn was on his feet in the room, crossing to the pad on the wall. "No. *Don't you dare kill* him—" Flynn cut off as a gunshot rang out, audible even from the camera feed. "Fuck!"

Umbra had me by the shirt. "Get back inside."

He looked wild.

"B-but he's..." He was dead.

"Get inside!" He was shoving me through the door despite his trembling.

31 had died. Our pack mate...

We should have splintered into a million pieces, but somehow... we didn't.

Flynn balled his fist, and the rest of the pack was on their feet. "Do you know how much I had riding on this?" he snarled into the comms. "I don't care how many people it takes to get him back in the cage. They weren't *supposed* to get out—and they weren't supposed to *fucking die—*"

"Wait—*wait!*" Eric looked down at his phone, then back up at the screen. "It's not over."

"How?"

"They... said the bond didn't break."

There were only two of us left in our pack, something that should have been impossible. And in the centre of it, was Umbra. My rock.

The one who kept us together.

"We just can't do that—"

"I'll double my bet." Flynn cut off the voice coming from the intercom.

There was a pause. Eric and Gareth had frozen, staring at Flynn. Then the static rang out in the room again. "*Double* it?" the voice asked.

"I haven't got much choice, do I, since you killed their fucking pack member."

"We don't usually take this route until later—"

"There isn't a later. You said if they survive the poison, they stay in?" Flynn demanded.

"Yes," the voice replied. "But with only two members, I mean it's unheard of. And the risks—"

"I don't care about the risks."

"That's a lot of money, if you lose," Eric said to Flynn, looking unsure. "And if they kill each other it's over—"

He cut off as Flynn slammed the comms button. "Just give them the fucking poison."

Atropa's poison crept into my mind, ruining me. Turning me on my brother. My fists were tight around his throat as I shook.

"What's he doing?" Gareth demanded. "Fight back you fucking oaf!"

"He's just going to roll over?" Eric asked.

Flynn was standing before the screen, a scowl on his face as he watched.

Umbra didn't fight me. His hand came up, brushing my cheek.

Terror and confusion collided, and then I was reeling back, letting him go. I knew who he was. He was my brother.

My pack.

And he would die before he killed me.

"Yes!" Eric was laughing. "That's it. We just *killed* the odds."

They were celebrating.

. . .

I clutched Umbra, bones quaking.
My brother.
And I'd nearly killed him.

"My lucky pack," Flynn was saying. "Tell them I'm in—*all* in, and bring us more drinks." The doorman bowed his head, then left.

"Damn, for a moment there..." Gareth blew out a breath.

"Flynn called it," Eric was saying. "Pack five is our golden ticket."

"At least 68 fights back. Won't roll while he's choked to death." Flynn barked a laugh, words slurred. "What kind of shit *was* that, anyway? Fucking pathetic."

The days flickered by, and the Lincoln pack returned, week after week as we suffered.

Umbra was losing it.

He pinned me to the bathroom floor, a plastic fork digging into my skin. I curled up, trying to find solace in the knowledge they wouldn't take him next time.

"You've got to be joking?" Eric laughed. "Trying to get himself picked?"

"He knows, right?" Gareth asked. "He's got to know."

"I think he does," Flynn snorted. "But I don't give a shit what he does. It's fucking working."

Umbra was gone.
They'd taken him.
After everything, they'd taken him again.

I lost it, aura flaring, the world burning around me as I felt his pain and fear through the bond. I threw myself against the walls until I was black with bruises, until I hurt so much I couldn't feel him anymore.

"He didn't see that coming this time? How fucking thick is he?"

That was the day the Lincoln pack were brought a black suitcase. That last day they had visited.

Inside that case was what they'd stolen: the missing piece we'd been hunting. But no words were exchanged on the video feed, addressing what was inside. When it was set on the table before Flynn, Eric clapped him on the arm.

"Beat more than just the odds this time."

SHATTER

My own mates entered this horrifying picture.

I learned, at last, what role they had to play. With every line, I read the truth.

My pain, it was the smallest piece, there was more, spanning further than I could have imagined.

"An observation room?" Ransom asked, voice rough as he read behind me. "They were watching while they... they ran experiments on you?"

Dusk's expression was twisted. "They were betting."

"It wasn't just that," Decebal said. "They made sport of it, but they were there for a reason. We don't know the full story, but they were there for the experiments as much as the bets."

"*Her*... mates?" Ransom asked.

"All the major players involved are dead or insane, so they're all we've got. We know they took something, we just don't know what it is. The day they left, they walked away with a suitcase. We don't know what was inside—"

"We hope whatever it is, it will give us answers," Dusk added, catching Ransom's expression. "Thought it was the winnings at first, but those were deposited into an offshore bank account Decebal's pack mate dug up."

"Whatever's in there will help you get better?" Ransom asked.

Decebal nodded.

"And they didn't recognise you at the academy?" I asked. If the Lincoln pack had watched...

"The feeds weren't detailed," Decebal said. "And neither Umbra nor Dusk..." He glanced between them apologetically. "They looked *different* back then. Hair was short, and they weren't... well. Their names were their own choice, the facility never had those."

I understood. Even that picture of me in a white gown with my hair up and expression drawn. It was all but unrecognisable...

"They're our last lead," Dusk said. "But we know they're close to it. What happened the other week, when I collapsed, it was because Flynn touched me."

My gaze snapped up to him, throat dry.

What had he just said?

Everything that had happened, was because Flynn had *touched* him? My mind was racing in a thousand directions, a thousand puzzle pieces trying to fit together all at once.

I... needed to read these files again.

"Who?" Ransom asked.

"Their pack lead. He put a hand on my arm, and—"

"And you nearly died," Decebal said.

What the hell did that mean? There was more to this... More even than Decebal's notes showed.

"Question is, how do you plan on dealing with them, if you can't touch them?" Decebal asked.

"*He* can." Dusk said, nodding at Ransom. "He was never a part of the experiments. He touched Flynn in the apartment, too. Nothing happened."

"So whatever happened is contained to you and Umbra?" Decebal asked. "I'll take any good news."

"Why are we fucking around with academy enrollment?" Ransom demanded. "We know where they sleep, just—"

"No," I cut him off, worry rising in my chest. "We don't know how they're connected."

"Then grab them and make them tell us."

"Decebal shut that down," Umbra muttered.

"Why?"

"Because they're it," Decebal said, leaning back in his chair. "If they panic and lie, we have no way of knowing. We don't even know if the answers are actionable. I suggested the academy. Bugging them and getting close—"

"That turned out fucking stellar, didn't it?" Umbra asked mildly.

"Well, you can't control your temper, and I wasn't expecting an omega scrambling Dusk's brain."

"Fuck you," Dusk muttered.

"What about now, with Shatter?" Umbra asked. "She knows all about Arkology shit. She'll know if they're telling the truth."

"No—no. Not enough." My voice was weak. "I still don't... I don't understand what all of this means. I've never read anything like this before."

"Thank you." Decebal waved at me. "Plus, once they know, there's no going back, and you're on your last goddamned life."

I shivered at that statement.

"Okay. I'm with him," Ransom said quietly.

"Oh, for fuck's sake," Umbra groaned.

"So what's the plan now? We just go back there and wait?" Ransom asked.

"Yes. You'll be close if we turn anything up. And the moment they find out she's their scent match, it's not like they'll be going anywhere—" Decebal cut off at the growl from Dusk. Panic spiked my system, setting me on high alert.

"They only find out if Shatter wants them to."

Every eye was on me.

What did I look like right now?

Not good. I nodded, trying to swallow back my terror. Instincts still warned of danger, the desperate need I'd harboured to keep that secret when I was in Flynn's room, praying my scent blockers wouldn't lapse; it lingered like a bitter taste.

I took another breath, feeling Umbra's warm touch trailing gently up and down my arm. I was safe with wolfsbane and blood. Midnight opium. Lily of the valley.

I *was* safe.

I realised I'd withdrawn in the bond, curled up and afraid, but I opened it up again, gently reaching out and feeling them there.

I *was* safe.

I was... but... I felt a sudden wave of nausea, and for the first time since I'd run from Eric, the first ripples of hatred. *I* was safe, but they weren't.

What they'd given me, their words, their actions, the pain—it had made me feel so small. I wanted to turn my back on my own reflection, frightened of how weak and pathetic and worthless I was.

They'd done that to me, and they'd done it before. The very people that made up the fortress at my back, that gave me the strength not to run...

They'd tried to do it to them, too—my pack.

Tried to make them nothing.

My mates had laughed as Dusk and Umbra had been ripped apart—had stood in that room, speaking as though they were less than human. Making bets, and reducing them to nothing but a game. A bet.

I gripped Umbra's hand tight, looking back at the papers before us.

What they'd taken from my pack, they still had it, and my fear... it was nothing in the face of that.

TWENTY-SIX

RANSOM

The look of absolute fury on Shatter's face as Decebal had reached out to collect the stack of papers was almost enough to get a smile from me—even when I felt sick at what I'd just learned.

She went from despair to protectiveness in a split second, a growl rising in her chest, narrowed eyes fixated on Decebal's hand.

Decebal drew back, eyebrows raised. "We have to destroy them."

"Destroy them?" In moments, she'd seized every piece of paper from the coffee table, clutching them to her chest like someone had threatened to steal her firstborn.

"I have the same data in my safe at home," Dusk told her. "But if the Institute gets a hold of those papers—"

"They'll... take you?" She stared at him in horror. "Like Uncle was worried about me being taken?"

"If that's all they did, we'd be lucky," Dusk said.

Again, Decebal tried to tug the papers from her, but she wouldn't let them go.

"Just wait. I'm not *finished*. There's... so much information, and I need to fix it." She pulled it back from Decebal's grip.

"Fix it?" Umbra asked.

"When I read textbooks, everything is in order. This is a *disaster*, nothing is together right."

"You think we're missing connections?" Decebal asked with a frown.

"Everywhere."

He glanced at Dusk, but Umbra looked unexpectedly happy. "She's a genius. You need to let her have them."

"Genius?" Decebal asked, and I echoed the surprise.

My omega was a genius?

I peered at her. Her hair was wild, eyes wide as she clutched those papers to her chest desperately.

Of course she was.

And... *could* she help, perhaps? Offer something they didn't know.

I needed something other than despair.

"You know you said you didn't know where she got those entry exams?" Dusk asked Decebal.

"Yeh."

"She took them."

He looked taken aback. "Those numbers were hacked. There isn't even a record of scores that high."

"I *did* take them." Shatter's nose wrinkled with indignation.

"Lucky," Decebal said. "It's the *only* reason they overlooked the rest of your admission disaster."

"I worked *really hard* on my admission," she said.

"You didn't fill in a last name."

"I didn't *have* a last name."

"Well, *now* you do, since Dusk asked for—" Dusk coughed loudly, and I noticed him shoot a glare at Decebal.

"What did you ask him to do?" I asked.

"You can keep the papers," Dusk said to Shatter. "And if you figure something out, we can just add them to my safe back at the apartment."

Decebal frowned. "Dusk, you know it's risky to just leave them around—"

"She thinks she can figure something out," Umbra put in. "She *should* look."

So, that was that. Shatter gathered the intel up like an omega possessed and got to work.

It was comforting, feeling her determination down the bond. It was enough to distract her. And I would live through her feeling of *doing* something.

I'd barely kept up with the conversation.

All I knew was that my pack was sick—still. It was getting worse, and the foul pieces of shit who'd hurt my omega were involved with that, too.

I helped the others put lunch together while she worked, and as afternoon rolled in, Dusk clapped me on the shoulder and nodded toward the games room.

I followed him down the hallway, making sure he could feel me poking at him through the bond. He was still vacant.

Was he upset because he'd bonded her?

It was clear as day that he loved her. God, we all did. She was the only certainty since I'd woken. I mean, *sure*, it was a dark bond, but Umbra had told me it was the only option.

A technicality.

It just made it easier to keep her safe.

"You're back... fully?" Dusk asked as he lifted a pool cue from the rack on the wall and tossed it to me. The familiar weight of it in my hands was comforting. Another little piece of reality to remind me that it was over.

"I... yeh." I thought I was, anyway.

I could see already that he was afraid I might disappear again. But... but I didn't think I would. Everything was different, now. What she'd done didn't feel like a temporary fix.

"I haven't had a chance to slow down since you woke," he said quietly. "And you're... okay?"

"No."

Dusk paused as he pulled the coloured balls from their pockets on the table.

"I thought... I was dead, Dusk," I said quietly. It wasn't just that she had brought me back. Every moment I surfaced, even for a second, it was a nightmare. "Until her."

Our perfect omega.

"I won't be okay until my pack is. You, Umbra, and her."

And she was going to save them. I just knew it. She'd been sitting on the living room floor for hours now, commandeering the entire space, having shoved the coffee table, couch, and recliner to the walls. She'd spread Decebal's intel everywhere, her side of the bond locked down tight for the first time as she frantically read and re-read every page before placing it in its own place on the floor.

She shot Decebal reproachful looks every time he so much as coughed, as if he might come and sweep them all away.

Umbra seemed content to hangout by the kitchen island to watch and feed her. He told me (rather knowingly) that he believed the pieces of paper tilted at the most extreme angles upon the floor were the ones she deemed most important. We couldn't tell because she hissed like a cat everytime one of us tried to peek, a furious tide of omega indignance surfacing violently for a second.

I could have watched her all day, too. She *was* my solace.

She changed us—the pack I remembered. Before, every new

weight threatened to tug us under. *With* her, the world felt brighter, more manageable, somehow.

Even now, a room away, I could feel my dread creeping back, the trauma too fresh. That stomach turning darkness, like a demon had me in its grip.

I hadn't just been gone; I was trapped in a body that wouldn't work.

There were flashes of brightness lighting up that darkness for brief moments. Memories lighting so briefly, like Dusk with his arm around my shoulder, holding me against him. There was a whole world out there, one that continued turning for all the seconds I'd been gone. But for me, this was it. This was my world: Umbra, Dusk, and now her.

I watched as he set up the rack, letting me work through the silence.

I just drank it in. The scent of midnight opium, an edge of bitterness spiked like strong coffee, overpowering the softer side of amber and vanilla.

He was on edge; I could see the clench to his jaw, even as he set up our game.

I loved Pool.

I used to play with him and Umbra for hours in the slices of reality I'd had before sickness took me completely. This room was one of the last memories I had.

"Sometimes you would come, right? Or Umbra would spend the night?" I asked, trying to keep the desperation from my voice. He tilted his head toward me as he placed the last ball.

"You... remember?"

Relief washed over me. I hadn't imagined it, after all. "Fragments," I said.

I would never tell him it was a worse nightmare when I did wake. When I surfaced for a few brief moments to see cuffs on my wrists. Aware for just one second too long. One second was enough to know what had happened to me.

Enough to know that I was going back in any of my next breaths.

It was hard to describe that horror. Like running in a dream, but you never moved, only a thousand times worse. Every time I blinked and woke, it could have been months—Dusk looked more gaunt, or Umbra's hair was a different length.

Sometimes I would linger long enough to know what it cost my brother to come and see me. His scent would douse the room until I lost it, and he'd wake to my fist around his throat...

Dusk tossed me the chalk, and I caught it just in time, nodding for him to start. I ran it over the tip of my cue, still trying to drag my mind from the darkness. To dispel the tremor from my hands.

How many times had I wished I would die, so I didn't risk hurting them again? So I wasn't more of a burden on their lives that I had already broken beyond repair.

The demon's claws had sunk deeper, with every memory, making every waking moment sickening and stomach wrenching.

Until her.

I thought, when nightshade seeped into my senses, waking me at last, and the demon was gone, that I had died at last.

My reaper. The beautiful angel that freed me.

Dusk made the breakshot and pocketed a solid. He'd feel me spiralling, but he said nothing as he sank another two.

"You got better," I said. My voice was hoarse.

He surfaced in the bond, yellow eyes meeting mine with a grin, a rare moment of the part of him I'd so rarely seen, a moment of youth and happiness. He turned back to the table and sank another, and I had to clench my jaw to fight the tears that burned my eyes. Despite everything I'd just learned, he was happy.

He might die, but he was happy because I was here.

I'd grown up with obscene wealth and total and utter isolation. I'd known nothing but connections borne of dependence... need... money... Conditional and cold.

Dusk and Umbra had been here this whole time, fighting for me when I could give them nothing. If I'd died, they would have inherited my wealth.

They'd fought for me for no other reason than because they loved me.

Despite every agonising second of darkness, it was worth waking up for that.

A stiff smile curved my lips as I watched him play. Pocketing five of the solids before the cue ball scratched.

"Ah. Fuck." He leaned back. "Go on then." He sighed, sitting on the wing of the couch.

I stared at the table for a while, tapping my finger on the cue. When I finally lined it up, I knew the shot I needed.

I sank my first striped ball. It was therapeutic, focusing on the angles, measuring the table and distance, or where to stripe the cue ball, knowing I could rely on instinct here. The only place I could.

But as each stripe hit the pockets, dread dug its claws deeper.

Finally, there were no more stripes without the hint of a foul.

It took me too long, and I almost expected it to fail. It felt like it *should* fail, but I sank the black ball easily, ending the round.

Dusk snorted. "Four fucking years to get ahead. Still not enough."

My heart sank.

I'd won. My sickness hadn't taken this from me, and all I felt was disgust. Shatter was in the next room, dealing with shit that actually mattered.

What was I good at? Sinking pool balls and getting shit-faced without a hangover? "I'm…" I trailed off. "I'm fucking useless," I muttered.

"That's a bunch of crap."

"She's going beautiful mind on this shit, and I'm just—"

"You *just* woke up—"

"Exactly. I just woke up." My voice shook. "All this time you were sick, and I was taking all your—"

"Ransom." Dusk's voice was sharp.

I spun on him, my voice more aggressive than I meant it to be. "What?"

"Shut the fuck up."

I opened my mouth, then shut it, blindsided.

Dusk snorted, setting his cue down and shoving me in the shoulder. "I didn't keep your spoiled ass alive for years just so you could wake and whine my goddamned ear off."

I chewed on my cheek, knowing there was a bitter expression on my face. He raised a finger and jabbed it at me. "Oh no. No fucking sulking. You know what? We did you a favour mate, neither of us warned her you were a spoiled little shit."

"It's true." I glanced to the door to see Umbra leaning against the frame, watching us as he popped open a bag of chips. "Sun shines out of your asshole as far as she's concerned."

"So, do us a favour, and quit moaning."

I choked a laugh before I caught myself. But then Dusk had tugged me into a hug. "Bench it for five seconds and let me be happy you're back."

"Alright." My voice was weak.

I held onto him too tight, Dusk dragging me back to the ground when I was otherwise in freefall, just like he always had.

It was evening, and Shatter showed no signs of freeing the living room from crime-scene-investigation classification.

Umbra was still out there with her, watching with popcorn like it was a show. Dusk and Decebal were in the games room watching TV.

That meant I had no excuse to avoid tackling the thing I'd been dreading dealing with since I'd woken.

"*Fuck.*" The brush got stuck in my hair as I tried to drag it through my locks.

Dammit.

Four years without a single hair mask. Not a surprise. It wasn't like Dusk knew what good hair products were. The issue was, I had an omega now.

My hair couldn't *literally* be matted.

I had to talk to her at some point—properly, actually, talk to her. I'd woken in a state of panic, the tail end of a rut in my system, and every time I caught sight of her all I wanted to do was jump her bones. By the way her scent hit the air every time she looked at me, she wanted the same.

Maybe talking was overrated.

She was mine. We were going to be fine.

I tensed with a snarl as the hairbrush snagged again.

"*Dammit.*"

But I jumped as I caught sight of a glittering golden flash in the mirror. I spun to see her at the doorway, peering in curiously. My heart thundered out of control as her scent breezed in, white petals of nightshade like a cool breeze on a summer's day.

She stepped toward me, fists bunched in her T-shirt.

I tugged at the brush.

Thoroughly *stuck*.

Well.

Shit.

She reached me, eyes wide as her gaze flickered from my face to the brush, something nervous in her expression.

I tugged at the brush again.

Nope.

This was the first time we'd been around each other without something fucking insane going on. Literally, kind of our first actual... meeting. This was the worst romantic introduction in the history of ever. Period.

"Uh..." I trailed off, totally lost for words. I didn't get nervous around girls, but she was so fucking pretty. Her nose had a cute curve to it, and wrinkled adorably when she was snarling at Decebal earlier. Her cheeks almost always had a little blush of pink, and her eyes. I could get lost in her eyes. I had. I remembered the first moments, an angel with golden eyes.

She was still staring at me, then at the brush, and her scent was getting oddly... possessive.

She lifted her hand, then drew back, rapping her knuckles against each other anxiously like she was about to do something she wasn't sure about.

"You're... having hair trouble?" she asked. Her eyes shone—and when had her pupils blown that much? Even in the bond I felt her tumbling far from the intensity she'd had when she was studying. If I had to name it, I'd say she was on the edge of feral.

I nodded.

Another wildly strange beat passed, and a smile wobbled on her lip for a moment. Then she leaned up and drew her jaw along my cheek so gently I wouldn't have known what it was—until nightshade drowned me.

That was a scent mark.

Then she had me by the arm and was dragging me from the bathroom. She stopped me in front of the bed and was making me sit rather aggressively.

What was going on?

Then she got to work, plucking strands of my hair from the hairbrush. Even more oddly, little purrs kept rumbling in her chest.

Once she was done, she scent marked me again and began to brush my hair gently from the ends to the roots. It was going to take a while, but she didn't seem to mind.

A number of times I opened my mouth to speak, then shut it. I didn't need to. This was fine, even if I had no idea what was going on.

Then I felt her prodding at me through the bond. I made sure it was open for her. It was hard not to feel calm with her scent everywhere and her touch occasionally brushing my neck or cheek as she worked through my hair.

"You're done with the information, then?" I asked at last.

"Oh no. Um… You seemed a bit stressed… in the bond."

My hair stress was that obvious?

Sure. Right, that was my problem. Not the looming threat of the death of my packmates I'd just been delivered by Decebal.

I let her continue detangling my hair for a little longer before I dared ask. "What's the takeaway?"

There was a long pause, and when she spoke, it was in a small whisper. "It's… bad."

My heart sank.

I'd looked through the papers, I'd processed it—to the best I could, though I didn't have the mind she obviously did.

"Will you help me save them?" She sounded anxious. "Both of them."

I froze, and the hairbrush halted its movement.

"What do you mean?" I asked. The meeting we just had was proof enough that saving them was exactly what we were trying to do.

"Dusk is…" She trailed off, hairbrush falling away, and I shifted so I could see her. She settled on her knees before me, something pleading in her eyes. "He spends so much time thinking about you and Umbra and... and me, that anything he's planning might..."

"Leave him behind?" I asked.

She cocked her head, the look in her eyes confirming it as she examined me. Her wide eyes were a storm of nerves and ferocity the likes of which I'd never seen.

"There are other options he didn't have before—ones that could help, but he's not going to want to try them."

I narrowed my eyes. "If it helps Dusk, it helps Umbra. He'll be in. Why don't you want him to know?"

She chewed on her lip, eyes calculated. "Because they involve me."

I considered that, but I didn't think it was the full truth; not if she was coming to me instead of him. "You mean they might hurt you?"

"No. I mean..." She tugged on a lock of hair. "Not necessarily. But my... my scent matches are involved. I think he's going to shut down anything that might make me a part of it."

"They hurt you." That fact was a hot coal, constantly present in the pit of my stomach, igniting rage at every reminder.

Her brows drew down and the nightshade in the room turned sharp. "They're hurting Dusk and Umbra."

"But you think it might put you at risk."

"I don't know. I need to go through some of my Arkology books, but I have some ideas..."

"I don't want you in the firing line, Little Reaper. You're already more a part of this than you should be—"

I cut off as her hand snapped out, grabbing my shirt in her fist, eyes blazing. "You didn't see them the day Dusk collapsed. You didn't see how close to death they were—what Umbra was doing to stay alive." Her voice cracked, tears filling her eyes. "I think that's where they're headed, and we can't risk being too late."

I stared at her, hating, once again, how much I'd missed.

"This is it for me, I'm already a part of it. You—*they*—are my pack. My family. It's all I've dreamed of. I won't..." She took a breath, voice shaking. "I'm not going to let them die."

Warmth spread through my veins. With every corner I turned and every new thing I learned about her, she became more extraordinary.

"Okay," I said. If being her support is what I had to offer this pack, I would do that. And I would make damn sure whatever insane plan her crazy little brain came up with didn't get her hurt in the process.

"Okay?" she asked, as if she hadn't expected it.

"I'll help you protect them."

Her smile was enough to stop the world.

"Kiss me," I told her.

I'd done it before, and I'd craved it since. The command lit between us, igniting the bond that made her ours. Her palms brushed my cheeks, her energy through the bond—anxiety, anger, fear—it all drained away for peace as she melted beneath the command, submitting it in a strange moment of freedom.

Her fingers wove through my hair as she pressed her lips to mine, and I realised she'd brushed out every last tangle.

TWENTY-SEVEN

UMBRA

Shatter had been obsessive about those files for too long. It was ten in the evening, and she'd barely stopped—ducking out only once for a short time to see Ransom, but she'd been back at it the moment she'd reemerged. The living room looked like a bomb had gone off in it.

Her anxiety had switched out for frenzy, and while I loved that she was trying to save us, it worried me.

I sat down on the couch that had been shoved backward so she could have more floor space. She was chewing on another pen since her first had exploded all over her earlier. There was still evidence of that in her hair.

She glanced up at me, then back down at the papers, a shiver of nerves taking flight from her end of the bond. They did that every time she stopped for too long. Every time the papers in front of her stopped offering solace amidst obsession.

The bond completed my picture of her—the things I'd suspected but couldn't confirm. Shatter was someone who'd been running from her fears for as long as she had memory. With every victory came a dozen failures until her world was made of nothing but doubt.

And now our pack was at risk of being one of those failures.

She was afraid, not just of this, but the trauma that was chasing her, the pain from her mates that she hadn't had time to process.

"Are you... are you okay?" she asked, looking up at me while fidgeting with a stack before her. Shifting it back and forward, eyes snagging on words like she couldn't quite look away.

"I could use some cuddles," I said.

"Oh." She reached out, beginning to gather up papers.

Oh ho ho, I didn't think so.

"*In* the hot tub."

She opened her mouth to argue, but I quickly added, "Hot tub cuddles are my dream."

I had a lot of dreams, but she didn't need to know that.

Her jaw clenched as she looked down at the papers, as if trying to figure out how she could make them waterproof.

"For a bit," she said.

Psh.

I'd cuddle her for as long as it took for her frenzy to die down. She'd asked for the dark bond. I wasn't going to throw around commands like Ransom, but if it was necessary to order her to keep cuddling me so her very important brain didn't melt out of her ears, then that was just life.

And *that's* how I found myself climbing into the warm tub beneath the stars with my sweet little siren nightshade.

I was right, too. She wasn't better. The frenzy had been a mask. She kept her T-shirt on, scared to show me what was beneath.

Her scars. The bites.

I knew.

Schooling and me, well, we might no longer be friends, but I wasn't totally stupid.

Yet, those scars were hers, and I didn't need to see them unless she wanted to share. I had spotted a dressing peeking from beneath her T-shirt sleeves, though.

"Can you keep them out of the water easily?" I asked, suddenly concerned.

"Oh, yeh. They're uh... they're higher up." She got all flighty when she said it, even in the bond.

She needed to know she was safe with us, no matter what.

I could do that. One little bit at a time.

The water bubbled around us as I drew her close, savouring the feeling of her arms around me. Her body pressed to mine. Her scent tangled with the hot tub and earth and pine from the trees beyond.

We sat for a while like that, and I felt her unfurl like a flower in the bond. Frenzy fading for that fear again. It wasn't nice, but it was good. If she stayed curled up tight like that, it would eventually start tearing its way out from the inside.

"I love you," I breathed as the bubbles died down, running my thumb up and down her waist where my hand rested.

She leaned back, something so sad in her eyes that it broke my heart. "What if you and Ransom see, and you don't want me anymore?"

"That, Nightshade, is never going to happen."

I caught her wrists gently, lifting her hands and pressing her palms to my chest. I lifted them slowly so she could feel every bump of endless scars that marked my body as the canvas it was. My payment.

And she'd never run from me.

She shut her eyes, the soft wing of a butterfly smothering gold as a tear tumbled down her cheek, glittering beneath the stars and the moon above us.

I wiped it away, cupping her face as I left her hands pressed to my chest.

"You're strong, Shatter. You're going to be okay."

I know she didn't believe it, but I knew it.

"Will *you* be?" she asked.

"I've decided… yes." Dying wasn't an option anymore. "I need to see you in glasses."

Her brows bunched, all cute-like. "My eyesight is actually quite good…"

"Might not be when you're old. I'll wait."

A smile trembled on her lips for a moment, and then she settled back against me.

"You haven't used the dark bond," she whispered after a long time.

"No."

Surprisingly, I felt a trickle of worry from her.

"Would you like me to?" I asked.

There was a pause. "You didn't want it, did you?"

"I didn't want anyone taking that choice away from you," I replied.

"He didn't."

I knew that now. "I want you," I told her. "That's what matters."

"I know I was running from it before… but then…" She trailed off, as if she wasn't sure how to explain it.

That was okay.

I could see her.

Everything she'd placed on a pedestal had turned to dust. The script had flipped—and this, *this* bond was the only part she could control when the cramped world of dreams that she had left had been torn from under her.

That was going to have to change. I wanted her to build her

world of dreams and choices that was bigger than she could ever even imagine.

"I'm... I *am* okay with the dark bond," she whispered.

A purr rumbled to life in my chest as I drew her closer. "That's trust I don't know what to do with."

She leaned back, finally brightening a little. *Truly* brightening and not just in a frenzy. She drew me close, pressing her lips to mine.

I slid my dripping fingers through her hair, ignoring how they tangled in her locks, and drew her against me further, lifting her and kissing her.

She took one of my wrists, her other hand still holding me in a kiss and ever so slowly, drew it beneath her shirt, lifting it higher as if she perhaps wanted me to know. Wanted to risk letting me find her wounds and discovering I might push her away.

Never.

She broke the kiss, eyes holding mine, wild hair backlit by the moon, a shadow cast across her face, golden eyes glinting dimly like a dying firefly at night. She'd paused with my hand at her ribs. Her lip caught in her teeth, and her breaths came sharper.

I felt her delicate fingers shake.

"You don't have to, Nightshade. Not until you're ready. I won't love you any less."

One more beat passed, and then she curled in on herself. I dropped my hands, pulling her tight against me once more.

She was so small.

It was hard to reckon with what had happened. To imagine anyone hurting her.

I shut my eyes, violent hatred lurking between the cracks splintering across my mind. The only thing keeping me tethered was the cool petals of nightshade tangling with the hot tub chemicals, and the earth and pine in the forest beyond.

Just enough to lull to sleep that dormant beast. The half of me that had lived in the Cimmerian Vaults. It had woken once for her, already. When I'd seen those alphas with their hands on her... without a care for her fear, or spirit or soul—what made someone important. Creatures like that, if they were no more, karma had no complaints.

She had to understand, though, and I don't know if she did.

"They're going to die," I said.

She was gentle, but this wasn't something I could protect her from.

"The price cannot be you," she whispered.

"I know."

"Glasses, remember?"

The fact was, I knew I was broken. But before, I'd been so broken, that I'd never cared that I was.

But now?

I cared if it meant not being enough to protect her.

There was a gift in there somewhere, the frightening fragments of a person long gone. A piece to claim back. As dangerous as it was tempting, and equally impossible to ignore.

I was a shell, left to scrounge from the rubble of a person I would never be again. There had been a monster before the experiments, a monster from the Cimmerian Vaults but that wasn't where the rubble came from. The rubble came from destruction before that. The faintest flash of memory and life I felt when I rubbed a coin between my fingers, or shuffled a deck of cards. In the moment I'd watched a young boy tumble from monkey bars when we'd brought Ransom to the park, or when I caught the sweet scents of a candy shop.

The rubble came from there. And it was in black and white on the document Decebal had dug up on my past.

Dusk used those files as motivation: a prize for the moment we were free. I would never look. I'd burn them the second Decebal handed them over.

That hadn't changed, but the reason... *Shatter* had changed the reason.

Before, I knew there was no point to knowing. Now, I didn't want to because I couldn't risk it. I couldn't risk breaking again, when I had something to heal for.

"We're going back tomorrow," she said quietly. The silence had stretched for a long time. I drew her closer.

"I promise, Nightshade. You won't be rushed into anything."

When we returned to Rookwood Academy, she wouldn't face her monsters alone.

TWENTY-EIGHT

DUSK

Decebal had got everything sorted with the Dean. Shatter was going to stay in the apartment with Ransom for the week under the guise of catching him up with course work. Well, she *would* also be doing that since we were committed to the Academy for longer now.

Beyond that, I wasn't sure. I would be damned if the Lincoln pack ruined her studies. We'd never planned on actually staying at the academy after we got what we needed, but she was our omega now, which meant if she wanted to see her classes through to the end, that's what we'd be doing.

"Dusk?" Decebal caught me in the doorway as I was making for the car. The others were in, and we were ready to leave.

"Yeh?" he asked.

"I just had a thought. You said Shatter was different to any omega from the first time you met her?"

"Understatement," I replied.

"Now she's woken Ransom, and saved you and Umbra after Flynn touched you."

"Right."

"What if it's because of what happened to her at the facility? She got injected with something she shouldn't have. The poison they were using while you were there—her scent even matches it. What if it's tied with how she's healing you?"

"What are you getting at?" I asked.

"Vandle."

I froze, staring at him. "You think her scent—?"

"She brought you back. What if she could—?"

"I *won't* take her into that place." My voice was low. "Even if we wanted to—?"

"We wouldn't have to," Decebal said. "All we'd need was her scent."

Shit. He was right.

"Alright. Book a visit."

I was left to ponder that as I drove us back to the academy. Shatter was in the back with Umbra, playing cards and Ransom was at my side. He was quiet again, but I thought he was less down. I hoped he'd heard me. I got it, feeling helpless, I really did, but he'd suffered enough.

The closer we got to the academy, the more nervous Shatter was through the bond. Umbra noticed, too, because he even let her win a game. I *knew* he had because that was a trick deck, and she literally couldn't win unless he wanted her to.

Upon her victory, they stopped playing, and she curled up under his arm, fading away in the bond as if she didn't want us knowing how she felt.

I still hadn't surfaced either. I should, I knew that, but I hadn't got a grip on my own feelings about dark bonding her, and she was so happy to be a part of our pack, I didn't want her getting a flicker of it.

When we pulled in, it was already starting to get dark. Shatter didn't put her contacts in, but she did tuck a scarf around her neck and pull the hood of Umbra's oversized hoodie up.

We got back to the apartment without many witnesses, which meant she was free to hide here until she was ready to leave.

When I opened the door, it was to find an omega on our couch. I'd offered to let Roxy stay, but I still hadn't turned my phone on, and I don't know why, but I assumed she would have left by now.

Roxy scrambled up, dropping the blanket she'd been curled up in on the couch, turning from the baking show playing on the TV.

"Shatter!" She looked more of a mess than I thought Roxy Vasilli could look, with hair in a messy bun, and bags beneath her eyes. Her phone slipped from her hands, and she was racing across the room, throwing herself upon Shatter before she made it through the door. "I'm so sorry."

Shatter held her, eyes wide with alarm. "It's okay," she said.

"No, it's not."

"I lost you your sponsorship—"

"They can burn in hell for all I care," she hissed, drawing back. "All that—" She cut off, her face blanching. The scarf Shatter had been wearing had tumbled off in the hug, revealing the poisoned mark across her neck.

Shatter's hand jumped up, and she looked panicked. "Uh..." She glanced at me desperately, which was when Roxy unfroze, a growl rising in her throat as she tugged Shatter away, absolutely vicious.

Shit. She was going to think—

"W-wait!" Shatter said, tugging on Roxy's sleeve.

I frowned. What *would* she think? Actually, I needed to know.

My voice was quiet as I stepped past them both. "Shatter. Not a word. Go to your nest."

Shatter's eyes widened at my tone and the dark bond command. She took a shaky step back before halting. I didn't feel the pain myself, but I *knew,* somehow, that it rolled through her body, an alert that she was fighting my command. Her jaw clenched, and her look was beyond hurt.

Shit.

I hadn't meant for that to happen.

"Go." I said again. This time it wasn't a command.

"How *dare* you!" Roxy snarled.

I shot Umbra a look. He examined my expression for a long moment. "Come on, Nightshade," he said. "Give them a minute." Shatter frowned, but she let him lead her away.

"Fuck no." Roxy was stepping after her, but I caught her by the arm.

"We need to talk."

"Don't touch me, you foul—"

"*Don't* test me."

Roxy froze, eyes hateful before she glanced down the hall to Shatter, clearly worried my words meant I would take it out on her. I didn't correct her. I needed to see this for myself, because this might be the other shield that protected Shatter now we were back.

"Ransom," I growled. He'd been frozen in the doorway behind me, caught between anger and confusion. I nodded down the hall where I heard Shatter's nest door shut. She was still completely vacant from the bond. He glanced between me and Roxy one last time, but thankfully followed the others.

The moment he was gone, Roxy turned on me. "I trusted you," she spat as I stepped into the kitchen and opened the fridge, thankful that Umbra's beer was still there.

Thank *fuck.*

I'd just hurt my omega with the dark bond I should never have given her.

It had been thoughtless.... too easy...

Roxy rounded on me. "I came to you to protect her!" she hissed. "And you do *this*—after everything she went through?"

"I need you to be aware of two things," I said, crossing my arms and tapping my finger on the edge of the beer as I leaned against the fridge. I could trust Roxy, I believed that. But I needed this from her first.

"Shatter is scent matched to the Lincoln pack."

Roxy froze, staring up at me with wide eyes, her mouth working soundlessly for a moment. "Why—why didn't she tell me?"

"Because," I said. This was the second thing Roxy deserved to know for Shatter's sake. "I've been drugging her every morning before school so that they would never catch her scent. The decision not to tell anyone was mine, not hers. She never had a say in the matter."

Roxy looked about as disgusted as I expected. "Why?"

"Because I think the universe made a mistake. They don't deserve her."

I could see it in her eyes: she thought I was right. Though now she didn't think Shatter belonged with *me* either.

I cracked the beer and crossed to the couch, reaching for the remote and turning to the TV to flick through channels.

Roxy was having none of it, following me and ripping the remote from my hand before throwing it back on the couch.

"You dark bonded her because of *them*?" she snarled. I could see her working through the new information, piecing it together.

"She's mine," I said quietly, cocking my head and fixing my gaze on her. Roxy leaned back, lip curled in a snarl. Her scent was an assault in the room. I'd noticed she'd been using a dampening spray so her scent was muted, but now it was like being smothered by an angry Christmas tree. Really quite unsettling, actually.

"That's what this is?" she demanded. "You can't stand that

she's matched to them after what they did, so you had to one up them?" Her eyes were wild with fury. "You're fucking sick."

I stared at her, working through that.

"It wasn't her fault," Roxy hissed. "She must have been..." She trailed off, eyes wide. "If they're her mates?" She looked like she wanted to throw up. "It must have broken her—and you go and fucking break her some more—" She shoved me "—for the sake of some stupid alpha pissing match?"

Okay.

Right. That... that was good.

But Roxy was far from done. "You can't hide that she's gold pack—everyone is going to know you stole her freedom—that she was just caught in fucking middle."

I breathed a sigh of relief, running my fingers through my hair. I dropped down to the couch, all the energy draining from me as I took a swig of the beer.

Good.

"That's it?" Roxy demanded. "You'll stop me from seeing her and—"

"You can see her." My voice was rough.

"But you—"

"I have no intention of hurting her." I shut my eyes for a second. "I just needed..." I trailed off. "Shatter asked for the bond. She was upset, and I was... I was weak."

Irrational.

Foolish.

Roxy was staring at me in shock. "Why... didn't you say that at the start?"

"I just needed to know..." My voice was strained. "When the school finds out, I don't want her hurt again. I needed to know everyone will blame us, not her."

She'd gone through enough. Everyone had seen the video.

"You're worried about her image?"

"She has enough going on without having the whole academy hating her," I said. "And if everyone thinks she's the victim, then..." Well, it was the best of all the bad options.

"Shit."

"What?" I asked, glancing up again.

"The Lincoln pack," she said. "If everyone finds out they're her scent match, they're going to look..."

"Like the fucking monsters they are?"

This was about more than image. When she returned with us, they would be angry. If the whole school saw me as an enemy, the Lincoln pack would too. It would shift their attention from her.

And the fact that they would be ruined if the scent match ever became public? Silver fucking lining. It was a tiny thing in the bigger picture, but I was going to relish the looks on their faces when they realised how badly they screwed up.

"You're going to stop hiding her scent, then?"

"When she's ready."

I wouldn't push her on that. It was her choice.

Roxy was already backing up to go see Shatter.

"One more thing," I said, halting her in her tracks. "The Lincoln pack—"

"It's over. I got an email saying they'd dropped me for inappropriate conduct. They're claiming I sabotaged political relationships. Goes against the contract." She sounded resigned.

I had underestimated her. For some people, getting dropped would have been the end of the world. Getting chosen by a pack meant her tuition would be covered, but if they were claiming Roxy violated the contract, they could withdraw it. It would also wreck her reputation. But instead of leaving, or going to a bar and drinking, or going back to her family for the weekend to mope, she'd stayed here, waiting for Shatter. By the gaunt look in her eyes, she hadn't slept much.

"Stay here tonight. I've talked to the Dean. There's an open apartment two down since the Rodger pack merger. It's yours."

"That's alright. I'll find a place off campus."

I narrowed my eyes. "Why?" Was she scared of the Lincoln pack?

"Getting into this school, it was great, but it's not cheap. I know some omegas sharing a place, I can see if they have a—"

"It's covered."

Roxy folded her arms. "I can deal with student loans like everyone else."

"I wasn't asking."

There was a long silence.

"You gave up the Lincoln pack sponsorship because of my pack," I said. "To protect *my* omega. It's covered. Plus, I'd rather you were close in case they're a problem." It wasn't like the Lincoln pack couldn't catch her entering and leaving campus. At least this way I could keep an eye.

"She's probably tearing her hair out waiting for you," I added, seeing her brewing a stubborn argument. She ran her tongue along her teeth, then sighed and nodded, heading down the hall to Shatter's nest.

TWENTY-NINE

SHATTER

"Shatter!" Umbra grabbed me around the waist and hauled me away from the bookshelves.

"But I—"

"No."

"She's going to—"

"Think your nest is awesome. Because it is."

I glared up at him, pouting, hyper-aware of the oddly angled stacks of books on the floor beside the bookshelf. They were too perfectly positioned for Roxy not to know it was on purpose.

Umbra had been pissed about the whole 'dark bond command from Dusk' thing, but I wasn't. I'd felt his spike of panic when I fought his command. I knew he hadn't meant it.

"He called the shots for years," I'd said. "He's not used to having to be careful about that."

And the pain had been... Well, it wasn't the worst thing I'd ever felt, but the bar was high for me.

But now the true issue had arisen, since—despite the dark

bond command situation—we all knew Dusk had a plan, and that meant Roxy was going to be coming in here at any moment.

To my nest.

And all of its madness—A KNOCK sounded on the door.

"Shit." My gaze snapped up.

Ransom, who'd been watching the fight between me and Umbra from my desk chair, got to his feet and crossed to it in an instant.

Oh *dammit*.

She was here.

She was here and my books were all—I squeaked as Umbra (noticing me sticking my foot out to at least knock the stack over) grabbed me by the waist and tucked me under his arm like I was a misbehaving puppy. Then he walked me across the room and set me down before a rather startled looking Roxy, who was standing at the door.

"Hi..." I said, straightening my shirt and trying to fix my glare.

Roxy stifled a smile, looking between me and Umbra. "Can I come in?"

"Um..."

"Yes." Umbra spoke for me.

I wrinkled my nose. "Fine. But you have to go." I tried to shove him out the door, and was about as successful as if I'd tried to move a brick wall.

Ransom, at least, had the decency to exit without *rudeness*, giving me a little kiss on the forehead before he left. See, *that* was sweet, and not embarrassing.

"I'll go," Umbra said, "But Roxy needs to know the nest rule."

"Nest rule?" Roxy asked as she stepped in. She was looking around at it. At *all* of it.

"Nothing can be straight," he declared. "Not ever. Not even a little bit—"

"Shut *up*!" I hissed.

With a broad grin on his face, Umbra exited the room, offering me a smug little salute as I slammed the door in his face.

Oh *bother*.

"It's amazing," Roxy said, staring around.

"You don't have to say that to—"

"I'm not. I'm jealous. Your instincts are off the walls."

I shrank. "I know." My voice was quiet as I tugged at my hair.

"That's a good thing, Shatter," she said, looking back at me.

"Oh. But I mean, it's not like... normal... and Omega Studies—"

"Wants to train omegas to fit into little boxes so that they all like the same thing, and behave the same way. Only keep the instincts if they fit. Truthfully? Most alphas don't even want that, let alone the fucking omegas." She smiled as she stepped up to the bookshelves, peering at them curiously. "I grew up learning that. It's a fucking task to undo all that work. I wish I knew who I was, like you do."

I almost laughed, but caught myself because she seemed serious.

I didn't know who I was. Literally, figuratively...

"No wonder they're obsessed with you. You are what real alphas look for."

"Real alphas?"

"I don't know." She shrugged. "Any alpha worth being with."

Hmm.

Okay.

That was definitely a compliment.

"Are you okay?" she asked. Her voice turned more serious, and my stomach flipped.

"Um..." I tried to ignore the dark cloud that threatened to return as my mind scrambled for a response. I straightened and unstraightened my pencil case on the desk. "I mean... I'm going to be." Shit. The notebook wasn't quite right either. If Umbra insisted on me leaving everything off kilter, it could at least be off kilter the *right* way. "And uh... Dusk's sorting it all out," I said. "Ransom's behind in classes so the Dean is letting me tutor him for the week." I frowned, adjusting my candle beside the new arrangement. Also, my words were coming out so fast, but I couldn't seem to slow them down. "Bolin's going to drop off the coursework, so I won't... I won't have to go out for a bit."

And see everyone. All the people who had seen that video.

And Roxy knew...

Oh my God, Roxy knew...

"The library, I..." Fuck. My cheeks blazed, and I ran my fingers through a tangled lock refocusing my attention on the pencil case. It *still* wasn't right. "I swear I didn't—"

"They're your mates," Roxy said quietly. I looked at her in shock as she sat down on my desk chair right beside me. "Dusk told me."

"It doesn't make it okay."

"Not okay, like... having sex in an open library?" she asked.

I chewed on my lip, shrinking down.

"I didn't watch it," she said quietly. "But I uh... I got enough context before I turned off my socials."

"I was..." I chewed on my lip as Roxy examined the items on the table, then reached out and turned the pen at an angle. It fixed the puzzle, perfect unevenness, removing the tangent lines and dead space just right.

"I imagine you were quite confused," she said quietly. "That Dusk wasn't your mate, and he seems to care, and Eric was, and he's... Well, he's a vile piece of garbage not worth the alpha title he was born with."

With nothing left to distract me on the desk, I glanced up at her. "I didn't... I didn't see that in time," I whispered. "I... I'm so... so s-stupid." My voice cracked and then Roxy was on her feet, drawing me into a hug.

"No, no you're not, babe. I would have been so mixed up too if they were my mates."

I hadn't had a hug like this since Aunty Lauren, with slender arms that packed the same power as Umbra's.

And it was okay to cry in front of Roxy. Not that I didn't trust my pack, but they ached for this almost as much as I did. The undercurrent of rage in the bond that they had for me, it was... comforting. It made me feel so much less alone, but it curdled with their pain. Instead, I could cry to her, as she led me to the bed and held me tight.

So I did.

I cried so hard that it was hard to breathe, and she had to rush to grab tissues from my desk before hugging me again.

It took me a long, long time to get it out of my system, and Roxy stroked my hair, something sorrowful in her cosy scent of fir trees and oranges.

When I finally looked up, I saw there were tears in her eyes. "I'm sorry, Shatter. I tried to..." Her voice wavered. "I tried to find you, the second I knew—"

"I know."

It was why I loved her voice. It was the only voice I'd heard when I was in that room. The only voice that wasn't theirs.

It was the moment I'd realised she really cared about me.

I had a friend.

And she'd blown up her contract with the Lincoln pack to get to me. She'd been here all weekend, and she'd...

I frowned.

What about all her stuff? Classes were tomorrow morning, and her things must still be in the Lincoln pack apartment.

How would she study properly?

Wait wait wait.

I stumbled from her arms and launched myself across the room in an instant, pulling open the drawer of my desk before I found what I was looking for. I grabbed the pencil case and rushed back, holding it out to her. "I have a spare one—I-if you need it."

Well.

Actually, I'd have to put together another one, since mine was gone. But that was okay. Umbra had saved my registration card, and that's all that really mattered.

Roxy took it from me, a smile on her face that dispelled the building nerves. "Thank you."

"And... obviously anything else you need until you can get your stuff."

"Thanks. Dusk offered to set me up in an apartment on this floor. I don't know when it'll be ready."

My heart lifted. "You'll stay over tonight?"

"They seem alright if I take the couch—"

"No, I mean like...?"

Roxy's eyes lit up. "Like a slumber party?"

A... A what?

"Yes. I mean... I-I don't know if my nest is good for that—"

"It is. I love it in here."

"Oh. Okay."

"So. Pyjamas. Gossip. And we'll need slumber party food."

My mind emptied of everything but pure alarm. "R-right. Well, my Pyjamas are in the closet. Do you want to find us some, and I'll go get the slumber party food?"

Slumber party food?

As soon as I was outside and the door was shut I panicked. I ran down the hallway so fast I almost tripped right into the living room on my face.

"What's wrong?" Dusk looked alarmed as he crossed toward me, eyes scanning my expression. "Shatter, about earlier—"

"No no no, *help me!*" I hissed. "Roxy wants a slumber party, and she said there needs to be food."

"We can get food," Dusk said.

"She said *slumber party food*. What does that mean?"

It sounded like code.

I didn't know codes.

"I think it's just snacks—"

"You're *boys*. *Alpha* boys. What if there's a secret language, and I'm supposed to know it?"

Ransom snorted, and Dusk was grinning, but Umbra—the *only* rational one—was pulling out his phone. "I'll look it up," he said.

Thank fuck someone was taking me seriously.

Oh...

Oh dear.

"She's gonna know I've never had a slumber party before."

"No. She isn't," Dusk said. "Umbra will sort out the food, and I'll bring in the TV from my room so you can watch chick flicks."

"That's a thing?"

"It's a thing."

"What if it's only a thing in alpha slumber parties?"

"I..." Dusk looked so stunned that Ransom beat him to answer.

"She has a point." Ransom folded his arms. "Do we *truly* know there isn't a significant divergence of features between alpha and omega slumber—*OW!*" He cut off as Umbra, who was still scrolling through his phone furiously, leaned over and flicked him in the ear hard enough that he yelped.

Dusk snorted but was already heading back to his room.

I rushed after him, heart in my throat.

I was almost tearing my hair out by the time he was unplugging his TV. "W-wait."

He set it down on his bed, turning to me.

"What if it *is* a divergent feature? Then she'll think I'm like...

an alpha or something." Would that be worse than her thinking I'd never been to a slumber party before?

My *friend* was inside my nest right now, ready to have a slumber party.

"It sounds more serious than a girls' night," I went on. "It's like... like a whole party. Do you *usually* watch movies at a party?" Snacks sure—Pyjamas... that was a little confusing, but movies? I mean... were we supposed to watch while the music was playing? I'd never even heard of a party without music. Or was it like an interval thing? And if so, what kind of interval? Would she figure it out when I got the wrong ratio of movie to music time?

"You're going to be fine," he told me.

"Dusk." I seized him. "I *need* you to be sure. This is not a mop." That was the wrong word.

"A mop?"

Drill. *"This is not a drill."*

"I am absolutely completely certain that chick flicks are not an alpha-slumber-party exclusive feature, alright?" he asked.

"You didn't even look it up."

Umbra was looking things up.

I changed my mind.

I needed a phone.

"Gem." My eyes snapped to him as his grip closed around my chin. My breathing settled instantly.

"Y-yes?"

"I'm going to set up the TV. You are going to tell Roxy that you want to hear what her ideal slumber party is, what her favourite snack food is, and what movies she likes. You're going to collect the data she gives you and figure out the right move from there."

"Oh. Okay." That sounded surprisingly doable.

A plan.

I could execute a plan. Especially when data was involved.

Later, I was curled up with Roxy in my bed. The movie on the TV was far more educational than I was expecting, with really pretty blonde girls explaining social cues and complexities in a way that was really easy to understand. I took mental notes. I had to watch more of these.

There was a tray of tea on the bedside table, and two huge baskets of snacks, from chocolate bars to popcorn, and a variety of chips.

Roxy had all but pounced on the chocolate bars when they'd arrived, which meant Umbra had picked right, and I was starting to get the impression that music wasn't a necessary feature of a slumber party even though it was a party—since Roxy hadn't brought it up.

Finally, Roxy got sleepy and curled up at my side, pillow in one arm, stack of chocolate bars in the other.

I buried myself between the covers and pulled the duvet over us.

"It was the perfect slumber party," she said with a yawn.

Was it?

"Oh. Good." I ducked my face into pillows so she wouldn't see my stupid smile.

"And I like your scent. It's really... calming."

"Calming?" I asked. That was new.

Maybe bonding alphas really had toned it down like Uncle had said it might.

"It's like jasmine and earth... a little deadly. I like it."

"Thank you," I whispered.

"It's unique... different..." She yawned again, a small smile on her face. "Everything they're going to hate when they find out... When you're ready..."

I frowned.

Would I ever be ready?

I was still so scared of them.

I wasn't scared of the idea of them hating my scent, though. I thought maybe that *was* a little satisfying, actually.

"What about the ball?" she asked.

"The ball?"

"Next weekend. It's the charity event they're hosting."

Oh. Right. I'd totally forgotten.

"What about it?"

"I don't know... if you were ready by then, you could ruin them at a ball."

"Ruin them?"

"You have their secret, Shatter. One that will ruin them worse than they could ever ruin you."

"What do you mean?"

"What they did to you—publically—when people find out they did that to their own scent match... Money won't be enough to save them. No omega will go near them again."

"You... you really think so?" I asked.

"We could go shopping, get you a revenge dress."

"A what?"

"Like... the sexiest dress in the world. And then you walk out for the first time since they saw you, looking like a goddess, scent out, and then they realise how badly they fucked up."

I mulled that over, enjoying the flash of vindictiveness in her eyes as she said it.

"If you're up for it, babe. You don't have to."

"I know."

I didn't know if I was bold enough, but the idea did make me feel a little warm inside.

"Roxy, I...I'm sorry that being friends with me meant—" She frowned.

"I'm *not* sorry I'm friends with you." Her fingers tangled in mine and she squeezed tight. The fir trees tangling in the air around me wilted. "I stayed with them longer than I should have.

My mom and sisters kept telling me what an amazing opportunity it was, and I should have been grateful to land a pack and have my tuition covered. No one ever walks away from something like that. But they weren't..." She swallowed, like she wasn't sure how to say it.

Ice slid through my veins.

But... she was Roxy. She knew what she wanted and how to manage alphas. "They didn't... hurt you, did they?"

Had I missed that, somehow?

"Not like..." She swallowed. "Not like they hurt you. But they weren't very nice. They'd find little ways to punish me if I wasn't what they wanted."

"I'm sorry."

"I'm really happy it's over. My family is going to be upset—they care a lot about reputation. But Dusk said he was going to cover my tuition anyway, so they can't be that mad."

"He did?"

"Yeh. I mean. I told him he didn't have to but uh... he seems like the stubborn type. I also got the impression it might already be done."

I snorted before I could catch myself.

Roxy gave me a wry smile, closing her eyes and squeezing my hand again.

Her scent settled, a peaceful Christmas morning, fresh orange and fir trees out the window. "I think I would have stayed if it hadn't met you, and I think I would have changed into someone I wouldn't recognise," she said.

"I'm glad you're free."

THIRTY

RANSOM

I woke in Shatter's bed to the softest touch against my skin. I didn't move as she gently brushed her thumb along my cheek. Nightshade was a drug in the air, and I could feel her in the bond. She felt safe and warm and... and very possessive.

I kept my eyes closed, trying not to smile. If I smiled, she'd know I was awake.

I still needed to get to know her properly.

Roxy and Shatter had spent most of the day together yesterday while Dusk and Umbra went to school. In the evening, we'd helped Roxy set up her new apartment. Maybe I was being a coward, but Umbra had let slip how important Roxy was to Shatter, so I didn't want to interfere. That, and... *maybe* I was nervous.

Shatter kept breaking rules. I didn't *get* nervous over women.

It didn't matter how nervous I was, today I had her all to myself. And the best way to get an insight on someone was to see what they did when they didn't know they were being watched.

Based on the dissatisfaction and boredom down the bond from Umbra and Dusk, I guessed we'd overslept the start of classes.

I watched through mostly closed eyelids as Shatter sat up in bed, rubbing her eyes. When she settled, she began tapping her finger anxiously on her thigh as she peered around.

"You have a pack now…" She trailed off, more of her internal conversation clearly happening in her head.

Oh, she *talked* to herself?

That was unexpectedly delightful.

"…Or what will they think? Or if there's visitors—?"

She cut off, and then she was out of bed like a shot, and I thought I spied alarm on her face as she hurried from the room.

I sat up, considering that.

Why had no one warned me she was this cute?

It didn't feel out of place… Flickers of memories drifted in from when I was waking up. We'd had a heat together. I remembered something about her wrestling sweatpants onto me… That was definitely a little funny, but that memory merged with the next, which was my taking a swing at Dusk before throwing him into the TV.

I grinned, getting to my feet and walking to the door, then I cracked it open and peered out.

I could see half the living room and kitchen down the hall.

What was she doing?

Scrambling around in nothing but a T-shirt, tanned legs on full display, she grabbed couch cushion after couch cushion and—oh. I chuckled.

She was drawing her chin along them.

Scent marking them.

All of them.

When she was done with the couch, she hurried to the kitchen, where she opened drawers and scent marked (seemingly) random handfuls of cutlery, bowls and plates, the toaster oven—she had to bend over the counter for that, which gave me a wonderful view of her ass hugged in lace—and whatever else she could find. Then she hurried up the steps to the balcony.

Yes.

She wasn't going to leave our rooms untouched. She vanished into Umbra's first—I could see up to her knees at this vantage—then she made for mine. I hoped she marked every pillow and blanket and item of clothing...

I backed up around the door as she came back down the hallway for Dusk's room. Once I heard the latch from across the hall click, I dared to peek back around.

She was standing in his doorway, more tentative now.

Why was she hesitating?

"...Hmmm..." She shrank a little, fists balling in the hem of her shirt and tugging at it. "On one hand, he's mad at you for convincing him to dark bond you..." She trailed off. "But he's pack lead, so... I have to, right? What if he thinks it's rude that I haven't?" She straightened at that and then charged into his room in a rush.

The smile on my face was broad as I watched her pick carefully through the pillows on his bed, as if Dusk had a preference to which she left her scent on. What a ridiculous notion. He'd want her to mark them all.

Then she vanished—into his closet, maybe?

Finally, she returned to his bed, traced a finger along the lamp shade, before leaning down and marking it. Her face fell the moment she'd done it. "Oh... He's going to think you're so weird..." She tugged at her hair.

Next thing I knew, she grabbed all the pillows she'd just scent marked and shoved them under his bed.

Then she vanished again to his closet, returning with an armful of clothing. For a moment she seemed to second guess herself, eyeing the doorway and forcing me to duck away.

Was she considering removing them completely?

When I dared peek back around she'd clearly decided not to, stuffing them under his bed also—and giving me another fantastic view of her from behind. Finally, she stopped at the lamp. She stared at it for a long second. Then she grabbed a handful of her shirt and tried to rub at its surface as if that would neutralise the scent mark.

I contained my snort with immense difficulty.

She looked so genuinely concerned. Finally, she unplugged the lamp and stuffed it under the bed with everything else.

Very subtle.

I'm sure Dusk would never notice.

I backed up from the doorway when she looked like she was done, and sat down on the edge of the bed so it looked like I'd just woken up.

She was... well, she was... incredible. How had we managed to find an omega like this? And what was she so worried about, second guessing everything?

The door creaked open, and I glanced up to see Shatter slip in. She froze when she saw me, cheeks going pink. "You're awake."

"I am."

She reached me, and I couldn't help reaching out and tugging her closer by her hips. She was so fucking beautiful I could stare at her all day.

"I'm sorry—it's my nest, and you didn't even wake up with—"

She cut off as I put a finger to her lips.

"I'm going to need you to stop doing that."

"What?" she asked, eyes wide.

"Doubting yourself. Your instincts make the rules, alright?"

That, and anxiously warning me when we got back to the school that we were going to meet 'real' omegas as if I'd catch sight of one and regret she was ours. I'd been sick for a few years, not born yesterday. Probably best not to tell her I'd spent far too many of my teen years drunkenly partying.

"My... instincts?" she asked.

"Yup."

"Well..." She looked concerned. "I'm going to have to read through my omega studies textbook again—"

"No." Absolutely not. "I don't want a commercially packaged omega. I want you."

"You don't understand, I'm not... I spent a lot of time hidden from alphas, and my instincts—"

"Are everything we need. No study. No nothing. They're perfect. If you feel you need to do something, I want you to do it."

"O-Okay." She glanced at the door, clearly cycling through everything she'd just done and wondering what I might think.

"Good." I tugged her closer, pressing a kiss to her stomach over her shirt. "Now. What are we going to do today?"

"I have a plan for studying—"

"I want to go shopping first."

"B-but we can't study while shopping."

"Exactly."

"But Dusk said—"

"Fuck Dusk and his rules," I snorted. "I'm years out of date. I don't even have a phone."

"Won't he be upset?" She shrank a little.

"I hear it's quite the show when Dusk is upset with you."

Her whole face went beet red. "I don't think... he's..." She trailed off, and I grinned.

"Come on. Get dressed. We're going out. We'll grab breakfast on the way."

SHATTER

He'd stopped at a breakfast place on the way to the mall, and I'd had a stack of pancakes, which tasted amazing.

Now we were wandering about, and I was out in public with my alpha.

It was refreshing to be away from the academy, but it was more difficult than I'd anticipated. People kept looking at him funny, which I got, but he was kind of mine now. Or... I was his. Whatever. It should mean something.

Was it *normal* for people to stare at someone as much as they stared at him?

He *was* good looking—like a magazine model, tall and lean, with tanned skin, and his brows were dark, which contrasted the rich green of his eyes. He always had a casual mess to his auburn hair that fell from his bun just in the right ways to seem deliberate (though I'd watched very carefully as he tied it up this morning and was disappointed to find he didn't do anything special).

Everyone's eyes seemed to snap to him, to me, then to the dark bond on my neck, and then right back to him.

We entered a clothing shop, and there was a very pretty omega who was helping people pick out fashion. She reminded me of Roxy a bit, with glossy hair and a beautiful smile. Except, when she approached us, she placed a hand on Ransom's arm before spotting me. She withdrew it until she saw my dark bond, then she returned her gaze to Ransom like I didn't exist. When her hand touched his arm the second time, I growled before I caught myself.

I cut it off in an instant, embarrassment flooding my system, though she flinched back, eyebrows shooting up.

I couldn't shake the red from my vision, the world a blur of rage that I tried really hard to manage. I did, though. Uncle had been right about one thing; the bond had balanced out my instincts a bit.

I didn't settle until Ransom led us out of the store.

"Hey, Little Reaper, look at me."

His palm cupped my cheek, and I snapped my gaze up to him.

It was hard to miss the delight down the bond from him, even when he was trying to keep his expression serious.

"Why... why did she do that?" I asked.

"Some people rank bonds like that. You'd own a princess bond. We'd both own a normal bond, but the alphas own a dark bond. The direction of the claim means some people think we're open for—"

"Flirting?" I asked, my lip trembling.

"Something stupid like that."

"No." My voice was an embarrassing whine, and I glanced around to see a passing couple shooting me funny looks. "Dusk said I seduced him into the bite. That means it's mine—you're mine." Ransom had difficult hair, just like me—that ranked the same as a scent match, right?

Ransom's smile soothed my nerves. "I am," he said, leaning down and pressing his lips to my forehead.

I swallowed. "I'm sorry for embarrassing you like that."

"Please," he snorted. "Growl at omegas all you want, but know I've got eyes only for you."

"Okay." That was good, I thought, because it hadn't felt optional when I'd done it.

"And I've never been so turned on in my life."

I snapped my gaze back to him and saw the truth in his eyes. "Really?"

"Uh-huh. Just like all the scent marking I found in my room when I grabbed my jacket."

Oh... Well, I hadn't expected him to find it so quickly. My heart still raced thinking about it. "That wasn't too much?"

"I loved it."

My chest warmed with pride at that. Okay. Ransom liked it. Maybe Dusk wouldn't be mad after all. I wasn't very good at giving my alphas space.

Next, we stopped at a beauty shop and Ransom picked out a

bunch of hair products. It definitely cheered me up when he told me half were for me, though I'd have to get him to explain how to use them, though.

Last on the to-do list was apparently tech, and when we entered the phone shop, Ransom looked about at all the phones with a rather lost expression on his face.

"I'm behind," he said. "What model do you have?" he asked me.

"Uh... I don't," I said.

"You don't have a phone? Oh, for fuck's sake. Why didn't Dusk get you one?"

"He... he thought I was going to run away. And anyway, I don't know what I'd do with a phone."

Ransom rolled his eyes and bought each of us one based on the shop worker's recommendation. Then he bought us both laptops—despite my protests that I didn't know how to use one.

"It can help you with your investigation," he said. "Plus, the guy said this one is simple to use."

Investigation definitely meant the Dusk and Umbra stuff.

"I've got all my textbooks now."

And I had a list of things I needed to recheck. The untethering, for example, and how exactly bonds and auras interacted with a pack breaking. They'd lost their third member and stayed intact. I needed to understand the mechanisms behind that so I knew where they might have diverged from the normal.

I had Bolin's list of course work, so I wouldn't get behind, but honestly, it was a lot of stuff I was already familiar with. Instead, I planned on using my study time to do a deep dive into a few things I needed to brush up on in order to hash out some of my theories on Dusk and Umbra.

"Well," Ransom said. "With a laptop, you can find studies that aren't in the textbooks, and with a phone, you can text Decebal and ask him if he can dig up any more secret studies that the textbooks will never publish."

"Secret like... banned?" I asked.

"Doesn't the Institute have a running list of shit they don't want accessible?"

"Yes..."

"Decebal's pack mate can get into all sorts of shit like that."

"Really?"

"Yup."

Dammit. I *would* have to learn how to use the laptop. I had been watching when Umbra tried to show me my way around it; I'd just not wanted to.

But secret Arkology studies?

"Fine."

We arrived home with bags and bags of shopping. Dusk looked up at us from the couch, where he had his textbook and laptop out. "A really productive way of studying," he said.

"We... we're going to do it," I said quickly. "I swear."

I hurried Ransom down the hallway to my nest and gathered up all the right textbooks.

"Okay. So." I settled on the bed with a stack of books. "I have all the chapters that we absolutely have to go through to catch you up. Maybe I can read them out, and then I can ask you questions about it to make sure you've got it sorted."

"Sounds like a plan," he said, settling beside me.

We read for a while, and he focused at first, but after two chapters, he looked bored. That was okay. "The uh... the next bit's really interesting. It outlines the connection between aura size and—" I cut off as I felt his touch trail along my waist and looked back at him.

"Keep reading, Little Reaper," he said, shifting behind me. The command settled in the bond, and I glanced back down at the words, trying to find my place. "It's really cute how much you get into it."

I opened my mouth, reading the next sentence, as he readjusted my hips. "On your knees, baby, and keep reading."

What?

"Um…" I tried to stammer out the next sentence as he shifted behind me, sliding his hand down my back and pressing me into an arch as I clutched the textbook, propped up on my elbows.

"…the… the difference in aura size can alter the… the outcome, which is why precise equations are… are…" I let out a little moan as he tugged my panties aside and pressed his finger into me.

"You said the chapter was crucial."

"I-it is."

"Well, I've decided using this sweet cunt of yours is also crucial."

"But… you won't learn anything—-"

"Eyes on the book. I need my education."

The command seized me again, and I stammered out the next half of the sentence before he tugged my panties down, and I felt his tip at my entrance.

"You're doing so good, don't stop."

He slid into me, and my blood lit with lust as he filled me up. I moaned, stumbling over words that were still tumbling from my lips, beyond my control.

"*Fuuckk*, Little Reaper, keep going."

My blood hit a boiling point as I stammered, eyes fixed on the book as his tip slammed into that perfect spot deep in my core.

Finally, the words jumbled as bliss threatened to overtake me. I was panting.

"You're going to finish the chapter before you finish," he growled.

I whined, my body shaking from need as I searched the page for my place again.

"R-Ransom," I begged. "I can't... mmm..." I trailed off as he drove into me again and my body shuddered.

"You're almost done, and you squeeze me so fucking tight when you're right on that edge."

More words came out, finally losing their meaning as my brain turned to mush. I was trembling, desperate, and each time he sank into me, his knot would stretch me out just a bit, his tip pressing into my core.

I could hear his low panting as if he was holding off, too.

Finally, I panted out the last word of the chapter. His fingers closed in my hair as he shoved me down against the page, driving into me so hard that I saw stars.

I cried out as the orgasm that had been building surged through me. Each stroke was another jolt of pleasure, and low whines sounded from my chest as he drew it out over and over, his own release warm in my core as he filled me up.

"Fuck, you're so sexy," he growled as he pressed into me again. "Now. Next chapter?"

THIRTY-ONE

SHATTER

Dusk was at my side on the couch the next evening, head buried in a textbook. For the last hour, I'd been edging closer on the couch as he studied.

Things were getting better. But I knew he was still reserved with me because of the dark bond.

"How's the week going?" I asked, peering at his *Arkology: Genetic and Genomics* homework. "Have you seen them?"

It was Wednesday, and I knew they had a lot of classes with the Lincoln pack.

He nodded, turning to me. "I'm doing alright, but Umbra was never good with this to start with. He's about ready to crack."

"But... he can't go near them —"

"I know. I'm thinking of requesting a transfer. We might be at this academy for a while if you want to stay, so better to find him shit he's actually interested in. Or he could drop some classes entirely if he wanted. We intended to get close to them, but that's off the table now, anyway."

"Would *you* drop them?"

"No." He glanced down to the textbook. "I'm actually not hating it."

I brightened at that. "Really?"

"Yeh."

"I could… help you study some time?" I offered.

He grinned. "Once you're done helping Ransom, maybe."

I nodded, but a blush was creeping up my neck.

"What?" Dusk prodded, but Ransom had emerged from his room and was making his way down to the kitchen.

"It's not going so well on the studying front," I whispered.

We'd tried again this morning but it had ended in a lot of sex. Study sex. I couldn't lie and say I didn't like it, but… "I don't think he's going to catch up," I whispered.

There was a small smile curving the edge of Dusk's lips. He dropped his voice to match me. "Does he need to transfer, too?"

"I'm doing my best. But uh… we'll have to see."

He nodded. "What about the ball?" he asked. "You don't have to go, but Ransom mentioned you brought it up…"

"Roxy said something about a… a revenge dress?" I eyed him, wondering if that meant anything to him.

He cocked his head, leaning back a bit, a little twinkle of malice in his eyes. "*Did* she?"

"But if Umbra's having a hard time—"

"It's on Saturday. Decebal just texted, and we've got to follow up a lead. He's booked it for the same night as the ball. I could ask Umbra if he wanted to join Decebal, then he won't have to sit in the same room as the Lincoln pack."

"What's the lead?" I asked. He'd put the files we'd brought back—the ones with all my notes on them—into his safe, but I had them all organised in my head like a textbook. If there was more information, I needed to figure out where to file it.

"I'll give you all the details, but it might be a dead end. I don't want to get your hopes up."

"Okay. Well, maybe that would work... Would you want to go?" He'd implied it was hard for him too, to see them.

"Shatter, if you want to ruin that pack, I will be at your side every second. Sounds like Roxy will be too."

"Okay. I mean, I'm not totally sure yet." But I was going to emerge from here eventually, and every spare moment I'd had this week had been working on figuring out what had happened to Dusk and Umbra. It was therapeutic.

I hated them. It was new for me, to hate anyone that much, but their taunts, what they'd said about Umbra and Dusk while they were watching them being ruined—when one of their pack had died...

Vile sickness turned my stomach every time I thought of it.

Decebal had told me he'd get me secret articles as soon as he had some. I'd given him a list of topics I was most interested in.

"Only if you're up for it," he said. "You can change your mind as much as you—" He cut off at the sound of a strangled growl from Ransom in the kitchen behind us.

"Where the *fuck*—?"

I spun on the couch to see him rifling through the cutlery drawer desperately before slamming it shut. On the kitchen island was a bowl of leftovers.

"What is going on?" Dusk asked.

"The... the cutlery... there's no more... *Argh*." He looked furious.

"Umbra reorganised it last night," Dusk said.

"*Umbra?*" Ransom demanded. "That greedy *bastard*," he hissed under his breath, and then he was taking the stairs by threes.

We both watched him cross the landing and then bang on Umbra's door loudly.

Umbra answered, and it was hard to hear them through angry

hisses, but I swear I heard Umbra say something like: *"Well you took the toaster oven."*

The... toaster oven? I glanced back to see that, sure enough, it was gone from the kitchen.

"I did *not*," Ransom's voice rose with outrage.

Wait... *The toaster oven?*

The cutlery?

I froze, cheeks going bright pink as memories of me rifling through this kitchen and scent marking everything at random came floating back into my mind.

Oh dear...

Dusk was craning his neck and peering into the kitchen, clearly also noticing the vacant spot where the toaster oven had been.

"Here," Umbra was saying. "Make it a deal: coin toss. You win, you get all the shit I took, I win, I get all the shit you took."

There was a pause, then Ransom folded his arms. "Alright then."

"Oh..." I reached out from the couch, but it was late.

"Tails."

A minute later, Ransom (now a seething demon of alpha indignation in the bond) was hauling the huge toaster oven into Umbra's room.

"Might as well bring the game consoles, too," Umbra said, a smug grin on his face. "Since I assume we'll be playing in here."

"*Fuck* you," Ransom snarled.

"Shatter," Dusk said, making me jump. "Do you have *any* idea what is going on?"

"No." I shook my head instantly, trying to keep my voice serious. "None at all."

"So it couldn't *possibly* have anything to do with the fact I unearthed half my wardrobe and a lamp from beneath my bed yesterday?"

"I... I don't have *any* idea how that happened."

He raised an eyebrow. "Come here."

I was shifting toward him in an instant and he pulled me onto his lap.

"Are you lying to me?" he asked. "Because you know what happens to lying omegas in my pack?"

"I..." My lips parted as he squeezed my butt, dragging me closer. My pulse began racing as I stared into his piercing eyes, body growing hot. "I mean... I *might* have scent marked a few things around the apartment..."

"The cutlery?"

"Some of it."

Dusk raised an eyebrow. "The... toaster oven?"

"Umbra bought it to make me breakfast."

And he was getting way better. Yesterday morning he'd roasted tomatoes and had only overcooked the eggs a teensie bit.

"I just thought I should make sure the home was ours. I know you have doubts about... the bond."

His fingers wove through my hair, dragging my neck back. I froze as I felt him press his teeth to the bond.

"I love you, Shatter," he breathed. "You belong in this pack. That's the end of the conversation."

He drew back, still holding me. I bit my lip, unable to take my gaze from him. He was far too good looking, with his gorgeous deep amber skin and bright yellow eyes.

"But we are not stable alphas. Keep scent marking kitchen appliances and cutlery, and you might drive us all back to insanity."

"Noted."

"I'm not saying you *shouldn't* do it. I'm just saying we have to be more careful. If you do feel you need to, you can, but—" His eyes twinkled with mischief as he leaned close, breathing in my ear—"You leave it in *my* room when you're done."

The command locked in place through the dark bond, surprising me.

"But the others—"

"You won't tell them about this command."

My lips parted as that locked in, too. *"That's cheating."*

His grin was wicked as he leaned back. "I work smart, not hard, Gem."

THIRTY-TWO

SHATTER

"Tonight is the night," Ransom declared.

Umbra looked determined as he rubbed his hands together, waiting for the popcorn to pop in the microwave. "If we don't get RedEyedBandit off my scoreboards—"

"We'll do it." Ransom was absolutely determined.

It was Thursday evening, and Ransom and Umbra had told me they'd show me how to play the game the two of them had been obsessed with since we'd returned from the cabin.

It was full of duelling monsters and looked pretty challenging, to be honest. But they'd been battling each other almost every night since we'd arrived, and it did put a smile on my face—watching them get competitive over it.

On the other hand, Ransom's catch-up studying had been abandoned entirely. He'd taken me out for lunch today, which was great, and we'd fucked again, but he had retained nothing at all. He was smart, but it wouldn't be enough at this rate.

Instead of pushing it, I'd happily joined Roxy this afternoon.

She was still setting up her new apartment. Since it was pack-sized, she had room for a nest.

She swore blind she'd never been happier now she was enrolled without needing a pack about, but I thought her week had been rough when it came to the Academy. She wouldn't go into detail, but she'd mentioned something about the other omegas, and I wondered if they were pushing her out.

I'd also prodded her to tell me what people were saying about me. I'd been so careful, even just hurrying down the hall to Roxy's place, since I didn't want to see anyone, but my time was running out. I needed to know what I might be facing. She hadn't wanted to give me the details, but I'd convinced her to give me the gist of it.

Everyone was, apparently, going with the Lincoln pack narrative, since I haven't been spotted. I'd tried not to imagine what people thought of that.

That I was the crazy stalker that was obsessed with them. That I'd wanted to be with them like that... I'd been seen coming into their party—even going into that room with Eric...

"You're in tonight, right?" Ransom asked Dusk, dragging me from my spiral. Dusk was standing from the couch where he'd been studying.

"Actually, I'm going to turn in." There was something odd about the smile on his face.

He'd been in and out of the bond more today, but now he was gone. I frowned, his figure departing down the hallway. I tried to refocus on what Ransom was saying. Umbra had caught my eye, though, and I realised he was a little worried about the bond.

Umbra nudged me. "You want to go?" he asked. I looked back to him and Ransom, who had settled happily under a blanket—which was definitely one I'd scent marked on my rampage. He nodded in agreement, eyes darting after Dusk too.

"We can show you another night if you want," Ransom said, clearly noticing something was up.

I considered that, staring down the hallway after Dusk. "Maybe..." I chewed on my lip, then got to my feet. There was something off about Dusk tonight. "You sure?" I glanced back at them.

They both nodded.

"Alright." I followed Dusk down the hallway. I was their omega. It was my job now to be paying attention to things like this.

I stood before his door for a long time, trying to figure out what I was going to say. I'd never actually... visited him like this. Like... like I wanted to spend time with him or see him.

Would he think it was odd? Did our relationship have room for that?

I took a breath and knocked, realising I'd been there for a while. I heard movement from within, and then the door opened. There was a little spark of confusion in his eyes as he peered down at me.

"Is everything okay?" he asked, glancing back down the hall to where Umbra and Ransom were already shouting over the game.

"Everything's fine. I just thought I could see what you were doing?"

"They were going to show you how to play," he said, frowning.

Hmm. Maybe I'd read it wrong. "I mean—if you'd rather be alone—"

"Never," he said, catching me off guard. "Would I rather be alone than with you."

"Oh." A whole different kind of buzz unsettled my stomach at that. "Okay."

There was a curve at the corner of his lips as his gaze dropped to where I tugged at my hair anxiously, then he stepped back in invitation. The first thing I noticed when I stepped in was the folder on the bed—the one with all of our data.

It was open, with pages scattered around.

His mission. Our mission.

I sat on the bed, watching as he took the bed beside me, eyes darting to the papers with a hint of yearning.

"You looked after them for a really long time," I said.

He raised an eyebrow, analysing me. "I did."

"Did you ever get tired of it?"

He let out an amused breath. "Quite the contrary."

I tried to detangle that, looking back at the pages. "You were uh... studying this again?" I asked, nudging the analysis on Ransom's sickness that I'd already committed to memory.

"If I read them out of order it helps me see it in a new light. And I'm going through your notes."

I nodded, considering that, and building up the courage for my question. "What... what would you be doing if you weren't doing this?"

Dusk barked a low laugh, fixing me with a curious gaze. "I'm a codependent shell. I don't think there is anything else."

I blinked, taken off guard by those words.

Dusk didn't talk about himself much. Actually, he never talked about himself. I'd never noticed that until those words settled over me, digging up more meaning with every second of silence that passed.

He didn't seem sad or upset, like the words might imply. He was carefully watching my reaction.

"They get on really well with each other," I said slowly, eyes drifting to the door for a second before returning to him.

He nodded. "They do."

"And they're healing each other."

A trace of humour crinkled his eyes as he drew back a little, taking me in more completely. "They are. It's good."

"And they don't need you... l-like they did before."

"No."

"You give me... balance." The word slipped out, as true as it was unexpected. Dusk had been the balance to my instincts at every turn. Ones that were supposed to be impossible to tame. "I... I need you."

There was a long beat. "It would be entirely unhealthy for that to make me feel better."

"Does it?" I asked.

A smile played on the corners of his lips, but he didn't answer.

"If they're healing each other," I said. "Who's healing you?"

"I don't know if there's anything that needs healing," he said.

I frowned. I didn't think that was true.

He was broken in his own quiet way.

"But you don't think you have anything else outside of... this?" I glanced at the papers across the bed.

"I suppose not." He looked at the pages too, his expression drawn. "I don't know when it happened. I just looked behind me one day and..." He trailed off, searching for words, but my whisper tumbled out.

"And it was spring, but... but the last thing you saw was snow..." I realised it might not make any sense at all, but his yellow eyes were fixed on me more intently than they ever had. "I... I'm just saying... there might be a way back from that."

It was the path I was on right now.

"I would like that."

I wanted to be theirs. And that meant it was my job to take care of him.

"But there are more important things to discuss."

"There are?" I asked. I looked to the papers on the bed. Had he made a breakthrough?

"Yes. Like the fact that you scent marked half of my clothes and shoved them under my bed—and then tried to lie to me about it yesterday."

"Um..." My gaze snapped to him, eyes wide.

"Why did you hide them?"

I don't know what I had been thinking. It had been a haze of instincts, and then panic... "I just thought... you're annoyed at me for talking you into dark bonding me—"

"I'm not annoyed at you."

"You... you aren't?"

He cocked his head. "I'm annoyed at myself. Not you."

"You shouldn't be."

"I don't want you second-guessing those sexy instincts of yours," he growled. "Understand?"

I nodded.

"I have to punish you for that. And the lie."

Something molten trickled into my core. "Y-you do?"

"But first, we're going to discuss my command the other day."

"Oh..."

"When we came back and Roxy was here, I need you to know I didn't mean for you to get hurt."

"I know," I replied. "You didn't know I was going to fight it."

"I should have, and I'm sorry," he said. He looked so earnest that I was getting all odd about it. I still wasn't used to Dusk apologies. "I'm going to be more careful."

I nodded. "Thank you."

"Now." He leaned back where he sat, raising an eyebrow. "Tell me why, when Ransom commanded you to kiss him back in the cabin, you got all hot and bothered."

Oh... I swallowed, suddenly finding his gaze very hard to meet. "Well..." I tapped my finger on my thigh. "It was sexy."

"I'm going to need a little more than that, Gem."

"It was like... I don't know. He's interested in me, and I like it when..." I trailed off, embarrassment making it impossible to meet his eyes.

"When what?"

Was I really about to admit this to Dusk?

"When he takes charge."

"Just Ransom?" he asked.

My voice was small as I wrung my shirt in my fists. "No."

"So. Tell me if I'm wrong: you like praise, you like it when I'm in charge..."

Oh shit. We were really going to talk about all of this?

"What about when I don't let you finish?" he asked.

"I don't know why that's so hot," I whispered.

He grinned. "A little praise and a little degradation. You're so sexy, Shatter."

That settled my heart a bit, even though it did seem like such an odd thing to like.

"I like it when... you get off too," I added. If we were already here, I might as well admit it.

"When I tell you that you can't?"

"Mhmm." My cheeks had never been this hot before.

"So it's a turn on when I tell you I'm going to use your sweet little body until I'm done?"

I chewed on my lip with another nod. There was slick pooling in my panties.

"Did you like it when we were out in public and you could get caught?"

"A bit."

"Did you like the idea of getting caught, or that it wasn't allowed?"

"Um..." I frowned. "That it wasn't allowed."

"And when I woke you on my cock?"

Oh... shit. My scent shifted at those words; his grin was enough to confirm that.

He adjusted so he was sitting beside me, and I had to look up into his eyes. "You're so perfect," he breathed, curling a finger beneath my chin. "But you are going to say if I ever have a command that makes you uncomfortable—from me or the others."

"Okay."

"And I need to know if there is anything you don't want to do."

I frowned. "Like... what?"

"I need to know if there's anything you don't want, or if anything has changed."

Changed?

It took me a moment before I realised what he meant.

The Lincoln pack.

For a second, my mind flashed back to that room, but I dug my nails into my palms to ground myself. "Did you uh... did you watch the video?" I asked, my voice quiet.

"No."

Oh.

Okay. That was... unexpected.

That was another thing I was going to have to face. A school of eyes that had seen that. Had seen Eric... Again, nails dug into palms.

"No." I shook my head. "Nothing has changed."

Not between me and Dusk. Not now he'd taken my scars. "I want... I want you to take it like you took... the scars."

I saw a flash of rare vulnerability in his eyes, as if he hadn't expected that.

"Is there anything else I should know about?"

"I..." I tapped my finger anxiously again. "About the uh... the punishments..."

Maybe I really shouldn't tell him this.

"What about them?"

"They make me really want to..." I winced. "...To fuck you."

Something humorous twinkled in his eyes. "The first time I bent you over the couch you were literally dripping through your panties for me."

"Yeh, but you... you pressed your dick against me, and I'd never been touched by an alpha—and then the other times you're always so... so I don't know... you always did other things at the same time, so I just thought—"

"Shatter, your scent gives you away if I even say the word punishment."

"You knew?" My voice was weak.

All this time?

I was going to die.

"You gotta quit being so fucking cute. I have a plan for the evening, and you're about to derail it."

"But it's not weird that I want you to... I don't know. That I like it?"

"No." He snorted. "And for what it's worth, I dream of turning your hot little ass pink and then fucking you until you scream my name." He leaned down and nipped my ear. "I love claiming you and ruining you—and doing it on my own terms."

Goosebumps rippled on my skin as his thumb brushed across his bite.

"Now, you're going to go into your nest and find the sexiest lingerie you can find. Then you'll go to the living room and wait for me in your usual place on the couch."

"Out there?" I asked, eyes wide.

Ransom.

Oh fuck. He was going to see at last.

"Yes."

"Can I cover up my bites—"

"Always," he said. "Now. Go and give them a show."

I was standing before I realised it, finding it so natural to give into his commands when I was this turned on. It didn't take me long to find something to wear.

Umbra and Ransom both looked up from the TV as I made my way down the hallway in black lace and a cream shirt that cut off at my waist.

I didn't meet either of their eyes as I stood at the edge of the couch, and then leaned forward, lowered my chest to the couch cushion below, my palms pressed at my sides.

The game paused, and wolfsbane and lily of the valley turned possessive.

"Little Reaper, *what* are you doing?"

"Waiting for Dusk," I said quietly.

I took a breath, relaxing in that position, relief coiling with anticipation as I waited.

DUSK

I found her waiting, with perfect obedience, in the living room. Her head was turned to the side, cheek pressed against the couch, and her stunning golden eyes found mine.

"Good girl," I purred, stepping up behind her and letting her feel how hard I was for her. She shifted back just a bit. I would never get tired of looking at her. Honey hair scattered about her in waves as she waited, presented like this.

The video game had paused, and Ransom was eyeing us both with interest while Umbra had his arms crossed, watching like it was a show he'd been waiting for.

"Tell them what you did, Gem?"

"I... I scent marked your room and then hid your stuff. And then I lied about it."

"And next time."

"I won't second guess my instincts."

I squeezed her ass, loving the way goosebumps rippled across her skin at the faintest touch. I'd let her wait for a while, knowing the anticipation would get to her.

She loved my punishments, and hearing her admit that at last was music to my ears. Now she was buzzing with contentment and relief. I monitored that closely as I flicked the clasp of my belt. She went extra still at the sound, and there was a definite spike of anticipation from her.

I tugged it off, withdrawing the small pot of massage oil from my pocket. I could swear she lifted her hips slightly, stifling the beginnings of a purr as I rubbed oil into her skin.

"Five, Gem," I warned her.

I had plans tonight beyond just this, and I didn't want to wait long to fuck her.

She let out a little whimper at the first strike, and I watched her skin turn pink from the mark.

"Good girl," I purred as I massaged the spot again. I dropped my finger to her panties, slipping my thumb into her cunt just to hear her moan. "Prop yourself up, let them see you properly."

Umbra growled with approval as she lifted herself up. His hand cupped her neck, pupils blowing, and wolfsbane was a drug in the air. Ransom had cocked his head, staring with utter intensity as he watched. In the bond, he was a mess, half shock, half lust.

"After you take your punishment, you're going to let me use your holes without complaint, aren't you?" I asked.

"Yes," she said, breathless.

"And you won't come tonight, not until I knot you."

I felt her shiver again. "No, Alpha."

Sweet mother above. I was done for if she started to use that term in earnest. Ransom's whole body was tense, as if he wanted to pounce on Shatter and sweep her up for himself. I felt a little shudder of that feral part of him surface, the unbalanced, possessive alpha that had grown up an only child, watching his omega being touched by someone who wasn't him.

Not just touching her, but turning her perfect skin pink.

I grinned, then leaned back, examining her. I shifted the shirt further up her back so I could see the way her ass tapered to her hips, and the goosebumps along her rich skin which glistened with the oil I'd rubbed into it. The black lace was barely present, a thin thong that shaped around her butt, accentuating her curves.

I readied my belt again, stepping back. Umbra had eyes only for her as he cupped her neck. The game controllers were left forgotten, and I watched as Ransom's slip to the floor without him noticing.

She let out another whine as the belt made contact with her flesh again.

By the time I reached the fifth, she was shivering, one hand gripping Umbra's wrist as she panted lightly. Slick was dripping down her thigh already.

I stepped back, and she straightened, turning to me. Her eyes were wide and dazed, lips parted. I cupped her chin.

"You're going to go back to my room and put on the blindfold that's on my bedside table. Then lie on the edge of my bed and play with yourself until you're about to come." Her mouth dropped open, but I wasn't done. "Then you'll switch to fingering your sweet pussy until you're close again. You'll keep doing that until I tell you to stop."

All she could do was nod, eyes wide.

"Go on."

She took a step backward, darting her gaze to Umbra and Ransom before hurrying back down the hall to my room.

Both of them turned to me, and I buried my smile at the look of utter shock on Ransom's face.

"We can watch, right?" he asked weakly.

"Absolutely not."

"But we're pack."

My grin widened. I swear at the sound Shatter made on the third strike, I'd felt a flicker of murder from him. Lust—absolutely, but I got the impression he had been on the edge of wrestling the belt from me to take over.

"You can dream about it," I said.

"You're going to… stay in here while she…?" Ransom trailed off.

"God no. I'm going to go and watch."

The sight that met me when I entered my room put to shame every imagining.

Shatter lay on my bed, knees up as she dipped two fingers into herself—which meant she'd come close to the edge already. Even from the doorway, I could see her body shivering.

I watched for a while, in a constant state of war with my own self control. She was hottest when being edged. Her whines became so desperate, and then the orgasm she got at the end was beautiful

Finally, I joined her, crouching down and pressing my finger to her entrance. She jumped, a moan sounding from her chest.

"Dusk?"

"Yes," I answered, dipping into her with a second finger, watching her arch against the sheets.

"I…" Her voice shook. "I want your knot."

"You're going to take my knot, beautiful, but I'm going to play with you first."

I stood and removed the rest of my clothes.

"You can stop touching yourself," I said. She uncurled from her position, already shaking with exhaustion.

"Stand up."

I helped guide her to her feet, so she was before me, then I pressed her hands to my chest. I paused for a moment as she ran her touch up and over the healing brands. Then one of her hands dropped to my cock and circled it as she pressed her lips to the mark I'd made for her.

I growled, almost pinning her to the bed and claiming her right there.

"I want..." Her voice was breathless. "I want it to be like when you used to punish me."

I nudged her chin up. I knew what that meant to her. I hadn't seen the video, but I knew what it contained. I knew what Eric had done.

She wanted me to take it back from him, like I'd taken the scars.

"Tell me who you belong to," I breathed.

She hesitated only a moment, brows creasing at the unfamiliar question. "You."

"And these perfect lips?" I asked, thumb pressing against them.

"Yours, Alpha," her voice was quiet, almost sultry, and her scent had become more needy than ever before. There was a warmth to it that was new, a side.

It read, to me, as safety.

Trust.

Something more absolute than I'd ever felt from her.

There was a low rumble in my chest.

"You're going to use them to get me off," I told her. "You're going to keep playing with yourself, and the closer you get to your orgasm, the more you're going to choke yourself. I want to finish in your tight throat before I let you finish. Is that clear?"

"Yes, Alpha," she replied, lip caught in her teeth, nightshade becoming an aphrodisiac.

It wasn't that I had to use commands. I knew she would do what I said, but the feeling of her submitting to me like this, it was a high I had never anticipated. It was more than just about how hot it was; it was her trust, and the safety she felt whenever she allowed herself to be swept away by the command.

Her scent was a storm of lust in the room as she sank to the floor, fingers not leaving my length as she did. I groaned as she took my tip between her lips and began to work my cock.

I closed my fingers in her hair and around the blindfold so I was everywhere for her, but I let her do the work, my command driving her onwards.

It wasn't long before she was shaking as she neared her own orgasm, taking me deeper and deeper. Knowing that drew me right to my climax, and the nails of her free hand dug into my thigh as she dragged herself over my cock.

"Fuck, you're so goddamned beautiful," I groaned, tugging the blindfold from her.

This was on another level, feeling the command between us, seeing her eyes water as she desperately choked herself on my cock, shuddering with an orgasm she couldn't reach.

Her nails drew blood along my thigh as I came, grip rough in her hair as I unloaded down her throat.

She was panting when I released her, and I had to help her to her feet before I lifted her in my arms and set her down on the bed near the headboard. She let out little moans with almost every touch, and with what strength she had left, she tried to drag me closer.

"I want you," she whined.

"You'll have me, Gem. I'm going to take care of you." I pressed kisses along her skin, careful around the healing wounds. "When you were out there, did you want them to join in?" I asked.

"Yes." She'd chosen me tonight, and I would be just a tiny bit selfish about that. I would keep her to myself, but not forever.

"You're going to take us all, aren't you? There are so many ways we're going to ruin you." I drew her closer, lifting her hips enough that I could line it up against her entrance.

There was a low, feral growl in her chest as she felt me, and her back arched, trying to take me sooner.

"I'm going to enjoy watching Ransom and Umbra take you while I claim your throat," I breathed, pressing into her all the way. I leaned forward, cupping her neck, my thumb brushing the bite I'd given her as I rocked into her. "Squeeze me, precious."

"Mmm," the sound that rose in her throat as I felt her tight cunt clench over me like a vice was so hot.

"Fuck." I almost came right then. "Would you be able to take us all?" I asked as I slid out of her slowly. "Your whole pack at once?"

She nodded, a needy whine slipping out at the words. Her fingers dug into my hair to the point of pain as I slammed back in and set a pace to leave the whole bed shaking. The sounds coming from her with each stroke were so hot, more so, knowing they'd be loud enough that Umbra and Ransom could probably hear.

"Would you like that? Letting them fill you up while I told you to fuck them however I want?"

"Yes," she whined, arching against me so she could take me deeper with each thrust. "Please," she begged. "Knot me, Dusk."

She was shaking, each exhale accompanied by a little moan.

That was enough to send me over the edge. I slammed in. She cried out, her whole body seizing over me as I pressed my knot into her.

Fuck. Me.

My grip was punishing on her waist as I rutted her with my knot buried deep, finishing violently as her whole body arched, grip enough to tear my hair out as she was wrecked by the orgasm she'd been denied for so long.

I turned us so she was resting on my chest, and I propped myself up at the head of the bed. She curled up against me, still shivering with little aftershocks.

I wrapped my arms around her, pulling covers over us and

holding her close. It was a long time before she surfaced, and still her eyes were dazed as she peered up at me. I traced circles on her skin with my thumb ever so gently, almost touching one of her wounds. I had helped her treat them again this morning, and they were healing bit by bit.

"I want to go out with Roxy tomorrow," she whispered. "To pick out a dress."

"For the ball?" I asked.

"Yes."

"You've decided?" I asked.

"I... I need to do it. I want to."

"Alright. Then we're going." I'd already checked with Umbra, and he was good to visit Vandle with Decebal. If Shatter wanted to ruin the Lincoln pack at the ball on Saturday, I would hold her hand the whole way.

THIRTY-THREE

SHATTER

I gazed up at the fancy dress shop through Roxy's car window. It had that high-end look, and I always pictured Aunty Lauren shopping at places like that.

Nervous, I'd kept my contacts in and my hoodie up, hiding my bond when we left the apartment, and don't think anyone noticed me.

Dusk caught up to us when we reached Roxy's car, insisting he could drive and wait outside, but Roxy practically beat him back with her handbag then bundled me into the passenger side door.

Ransom had given me one of the plastic money cards he used at the mall, along with the secret four-digit number. He said I could buy whatever I wanted. I thought that was a good thing, but when I told Roxy that at Starbucks she nearly choked on her cream-topped drink.

"So. Revenge dress?" Roxy grinned, eyeing me. I nodded, ready. "I need to know I can face them. And if I'm doing it, I'll do it with all the strength I can muster. You need one too."

"A dress?" she asked.

"A revenge dress." I'd looked it up. We both qualified for one as far as I could tell. The Lincoln pack had dumped her, right?

"Both for the same pack?" Roxy's face lit up. "That's going to be amazing."

In a huge changing room with light pink decor, we had a dozen dresses to try. The woman at the front eyed my oversized hoodie (Umbra's), but Roxy looked like she belonged, so they let us in.

Roxy went first, pulling the curtain back every few minutes so I could see her in dress after stunning dress while she gave me a rundown on the ball politics.

"It's a charity ball," she was saying as I heard her wrestle with fabric behind the curtains. "The Lincoln pack announced they're officially open to omega applicants, and there was an announcement that they made an 'exceptional donation', so they get honorary seating."

"What does that mean?" I asked.

"Probably that they're put up at a head table. I'm sure they want to look like they rule the place. But—" Roxy cut off with a little hiss of frustration. "One sec. Zipper." She drew the curtain to reveal a pretty, sapphire blue dress that was half done up at the side. I helped her hold it together so she could tug it closed. "The event organisers are apparently in a scramble because there was another last-minute donation. They're setting up honorary seating for another pack."

"Another pack?" I asked.

Roxy gave me a sly smile before adjusting the dress over her bra. "Your pack. Definitely."

I considered that. If she was right, we were going to be front and centre. I was going to be making a statement.

Roxy glanced at herself in the mirror. "A bit bulky I think. I'll be sweating."

"I love the colour," I added. "Matches your eyes."

I sat on the pink vintage couch as Roxy requested a less bulky dress in the deep sapphire colour, mulling over what she'd said.

I glanced at the rack of dresses I'd chosen, eyes falling on one in particular. The most daring one.

Could I...? I wondered.

"If I arrive at the ball dark bonded, with golden eyes on display, they'll think it was Dusk, won't they? They'll think I am the victim?"

Roxy looked over at me, a frown on her face. "I think... the moment the truth comes out, people will think that you were caught in the middle."

In other words, they wouldn't know any of this was my choice—that the bond wasn't my choice.

But the Lincoln pack already believed I was pathetic.

Roxy vanished behind the curtain to try on the dress she'd been handed, leaving me to think.

Decebal had sent me some studies at last, and I'd read some fascinating, if unfinished, studies on the correlation between aura instability and aura strength. The reason it had been cut short wasn't mentioned, but the last thing the study had listed was man-made impacts on unstable auras.

It would make sense that the Institute wouldn't want the knowledge of how to artificially destabilise auras to be public knowledge. But if they cut the study short, then it also implied they knew what the results might show.

I thought back to the trials that Umbra and Dusk had been in. Pushed to the edge. Caged up. Atropa's poison put into the very air they breathed.

Was that knowledge already in the hands of others?

People who were using it for their own gain. For money.

It hadn't just been about bets. What they'd done to Umbra and Dusk was deliberate and calculated. Decebal and Dusk had listed extensive theories, linking the bets to the tests, believing that they were studying endurance.

Weaponising alphas wasn't a new concept; there was money in that, and wars that depended on it. It wasn't a bad theory. Ransom had helped me figure out my computer well enough now that I'd researched the history of Atropa's Poison. It was a drug developed for war. Alphas were resilient to some of the worst chemical warfare, and their primary weakness, Agritox, was a reactive compound, and thus confined to physical forms like bullets. The compound, because of its unpredictable nature, posed challenges in large-scale production for warfare, requiring advanced facilities and expertise.

But Atropa's Poison could be used as a gas and, instead of killing alphas, turned them on each other. It was a way to take out enemy packs on the front line, not only neutralising the effects of aura-steroids banned by the Geneva Convention for front line use—but turning those very alphas against their own.

It wasn't at all far-fetched that the tests were weapons-based and were trialling alpha resiliency to different drugs or stressors. It would also explain their desire for alphas from the Cimmerian Vaults, as those might be in line with alphas on the front line if illegal steroids had been used. Their top theory was that the Lincoln pack were perhaps involved in funding to get the first claim of a drug that would make their auras stronger.

It wasn't a terrible theory. And alpha auras were connected with one another when they were in a pack.

Were they trying to find a way to... to replicate that outside of a pack? To take the strength of one alpha and give it to another?

Yet, the more I considered the tests, the less sense the theories made. The testing had been erratic. Umbra had been picked over and over again. He'd convinced them to take him instead of Dusk, but his repeated selection made it an unreliable benchmark.

I didn't think that they were intending to get stable data.

It didn't seem as though their pack was being measured at all. Rather, they were the ones being tested—pushed and pulled in one way or another.

To what, though? I had no idea, but I was close to a breakthrough. I could feel it. I'd been scouring texts on omegas balancing packs and how it worked.

I wasn't there yet; I didn't have answers, but from everything I understood about omega-alpha relations, my role was important.

I was an anchor in the pack.

There was a chance, if a solution presented itself, I may be the centre of that.

It was the part I would never say to Dusk.

Already, people thought so little of me at the Academy—outside of Roxy and my pack. I'd tried over and over to fit in, to be what they wanted me to be, and I'd failed.

And I'd found love anyway. My pack and my friend, they wanted me as I was.

Roxy settled on a stunning velvet dress in the same rich blue, and then it was my turn. I stood, crossing to the rack and lifting the daring black dress from it.

I didn't think I was going to take long.

This had to be the one.

It was the scariest thing I'd ever done, opening the curtain for Roxy to see me once I had managed to get it on, glad to find it was a perfect fit.

As I expected, her eyes went wide, face blanching. I braced for the worst, and yet as her gaze traced each mark across my chest and arm, the bites that the dress didn't hide, I realised the truth I'd been hoping for when it came to my scars—one I could never have known until this moment. It was a truth that no one else knew—not even Roxy.

These marks no longer belonged to the Lincoln pack.

Dusk had claimed every single one of them, and showing

them off, that, to me, was like showing off this bond that I loved so much.

No one else had to understand.

"Is it okay?" I asked.

"Shatter, it's beautiful but…" She trailed off, like she wasn't sure how to say what she was thinking.

"No one will believe I would choose to show these?" I asked.

I knew that.

"I don't believe in shame, Shatter. I don't, but if you don't want the narrative—"

"I do." Dusk wanted that narrative, and I knew now that I wanted it too.

"You do?"

"He… he wants to protect me with it. I agreed to that."

"They won't just think he claimed you, Shatter, they're going to think he's cruel."

I swallowed, glancing down at the smooth black fabric, and the bites that were on display. "That's okay."

Dusk didn't give a shit what anyone thought of him. He never had. I envied that about him. And it was my own little claim to something powerful in a way, choosing this, and knowing everyone would read into it exactly what I wanted them to.

Everyone was wary of my alphas. Dusk was an unknown, and people thought Umbra was unstable. If the world wanted to see me as a victim, as weak and pathetic and small, I would let them.

Because there might be a time in the future where I could use that to protect them, just like they protected me.

THIRTY-FOUR

UMBRA

It was late Saturday afternoon.

Ball day, and revenge dress day. Since I was going out with Decebal this evening, Shatter had told me she wanted me to see her before I left.

I stepped into Shatter's nest at last, as Roxy ushered me in. It was messy; the bed scattered with boxes of makeup, brushes, straighteners, and all the stuff Roxy had brought. But I noticed that for only the briefest of seconds as my eyes found my omega.

Shatter...

I lost my breath entirely.

Holy *fucking* shit.

She waited beside her desk, looking anxiously over at me.

Her dress was black, with delicately thin straps and a neckline that dipped scandalously low. It clung gently to slender curves before tumbling to the floor. It had a slit to her upper thighs, through which her smooth legs and golden heels peeked through.

I'd heard her debating with Roxy in the living room earlier over the heels; she liked them but wasn't sure she'd be able to stay upright. She'd decided to risk them when Dusk and Ransom swore they (or Roxy) would be with her the whole time so there was no chance she'd fall.

When she turned, showing it off for me, I saw the back of the dress dipped to her tailbone. Her hair was stunning, and it was still *her*, volume tumbling over her shoulder and down her back, but the honey brown mane was a silky jumble of curls and waves. I noticed by the way it fell right now, it was covering her chest. The place I knew the marks were.

Beneath, how much of the dress hid them?

I noticed she wore a necklace like the one she'd had before, only now it was golden. It had our pack's symbol and a new star, with Dusk's bite contrasted beneath it.

I'd crossed the room before I realised, stopping before her.

"Alright, I'll leave you two alone." That was Roxy, who I'd entirely forgotten was here. I glanced over to see her grabbing an armful of the beauty supplies. "See you there."

"You're sitting with us, right?" Shatter asked Roxy as she was leaving.

"Yup. Just gotta finish getting ready—and *don't* ruin the makeup."

I dragged my gaze from Shatter to see Roxy narrowing her eyes at me.

Ruin it?

Roxy couldn't rightly assist in making Shatter look like a golden goddess and then drop *that* bomb on me.

I was going to ruin my omega.

If the makeup wasn't good quality, that wasn't my fault.

There was another long second of silence as it closed, and Shatter's cheeks went pinker than ever as she looked back at me.

"I'm really not sure about the heels." She peered down at them, and I admired their beautiful gold shine that matched her so well. "I'm not good at walking in them—"

"I love them," I said quietly.

"Do you?"

"They're perfect," I told her. "*And* it means you can't get away from me," I added.

Bonus.

"You don't think it's too... too much?"

"You are going to steal the show." No doubt about it. I was seeing her now, since Decebal would be here in half an hour to pick me up.

Dusk had made that massive donation to get them a throne tonight, but it meant he had to go to the ceremonies beforehand and get thanked a bunch and all of that dull shit, while Ransom got to escort her in. So Dusk wouldn't see Shatter until she walked into the ball when it began.

By the look of her, I thought he might faint.

Shame I'd miss it.

And it wasn't just the captivating outfit and shimmery makeup—or even the way in which she wore it, with adorable excitement she deserved, it was the dark bond. The way it was on full display, and she was putting that on display for the world.

It made me rock fucking hard just knowing that.

"Okay. Well. Good," she said. "Because Roxy made it so pretty."

"And no scent blockers?" I asked.

She shook her head, a flicker of determination in her eyes.

Her hands were at her chest, pressing her waterfall of curls close. I could see shimmering golden swirls across her skin, over her collarbones, and... Something got stuck in my throat as I saw the trace of a wound peeking out from where her hair fell.

The marks she'd been too afraid to show me before now.

Gently, she took my hand and lifted it to her chest. "You... you can see," she whispered.

I held her gaze for a long silence, thumb brushing her skin.

Finally, I moved her locks, sweeping them back and over her shoulder, still holding her eyes.

It took every ounce of courage I had to drop my gaze.

When I did, the marks I saw across her skin sent ice through my veins.

I'd expected the worst, but I hadn't truly known what the worst might look like. I counted at least ten, and one mangled mark beside her collarbone that looked like it had been bitten twice. They were surrounded by swirls and patterns in gold, but I couldn't see that, not when those marks each symbolised her pain.

Her fear.

Fear I hadn't protected her from.

My monster stirred, howling and ready to kill.

I would *never* have bitten her like that. Alpha bites healed differently than normal wounds, the bite I'd given her at the start of term wouldn't scar—it wasn't deep enough, and it wasn't a bonding mark. But the Lincoln pack had ensured the wounds they'd given her wouldn't heal.

Her hand came to my cheek, scent calm in the air. There wasn't anything fearful in it like there had been in the hot tub.

"They're yours, not theirs," she said. It was the first time I felt a flicker of fear from her, as if she was making an offer she wasn't sure I would accept.

I forced myself to look back, to understand those words. The bites across her flesh—though vicious and cruel—were also beautiful. I saw the gold, now. Truly saw it. Roxy had used shimmering paint, and delicate lines had been drawn across her skin, outlining each bite like it was precious.

I looked again, following the marks as if they were constellations, realising that it was the same pattern Dusk now had across his chest.

"They're... ours?" I said.

"If..." She swallowed. "If you want—"

I cut her off so she could never finish that with uncertainty, pressing my lips to hers and drawing her close.

There was a spark of joy from her down the bond.

"Sit," I commanded.

I loved her, and she was everything right now, claiming those marks for us. I sank down before her and hooked my hands behind her knees.

Fuck, she was beautiful. A black and gold goddess, honey brown hair almost matching her tanned skin in the low light. She smiled, and a purr rose in my chest as her fingers tangled in my hair, forcing my head back so she could look into my eyes.

"I love you so much, Little Nightshade," I breathed.

There was shimmery makeup smudged across eyes, necklace, and bites. The distinct golden swirls reached down her arms, and there were even a few between the laces of her heels and up her thighs.

I traced my lips along the marks on her calf, easily drawing her closer as I kissed higher and higher. The dress was light, and easy to push up.

I could worship her forever.

She let out a little breath of pleasure as I dragged her closer so her butt was right on the edge of the bed.

I pressed her dress up again and tugged her panties down. Her legs tangled over my shoulders, and she let out the cutest little breath of pleasure as I found her clit with my tongue. She had to let go of my hair to catch herself on the bed, since I wasn't too concerned at all with her balance.

Nightshade flooded the room, dark and sweet.

She felt safe with me, even when I'd seen her scars.

That was all I needed.

I would never get tired of the taste of her, or the way she let out the sweetest little moans when I treated her just right, or when I slid a finger inside of her, working deep.

She was so sensitive that she was shuddering over me in less than a minute, which was good because it meant I had time to go again. This time I lifted us, laying down on the bed and dragging her over me.

It was easy to hold her steady and beautifully suffocating over my face, and I was in fucking heaven. She was shivering, whines so sweet I might lose myself entirely and say fuck the night and the ball and the rest of the world and just lock us in so I could keep going.

I worked my fingers deeper this time, and with a deep shuddering moan she came again, spilling juices over my face.

Fuck.

Yes.

When I drew away, she was panting, cheeks pink and cute.

I wished we had more time tonight. How I wanted to see her come apart for me until she broke for me again. I loved her.

I loved that, even in this dress, she was shy, anxious Shatter underneath it all. My omega.

It made it so much sexier.

Also, Roxy's makeup was perfectly fine, so she wouldn't have my head.

When I stood, she also got up, even if she was unsteady with the heels and her climax. "It's not dangerous, what you're doing tonight, is it?" she asked.

"Nothing like that." It was a long shot more than anything else, but now I had dreams of glasses and banana splits, so I'd try whatever there was to try.

I tugged a handkerchief from my pocket.

"This is the one to scent mark?" she asked.

I nodded. She knew I was trying for answers tonight.

She drew it along her jaw, her scent dousing the air. I tucked it into my pocket.

"I love you."

Warmth bloomed in my chest, hearing her whisper those words to me, and I seized her by the hair, drawing her up into a kiss, a growl in my chest.

For a moment, I forget everything else.

I forgot the weight I carried.

I needed answers from Vandle because I couldn't hide the truth from her forever. It was a truth that even Dusk hadn't noticed.

I was at the front line.

The sickness always reached me first.

I hated it, and it didn't make sense because I knew Shatter was perfect. She'd saved Ransom—saved us all.

But when Shatter had entered the bond, it hadn't stabilised.

At first I thought I must be imagining it, but with every day that passed, it had become impossible to ignore. My nightmares grew like stretching shadows in the evening, claws extending, a darkness getting closer and closer.

Even now I had to check that my blade was in my pocket.

The thing that kept me safe when I had to leave her side.

Because since Shatter had joined our pack, my sickness was getting worse faster than it ever had before.

And tonight, I had to get answers.

THIRTY-FIVE

DUSK

The ballroom was decorated similarly to how it had been the night of the choosing. Crystal chandeliers adorned the ceiling, their lights reflecting off every surface to bathe the room in a warm glow. The second floor had been opened up as the guest count went beyond just academy students.

The main floor buzzed with a low energy already. There were staff members setting things up, and early guests, which included me, the Lincoln pack, and the charity event organisers and representatives.

The Lincoln pack's setup mirrored ours: our seats were stationed on raised platforms against the wall, with lavish decor leaving them looking something like thrones. Beside the setup was a long table with four seats for us to take when we wanted to eat. Thank God, since sitting here alone made me sick of this obscene display—designed, I was sure, to encourage such donations like the ones we'd made.

The Lincoln pack were far enough away that I could see them —which I much preferred—but couldn't catch their scents.

Good.

That meant Shatter would have more control when she arrived. They wouldn't catch her scent straight away.

It had been a dull few hours. I'd been thanked repeatedly for my donation to the New Oxford Arkologic Research Foundation. The foundation members and other donors were socialising already, drinking champagne before the main event, and—from what I'd heard—discussing things like upcoming research strategies and the impact of new studies on prevalent diseases.

The staff, who were flitting around and setting things up, were dressed in formal attire. The room smelled like the subtle muted presence of scent dampeners and flowers, which were arranged on every table.

It was about half an hour from the official opening when I spotted Roxy enter. She wore a deep blue dress, ideal for the revenge Shatter had told me she was also claiming tonight.

We were over halfway through the first term, which meant seeking partners outside of those that were originally chosen was back on the table. The politics were a bit more messy, as packs didn't often like to announce they were dropping their omegas ahead of time—and most didn't do what the Lincoln pack had, which was considered quite extreme.

I didn't think Roxy would have trouble finding a pack, but I didn't think she was looking for one. I had helped Umbra and Ransom carry some of her new furniture into her apartment over the last week, and when I entered, it was hard not to look around for the Christmas baking and gifts beneath the tree. I swear she'd left her festive scent mark on every surface. She'd thoroughly claimed the whole damn place, and I got the impression that she was very happy being pack free.

"How is she?" I asked as Roxy plucked a wine bottle from the table beside us and poured herself a tall glass.

"Nervous." She took a seat, her orange and fir tree scent was present, though muted beneath scent dampening spray. She chose the seat beside me as, with the two of us, it would look odd for her not to. I didn't mind, besides. Shatter had extended the invite, and she had proven she had nothing but Shatter's best interests at heart. "But she is going to devastate them," she added. "You just wait until you see her."

Roxy looked the picture of vengeance as her gaze slid, just briefly, to the pack across the hall. I followed her gaze to see the Lincoln pack were in utter shock. They were staring, the whites of their wide eyes clear as day, even across the room. Flynn's mouth had dropped open, and Eric had frozen with a glass to his lips.

"That's a pretty sight," she said.

"I agree." The first blow of the evening, seeing Roxy join me. They'd think this was the play. That we were claiming her after they'd dropped her.

"They aren't ready for tonight," she mused.

"I don't think so." It was a pleasant thought. Before this, I thought I was nothing more than a hunter. It was part of who I was, chasing down those who had wronged us, who had caused the death and suffering of every alpha at that facility and making them feel that same pain before they died. But what Shatter was about to do to the Lincoln pack? It was satisfying in an entirely different way.

I would take anything, since I, quite literally, couldn't touch them.

I was still working on ways around that.

"It was a good play, out donating them," Roxy said. "I bet they weren't happy."

I grinned. "I've been told I have a flair for the dramatics." The Lincoln pack had been giving me smug looks all week, which didn't help the constant urge I had to tear them into little pieces, but this afternoon they'd been stiff as I collected the majority of the praise by doubling the donation they'd made in order to secure the spotlight for the day.

And they didn't yet know that it was a spotlight I'd claimed for her.

Despite the occasional tremor from Shatter through the bond, there was enough conviction to drown it out. A determination that had been building since she and Roxy had gone shopping yesterday.

Tonight was everything.

The Lincoln pack would realise what we'd taken. It was a part of the torture I needed them to carry: to know that they'd failed—that she was stronger than the pain they had given her.

They would know their own loss before I finished them. And Shatter, my omega, she would be free. Free of the foul mates the universe had destined for her. Free of the torment they'd believed had been enough to leave her crushed.

This was everything I wanted for her, and I would be at her side every step of the way.

Today, she was brave enough to face her monsters.

And if Shatter wanted to claim tonight to destroy the monsters who believed they could break her, then I would make her a queen and put her on a fucking throne.

UMBRA

Where Decebal and I were going tonight wasn't the sort of place I ever wanted Shatter to step foot in.

We parked before a daunting-looking building. It was out of the city and far from prying eyes, a place so isolated that everyone else could forget it existed.

That's what everyone preferred to do with things like this—things that didn't fit.

Hide them away and pretend they don't exist.

Shut the doors and close your eyes...

It was mid-afternoon when we arrived, and the weather was miserable. Huge, angry waves smashed into the rocks and beach below, and the wind howled.

Appropriately ominous, I thought, as I looked at the huge building inset just a bit on the cliff edge. It looked like an old fortress, forest on one side, ocean on the other.

There was nowhere in that building where crashing waves couldn't be heard, or the tang of ocean salt and washed-up seaweed wasn't present in the air, strong enough to taste. Out here it blended with the damp earth and forest that stretched behind.

I knew that, and didn't know that all at the same time. I had no memories, just a certainty that it was so.

I also knew the darkness within. The thick walls of stone. Cages of metal designed to keep alpha auras contained.

When we stepped up to the front doors, we were met by guards. I let Decebal deal with the formalities, instead staring up at the weathered walls.

We were made to sign a waiver, show our IDs, and given a long speech about safety and regulations that I tuned out entirely before we were accepted inside. I don't know who Decebal was pretending we were. Probably should though, in case they asked. It was alright though, I could just act stupid and let Decebal do the talking.

Dusk had been with us when we'd come last, and he'd hated every moment. I'd found a strange solace here.

It was cold inside—no amount of heating could truly warm up the bones of a place like this. But cold was a sanctuary after the harshest of burns...

For Dusk, this place was the face of an old enemy.

For me it was an old friend.

Our footsteps echoed with strange familiarity as we entered a hallway with dim, flickering lights that looked out of place against the stone. Even the electricity in here struggled to contend with the atmosphere, with a building that was truly a living, breathing creature. The faint metallic smell of old metal bars and aged electrics that struggled to survive lurked in every inch of this place.

It wasn't long before I heard the faint howling from within. Screams and cries; the sweet serenade of insanity. It was an old companion, a dream always just out of reach... I'd never quite been there, I didn't think. Always yearning, yet never arriving. Not like some, whose world was washed away, and when the tide drew back the lines in the sand were gone, completely.

All payments.

All debts.

The immortal vice, unbound at last...

"You alright?" Decebal asked, glancing at me.

I realised I'd started humming.

"Yup."

More than.

I did quite like it here, and I'd forgotten the comfort it offered. I'd never found that again—well, not until Shatter, anyway.

I smiled at the thought of Shatter, and the guard who was leading us into the gaping mouth of my oldest companion gave me a strange look—likely because I'd begun humming again.

He didn't recognise me. Dusk and I were completely different people than we had been before, and Decebal had checked the staff. They turned over guards far too often for that to be a concern.

He led us up some stairs and down a few more hallways, and all the while the howls and screams of prisoners grew. As we stepped through a colonnade, I peered down at a courtyard. It was empty right now, broad, with large metal structures, for exercise. And the gates on either end were barred. It was all made with the same metal. The kind that stopped even the strongest of alphas, auras and all.

What a cost it must have been, building a place like this. It's why the prison was a fortress made of stone, I was sure. So they could minimise the amount of metal they needed.

Finally, we stopped at a door, and the guard dug in his pocket, pulling out a set of keys. He unlocked it, opened it, and waved us through. A few of the howls rose louder in the air, their owners clearly now far off.

"Cell twenty-three."

Decebal thanked him, and we entered. It became warmer as we stepped in, diverted into the limited capacity they had for the living spaces.

The hallway was wide, and understandably so, as the cells were on either side. Flaking paint along the floor marked the safe-zone the guard had warned us about at the gates. A flailing few arms, taut as they reached from between cell bars signalled the cost of a misstep. The auras were thick in the space, though there was a heavy mist of scent dampeners in the air, a small attempt to limit chaos. The scent of dampeners didn't hide everything, though, not the musty dampness that lingered in every crack, or the acrid tang of sweat, fear, and madness from the alphas within.

Decebal led the way, and I lingered, unable not to peer into every cell we passed, to meet the vacant eyes of the alphas within.

And each was a harrowing mirror of what I knew I'd once been.

THIRTY-SIX

RANSOM

"Am I going to have to carry you in there?"

Shatter was very cute to watch, stumbling up the pathways to the main building, continuing to let go of me so she could get her practice in before the ball.

"I think I basically got it—oop!" She caught the back of her heel on her dress and stumbled. I caught her before she fell, captivated by the grin on her face.

Once we got to the entrance hall, she made me escort her to the bathroom so she could check her makeup and hair before she took off her shawl.

She might be smiling for me, but inside, she was a ball of wound-up anxiety. I peered around while she was inside, noticing a worker tugging open the entrance to the stairs, opening up the balcony above, a rather cheeky idea popping into my head.

When he returned, I swept her into my arms, ignoring her squeak of surprise as I carried her up the side stairway instead of through the main doors.

"What are you doing?"

"Detour," I told her.

She was too nervous, still.

I could fix that.

I set her down before the balcony railing that overlooked a beautiful ballroom. The evening had begun below; music played, and the party had begun with drinks and dancing. The low sound of chatter rose in the air. I'd picked a spot on the balcony that was above the side of the room where the platformed seating was set up. That meant we could neither see the Lincoln pack nor Dusk.

Good, and good, since he'd denied me the opportunity to watch them the other night.

"Hands on the railings, Little Reaper," I told her. "And don't let go."

"Uh... Why?" Her voice was suddenly nervous as I used the bond.

If she was starting to believe dark bond commands meant sex, she was dead on. I enjoyed how blindsided she was by everything, though, so I didn't say anything. "Tonight, Dusk is going to put you on a throne, so I'm going to fuck you in front of all the peasants."

She let out a breath of shock. "*Ransom*. That's really rude."

I chuckled, nipping her ear, cupping her neck. Fuck, I loved how she melted against me at any sign of dominance, the faintest vibration of a purr in her chest like she couldn't help herself.

"Hold up," she said, as if trying to fight her reaction to my touch. "Aren't there people up here?" she said. "And anyone can look up and see us."

She was so precious. "They can, can't they?"

"But we'll be late," she whispered, eyes still darting about for passersby.

"You know, Umbra was right. Seeing you and Dusk was quite the show. But I can't say it didn't make me a little jealous. If I delay him seeing you like this because you're—what were his words... letting me use your holes without complaint? I think I can live with that."

"Right now?" she asked.

I tugged at her dress. The silk was cool and thin enough that it was easy to shift the slit over her hips without revealing her to the whole ballroom.

"Arch your back for me," I breathed. The heels were perfect for this, getting her so much closer to my height.

"You can't," she pleaded as I tugged at her panties.

"You're tense, Little Reaper," I breathed. "I'm going to help you relax."

"Umbra already did."

I laughed, pressing a kiss against her neck, freeing my own cock with a decent amount of subtlety beneath the waves of black silk. "Tell me the truth. Do you really not want me to fuck you?" I asked.

"I..." She let out a little whine of irritation at the command. "I always do, it doesn't mean we *should*—" She cut off with a breath of shock as I drove my cock into her without warning. When she whined like that—it didn't matter if it was rage, or brattiness—I just needed to fucking claim her.

"You take me so good, Little Reaper," I growled.

"Wait—!" Her voice was breathless.

"Yes?" I asked, pressing into her deeper as I cupped her neck and ran my teeth along her jaw.

"We're right in the middle of the party." Her voice was weak.

They wouldn't. We'd arrived just as they were opening the balcony, and I'd told a worker to close it off for another half hour before letting anyone else up while she was in the washroom.

The only view anyone was getting was from below, and they wouldn't see much. Not that I was against that at all, but she was ever so shy.

"Was Dusk lying when he told me you're wet for him when he plays with you around the academy?"

"Well…" She swallowed. "He's…" She trailed off. "He's Dusk."

"So you're happy for someone to catch you being claimed by him, but not me?"

"That's not…" She let out a breath as I slid into her. "Not what I meant. And we weren't in the middle of a—a party."

"Well, maybe it's a bit more my thing." I'd fuck her on a stage with an audience and wouldn't blink but I think that might make her faint. "Turn around."

I drew out of her, careful to keep track of her dress so when I lifted her and set her on the railing, she was covered.

"What—Ransom!" Her arms wrapped around my neck, and she glanced back over the ledge.

"You think I'm going to drop you?" I asked with a grin, letting my aura flare slightly as I stepped close, nudging her knees apart. With one hand tangled in her hair and the other at her hips I drove into her.

She let out the sweetest little moan, slender arms still wound around my neck. I saw her glance over her shoulder again, eyes wide as she took in the crowd below.

"Do you want me to let you down?" I asked.

Her eyes snapped back to me, and I saw a flicker of a thrill in them.

Oh, she was so very into this.

I grinned, and she let out a little gasp as I dragged her back over my length roughly.

"Good girl," I breathed, driving into her again, palms resting on the small of her back, feeling her heels dig into my back as she wrapped her legs around me, too.

She was so beautiful, though the bond and ball of nervous energy, flitting between humiliation and thrill like she couldn't make up her mind.

"They'll kick us out—ugh!" I drove into her roughly, cutting her off.

"I've never been kicked out of an event in my life," I growled. "I'm Ransom Kingsman, and you're my omega."

I took her like that for a while, taking my time, loving the sweet little sounds she made as I fucked her. My own thrill rising every time she tilted her head, clearly trying to watch for passersby, or to glance down at the ball below. Whenever she did that, she'd clench over me so tight, and I wasn't sure if it was fear or arousal.

"You know what I want to do tonight, after we go home?" I asked as I slid into her. She was shaking, and I could feel the slick dripping down her thighs.

"I want to fuck you like this with Umbra and Dusk. I want to see how you take them, Little Reaper. And I want to know if you can take us all."

She groaned again as I rocked my knot against her. I felt her clench around my length and stayed right up to my knot, enjoying her tightness.

"Do you think you would like that?" I asked.

"I..." She moaned, tensing again as I pressed my knot a fraction further.

"Wait—Ransom!" Her voice was frantic. "You can't—"

"Answer me." I drew back before feeling her stretch over me again, almost all the way.

"Yes," she breathed. "I want you."

"Together?" I drew out and pressed back in.

"Yes."

"Say it."

"I want..." She was panting as I drove into her, each time. "I want all of you."

"Come for me, Little Reaper," I growled.

Fuck.

She seized over me, trying so hard to be quiet, the sweetest groans trapped in her chest as she came apart. I fucked her with long strokes, spilling into her, my orgasm was so blinding that I stepped back, leaning against the pillar to our left, suddenly not trusting myself to hold her steady.

It wasn't hard to hold her, though, she was clinging to me like a koala, lip caught in her teeth as she watched my orgasm as if she was very proud of herself.

I set her down and helped her get her bearings, tucking her hair behind her ear and almost losing myself in her dazed, golden eyes.

"I can't believe you did that," she whispered, but I could see the hint of mischief in her expression.

I grinned. "I'm going to have to be creative to keep up with Dusk and Umbra. They've had much longer to steal your heart."

Her brows drew in a frown.

"You don't have to do anything to be important to me," she whispered.

I stared at her, something suddenly caught in my throat.

"I love you already," she told me.

It warmed my blood to hear her say it.

"But was that about you making me feel better, or you?"

"You," I said indignantly.

"Sometimes when you see me with Dusk, you're sad," she said. "Are you jealous?"

I considered her. "Yes. But not... not like it sounds."

She frowned up at me, eyes imploring me to tell her. "If you're going to fuck me on the ballroom balcony so I'm less nervous about going in, then you have to tell me, too."

Ah. So she had seen through that.

I snorted, wincing a little at the words about to come out of my mouth. "It's hard not to feel useless. To try and figure out who I am, or... find my place."

"You're the centre of this pack."

"Oh no, that's you now," I said.

She considered me. "I don't..." She swallowed. "I don't know who I am, either," she whispered. "I never... never got my memories back. I don't think I ever will. It's like... I'm... no one."

"Shatter..." I stared at her. "You truly believe that?"

"I have no memories—"

"And I have all of my memories. Of school, and friends who never saw me for anything beyond a bank account, of nights getting drunk at bars because I didn't know what else to do with my time, or what I wanted from my life. Of a father who turned out to be a monster. I have a lifetime's worth. I have all of that, and I am stranded. But you—you are the most fascinating person I've ever met," I told her. "You know what you love, what you want, and what you love you are good at. You fight for your dreams when a thousand others would have given up. And you aren't just caring and protective over the people you love, you're brave, choosing to face your monsters when no one would judge you for running—what more to a person is there?" I asked. "Nothing that could be found on a piece of paper."

She stared at me, and even through the bond I felt her stunned silence.

"I intend to follow you around like a lost puppy so I can learn some of your tricks."

A smile wobbled on her lips, though her eyes were still dazed, as if she were still trying to untangle what I'd said.

"Until then, you'll let me help you save them, so I can feel like I'm doing something. You tell me what you need, I'll do it. Anything."

"You should be studying Arkology."

"Anything but that."

Her smile widened, and I drew her into a kiss.

"Are you ready to go in now?" I asked.

When I pulled away, she looked anxious again, eyes darting down to the ball below. She nodded, still tense.

"What is it?"

"You said I was brave." She swallowed. "That's not true, I'm… I'm really scared of them."

I knew that.

I'd been in her nest nearly every night this week. She had nightmares, her breathing picking up until I tugged her into my arms and purred for her. She hadn't even woken up.

I drew her close, my voice a whisper just for her. "If you weren't, Little Reaper, then it wouldn't be called bravery."

THIRTY-SEVEN

SHATTER

Entering the ball with Ransom was one of the most unnerving experiences of my life.

I'd never felt so many eyes on me. Eyes that lingered in shock, as they met mine, and then widened some more as gazes trailed down to the bite on full display on my neck.

For one wild, brief second, I wondered if anyone had seen us on the balcony. I looked up and was horrified to see that it was really quite visible. But then a nervous giggle bubbled up my throat. Spotting Ransom fucking me on the balcony wasn't going to be anyone's takeaway from tonight.

No. It was mine. Another thing I could claim while they were all focused on the things my pack would never let define me.

My neck and eyes.

At first, there was a stunned silence. All I could hear were the musicians playing and my own heels clipping the marble floors. Then I heard a crescendo of whispers rising through the air.

It was okay.

Ransom's arm was in mine.

I saw the Lincoln pack first, beyond the dance floor with its milling crowds and dancers, to the circular dining tables around which packs loitered and socialised. All three of them were on a raised platform, their seats like thrones.

Gareth, Eric, and Flynn were just like I remembered them at the choosing. When they'd been different people in every way possible to the monsters I now knew them to be.

They must have caught sight of me at the same moment I saw them, because I saw Flynn lean forward in his seat, lowering his glass, eyes fixed on me. Eric said something, and Gareth cut off his conversation with an omega who was perched on the arm of his chair, head snapping in my direction.

I heard an echo of Gareth's laugh. The cold tip of a marker pressed against my skin. Eric's fist was painful in my hair with Flynn's weight at my back. Teeth threatened, a cruel prank that toyed with my freedom...

I almost stumbled, but Ransom drew me closer, arm winding around my waist. We'd used scent dampening spray—not enough to stifle our scents entirely, but enough to mute them, which was event etiquette. But with every deep breath, my fear was offset by lily of the valley, a cool forest with damp earth, just like the trees outside that cabin.

He was here, with me. We'd just snuck onto the balcony so he could claim me.

My eyes scanned the room momentarily and I realised that where he'd claimed me was right above the Lincoln pack's seats.

I felt the echo of a smile on my lips.

Right over their stupid thrones, he'd given me everything they'd tried to steal.

Everything they'd sworn I'd never have.

Now he led me swiftly away from the Lincoln pack, and I felt the brush of his breath at my ear as he leaned close. "There are much sweeter things to be looking at, Little Reaper."

I glanced up at him, then followed his gaze across the ballroom. My heart tripped over itself as I saw the Kingsman pack were seated just like my mates. Roxy was waiting, and Dusk...

My smile grew at the sight of him. He was frozen, on his feet before his chair, lips parted as he stared at me. Just like Ransom, he was dressed up in a really smart outfit. With the shiny shoes, and a black button up that was cut all stupid perfect around his shoulders and figure and made him look almost as devastating as when he was wearing nothing at all.

"You've got him speechless," Ransom murmured. "I don't think I've ever seen Dusk—oh." He cut off with a chuckle as Dusk finally unfroze himself. He took the steps from the platform by twos, eyes wide as he began toward us. I stopped, drawing Ransom up, suddenly as unable to take my gaze from Dusk as he was from me. He was weaving through the crowd, almost knocking people over, still not sparing a glance anywhere else.

Then he was before me, midnight opium a roiling storm of passion, sharp edges of amber smoothed by traces of dark vanilla. He cupped my cheek, still something dazed in his expression.

"Fuck." His growl was low. "Shatter..." He swallowed, gaze dropping to my neck again.

To his bite.

To the scars—*our* scars.

All my fear was gone. With Ransom and Dusk, and Roxy, waiting.

"You are..." He was lost for words.

"Yours?" I whispered.

The sweetest smile curved his lips, and then he leaned down, kissing me with complete abandon for the people and ball around us.

Then he hooked his arm in mine on my other side, and he and Ransom both led me up to our seats.

What followed was a small fight, since I wanted to sit next to

Roxy, which meant I couldn't sit next to Dusk *and* Ransom. Naturally, Dusk won, pulling a pack-lead-command like I'd never heard him do before. Ransom wrinkled his nose, clearly debating whether it was worth fighting (not the end of the world, but it could contribute to pack imbalance) before slumping down on the end seat at Dusk's side.

Roxy was giggling at the whole thing, a half-finished glass of wine in her hand, her eyes sparkling and her cheeks a bit pink. She seemed so happy it was making me smile.

"Did you *see* their faces?" she asked. "Eric looked like he was about to throw his drink. And I think they scared off all their interest."

I dared another glance only to see that they were still staring, and Roxy was right, there were no longer any omegas nearby.

They'd seen the dark bond, and they knew I was gold pack. Which was more shocking to them, I wondered?

If it was the fact I was gold pack, what would that mean?

I realised it didn't worry me.

A breath released from my lungs, something pent up, building since the moment I'd run from Eric.

They could see me. They could see my scars, my eyes, and my bond.

They had, and so had everyone else.

I wore every insecurity on display, and I was still in one piece.

The world hadn't fallen apart.

The only thing the Lincoln pack didn't yet know was that I was their scent match.

That could wait for now as I settled in. Content to watch the dancers on the floor, and the many groups that flitted about, even if I could still feel a thousand gazes flickering my way. I knew the chatter would repeat my name, would paint a picture that wasn't true, and that was okay, because that was mine, too.

A weapon I could use.

With the scents around me, I had nothing to hide from anymore.

I had my best friend, I had my pack, and it was everything I'd ever dreamed of.

UMBRA

Vandle was a loose end that the Institute had left alive.

The clear reason for that was staring us in the face.

The alpha in the cage we'd reached was tall and slender, but right now he was curled up in his bed, eyes staring sightlessly at the wall. I knew he was prone to violence at the slightest provocation. During our last visit, he'd nearly taken out Dusk's eye.

That time, he hadn't said a word.

He was the only alpha we knew of who'd ended up back here after being in the experimentations. The best we could tell, he was part of the early trials—which had failed, and somehow he'd escaped.

He might never have been caught, except he'd returned to the facility after it was shut down. He'd returned when the Institute had taken over and continued a different set of experiments on omegas.

He'd sabotaged them, and now we knew that meant he was the reason for Shatter's curse.

The reason she'd been injected with Atropa's Poison.

Whatever they'd done to sedate him after that, it had been the last nail in the coffin. His sanity had cracked, and instead of killing him, they'd thrown him back in this cell.

A fate worse than death for most.

He knew things that even the Institute didn't—that was Decebal's theory. They didn't want to end his life, in case the information he had ever became crucial for them to know. But in the meantime, he posed no threat.

At least, they didn't think so.

I stepped up to the thick bars, releasing my aura into the space.

Vandle flinched, eyes snapping to me, but he didn't move.

"Careful," Decebal murmured.

I waited for a long moment. Finally, Vandle shifted. He placed his feet carefully on the ground, sitting up, head cocked as he stared at me. Every movement was slow and deliberate.

His face was gaunt, skin pale and sickly. His clothes were baggy and worn, and his eyes bloodshot.

I could see the distinctive colours. One white, one red. His hair was shaved short. That's how they *all* were in this place, and how it had been at the facility too.

Easier to manage.

From what I could see of it, it was silver.

Vandle was a seer.

He could visualise auras. In another life, he could have made good money working with the Institute and selling that skill. They were rare—though I knew Decebal also had one in his pack (the RedEyed*fucking*Bandit that had ruined all my scoreboards while I'd been in the throes of my sickness).

Vandle watched me intently, head tilted back, a snarl forming on his lips as he bared his teeth.

That was the reaction we'd got last time. He could see my aura. I wonder if he could see how broken it was. How much we were both alike.

Last time, it had made him stir, even if it was not enough to pull him back.

Decebal shifted at my back, tugging the metal cigarette case from his pocket. It was empty since they'd made him throw the last few out at the gates. We were allowed no contraband, and no alpha scents—we'd been doused with scent dampening spray as we entered.

And absolutely, under no circumstances, were we to bring in omega scents.

Decebal, however, flicked the bottom compartment of his cigarette case open and withdrew the small silk handkerchief that Shatter had scent marked.

Would it be enough?

I didn't *like* handing her scent to the alpha who'd ruined her life, but it could mean saving us all.

Protecting her...

I had a lot of hatred to go around recently, but it was hard to place it at Vandle's feet. He was an alpha long broken.

Seconds after Decebal handed me the piece of cloth, Vandle was on his feet, eyes wide. His aura flared—or... tried to. Like so many here, his was broken and fragmented. It was nothing more than flickering shards of energy shuttering in and out, trying to cling to life. Some harrowing in their power, never lasting long.

He crossed toward me in an instant, seizing the fabric from my fist, eyes wild as he examined it.

I narrowed my eyes, watching carefully.

He was shaking, I noticed, as he turned the fabric in his grip. More, with every second that passed. Still, I almost jumped when a burst of cracked, insane laughter broke from his lips.

THIRTY-EIGHT

SHATTER

"I don't have to dance, do I?" I whispered, clutching Roxy's arm as we headed into the bathroom. I was getting better with the heels, but certainly not enough to dance.

"I hope not," she snorted. "Take me to a club, then maybe. This is much too fancy."

"Some of those packs out there are really good," I noted. There were some very pretty ballroom-like dances going on.

We were about an hour in. Beautifully dressed omegas and beta women were filling the party, and for once, seeing them didn't make me worry.

I had seen the love in Dusk's eyes as he'd reached me, the stunned, absolute passion as he took me in head to toe despite everyone else here.

I was enough for him, Ransom, and Umbra.

That was what mattered.

I was done checking my hair, and was waiting for Roxy by the exit when I heard words from around the corner that drew me up.

"What do you make of the dark bond?"

I froze. That was Oliver's voice floating from the hallway beyond.

"That was a power play," Jasmine's voice came in reply, which wasn't a surprise since they were often together.

I shrank against the cream wallpaper, the texture of its flowery swirls pressing against my back where my dress dipped down. The last I'd seen or heard from them was that night at the party.

They were talking about me, no doubt about it.

"Showing off her eyes *and* a dark bond in one night? And if what the Lincoln pack said was true about her pining over them?" Jasmine laughed. "Here—" She cut off. "Check the back straps, will you? I don't think they're right."

I heard a muffled sound, and then Jasmine continued. "If you ask me, they were toying with her, acting to the school like they're obsessed, but I think they were taunting her. When she tried to make a run for it to the Lincoln pack..." She trailed off. "They're predators. The only interesting alphas in this place."

I chewed on my lip. That was good, though. It was exactly what I wanted. What Dusk wanted.

"You think so? The way Varis was looking at her—"

"She's his prize. Of course he was—"

The conversation halted as heeled footsteps approached. A brunette beta with a shimmery black dress and matching purse came around the corner, giving me a little smile as she passed me into the bathroom.

At that moment, Roxy appeared at my side, ready to go, but I put a finger to my lips, giving her a meaningful look. She closed the last few steps with a frown, careful about keeping her heels as quiet as possible.

"You believe what they said about her asking for those bites?" Oliver asked after a moment.

"Come on." Jasmine sounded amused. "You've seen her. She's

pathetic, actually admitted to following them around and watching in? And if she thought it was going to get her a bond from them? Plus, someone said her scent is god awful so she probably is desperate."

"Yet, you want to take a run at them tonight?" Oliver asked.

"That was the plan," Jasmine replied.

Roxy's eyebrows shot up and I frowned. *Jasmine wanted to try for the Lincoln pack?* She already had a pack, a good one.

"You're not worried about how they look after that?"

"Like I give a damn. Besides, I don't think that gold pack slut knows how to handle alphas, anyone can see that. Give me a run, I'll have them around my little finger. I want to show her how a real omega does it. She was a mess in that video, stammering all over the place—and she thought they might keep her?" I could hear the sneer in her voice.

The old, wounded part of me wilted, the part that was always worried about never being good enough as an omega.

"She gives us a bad name," Jasmine went on. "Plus, the North Prince pack are so dull. I need a challenge."

"No way for you to take your shot without the whole room seeing," Oliver replied.

"That's fine." Jasmine laughed. "The North Prince pack know I'm trying for it."

"They're okay with that?" He sounded surprised.

"Told them if I failed tonight, I'd stick around for my heat. Dan hasn't got a clue I've been winding him up on purpose. He's near a rut. He told the others to shut up about it if they had a problem."

Roxy wrinkled her nose in disgust, but Oliver laughed. "*That's* how you got them so obsessed with you?"

"Piece of cake."

Their talk died down as I heard more footsteps passing.

It sounded like a group of girls who'd had a bit to drink. They were giggling and I could hear snippets of their conversation even from here.

"...dresses and makeup are iconic. Talk about an entrance. They both look like queens."

"I wish I had an alpha to put me on a throne," another said. "Gold pack or not, I'm jealous."

"You think they're going to match the Barclay?" That was the first female voice. "Get two omegas."

"If they have a dark bond, they can't have two."

"Some get a second by title, though, not unheard of..." The voices trailed off and there was a long silence.

"Two omegas?" Oliver repeated into the silence. "You know, I don't think it's impossible that's what they're going for."

"Let's go back in. I need another drink." Jasmine sounded bitter. "You watch. By the time I'm done, no one will even remember that gold pack shit."

We waited for the sounds of their footsteps to vanish entirely before Roxy spoke. "I bet she was planning on being queen omega tonight, securing a spot with the Lincoln pack and being the centre of it all."

I was silent.

I knew they'd taken pieces of that video and put it together all wrong. I knew that the Lincoln pack were getting attention tonight, that omegas had been approaching them for a chance to join their pack before my very eyes.

Yet, hearing it like that, how easy it was for Jasmine to write me off, to claim I'd *wanted* the Lincoln pack to bite me like that—

My thoughts cut off as Roxy's hand squeezed mine.

"She's delusional," she said. "And for the record, you manage your alphas better than I ever thought was possible."

I smiled, trying to shove away the ache in my chest. "It's okay," I told her. "We knew this was going to happen."

"You still shouldn't have to hear it."

We'd waited long enough for them to be long gone, and headed back. Ransom was waiting by the doors back into the ballroom, his hand slipping around my waist as he drew me from Roxy's supportive grip.

I leaned my head against him, happy to inhale his cool, earthy scent.

I took my seat between Roxy and Dusk again, tuning into the conversation between an alpha named Percy, who I recognised as the lead of a pack that had a booth in our Arkology classes. He was talking to Dusk with enthusiasm.

"...foundation has real personal meaning to me. Thank you again, and..." His eyes slid to me, snagging on my neck before he forced them back up. He gave me an odd smile, then frowned as if he wasn't sure he should have. "And uh..." He returned his attention to Dusk. "Congratulations to your pack for the new bond. All of you." He made sure to nod at Ransom, too, then awkwardly gave me and Roxy a half nod. I could see the effort it took for him not to look back at my neck as he did.

"Thank you," Dusk replied.

"No one knows how to react," Roxy said with a giggle once he was gone.

I only planned on one drink tonight, and I sipped it slowly, listening to Roxy's social commentary and forcing myself to relax.

I wasn't used to being on display like this, but the rich, deep amber of midnight opium grounded me, and Dusk's fingers tangled in mine, tracing my palm soothingly as the music played on.

I'd tried so hard to ignore the Lincoln pack, but it was difficult. Their lack of attention didn't last long. There seemed to be a new omega speaking to them every time I dared glance. Every time I did, I saw, even from this distance, one of them looking at me. As if my attention drew theirs.

Once I swear Gareth cut off mid-sentence as his eyes met

mine, and the omega perched on the arm of his seat was forced to nudge his shoulder to drag his attention back to her.

My memories were still vile, recent enough that their thorns hadn't dulled. Not entirely.

But I didn't regret tonight. They had hurt me, but they hadn't broken me.

And now, they couldn't ever hurt me again.

They didn't have that power anymore.

I glanced down, finding a smile as I watched Dusk's finger trace my palm.

"Ransom's a total diva if you give him attention," Dusk chuckled. I glanced up. Ransom had gone to fetch us another bottle of red. "*Literally* strutting. Look at him."

I smiled, watching Ransom as he picked up a bottle from the long set of serving tables. He was getting stares as much as I was, and Dusk was right, I could practically see him puffing up at the attention. I pouted a little when I realised how much of that attention was from omegas.

"Don't be jealous," he snorted, catching my expression. "It could be a room of enraptured birds, and he'd bask in the attention the same. It's in his blood."

"I'm not jealous," I said, far too quickly.

Dusk grinned, leaning back in his chair.

Again, before I could catch myself, I saw a pretty blonde omega I didn't recognise join Eric. She was clearly enthralled by him, and he caught my eye, offering me a nasty smirk before I tore my eyes away.

I wondered when Jasmine would make her play.

She'd seemed so confident that it would work. I didn't know if I wanted it to, but I thought, perhaps, they deserved each other.

When we saw Jasmine next, however, she wasn't approaching the Lincoln pack at all.

Instead, she came sashaying up the steps toward us. At the

sight of her shimmery black dress and the sway of her glossy, high-ponytail, I tensed.

What was she doing here?

I noticed more attention on us than usual as Jasmine lowered her glass to her side, stopping between Dusk and Ransom, and holding her hand out delicately, fingers curled as if they were going to reach up and kiss it.

"Jasmine Lynn," she said. "I left you flowers but we never got a chance to speak. It's lovely to meet you, Dusk..." Her gaze slid to Ransom as if I didn't exist. "Ransom. I saw you at the party ever so briefly. That was an... impressive show."

I was absolutely still, every hair on my body standing on end as I stared at her.

The ball fell away, the dancers, the music, the thousand watching eyes.

"We aren't open for courting," Dusk said, his voice icy enough I'm surprised it didn't send her running.

Why was she here?

Jasmine pouted, drawing her hand back.

My lips pulled back in a snarl, fingers clenching on the rests of my chair. Blood pounded in my ears, but I remained frozen, holding on by the thinnest thread, struggling to keep at bay the rage that used to rule me. But it was lifting its ugly head, cracking the balance my pack offered me since I'd been bitten.

She wasn't here for them.

She *couldn't* be.

They were mine...

"You have a pack already, don't you?" Dusk asked. His continued coldness settled me by the slightest of fractions, but the thundering of my heart against my ribs was almost painful.

"Not one like this," she replied, voice silky smooth. "I would drop them in a heartbeat for a pack with a little extra..." Her gaze darted to me, sliding down to the dark bond on my neck. "Fun."

I saw red.

"Oh, you *little*—" Roxy began, but cut off.

I let out a primal growl, and, dress and heels notwithstanding, threw myself at Jasmine with all my might.

I took us both down, and we crashed into the marble, sanity forgotten in the seat behind me.

"They're *mine*!" My voice was guttural, primal instincts sweeping me away as my nails dug into her arms hard enough to make her shriek in pain.

Not enough.

I'd kill her.

"Shatter! Let go."

I realised my fist had closed around her stupid ponytail.

It wasn't a conscious decision to fight Dusk's command, but the red of my vision only intensified with the spark of pain that tore across my body at the defiance of the dark bond. I growled again, and then Jasmine whined in terror as my teeth sank into her neck.

My body shook with thrilling instinct as I held it there, and Jasmine went limp in my grip, a terrified whine in her chest.

What I'd just offered her was nothing close to a bond.

It was a threat.

The pain drained away as Dusk released the command, and then I felt his touch on my neck. Cupping it gently.

"Shatter."

No.

I wasn't done.

Jasmine was shaking beneath me, more pathetic whines sounding with each panicked heave of her chest.

"You won, Gem. You can let her go."

I frowned, then released my bite at last, knowing there would be blood on my lips. I didn't care.

I... I had what?

Won?

Won what?

Oh... Oh *dear*...

The world flooded back in and horror rose in my chest. We were in the middle of the ball. My gaze flicked up from the pooling blood on Jasmine's neck.

I'd bitten her.

The whole room was watching.

Dusk cupped my neck more firmly as he gently drew me back, further from Jasmine.

Jasmine scrambled back the moment she was free. "Get your filthy fucking gold pack b—"

"Finish that sentence, Omega—" Dusk's growl was more cutting than I'd ever heard it. *"—and I will finish what she started."*

He didn't even look at her. His yellow eyes were fixed on me.

Then, before I could even catch my breath, he'd dragged me forward by my neck and pressed his lips to mine. I melted into his touch, the kiss and its iron tang of blood returning my sanity. Then he was drawing me to my feet, not a care for the watching eyes of everyone in the room. When I glanced in Jasmine's direction she was fleeing, unsteady on her heels.

Dusk leaned forward again for another kiss, and this time his teeth caught my lip, a rumbling purr in his chest as he held me close. When he drew back he lifted a hand and wiped away what I knew had to be a smear of blood on my cheek. When he sat, he drew me onto his lap, arms winding around my waist possessively.

My whole body was hot with embarrassment as I glanced at Ransom and Roxy.

To my surprise, Roxy was failing to hide a look of delight, while Ransom was staring at me with blown pupils and a feral glint in his eye.

"Gem." Dusk cupped my neck, thumb running along my jaw

as he tilted my head up, his voice a low growl in my ear. "You never have to fight to prove we're yours. That's our job. I was about to tell Jasmine to fuck off."

"Keyword—*have* to," Ransom put in. "Like I said before—it's fucking hot."

Roxy's giggle drew a nervous smile upon my own lips. "If anyone was wondering about territory," she said. "They aren't anymore."

"I don't know what happened..." I whispered.

"You bit her *and* scent marked her. She'll be walking around with that beat-down all evening."

"*Marked* her?" Why had I done that... ?

Oh bother.

I needed to get better control of myself. Apparently, alphas were totally capable of balancing me in the bond—until they were the things my instincts were going nuts over.

"They're just going to think I'm even more crazy."

I tried not to pout.

I didn't regret it, I just couldn't fit in no matter how hard I tried.

Roxy chuckled. "I doubt anyone here has dealt with honest-to-God territorial omega instincts in their lives. A good dose of reality, if you ask me."

THIRTY-NINE

UMBRA

"You're like..." Vandle's voice was charred and cracked with misuse. "Like me." He met my gaze, head cocked, Shatter's scented handkerchief balled up in his fist.

"Yes." This was it, I realised, as I stared into mismatched eyes. The first breakthrough we'd had in forever. Vandle was awake.

"I was in the experiments," I said. "Like you."

He grinned. "They put you back together, so they could break you again..."

"Tell me what you know about that?"

"Too much," he rasped. "He liked me, you know? The Doctor."

"Dr. Wren?" I asked, heart racing. "He... he helped me."

Vandle's smile stiffened, the edges of a snarl drawing at his lips. "No. He toyed with you, with the others."

"Toyed with us?"

"That was his job too, you know? To push you. To see how far you would go to protect each other."

I felt my blood chill, but Vandle was going on, the cracks

working themselves out of his voice as he used it. Now he was, he couldn't seem to stop.

"But he cared about *me*." There was a madness and frenzy to his words. "He freed me when I should have died, kept my secret so I could help him spy the auras and give him more data. But no matter what I did or said, they never..." He flinched, scrunching his eyes shut for a moment. "They never stopped. Not until they were forced to. And they killed everyone..." His expression twisted into something sick. "Everyone... but you?" He frowned, but then shook it off. "And then, when I went back, they opened it again."

"The facility?" I asked.

"Why?" His eyes went wide, one blank white, one red, and he ran his fingers along his scalp. I could see red marks through his buzzed-short hair as if he did that often. "I went in. Took one of their white coats to make sure things had changed. I was going to leave forever after that. But..." His speech was getting frantic, the edge of a growl in his voice. "They had *omegas*. And I couldn't... I had to stop them. What they did to us, I couldn't..." His breathing came too quick, and I was worried he would slip back into silence.

"What did you do?" I asked. Keep him talking. I would know if he lied, which would be a good indicator of the usefulness of this conversation. I knew the answer already.

He was responsible for the mixed-up vial.

Shatter had been the one to pay, getting an injection that had broken her.

"I thought..." His breath caught. "I thought it would be enough to stop it. But... it didn't work." His madness broke for a moment, sorrow cresting his expression as he looked down at the handkerchief in his fist.

"You recognise her scent?"

"I was there when it changed. It was beautiful... But then... she didn't die."

"You meant to kill her?"

A low, wounded sound rose in his throat, catching on the way up like a dry, broken sob. He looked back to me, "I never wanted her to, but I knew if she did then so many more would be saved. But number One survived, and so did the experiments, and I was brought here..." He frowned. "How long has it been?"

He looked around the cell, at the cracked walls and bare room. I didn't answer, knowing if I told him that, we might lose him.

Instead, I digested what he'd said, sickness turning my stomach. And yet, I couldn't find hatred.

"She fought the poison just like you did," he whispered. "A survivor. One worth a thousand of me."

"What does that mean?"

"Do you know why they gave us that poison? The Atropa abomination?"

"Why?"

He stared down at his fist, where he held Shatter's scent. "Strength testing."

"What?"

"The kind of bond that remains if a pack survives that—well, they needed that strength. Not something I survived."

"Needed it for what?" I asked.

Vandle's fist closed around the iron bar of the cage, his expression turning into something so hollow that I feared I was truly about to lose him.

"You didn't survive?" I asked instead, trying to understand that.

"I... I killed them all."

Ah.

I swallowed, remembering the way the poison had felt the first time I'd been exposed to it. The primal fear it had instilled, telling me to kill—that I had to kill, or I would die.

"Your... own pack?" I asked.

"Of *course* I did." Vandle's lips drew thin in a snarl. "And then I was useless to them. If Dr. Wren hadn't taken pity on me, I would be dead too. Not because of them. No one... no one survives once the poison gets them. Kill them... then kill me..." His breath caught. "Dr. Wren wouldn't let me end it though... He put me to use..." He frowned. "But now... *look*." He took a step closer, examining me properly. "You survived—" He laughed. "—and you're free. You aren't supposed to be, you know?"

"Why?"

"You were *designed* for a cage. They would never have paid so much if they thought you would one day escape... If they thought you might find them."

"They?"

"Your better half. You're alive, aren't you—so you must have one."

"What does that mean?"

"You don't know?" A bark of an insane laugh slipped out. "Walking around with half a body and never even noticed?"

The words struck too close to the lurking shadow in the back of my mind. *"Tell me what that means."*

"You never figured out what they were doing with all of the tests?"

"They covered it up."

He grinned. "Well, it would have made locating sponsors too easy. It would have put their whole illegal operation at risk."

"What were they doing?"

"What do the rich hate more than anything?" he asked, his voice taunting. "What they can't control—what their money cannot fix. A sickness like a plague among them, and yet there is no cure outside... not outside of a scent-matched omega."

Ice seeped into my blood as I stared at him. "A scent match?"

"Nature punishes alphas who dare defy her..." Vandle whispered. "So they turn on her, warping and butchering her and forcing her to break."

I grabbed him by the shirt, trying to quell my panic.

Shatter was the Lincoln pack's mate.

What was he talking about?

But Vandle was in a frenzy, lips drawn as he spat the words with madness. "They don't want to wait for the cure that might never come—a scent-matched omega—a princess bond? That is a dice roll without the power they so dearly crave."

My mind was racing.

"The experiments were for a *cure*?" I asked.

"You," Vandle hissed. "You are the cure."

"For what?"

How serious was this sickness? How far would the Lincoln pack go to fix it?

Enough for them to gamble on an illegal fix...

There was a wide smile on Vandle's face as he stared at me, but he said nothing.

"Tell. Me!" My pulse was erratic, panic choking me.

Something only a princess bond with a mate could fix...?

Shatter was about to reveal her scent to the Lincoln pack *tonight*.

It might be too late already.

It was Decebal, in the end, who answered from behind me, his voice low and stunned.

"They were trying to cure aura sickness."

FORTY

> **Aura Sickness:** *A phenomenon where an alpha's aura begins to deteriorate until it vanishes entirely. An alpha without an aura loses the ability to forge pack bonds or omega bonds, leaving them strongly resembling betas. Traditional or dark bonds with a scent-matched omega have been known to cure aura sickness, with unreliable degrees of success. The only absolute cure for aura sickness is a princess bond with a scent-matched omega.*

SHATTER

We almost went the whole ball without an interaction with the Lincoln pack.

I finally began to enjoy the evening. I people-watched with Roxy, letting her explain gossip and politics to me.

Ransom, to Dusk's amusement, tuned in for Roxy's explanations with more attention than he'd had for any of our studies this week, claiming he needed to catch up on politics.

I think I could face my classes after tonight.

Actually, I was sure I could.

"Are you still going to take Omega Studies?" I asked Roxy as we reached the snack table with napkins in hand.

Now she was pack-free, it wasn't mandatory—though it was encouraged.

"I think I'll keep one of them. Otherwise, I thought of transferring into another Arkology class."

"Really?" I asked, eyeing a few pieces on a plate full of pretty cheese.

That sounded exciting. I knew Dusk attended an Arkology class on Tuesday and Thursday morning. Maybe we could take that class together, too?

I opened my mouth, about to ask if she would mind that, when a familiar, snide voice behind me drew me up.

"I had *no* idea." Eric's voice was obnoxiously loud. "If I had known it was a gold pack bitch at the time, I might have been a bit rougher."

I tensed, breath catching in my lungs.

It took all my courage, but I forced myself to turn.

Eric stood further down the snack table with the same blonde omega I'd seen earlier. Roxy was stiff, fury blazing in her blue eyes as she stared at him.

Then Dusk was there, stepping in front of me before I could do anything.

I caught the scent of midnight opium and lily of the valley, and my heart settled, if only a little. I still didn't want Dusk getting too close.

Eric grinned. "Did you see the video?" he asked, gaze shifting to Dusk. "I made it just for you—and Ransom Kingsman turning up in time to pick up my used trash—"

Ransom's aura split the air, and he closed the distance, fist in Eric's shirt.

I noticed security move from the edges of the room. I reacted before thinking, slipping past Dusk and closing my grip around

Ransom's arm.

"Ransom," I whispered.

It wasn't because I didn't want to see Eric hurt, but I could feel Ransom waver on the edge of that madness. The one I'd pulled him from in the first place.

My mates were not worth him tumbling back over that ledge.

With what looked like painful difficulty, Ransom released Eric's shirt. He didn't back off, though, his massive aura still shivering in the air.

Eric looked far too unperturbed. Perhaps he didn't think Ransom would attack him in public. Perhaps he wanted him to.

Everyone was watching, security hovering, but not yet intervening.

And then Eric went absolutely still, aura flickering in the space for a second as his gaze snapped to me.

Unwavering.

There was utter shock in his eyes.

It was the moment—I knew—he caught my scent.

My heart slammed against my ribs, nails digging into Ransom's arm to steady my breathing.

Endless seconds passed as we stared at one another, as if he couldn't understand what he was seeing. His face had drained of all its remaining colour.

But he knew.

He knew at that moment, gaze locked on me.

It was no longer a secret.

"What?" Gareth's voice drew my attention as he stepped up to Eric, and then Flynn was there too.

In an instant, both of their eyes were fixed on me, arrogance falling away from Flynn's expression, the smile vanishing from Gareth's.

This... This was a mistake.

They were so close. Their scents were here just like they had been.

Flynn's teeth threatened a dark bond. Gareth was filming me. Eric's weight pinned me to the bed as he took his time searching for another place to sink his teeth.

Panic rose its ugly head, but then Ransom's arm was around my waist. Their scents were here.

I was here with my pack.

My family.

My best friend.

I had claimed everything I had come here for, and I had done it without them.

"*No.*" Flynn's growl was low and furious, and in his expression was more rage than I had imagined.

He looked sick with it.

I shrank back. Ransom's arm dropped, but immediately I felt Dusk there, pulling me a step away.

"She's ours." There was something truly hateful in Flynn's eyes. It was more than hateful, it was... it was desperate. There was madness in that gaze as it darted from me, up to Dusk. A chill skittered down my spine at his words.

"She's *our* omega," Ransom growled. "You will not touch her."

"She's our mate—!"

"You hurt me." My whisper was harsh as my mind went numb. "You... You left me with scars and told me no one would ever want me again." My voice shook, my eyes burning, but I blinked the tears away.

I hadn't cried in front of them then, I wouldn't now.

"We didn't *know* you were gold pack," Gareth hissed. "You hid your eyes."

Hiding my golden eyes was illegal, but the dark bond on my neck neutralised the penalties for that.

"What is that supposed to mean?" Roxy demanded. I glanced at her, grateful she was at my side right now.

Eric had a nasty look on his face, but Flynn spoke before he could.

"We'll take her back." His voice was icy as he looked at Ransom. "What's your price?"

My lips parted in shock.

Flynn wasn't looking at me though, as he adjusted his cuff, dark eyes fixed on my alpha as if I didn't exist.

"Price?" Ransom asked, sounding as stunned as I felt.

"What do you want us to say?" Flynn asked. "Well played. You won."

"Won?" Ransom asked.

On pure instinct, I stepped closer to him, heart racing like a hummingbird in my chest as I stared between my mates.

Flynn looked at Dusk. "You knew she was ours, and you hid her from us. When she tried to escape and we didn't save her, you bonded her."

I frowned. *Save me?* But then I remembered what I overheard Jasmine saying. That she believed the Kingsman pack had been toying with me.

"Now you're dangling a scent match in our faces." Flynn's voice was stiff, as if he were trying to sound more casual than he was. "Well played. We lost. Is that what you want to hear?"

I felt Dusk's low growl vibrate against my chest as his hand slipped around my neck, cupping his bite as he drew me against him. Midnight opium quelled the rising panic attack as I watched my mates bargain for me like I was a trinket at a market stall.

"We'll take her off your hands," Flynn said. "Name the price."

"There is no price." Ransom's voice was strained with fury. "She's ours."

Eric looked between Dusk and Ransom as if searching for the

joke. Gareth laughed. "You can't be serious about wanting to keep her."

I watched Eric's eyes slide to me, lingering on the bites on my chest, his gaze slipping from amused to hungry for a moment.

Dusk drew me tighter against him. I could feel him through the bond, steadfast. A bastion I could cling to.

"She belongs to my pack." Dusk's voice was perfectly even. "Any marks she wears are mine."

Eric's eyes snapped to him and I saw a flicker of a snarl pull on his lips before he caught it. "We claimed her, she is worthless to—"

Dusk cut him off, each word slow and vicious. "You *attacked* your own scent match. Those marks might prove your foulness but they don't touch her worth."

I shrank against Dusk, and felt him draw me closer, and my shaking fingers were tangled with Roxy's and she squeezed me tight.

Eric took a step forward, but Ransom cut him off, his aura—which was still a smothering force in the air—flaring. "You bit her in that video, didn't you? The one you wanted everyone to see. You called her a stalker—too stupid to recognise your own mate." His voice dropped. "But you didn't claim her."

I felt Dusk waver in the bond just the slightest bit. Not with fear, but uncertainty.

I got that.

I didn't understand any of this. Even if I was their scent match, the only way to transfer the dark bond to them was through a princess bond.

The bond between mates.

But that was the opposite to the dark bond, it handed power to the omega. I know I thought I'd heard them discussing one all those months ago, but I'd written it off as imagination. The

Lincoln pack were not one who wanted to offer a princess bond to an omega.

"There is no price," Ransom said.

"There has to be a—" Flynn cut off at Ransom's growl. I'd never noticed until now quite how tall he was, rounding on them with ease.

"Take one more step closer to my omega, and I will put you all the way through the wall this time."

"This is *insane*," Flynn snarled, eyes darting to me. I felt a flutter of terror. There was a wild undercurrent of madness dancing in his eyes before Gareth grabbed him, dragging him back a step.

"Let's go," Gareth growled.

Flynn tore his gaze from me to Ransom, who was all but coiled to pounce—as were the security guards. Finally, he stepped back.

I watched them storm through the huge front door of the ballroom, my heart in my throat until they were out of sight.

"Do you want to leave—?"

"No." I cut Roxy short.

Not now. Not straight away.

They were out there, and I... I didn't want to run.

They were the ones running.

"Are you sure, Little Reaper?" Ransom had turned to me, aura vanishing in an instant.

I glanced around. I had to stay, even if half of me wanted to cling to Dusk and bury my face in his shoulder and let him carry me out of here.

But I couldn't.

They had fled, not returning to the seats they'd so dearly wanted.

I would return to mine.

Of course, every eye in the room was on us. Even the music had stopped.

"I want to stay. Even just a bit longer. If that's..." I swallowed. "If that's okay."

When we reached our seat, Dusk drew me onto his lap again. I'd made a step for my own, but I'd felt a flicker of discomfort from him through the bond, as if he didn't want me even that far.

"Something is wrong." His voice was low in my ear as he drew me close.

"That was..." Roxy trailed off, having taken the seat I'd occupied before. "That wasn't what I expected."

"What uh... what *were* we expecting?" I asked.

I was shaking. It was obvious as I looked down, seeing the rich, dark skin of Dusk's hands contrasting the rippling goosebumps on my arms.

"I don't know, but Flynn was..." Roxy paused. "He looked insane. I mean, I get it, scent matches are a whole thing, but they didn't strike me as the kind of pack that cared that much."

I couldn't shake the look on Flynn's face.

"How long do you want to stay?" Ransom asked.

I glanced around. The music had started up again, and everyone was returning to their dance or chatter.

"Not long." My voice was weak. "I just don't want to run from them."

FORTY-ONE

UMBRA

"*Decebal.*" My growl was desperate as I turned.

We needed to warn Shatter not to reveal her scent, but there was no reception in here. "If they find out she's their scent match—"

"I'm going." He was already backing up. "You get more information," he told me, before vanishing.

"All of this is about aura sickness?" I said, turning back to Vandle.

"Fascinating sickness," he said. "Really, not that devastating until ego's involved. Tell an alpha he won't be an alpha anymore? He'll burn the world down to change that. And you know what they say about it, that it's as random as a lightning strike? Yet, it's funny how, if you look, and I mean *really* look, lightning seems to strike cruel packs—though Dr. Wren thought there was more to it than that."

He rolled his shoulders, a grin on his face.

"*More*, like what?" I didn't know what I was seeking anymore,

I would take anything he would share. I didn't know what was useful.

"That thing about mother nature," Vandle breathed. "She doesn't break. She is vengeful, and, more than anything in the world, she protects her children."

"What do you mean?"

"Aura sickness," Vandle said. "That's what Dr. Wren used to say. Nature's way of biting back." He dropped his voice. "Vengeance for the pain of gold packs. But it's not so simple to track crime from punishment. He didn't think it distinguished alpha from pack. Its target could be any of them—and in that, I suppose, it is like a lightning strike."

I rubbed my face, trying to work through everything he'd said so far. "Do you know what they did to me—why we're sick?" I asked.

Vandle's oddly coloured eyes were calculating as he took me in. "You're 66, aren't you? I think I remember. Became a success the moment your pack mate died."

My blood turned to ice.

He remembered?

It was the greatest enigma—our survival when there were only two of us left in the bond. "How did the pack survive?"

"I think, because the bond registered a third member, even an unconventional one."

"What does that mean?"

"Your pack was born of theirs."

"It was... *what?*"

"They used your blood and a twisted binding. Not like usual bonds between alphas. But even then, as unnatural as it was, you still had to accept it. Do you remember the moment you connected? A moment of desperation to save your pack when there was nothing else?"

"I..." I trailed off, memories clawing their way back violently.

I had always known there was something wrong with that moment.

The bullet shredded more than just flesh. As 31's heart stopped, each one tore through our pack bond. Enough, by all laws of the universe, to destroy it.

No...

If the pack broke, I couldn't protect Dusk.

We wouldn't be of use to them anymore.

I flared my aura, reaching out desperately in the dark. Somehow, I found something to hold onto. Intangible and impossible, the energy was an anchor enough that I could hold on, even though it scorched me to the soul, unnatural and agonising.

I shuddered, cracks rippling through the very essence that made me an alpha; wounds that didn't feel as if they would ever heal.

"I... did this?" I asked, ripping myself from the vision before it pulled me from reality completely.

But... I had been right all this time.

This *was* my fault.

"You could not conceive of the power you handed to them when you did that," Vandle said. "The relationship was not symbiotic by design."

"Not... what?"

"They're feeding on you, 66. On you and 68. On your auras. A parasite draining you dry. A slow poison to wither you to nothing as you rot behind the bars of a cage."

A parasite?

"Once they knew you were going to succeed, he just had to take three injections of a serum with your blood, and the bond was sealed."

"That's what was in the briefcase?"

That's what this was? This sickness creeping in, devouring me.

The Lincoln pack... What they'd stolen they were *still* stealing.

"They needed powerful auras to handle the demand of that bond, and even then, only the strongest alphas survived the process."

"Is that why... When Dusk touched one of them—" I cut off as Vandle's eyes went wide.

"You *what*?" he asked. "Dr. Wren had theories about what might happen if contact was made."

"We... we nearly died. Our omega... she saved us."

Vandle nodded slowly. "And nothing happened to them?"

I felt the hatred twist my face. "No."

Decebal had checked the bugs. Nothing.

"It's designed to be one way. Aura energy displacement won't cross the bond. It will just... reflect it back at you."

"What the fuck does that mean?"

"You cannot touch him or hurt him. Any damage you inflict will only reflect onto your own aura. It was a fail-safe—since the lab rats were never supposed to get out..." He laughed. "To hunt him down and... and..." He cocked his head. "And what? What are you going to do?"

I was still trying to keep up. "Why do you keep saying... *him*?"

Vandle considered me. "You and 68 are only bonded to one—and his pack only by proxy. To bind to more than one alpha... well, not even Dr. Wren's experiments could manage that."

Flynn...

Did that mean I could touch the others?

"We have an omega, another pack mate, are they—"

"No. Just you and 68. It cannot go beyond that."

Okay. I nodded. Shatter and Ransom were going to be dragged into this fucked up bond.

"What do we do?"

"*Do?*" Vandle asked.

"If we kill them—"

"If he dies, you die."

"If..." I trailed off, those words sinking in like a nightmare. "*What?*"

"It wasn't built for you. It wasn't built for *fairness*. You were never human to them."

"So that's it? There's no way out?"

"Of course there is."

"What?"

"The bond was built for him, which meant there is a way out. But it will only break if he chooses to release it."

A growl loosed from my throat. I was sick to my stomach, every piece of hatred I'd ever tried to bury, surfacing at once. To free ourselves of this, Dusk and I were at the mercy of Flynn *fucking* Lincoln?

"You said you bonded an omega?" Vandle asked, ignoring my outburst entirely.

"Yes."

Vandle peered down at the handkerchief. "This omega?"

"Why... Why is it getting worse?" I asked, needing answers to that. "Since we bonded with her, the sickness has gotten worse."

It didn't make sense.

"It shouldn't be. She fixed us—"

"That *is* why it's making you sicker," Vandle said, a slight frown on his face. "She is balancing you—healing you. But the bond you have is parasitical. It cannot tolerate you being whole. In healing you, she's trying to sever the parasite. It cannot tolerate that."

Despite his words, a wild relief flooded my system. It had nothing to do with Shatter. There was nothing wrong with her at all. She was right... *too* right for us.

"What if she did manage to heal the bond?"

"Impossible," Vandle said. "Immovable object. Unstoppable force. There is no good outcome."

"So what is going to happen?"

"Your omega will continue balancing you, and, out of self-preservation the parasite will devour you whole."

I grit my teeth, trying to shove down more fury. If that happened, Dusk would die, too. He was a part of this. "How do you know?"

"You were a rarity, 66. How many failures did Dr. Wren see—did *I* see—before successes began? You think he didn't introduce a bonded omega to stabilise the connection? They always angered it. And the deaths always came sooner when it was a scent match."

I frowned. "She's... their scent match. Not ours."

"The survivor?" Vandle asked, peering at me curiously. "You think she scent-matched a parasite?" He held up the handkerchief. "*This* omega?"

"She did."

His eyes darted between mine for a moment as if searching for a lie, then his face split in a grin. "I don't believe it."

"Why?"

"I can't imagine what that would be like. Alphas like you and I, we can appreciate this." He lifted his fist. "But they aren't like us. I think... well, it might drive them insane, being bound to an omega with a scent like that...?"

"I don't understand."

He cocked his head, looking at me curiously. "It's called a *scent match*," he laughed. "You smell like blood and hers is laced with poison."

A harrowing silence passed between us, filled by the mad howls all around.

"You're saying... she's...?" I swallowed, my mouth dry.

I saw the faintest flicker of sorrow on Vandle's face as he read my expression. "It would make sense she defaulted to match the dominant pack if she met them first..."

The world around me, the constant mad howls, the scent of damp metal and stone, it all faded at those words.

We knew the Lincoln pack had walked out of that facility with something. We'd known they'd stolen from us.

"They stole... our scent match?"

Shatter.

Shatter was... she was so perfect. I'd known from the moment I met her. Dusk had known. She'd brought Ransom back.

I felt something crack deep within me, opening up a void, and this time, as it split, I knew it would never close.

It wasn't just me, or Dusk.

My omega.

Who'd fought her way to this academy for a dream that was never real. For mates that weren't supposed to be hers because they'd stolen from her just like they'd stolen from us.

All of this—all the suffering she'd gone through with the Lincoln pack, believing she was broken because she wasn't enough for them... For mates who had never been capable of seeing her for what she was.

And every scar she now carried.

It was because... it was because of me.

"Nothing is yours," Vandle whispered. "Everything yours is theirs. Even if she should be, she isn't. She's their mate."

There was a long, long silence as his words sank in.

"You love her?" he asked.

My voice was rough. "Of course I love her."

He cocked his head. "Then a bond was a cruel gift."

"The bond?" I asked.

No. It was the only thing we had been able to give her.

"I do wonder what your parasite thought when the cure continued after the facility shut down. He must be waiting for the miracle he gambled on to vanish. I can imagine he and his pack are searching for other solutions. Solutions like her."

"Never."

"Tell me. Does she love you?"

"Yes."

"And what happens if you dark bond another pack's mate?"

I frowned. "They... they can negotiate. The scent matches can make an offer to trade for the bond. But it's *our* choice if we hand it over—"

Vandal cut me off. "It's a princess bond... Which means she *also* has a say—"

"She hates them."

"And yet, they have the most powerful bargaining chip in existence."

I stared at him, the realisation dawning on me before he even said it.

"They hold the keys to your salvation."

"We would... still have to give up the bond." It would be our choice before hers. That was how it worked.

It was why the dark bond Dusk had given her offered her safety. Our bite meant she couldn't be bitten by another.

Mates were the one exception. They could offer the princess bond, but it wasn't just that she had to accept. *We* had to choose to give it up, too.

"I told you," Vandle breathed. "Nothing in this world is yours, 66, not your body, your soul, not your aura. What makes you think you could claim an omega?"

My aura flared, fear blinding me as I seized him by the shirt. *"She is not theirs."*

"They can steal her from you. If that pack bites her, it will be like your bond doesn't exist," he hissed. "And the moment they learn who you are, they will know that too."

FORTY-TWO

SHATTER

When I reached the apartment, I felt safe at last.

It was late in the evening now, and I'd survived the ball.

I'd faced my mates.

The whole world knew who I was—*what* I was, and that was okay. I had a pack who loved me at last, and neither my scent nor the colour of my eyes was something I ever had to hide again.

We said goodnight to Roxy, and Ransom wound his hands around my waist, drawing me close as Dusk tugged his keys from his pocket.

Ransom's voice was a breath in my ear. "We're going to ravish you in your nest, Little Reaper."

I shivered, desire sending shooting stars through my veins as I leaned back, biting my lip as I took him in. Dusk unlocked the door and then tapped his phone on. The light drew my attention.

I frowned at how his expression went tense.

"It's Decebal—*Shit*." he said. "Ten missed calls. You guys go ahead."

"Alright." Ransom turned back to me. The kiss he pressed to my lips was so passionate that my worries faded, and once again, everything was perfect.

Ransom dragged me closer, letting me tangle my legs around him with ease as he picked me up. His hands were firm on my waist and back, and I could feel his need for me through the bond.

I nipped his neck, impatience rising in my chest as he opened the door himself, and Dusk's muted voice sounded behind us.

Ransom chuckled, and as we stepped in, he pressed me against the living room wall, dragging rough kisses down my neck to my chest.

I moaned as his teeth found my nipple through my silk dress.

I think I was okay with Ransom claiming me right here, heels and all.

He could claim me anywhere he wanted to.

I was his.

There was a possessive growl in his throat. "I'm so proud of you, Little Reaper."

My fingers tangled in his hair as I drew him back, finding his eyes in the dim living room. "I faced them," I whispered.

And somehow, I'd—

Thoughts died as my eyes slid to the room behind him.

My blood ran cold.

Ransom, feeling me stiffen, turned, pupils constricting. A feral, guttural growl rose in his chest. It was the most frightening thing I'd ever heard, every one of my hairs standing on end.

The room was destroyed, furniture torn, and contents of the kitchen shattered everywhere. And the scent in here was wrong.

Traces of my mates, fading fast.

They had been here.

In my home.

DUSK

I heard Shatter's whine of terror from the hall.

My heart was in my throat as Decebal's voice in my ear faded in and out.

The words he'd spoken turned the world upside down.

"They can't discover she's their scent match, Dusk. Once they know, they'll never give up."

Too late.

But I drew up as I realised what Shatter's fear was for.

The apartment was in ruins, the fading scent of the Lincoln pack lingering in the air.

In *my* territory.

My aura split the air and I felt Ransom slip into madness for a flicker, hackles up, every instinct dialled to a hundred. He was holding Shatter against him, scanning every inch of the room.

My shoes crunched on smashed plates and bowls as I stepped in.

"Get her out," I growled.

Their scents were fading, but it didn't mean they weren't still here.

"No..." Shatter's voice broke. Then she was trying to throw herself from Ransom's arms. To the hallway... To...

Fuck.

Her breathing was ragged. *"Let me..."* She cried, almost wild. *"Dusk!"*

"I'll go first," I said.

I reached her nest to find the door off its hinges.

My heart tripped over itself as I saw what was inside.

The destruction of the rest of the house was nothing compared to what remained of Shatter's nest. There was almost nothing within that was recognizable. The bed was the only thing that stood within the wreckage.

The faded scents were of an alpha's fury.

"*What?*" That was Decebal down the line. "*What happened?*"

"They broke in."

I spun as I felt something. Nails digging into my arms. Shatter was there, her eyes wide as she reached the nest.

"*Wait—*" I tried to stop her, but too late.

Her sob rose in the air, the most broken sound I'd ever heard in my life as she saw what was within. It shattered me. Ransom drew her back, wrapping his arms around her.

"How did they get in?" he demanded. "The door was locked."

"*Fuck...*" My blood chilled, and then I was stepping back, turning and striding across the hallway to my room. The door was open, and I stopped at the doorway.

"Listen to me," Decebal sounded urgent on the phone. "*We know what they did.* If the Lincoln pack bites Shatter, they *will* steal the bond from you."

Steal the bond?

I'd bitten her. No matter how it had destroyed me, her safety was the only gift that had never brought me an ounce of regret.

Decebal's voice was faint, the phone at my side. "*You have to make sure they cannot find out who you are.*"

I stared around.

The room was ruined, and one of my windows was smashed in.

If they'd got in this way...?

"*No...*"

The world spun as I reached my closet door, tearing it open—

Before me was a huge, jagged hole across the drywall, as if something had been ripped clean out.

My heart turned to stone.

The safe—the place I'd kept all of the information—every truth about our pack.

The safe was gone.

End of Part Two

WHAT'S NEXT?

Want book two sooner? Join my Ream's Omega Tier. Chapters drop a few times a week until release on amazon! *(Discount code on my newsletter below to get early access for $3/month, leave whenever you want <3)*

Book 3

Join my newsletter at MarieMackay.com for: *Character art, updates, bonus content and 1st access to ARC calls!*

WANT MORE POISONVERSE?

WANT MORE POISONVERSE?
Havoc Killed Her Alpha - *Marie Mackay*
Forget Me Knot - *Marie Mackay*
Pack of Lies - *Olivia Lewin*
Ruined Alphas - *Amy Nova*
Lonely Alpha - *Olivia Lewin*
-
Sweetheart: A Bully Duet - *Marie Mackay*

Go to PoisonVerseBooks.com for more.

WANT A BULLY OMEGAVERSE?

READ SWEETHEART NOW
FEATURING MORE DARK BONDS...
Never let them discover I'm an omega.
Never let them discover I'm their mate.

Bitten and bonded against my will, I've become a ransom for the celebrity alphas I scent matched. They're my last chance at freedom, and I have to make them fall for me before it's too late.

Sent into their home disguised as a Sweetheart—a beta companion for aggressive alphas without an omega—I'm forced to keep my status secret until they fall for me, or until my heat arrives. But I grew up obsessed with the Crimson Fury Pack; they aren't just smoking hot celebrity actors, they're kind and generous. I know I can convince them to save me.

Only, once in their home, I learn all too fast that my mates are nothing like they appear in interviews and magazines...

What will they do when they learn the truth about the beta Sweetheart in their home...?

THANK YOU!

To my incredibly supportive author friends, you know who you are!

To my amazing alpha readers!

To my ARC team!

CHAPTER 15 SUMMARY

The Lincoln pack hold the FMC in their room. They film the interaction, and also bite her a number of times (non bonding marks).

Roxy comes to the door, but Eric doesn't let her in. They use a sharpie to write on her and then remove her from the apartment.

The FMC realizes during the scene that they seem to be changing; shifting from competition with other alphas, to obsessive about her. The FMC is worried that they might realize the scent match so she uses Dusk (telling them she wants him) in order to keep them in their competitive mindset, which she believes will keep her safest. She escapes without them discovering the scent match.

Before she leaves, Eric empties her pencil case onto the floor and tells her she won't be wanted by alphas ever again. The FMC runs, leaving her registration card behind.

You can continue reading from Chapter 16 in which there is a brief threat of SA that goes nowhere and is swiftly dealt with.

Printed in Poland
by Amazon Fulfillment
Poland Sp. z o.o., Wrocław